The Violent Century

LAVIE TIDHAR

The Violent Century

HODDER &
STOUGHTON

First published in Great Britain in 2013 by Hodder & Stoughton

An Hachette UK company

1

A CIP catalogue record for this title is
available from the British Library

ISBN 978 1 444 76287 7
Trade Paperback ISBN 978 1 444 76288 4

Typeset in Plantin Light by Palimpsest Book Production Limited
Falkirk, Stirlingshire
Printed and bound by Clays Ltd, St Ives plc

Hodder & Stoughton policy is to use papers that are natural,
renewable and recyclable products and made from wood grown in sustainable
forests. The logging and manufacturing processes are expected to conform to the
environmental regulations of the country of origin.

Hodder & Stoughton Ltd
338 Euston Road
London NW1 3BH
www.hodder.co.uk

The Violent Century

To Elizabeth, my own perfect summer's day

A gunshot in the fog.

A body floating, cold and white, in the water of the Havel River, a scrap of fabric clutched in a lifeless hand.

A woman hanging by the throat from the ceiling by her own bedsheets, her long black hair wet. We assemble the images slowly:

Tank's body strapped to a slab, electricity coursing through him.

Auschwitz.

The wolf man.

A plane crashing into a skyscraper. Red poppies in a field, as far as the eye can see.

A frozen golem, erupting from the ice.

Who do we focus on? Shadows flee from our gaze. To observe something is to change it. Still:

Oblivion, Fogg.

So much death.

A violent century. Where does it start? We sift through recollections, old footage, dusty manuscripts. Probabilities collapse. So much death, but wrapped around a love. We watch. So many shadows.

Where does it end?

The way it begins, perhaps:

1. DR VOMACHT'S FARMHOUSE then

The farmhouse stands on its own in a sea of green grass, white weathered stones like an ancient fort. Electricity had been installed some time back. Plumbing. A radio antenna on the roof. It is a shining bright day, the sunlight is blinding, a pure, yellow radiance emanating from deep blue skies.

Somewhere inside the farmhouse music plays, softly. A scratchy quality. A gramophone. A French chanson, each note hovering, for just a moment, in the air, before being replaced by the next.

Beyond the farmhouse lie mountains, outlined in chalky-blue in the distance. Insects hum in the grass. Summer. The smell of freshly harvested wheat from somewhere else, perhaps a nearby village, though we never see it. Smoke rises out of the farmhouse's chimney, white smoke against blue skies.

Idyllic. The word we look for, each time.

A girl stands in the field of grass, between the farmhouse and the skies. Her long hair is blonde. Her skin is white like clouds, her eyes are blue like sky. She wears a thin white shift, almost translucent in the sunlight. She is in motion, hands at her sides, trailing luminescent lines as she turns.

Are you watching?

A butterfly hovers in mid-air, between the girl and the farmhouse. A Clouded Yellow. It hovers almost motionless, it seems. Compound eyes look over the meadow. Antennas flutter. The Clouded Yellow has a distinctive mark on its wings, a white eye and a scythe-like scattering of black dots on the wing edges.

Are you watching?

Inside the farmhouse the music comes to a halt. The gramophone spins silently. The air . . .

The girl seems frozen in motion, her hands rise, as though to ward off something invisible. The farmhouse seems to shimmer, inexplicably, as though the level of agitation in its component molecules has been increased, all at once. A distortion emanates from the farmhouse. Silent, swift, it travels from the source and spreads in an outwardly expanding circle. The butterfly hovers, somehow changed. Were we to look closely we would see that its distinctive eye had turned from white to azure, the colour of a summer's skies. Time seems to slow, to freeze, then speed up again all at once. The girl completes her spin. Stops.

Lowers her hands. The butterfly flies away. The girl looks at the farmhouse.

Beyond, the distortion spreads and disappears. The girl stares down at her bare feet.

Green grass. Yellow sun. Blue skies. White clouds.

A perfect summer's day.

ONE:

THE HOLE IN
THE WALL

LONDON
the present

2. **THE SOUTH BANK** the present

Night-time. A cold wind blows from the Thames. London, the giant Ferris wheel spinning slowly, wreathed in lights. The South Bank: couples walking hand in hand, a man by the entrance to Waterloo Station hands out free copies of the *Evening Standard*. A homeless man under the arches sells copies of the *Big Issue* – stares at the tall fellow walking past him.

Unhurried. Tall, thin. Pronounced cheekbones. Handsome. Black hair, done expensively at some Kensington place. The man is in formal evening wear: black trousers, black jacket, a crisp white shirt, a top hat. He wears white gloves over long, thin fingers. In his left hand he holds a cane, ebony topped with an ivory handle. He doesn't whistle, but he seems to be enjoying the walk. Not too many people out. It's a cold night. Smokers huddle outside the Italian restaurant under the arch. The man crosses the road. Waterloo Station rises before him. In the distance, Big Ben chimes an indeterminate number of times.

Fog. It makes the man smile, as at a private joke. The man doesn't continue straight, to Waterloo. He turns left, onto Mepham Street, which opens on the backs of restaurants, on rubbish bins and delivery vans. A double-decker bus is parked kerbside, driver and inspector sharing a smoke by the open doors.

The fog intensifies. The man reaches out, as if stroking the fog. As though the fog were a cat, and the cat were an old friend. He smiles again, then lets it drop.

He stops.

Looks up at the sign.

The Hole in the Wall.

You could walk past it a hundred times and miss it. A London pub, hidden under the railway arches.

Grimy windows hide what's inside. If anything. The door is closed. Dim light seems to glow inside, however, indicating that the place might not be as deserted as it appears. Not welcoming, either, though.

Should the man be smiling again, right now? A look in his eyes, but whether it is anticipation or concern, maybe even apprehension, we can't tell. It is gone swiftly. The man climbs the three short steps and pushes the door open and goes in.

3. **THE HOLE IN THE WALL** the present

Entering the pub is like travelling back in time to the nineteen fifties. Post-war decor. Peeling wallpaper. Hardwood floor scarred by hard heels and cigarettes.

A long, dirty-brown leather seat runs the length of the right wall, stuffing poking out from open cigarette burns. It is facing a row of low tables on which thick candles, veined with molten wax, flicker with smoke. At each table sits a man. The men are as hard as the floor, as spent as a burnt cigarette. They are a mixed bunch, white and black and brown, like a Gothic painter's palette. Thinning hair. Bad skin. The eyes are uniformly vacant. They stare into space without seeing anything.

Beside each man, on the table, is a pint glass and an ashtray. The ashtrays are large and saucer-like, of a uniform industrial make, made of some cheap metal. In each ashtray burns a cigarette. The cigarettes vary only in their remaining lengths. The smoke rises into the air, collectively, a blue note in a grey post-war world. The smoke is like fog. It serves to obscure.

On the left of the room is a bar counter and behind the counter is a barman. He is a man in his fifties or thereabouts. Balding, with muscled arms, a broken nose mended awkwardly. We never learn his name. We never find out his story. What brought him here, to this place, this twilight. He is wiping a pint glass with a rag. There are rows of bottles behind him. There are draught beer taps on the counter. Facing the bar counter are a row of barstools, empty but for one. A solitary patron sitting there.

The tall man in the evening dress surveys the room. We get the strange impression he had not always dressed like this, that underneath the polish there is something rough, and hard. He doesn't say a word. Nods to himself, as though confirming something. Some suspicion, some expectation now fulfilled. Doesn't seem to mind the smoke. Walks to the bar. Leans his cane against the counter. Removes his gloves revealing long, slender fingers.

Sits down, two stools along from the single patron. Glances at him. The man sits hunched on his stool. Stares at an empty shot glass. Doesn't look back.

The tall man shifts his gaze to the barman.

– Bring me a brandy, please, barkeep, he says. Smiles, almost wistfully. Something old, and foreign, he says.

The solitary patron glances at him then. Face without expression. Picks up the shot glass in front of him and examines it. Definitely empty. Puts it down again. The mute barman looks at him, questioning with his eyes, and the man nods. The barman brings out a green bottle with no label. Pours the solitary patron a shot. The solitary patron gestures at the tall man in the evening dress. The barman's face reveals nothing, but he gets another glass and pours another drink and places it before the tall man. Then he picks up his rag and a pint glass and continues polishing.

The tall man in the evening dress smiles. Picks up the glass. Half turns it, watching the liquid in the dim light of the pub. Puts the glass to his lips and downs the drink and smiles again. We get the sense he does not smile often, or easily.

He turns in his seat, to face the solitary patron.

– So how have you been, Fogg? he says.

The solitary patron seems to start at the name. As though it had belonged to an old friend, presumed dead, or missing, or one you had simply lost contact with, had stopped exchanging even Christmas cards with this past decade or more. The expression looks odd, old on his youthful face.

– Oblivion, he says.

The name seems to fit the tall man in the evening dress. Fits him like the white gloves fit his slender fingers, fit like his Savile Row suit. Tailor-made, that name.

Oblivion.

He gives a half-shrug, a sort of *That's me* gesture.

The other man, we know, is Fogg.

– How long has it been, Oblivion? he says. Forty? Fifty years?

– Try seventy, Oblivion says.

– As long as that.

– Not since after the war, Oblivion says, helpfully.

– The war, Fogg says. He has a youthful, pale face. Black, unruly hair. Does anyone still remember the war? he says. Is there anyone still alive?

Oblivion shrugs.

– A few, he says. Then: There have been other wars.

Adding, a little reluctantly it seems: There are always other wars.

A silence falls between them. Behind their backs the solitary men with their solitary pints sit motionless, staring into space with vacant, milky eyes. The barman polishes the pint glass, over and over. Fogg grimaces, picks up his shot, downs it, motions to the barman. The barman fills it up again then, unbidden, also fills Oblivion's.

– You haven't changed at all, you know, Fogg says. You don't look a day older than you did.

– You haven't changed either, Oblivion says. Contemplates him with that hint of a smile. Something in his eyes, something affectionate or proprietorial. Or something less well defined, some nebulous connection. Warmth, a love. But what is love. Fogg looks uncomfortable under the other man's gaze. Shrugs. Yes, well, we don't, do we, he says.

– No, Oblivion says. We don't.

– Not on the outside, at any rate, Fogg says. Not quickly.

Oblivion shrugs. As if this is too metaphysical for him. Too . . . abstract, perhaps. He half turns again in his seat. Looks over at the silent men. Says, What's with them?

Fogg moves his hand and the smoke, from candles and cigarettes both, seems to rise, thicken, cling to his fingers. Looks at the men. Distracted. The men stare back. Vacant, like empty lots. Like buildings with tear-down notices posted on their doors. Fogg shrugs.

– Them? he says. They've been dead for a long time. They just don't know it yet.

Oblivion nods. As though he understood more than the words. Your smokescreen? he says, softly.

– It's just habit, Fogg says.

Oblivion nods. I remember.

– Old tradecraft, Fogg says. Sounds sheepish.

Oblivion grins. Suddenly, like a grenade. Must be harder, now, he says. With all the No Smoking laws everywhere.

Fogg shrugs. Looks like he's about to smile. Doesn't, in the end. Says, I'm retired – as though that encapsulates everything.

Which perhaps it does. Oblivion says, Yes, well. Raises his glass. *Salut*, Fogg, he says. They touch glasses, body to body with a sound both soft and hard. Drink, in unison. Bang their glasses on the countertop. Practised. Used to each other. Used to each other's habits.

– What are you doing here, Oblivion? Fogg says. Stares at him. Fog gathering between them like a mesh of cobwebs. What do you want?

Oblivion waits. Fogg, with a hint of anger: I told you, I'm retired. I left a long time ago.

A train goes overhead. Over the arches. It shakes the glass bottles lining the wall, and the heavy old tables. It runs and runs and runs. And disappears. The Hole in the Wall is awash in something like an expectant silence. Oblivion says, It's not as simple as all that, though, is it, Fogg?

Fogg waits him out. One of the drinkers coughs, the sound unexpected, loud in the silence of the pub. We don't retire, Oblivion says. Not really we don't. We don't have the luxury of it.

– For Queen and Country? Fogg says. It used to be for King and Country, in the old days. Stares at his empty glass. I don't serve any more, he says, quietly.

Oblivion, a moue of distaste flickering over his face, gone quickly. As though the task is unpleasant. What he came for. What he has to do. Says, gently, The Old Man wants to have a word with you. That's all.

Fogg says: He's still alive?

– And still old.

– And you're still his lapdog, Fogg says. Oblivion shakes his head, a tired gesture, not one of denial. He just wants a word, Fogg, he says. Gently, but with finality. Fogg says, No.

– No?

– No, Fogg says. I'm not interested. I'm out.

– He said you'd say that, Oblivion says. Fogg just shrugs. The same finality.

Oblivion doesn't seem to mind. Looks at Fogg. Looks like he's picking his words carefully. Says, He just wants to go over some details with you, that's all. An old file.

On his barstool, Fogg becomes still. The smoke thickens around him, beside him. Becomes, almost, a physical form. A grey shape, a shadow.

– What old file, he says.

Oblivion hesitates. A fisherman, moments before hooking the fish. Aware of what he is doing. Perhaps even having second thoughts. Fogg had to gut fish before. He knows. A slimy experience. Cold intestines sliding against human fingers. Scales digging into your skin as you grip the fish. Drawing blood. The knife sliding into soft belly. And that look in the fish's eyes. The look in Fogg's eyes.

– Well? Fogg demands.

Oblivion says a single word.

– Sommertag.

The fug of smoke crescendoes around Fogg, a beekeeper's protective mask. That single word, like a bullet with a name engraved on its side. Ricocheting from the walls. Another train rumbles overhead, its wheels chugging, multiplying that word, that name. Sommertag. Sommertag. Sommerta—

– Why? Fogg says. Why bring up the past?

– It's just routine, Oblivion says. Convincingly or not, we can't tell. Something's come up.

Doesn't say what sort of something. Fogg doesn't ask. Oblivion says, apologetically, The Old Man just wants to confirm some details with you.

Fogg stares at his empty shot glass. Better than a reply. Intensely fascinating, the glass. Its purity. Its imperfections. The way light travels through it.

Snatches it up. Whips around. Hurls it at Oblivion—

Who raises his hand. Calmly. We watch in slow motion – the glass airborne, travelling through space, through time, speeding up, like a bullet. Oblivion spreads his fingers, like *so*—

Something agitates the molecules of air and glass. Silica breaking into its atomic components, air separating into nitrogen and hydrogen. A strange smell, for just a moment, a hint of ozone, perhaps. We watch the glass. Avidly. With a certain fascination, if truth be told. Though we have seen this before, have studied—

It seems to melt. The glass. To separate into liquid strands, an object becoming a non-object, torn apart by an invisible force. The strands of milky liquid glass pass through Oblivion's fingers. Disperse further. Blink out. Just like that. Oblivion rubs the tips of his fingers together. Like a magician making a coin disappear. Scattering magic dust. The glass is gone. Vanished. The blank-eyed men at the back of the pub oblivious.

– Come on, Fogg.

– Damn it, Oblivion!

Oblivion doesn't reply. Stands up. He's tall, he almost has to stoop under the ceiling. But not quite. Pulls on his gloves. Says, Come on, Fogg. It's just routine.

Fogg says, Sommertag.

The name, if that's what it is, lights up the room. Fogg says, She was beautiful, wasn't she, Oblivion?

Oblivion says, Yes. She was.

As though something has been decided. As though there never was a question about it.

Fogg stands up. The silent men move their heads as one, watching him with their blank milky eyes. Oblivion picks up his cane. Twirls it, distracted.

– Let's go, Fogg says.

Oblivion nods. Is Fogg resigned? Defeated? We don't know. Something in his eyes. A light that shouldn't be there. The Hole in the Wall is grey, smoke stands motionless in the air. The barman still cleans the same pint glass with the same dirty rag. An automaton, like the smoking men. Fogg and Oblivion, Oblivion and Fogg. They walk to the door together. Their feet make no sound on the hardwood floor.

4. **PALL MALL, LONDON** the present

Night. It seems to Fogg it is always night, these days. London is his city, a city of fog. Sunlight hidden behind clouds even at midday. They cross the bridge, the Thames down below, the water eddies cold, treacherous. A Rolls-Royce Phantom II. Remembers this car, from long ago. Oblivion driving. That, in itself, is inconceivable. Remembers the car's driver. Samuel. Memory like a chalkboard, but you can never quite remove the images there, only smudge them. Sometimes beyond recognition.

– Did you steal it? he says.

Oblivion laughs. Not much humour. Inside the smell of old cigars and old polished leather. Fogg winds down the window. Looks down at the water. The Thames, brown murky water, fog gathering in clumps over the surface, as if the river is haunted by ghosts.

Quiet. A plane overhead, coming low, following the contours of the river. Heading to Heathrow. Passengers aboard, like so many sardines in a rations tin. Packed tight. Peering out of lit windows on a city burning with lights.

It's a short drive to Pall Mall. The tall buildings are dark. They have wide stone façades. Gentlemen's clubs. The Athenaeum. The Travellers. The Army and Navy Club.

St James's Palace. Fogg had met the King there, once, and the Simpson woman. Before the war. The Old Man had taken him to the palace. Secret meetings in secret rooms.

There is a shadow on the roof opposite the Bureau. Or does he just imagine it? The car comes to a stop. Oblivion stills the engine. They just sit there, the two of them. Like old times. Old men no less old for looking young.

– Have there been any new ones, Oblivion?

– You know the answer to that.

– Then no, Fogg says.

– No.

Just sitting there. Reluctant to get out. An old bond holding them together close as lovers.

5. **PALL MALL** the present

Fogg hadn't imagined the shadow, though. It's there, perched on the rooftop. Watching.

A young woman with old eyes. Dark hair. Dark clothes.

Watching the car. Watching the two men. Angry, now. Hawks up phlegm and spits.

Not quite in the way we would.

Normally a water-based gel. But this one's tougher. Her body's composition demands to be studied. *Has* been studied. Glycoproteins and water undergoing metamorphosis, becoming something hard and strong, like iron or lead. The globule of spit flies through the air, the shape elongating, hardening. Its speed reaches terminal velocity. It is aimed at the car. Like a bullet. Sometimes, everything is like a bullet.

It hits the back window of the Rolls-Royce.

Which shatters.

An explosion of glass and spit.

6. **PALL MALL** the present

The two men drop low in their seats. Cold air bursts in through the broken window.

Fogg: What the—

Oblivion: Stay down!

A second explosion. The passenger-seat window shatters inwards. Glass showers the two men. Oblivion kicks his door open. Slides out. Fogg follows. Crouching. Looking up, shadow on the rooftop. Something familiar about her. Fog starts to rise around the car. Tendrils of it. Obscuring.

The woman spits a third time. Phlegm like a bullet going straight at Fogg. Oblivion raises his hand. Something invisible emanating from him. The spit loses definition. Hesitates. As if confused. Caught between two states. Loses momentum. By the time it reaches them it has no power left. Flops, wetly, on the pavement.

– Spit.

She looks down at them. We can't read her face, from that

distance. She raises her hand, a salute, a wave. Turns and disappears into the night.

– Get up, Oblivion says. And get rid of the damned fog, will you?

Fogg does as he's told. Stands up. Stretches. The fog dissipates, slowly. He says, What the hell was that?

– That was Spit, Oblivion says.

Fogg says, What's her damned problem?

Oblivion twists his lips into something resembling a smile.

– I suppose she doesn't like you very much, he says.

Looks sadly at the car. Air gusting in through broken windows. Turns away.

– Come on, he says.

Walks away, towards the building. Fogg follows. Nondescript building. Can't really tell what, if anything, is inside. Could be a bank. Could be a warehouse. Could be anything.

They go around to the side of the building. A narrow alleyway. A door set in the wall. No handle. They stop in front of it. Stare.

– It's a damn shame about the car, Oblivion says.

Fogg, face suddenly animated: Too bad you can't fix things, isn't it, Oblivion. Only rub them away, like they never existed.

Oblivion turns his head. Too bad you . . . he says, but doesn't complete the sentence.

The door swings open. An absence of sound. Darkness beyond. Oblivion expels air. Never mind, he says. Walks through the door instead. Swallowed by the dark. Fogg, after a moment's hesitation, follows.

7. **THE BUREAU** the present

A dusty corridor. Bare. No windows. Never been cleaned, by all accounts. The door shuts noiselessly behind them. It's dark inside.

There's a small wooden table in the entrance, with a potted plant sitting on top of it. The plant's leaves are drooping. It seems half dead. Fogg touches it. Marvels at the feel of soft plant matter, the texture of the leaves. Says, Has no one watered this thing since the war?

Oblivion oblivious. Walks down the corridor. Fogg abandons the plant to its half-life. Follows. Says, What about the car?

– The car will be taken care of.

Fogg remembers this corridor. Remembers that same plant, decades before. Like them, it is one of the changed. Who knows where the Old Man found it. Fogg feels a strange sort of kinship with it. None of us choose what we become. Notices no dust on the floor, scuffed by the passage of too many feet over too many years – a clue that this place is not as abandoned as it appears. At the end of the corridor, a lift. No buttons to press.

– Hasn't changed much around here, Fogg says.

Oblivion says, The Old Man doesn't like change.

Which is ironic, Fogg thinks, but doesn't say. Doesn't plan on saying anything much at all. Plans on saying, in fact, as little as possible. Afraid, however, that they already know.

The only real question, then, simply, is how much.

The lift pings. The doors slide open. Nobody likes change, Oblivion says. They get in the lift. The doors close, sealing them inside.

8. THE BUREAU the present

Blinking lights. The first thing Fogg notices is that the technology has been updated. An open-plan space, deep under Pall Mall. Maybe below the level of the Thames, even. The Bureau. London has always been a warren underground, and Pall Mall is no exception: secret passageways, Tube tunnels, sewers, cellars, more of London under- than above-ground. The Bureau didn't build this space, merely colonised it. Ants in a warren. Or mushrooms, sporing. Take your pick.

Computer screens, office chairs on squeaking wheels. Desks with no personal mementos. Pens, note pads, yellow Post-it notes. In- and out-trays. Blinking server lights, fluorescent bars on the ceiling, dividing the world into neat black and white. A row of listening equipment. The listeners, mostly women, wear oversized earphones, like mufflers in winter. The sound of keyboards, a constant patter of typing, like rain on a corrugated iron roof. They go past the open-plan office, into another corridor. Lights flicker overhead. The same utilitarian design, walls sheathed in cheap durable plastic, hiding stone or earth or other Londons. Lights flicker, on and off, reminding him of the light in an interrogation room. Bad wiring, Fogg thinks. The corridor is quiet. They walk past a closed door. Fogg recognises it with a start. A sign on the door. *The Cipher Room.* Voices from behind it. Fogg stops, listens. Oblivion turns to him, half exasperated. Says nothing, though.

Voices crackly on a radio receiver. Faint. Broken by the hiss of static. Like echoes from the past. Pebbles on the beach. Like Fogg doesn't want to listen, but can't help himself. The voice rolls like a wave.

– Vomacht . . . North Sea installation . . . extraction team . . . aborted . . . snow storm.

Each ellipsis a burst of static. Can't tell who's speaking. Fogg tenses at the last phrase. Says, Snow Storm?

Says it like a name.

– Some operation in the North Sea, gone bad, Oblivion says. Shakes his head. Nothing that concerns you. Gives the door a tap. Like a warning. The sound dies abruptly.

– Come on.

Leads Fogg on. Fogg doesn't want to follow, but has no choice. Their feet the only sound in that corridor now. Reach the last door. No plaque. But Fogg knows it well, nonetheless. Takes a deep breath. Oblivion's sculpted face, turning. All right? he says.

Fogg nods. Let's get this over with, he says, futilely.

Oblivion opens the door and they go inside.

9. **THE OLD MAN'S OFFICE** the present

Fogg remembers a night in Paris. The room hot, stuffy, despite the cold outside. A fog knocking against the windows. Hiding them inside. A womb. A shelter. The room smelled of their sex. The bedsheets humid. A radio downstairs, playing marching band. He could mask the outside but he couldn't mask the music. It penetrated. War music, a truce inside the room.

Entwined. Did not escape into that other place. Stayed in the now. Her body hot, like an oven, the smell of freshly baked bread. Pressed against her. Excited again. People died, everywhere. They made love. The fog masked their sounds.

She was an innocent. He was convinced of that, then and after. The only one of them who could claim to be, despite everything, but he never understood her, in the way you never do, the ones you love. Maybe it was just the way he saw her, through a haze, a fog; perhaps, he thinks, he never saw her clearly.

Fogg comes back to himself with a start. Trying to avoid this room, its solitary occupier. The room is illuminated only sparsely. Bookshelves. A desk, a man behind it. Vintage posters on the walls. One shows a soldier speaking, his words spiral out of his mouth like a metal tongue, on the end of it are impaled three tortured figures, hands raised to their faces in agony. *Your Talk May Kill Your Comrades*, the poster advises. Another shows Uncle Sam pointing an accusing finger. Dressed in his customary cape and tights, a big fuck-off S etched on his chest. *Do You Have What It Takes? Uncle Sam Needs You.* Beside it, an old German propaganda poster. Rocket men soaring into the skies, right hands extended upwards, reaching for the heavens in a Nazi salute. A map of Europe below them, its borders marked, the long shadows of the rocket men falling on it. Underneath, a legend in English: *Every German is an Übermensch – Adolf Hitler.* Fogg remembers them dropping down from the skies in great paper clouds over London, during the Blitz.

Brings back memories. Paris. Leningrad. Berlin. Doesn't want to think about that.

A photo on the wall. A rare photo. The Old Man and a young Winston Churchill, shaking hands. Both smiling. Churchill with one of his trademark cigars. Long overcoats. Winter. Books on the shelf. Fogg knows them well. *Le Dictionnaire Biographique des Surhommes*, by Stanley Lieber. A default reference text. French edition. Banned for years in Britain. Even included some Bureau personnel within its pages. Stands right next to *The Super Man: His Myth, his Iconography*, by Siegel and Shuster.

A shadow stirs behind the desk. The figure leans forward. A deep, rough voice. Hello, Fogg, it says.

Fogg turns to face him, reluctantly. As though he could keep delaying, forever if he had to. As if he had the talent to stop time. But doesn't. Looks at him. An old man, still. Been old a long time. Unshaven. Powerful hands. Blue eyes, deep-set. Prominent forehead. Hair somewhere between black and white. Unruly. Sticks out somewhat. Fogg nods, cautiously.

– Old Man, he says.

– Sit down.

Gruffly. How long has it been?

But time no longer matters. Not in this room, this room without windows, and only one way out. Oblivion shuts the door with a note of finality.

Two chairs facing the desk and its occupier. Oblivion sits, on the right. The desk is strewn with papers. This room halts entropy. Exists like a pocket universe. Sealed, and Fogg is sealed in with it.

– I said sit down!

Fogg shrugs. Sits down, on the left, close to the wall. The Old Man sighs, leans back in his chair. I should have known you were going to be trouble when I first recruited you, he says.

TWO:
SHADOW MEN

KINGSTON-CAMBRIDGE
1926-1936

10. **KINGSTON UPON THAMES** 1926

Cambridge. But not yet. Before Cambridge. London boy. Well, that's a lie. Kingston, Surrey. Father a greengrocer in the market square. Burly men come in carts from the countryside, fruit and veg. Offloading. Fogg, helping. Puny muscles straining against the weight. His father a mixture of tobacco and parsley. You'll never amount to nothing if you don't . . . Shakes his head, says, Look at you. That disappointment. His son's weakness. Fogg Père lifting weights – at the Harvest Fair played the strongman. Once Fogg overheard two men in the market square. Terror of the town, one said. I still remember. Scared of him. I remember, the other one says. Talking about his father, he realised. Short where Fogg sprouts up. Wide where Fogg is not. Like the twin reflections in a funhouse mirror. Fogg Père would go into pubs and start fights when he was younger. Fogg's mother always working on the house, accumulating things, painting, the brick walls of the house each a different colour gave her sleepless nights. Three dogs, collies. Walks in Bushy Park. Henry, she'd say. Henry.

He hid in books. He was a quiet kid. Didn't talk much. No one wanted to hear. *Around the World in Eighty Days. The Coral Island. King Solomon's Mines.* Once came across one of his mother's secret books. *The Sorrows of Satan.* Marie Corelli. Didn't like it. His dad's shelf, a row of penny dreadfuls. *The Blue Dwarf,* Part Seven, gave him nightmares, the cover a hideous monster lurking beside a sleeping woman's bed.

Hid in books. Doors into other worlds. Had a secret place by the railway tracks, his own secret garden, would come back smelling of the rosemary that grew there.

But everything blurred, pre-Vomacht. He had one sister, Agnes. She died in seventy-three. So he was told. The world sharply divided, before and after. Even when it happened, at first he didn't know.

11. **KINGSTON UPON THAMES** 1932

Standing by the train tracks. He had cut a hole through the fence to get in. A bit old for it now but still, he likes to watch the trains go past. To Hampton Court, to London. Fog clinging to their metal hides. At dawn their lights shine like yellow eyes. Standing there. Rain falling, but lightly. The ground is not yet mud. A London summer. The ground rumbling underneath him. A train, approaching. Steam rising into the air. Beautiful things, trains. Something coming.

A bubble of silence rushing outwards, expanding. A distortion that has no name. Time slows, for just a moment. Henry reaches out, the fog clinging to his hand, that bubble of silence rushes in slow motion, envelops him, holds him, then pops.

Rushes onwards. Disappears.

And everything changes.

Just like that. The train passed him by. Faces in the windows. Each in their own bubble of silence. Each changed, in their way, but for most it is an undetectable thing, like a single spot of colour on a butterfly's wing.

Not so for Henry. Not with the fog around him suddenly alive. Suddenly . . . responsive.

Scaring him. Scaring him a lot.

When it changed.

12. **CAMBRIDGE** 1936

A blue sky stretches across the horizon. A yellow spring sun hovers in the sky. The black Rolls-Royce Phantom absorbs the light. Seems to shine. Brand new: and the leather's as crisp as a British morning.

Peacetime. Jack Payne and the BBC Orchestra. 'Happy Days Are Here Again'. The Old Man in the back seat. A folder in his lap. He uses folders the way others use guns. Awake eyes, the blue deep and startling. Fields go past. The road from London. Cambridge in the spring. Not many automobiles on the road. The Old Man looks at the folder. The photo of a young man stares back at him. In black ink, a name. *Henry Fogg*. The Old Man shuts the folder. We never learn his own name. He's buried it deep. Records can't be trusted, not any more. We only know him as the Old Man.

Samuel is driving.

Trinity College, Cambridge. The Rolls comes to a stop. A sea of grass. Students in groups, sitting in the sun. Samuel comes around and opens the passenger door. The Old Man climbs out. Stretches. Sun on his face. Opens a small metal box, extracts a cigar and lights it. Samuel closes the door of the automobile, softly. Students walking past, books under their arms. Laughing. The Old Man smiles. Then drops it. Like his face is not used to the expression. Turns his head this way and that. Searching for something. Hunting.

– Sir?

– Stay put, Samuel, the Old Man says. Walks towards the college entrance, a grand stone building rising like an ancient castle. The Old Man smiles again, to himself, and sees a fellow come hurrying towards him.

Youngish man. Good-looking in a Jewish sort of way. Tweed jacket. Glasses. A head of dark hair. Hurries towards the Old

Man. Stops. Reaches out to shake hands – the Old Man ignores the offer.

– Deutsch, the man says. Arnold Deutsch. Not proudly. Just giving out information. I've been expecting you.

Holds his hand out a moment longer. Then lets it drop. We study him, covertly. Deutsch. We know the name. A brilliant man. An Austrian. A Jew. A communist, too, but we don't find that out, not then. Not for a long time.

13. TRINITY COLLEGE, CAMBRIDGE 1936

The Old Man says, Where is the boy?

– He's waiting, Deutsch says.

– Then let's pick up the pace, shall we? We don't want to keep the young master waiting.

Deutsch nods. Calm, but can sense the hostility from the Old Man and, perhaps, not sure how to take it. Says, Of course not. Left unsaid: *sir.*

The Old Man blows out a cloud of smoke. Drops the cigar to the ground and grinds it with his foot. Come on, then, he says.

He starts walking. Long steps. Deutsch has no choice but to hurry after him.

14. TRINITY COLLEGE 1936

In a classroom abandoned by its occupants, a young man sits alone. There are no photos of this moment. Had there been, one might be amused by the formal suit, the bad haircut. That sense of fidgety motion even in a frozen image. But there are no photos. They have been destroyed. Windows blink in the light. The smell of cut grass. The sound of laughter. Sunlight coming in through the glass. One window is half open. Warm air wafts through. The boy – the man – fidgets.

The door opens.

The boy raises his head. Recognises the one man, but not the other.

– This is the boy, Deutsch says. Henry Fogg.

The name – *his* name – hangs in the air. Exposed.

Father had a stroke two years before. Mother took over the fruit and vegetables stand. Did better than her man, truth be told. Henry helped, but she said no. Her aunt died, or not an aunt, not exactly. A distant relative, with blood, and money. Left some of it to Henry's old mum, for the boy, she said. You married beneath you, don't let the boy suffer the same fate. Not much, Henry's mother says. Not much but enough. Blood and money will get you into Cambridge – blood more than money, for this is England.

You did well at school, Henry. You should go, she says, urgently, one night. Father in his armchair, staring. Lips moving. No sound. Drools from one corner of his mouth. His left. Henry's right. Father looks at him funny. Like he *knows*.

It's all arranged, Mother says. Shoves a piece of folded paper into his hands. He opens it, smooths it. It's a train ticket. Fierce pride, worry in her voice. Henry's sister's out, at a dance. He thinks. His memory of that period is hazy. It rains outside, banishing the fog.

They'd fenced the train tracks. On the Thames, swans mating, he watches the rowers going past, mud on the riverbank, black-berries ripe and black like eyes to be plucked. Just go, Mother says. So he went. Hushed enormous library rooms, books like an army of spirits raised from the dead. A shelter, he thought. An escape.

Until now.

Deutsch: Stand up, Henry!

He stands up. Reluctantly. Outside the windows, the weather begins to change. The sun fades, slowly. The man beside Deutsch glances at the windows, as if confirming something. Looks back. Deutsch gestures at him. Deutsch's Adam's apple moving up and down.

– This is— he begins to say.

– That's enough, Deutsch, thank you, the man says. You can leave us now.

– From *London*, Deutsch says. With a faint sardonic air. Defiant, somehow. Makes Fogg strangely grateful.

– I said that's *enough*!

Deutsch nods, once. Of course, he says. That same mocking smile, it reaches his eyes, too. Like he knows things even the Old Man doesn't know. As you wish, he says. Glances back at Fogg. Glances at the man beside him. The man from London. Good luck, Henry, he says. Opens the classroom door. Disappears outside and shuts the door behind him.

The two of them alone in the classroom now. Fogg and this old man. Like somebody's grandfather. Look at each other.

– Sit down, damn it, the man says.

Fogg watches him. Doesn't move. Anger, coming from somewhere deep inside. Been buried long. Says, Who the hell are you?

The Old Man smiles. Like Fogg's passed some sort of bloody test. Says, You heard Deutsch. I'm the man from London.

– There are a lot of people from London, Fogg says. Some of them are even men.

– I was told you had a rebellious spirit, the Old Man says. Already, even if he doesn't know it yet, Fogg is beginning to think of him that way. *The* Old Man. The Old Man. I like that. Now sit *down*, boy!

Fogg, if truth be told, is a little shocked at this show of temper. Sits down. The Old Man nods. Good, he says. Walks over to Fogg's desk. Places a folder on it. Opens it. Fogg's photo stares up at him. The Old Man runs his finger down the page. Marks. Family history. Makes Fogg tense. The Old Man says, It takes a lot for one of your lot to get into Cambridge.

– Excuse me?

– You will speak when I say you can speak.

Just like that. Conversationally. In control. Like he owns Fogg. Like this conversation is his, now. Fogg doesn't say a blasted word. Outside, darkness is settling. No more sun. A thick fog rises. Presses against the glass. It begins to slip into the room through the open window. If the Old Man notices, he doesn't give a sign.

– Your father is a greengrocer? the Old Man says. We have a file on him, you know, he says. He had run-ins with the law before, didn't he, he says. Still, a veteran. Got to respect that. Wounded in a gas attack in nineteen seventeen. Problems with his nerves after that, I understand.

Fogg doesn't speak. The only tactic to ever take against the Old Man, then and now.

What about your mother? the Old Man says.

– Leave my mother out of this!

Fog pressing in, sliding along the ceiling, under the desks. Fog like a living thing. The Old Man says, I couldn't care less about your mother. Goading him, though Fogg doesn't understand it, not then.

– As of today, the Old Man says, you are no longer a student of Trinity College.

Fogg says, What? Jumps up from his seat. It's dark in the room now. And cold. The Old Man resumes as though Fogg has not spoken.

– You have been . . . removed. Let us not use the word expelled. You are not Flashman. The Old Man chuckles to himself. Fogg looks at him in angry bewilderment. Your name will be removed from the official records, the Old Man says. For all intents and purposes it will be as if you were never here.

Fogg sits down again. Looks winded. What would we do under

the same circumstances? Is this the visit he's been dreading, all this time? Spring doesn't last forever – the first, and harshest, lesson we all learn.

– Why? Fogg says. Whispers. Who are you? What do you want?

The Old Man smiles.

– I want to offer you a job, he says.

15. **TRINITY COLLEGE** 1936

Grey fog rushes into the room. Clings to the furniture. Slinks about. Thickens like a cloud of ash. There's fog everywhere. It chokes out the light. It obscures the blackboard, the empty desks. It hides both Fogg and the Old Man. A smokescreen. The sound of a chair scraping. Then nothing.

The Old Man stands perfectly still. But smiling. Not pleasantly. We can't see it, but we know it's there. On his face. That motion of his head again, this way and that. Like he's scenting something. Like he's hunting.

And liking it.

Stealthy footsteps. Through the fog. The Old Man moves. With purpose. Like he can see perfectly clearly. The fog moves like a billowing screen, through openings we see snatches of images, the Old Man's movement, his hand reaching out.

See the half-open window. Fogg's face. His hands on the windowsill. About to climb out.

The Old Man's hand. Landing on Fogg's shoulder. A light touch, but Fogg doesn't move. As though he'd just been frozen.

– Call it back, the Old Man says. Softly. The words leave his mouth with a white cloud of condensation. The fog hangs in the air. I said, Call it back!

Snatches in the fog reveal them in this frozen tableau. Fogg's face white, bloodless. His eyes moving, restlessly. Trapped. The Old Man's eyes unfathomable. His grip on Fogg's shoulder. His fingers dark with blood, applying pressure.

The fog begins to lighten. To withdraw. Sudden, blinding sunlight pours in from outside. Shafts of light like prison searchlights moving through the room, eradicating fog. The air clears. Noise returns from the outside. The sound of humming bees. Students laughing. The smell of cut grass, again. The fog fades gradually, reveals the empty desks, the chairs where no one sits. The blackboard. A piece of chalk broken in half.

– I am going to release you now, the Old Man says. When I do, you will return to your seat. You will sit down. And you will pay attention.

But Fogg is frozen still. Doesn't speak. Maybe can't. Maybe the Old Man knows it. Says, Yes? and seems satisfied. Removes his hand.

Fogg, in motion. Like a trout released from a hook. Whirls around. Angry red patches on his white skin. Then stops, the Old Man watching him. Fogg walks back to the chair. Same chair, though he could pick any in the room. Sits down. Waits.

– Very good, the Old Man says.

He walks back to stand behind the reader's desk. The blackboard behind him. As though he's about to deliver a lecture.

– You think I can't see you, boy? he says. I can see each and every one of you, like bright pinpricks of light. Maybe not so bright, in your case . . .

Laughs at his own joke. Fogg frowning. Caught. He must know, he thinks. But how?

– You light up the map like beacons. I can see you, boy. I can see what you are, the Old Man says.

– Please, Fogg says. Please.

The Old Man tilts his head. Regards Fogg like a question.

– What are you going to do to me?

– I'm here to take you to a special school. For special people. People like you. Where you will be happy, the Old Man says.

Fogg, wanting to believe. Hope in his eyes. How easily it's taken away. But wants it to be true, so badly it hurts. Says, Really?

– Of course not, boy, the Old Man says. Don't be bloody stupid. I'm here to give you a job.

What is Fogg thinking right then? Is he feeling relief? Confusion? Anger? It's a lot to take in, this sudden shift in his life, in a way it is as great a divide as the moment the Vomacht wave hit him.

– This isn't an offer, the Old Man says. Maybe taking Fogg's silence for obstinacy. It's a given, he says. You'll work for me. Ultimately, you'll be working for the King.

– What? Fogg says. Where?

Doesn't understand.

The Old Man smiles. The Civil Service, he says. Then, into Fogg's bemusement, Now come along. We need to hurry if we want to make it back to London for tea.

16. **BERLIN** 1946

Old certainties ripped away, never to be replaced. What makes a man? It was Franz who asked him that. The memory jolts Fogg. Things he had not thought about, had successfully managed to forget, for decades. Good old Franz. Fogg's one-time informer, in post-war Berlin. What makes a . . . Franz hesitating, looking for the right word, in English. They are seated in a cafe in the Breitscheidplatz, near the Kaiser Wilhelm Memorial Church. What was left of it, after the bombing. Rat-people outside. That's how he came to think of the Berliners, after the war. Rat-people in the gutter, scavenging for food, love, identity papers, hope. The bombings and the loss. Robbed them of that perfect semblance of Germanic humanity. What makes a . . . Franz says again, thinking. Beyond-Man, he says, a little hesitant. Thinning hair, pinched face. Lost two toes on the Eastern Front. Round glasses with pale watery brown eyes behind them. No one's idea of an Aryan.

– Übermensch, Fogg says. Yes, yes, Franz says, a little impatiently. Hugging the cup of hot chocolate, unimaginable luxury. Fogg is paying. From what they call the Rat Fund.

Fogg isn't sure what Franz is asking.

– The Übermensch acts within the moral vacuum of nihilism to create new values, Franz says. Fogg realises he is quoting – or perhaps paraphrasing – Nietzsche. Shakes his head. Says, How the hell should I know what makes a man? What makes an Over-Man?

Pale sunlight coming in from outside. The remnants of ruined houses, craters in the street. Rats. Berlin. On the Eastern Front, Franz says, hesitates. Hugs the hot chocolate. Words come out haltingly. Like he's forgotten speech. On the Eastern Front the snow was broken by bomb craters. And yet it seemed to spread out to eternity. You know, Herr Schleier? It shimmered a pale blue, the ice did. And the sky, so black, a darkness undisturbed, so very strange, inhuman. Takes a deep shuddering breath, says, And amongst it, stars. So many stars, Franz says. Gulps down hot chocolate, Adam's apple bobbing up and down. So *many* stars. And each and every one is a sun, hiding multiple planets, worlds. War on each one, perhaps. He laughs. He rolls a cigarette between his fingers. Paid for by Fogg, from the Rat Fund. Franz lights it up. Takes a deep drag. We were all meant to be Beyond-Men, he says. A little sadly. We didn't know, Herr Schleier. That's what he calls him. Schleier for mist, or fog. We didn't *know*.

17. **THE ROAD TO LONDON** 1936

He is unused to this vehicle, the luxury is unimaginable. A machine from the future, this black shark moving smoothly across the road. Cambridge in the distance. Fields on either side of the road. Lone bird in a startling blue sky. The driver doesn't speak. But hums to himself. Looks back in the rear-view mirror, every now and then. Checking on Fogg.

The Old Man beside him on the back seat. The window open. The Old Man smoking a cigar. The smoke coalesces in the interior of the automobile. Warm air enters through the open window. Fogg with his hands in his lap. Silence from the Old Man. A waiting silence, wanting to be filled.

– What will happen to me? Fogg blurts out. The Old Man turns his gaze on him. Like he's been waiting. Says, Are you scared? But gently.

– How did you find me? Fogg says. Almost in despair. How did you *know*?

The Old Man, those deep-set, deceptively sleepy eyes. One can get lost in them. We know this. Says, Deutsch is a spotter. We pay his salary. Well, his second salary. When a possible candidate comes up, we're notified.

– We? Fogg says. The Old Man's teeth around the cigar. Uneven. Canines a little pronounced. Gives him the aura of an elderly wolf.

– As I said. The Old Man blows out a cloud of blue-grey smoke. It responds to Fogg. It whispers to him. That thing inside him that changed, that means fog and smoke are no longer natural phenomena but something almost *alive*, something he can, as ridiculous as it may sound, somehow manipulate. His Majesty's Royal Service, the Old Man says. More specifically, the Bureau for Superannuated Affairs.

Smokes and waits. A twinkle in his eyes. His grin a wolf's grin.

– I don't understand, Fogg says. Runs it through his head. Comes up with: The *Retirement Service*?

The driver smiles in the rear-view mirror. Samuel, though Fogg doesn't learn his name until much later. The Old Man says, Consider us a . . . pension scheme. For the Empire. Fogg shakes his head. The silence again. That waiting silence. Baiting him.

They drive along the road, automobiles pass them going the other way, in the field a horse pulls a cart heaped with hay. The farmer driving it turns to look at them as they pass, the Old Man turns his head sharply, stares, his intensity frightening. As the car drives on the farmer and his cart disappear in the distance, grown small like ants. The road continues ahead. The Old Man sighs, rubs his head as if it hurts, says, I thought I felt something.

Fogg is left wondering if one day, soon, that anonymous farmer, too, would receive an unexpected visit, would see the same Rolls-Royce glide into his path, making him stop, and stare, surprised and apprehensive.

– You said Deutsch is a spotter, Fogg says. Of . . . you mean there are others?

– What do you think? The Old Man says.

– I hoped so. But I never knew.

Relief in saying the words. Breathing in, deeply. The smell of hay from the fields. Passing a row of beehives, short squat boxes with a buzzing dark cloud around them. The Old Man, with unexpected gentleness: And you were afraid.

– Wouldn't you be? Fogg says.

– Fear is healthy, the Old Man says. Then catches the driver's eye in the mirror. Sighs. Says, Yes, I would be too. Says: I *was*.

A connection between them. Things unsaid. A world of meaning in those two words. *Not alone*, Fogg thinks. For some reason, thinks of his father. When he, Henry, was young. When his father seemed to him like a tree, so big and strong, and he loved him, unconditionally, even when love hurt. And he says, with wonder in his voice, So you're . . .

– In a small way, the Old Man says. Yes.

– What will happen to me? Fogg says, into the waiting silence. And the Old Man says, simply, You will serve.

NAZI FORCES INVADE POLAND

September 1, 1939

WARSAW Nazi forces have invaded Poland in a move drawing wide condemnation across Europe. Reports suggest the attack began with the German battleship Schleswig-Holstein opening fire on the Polish garrison of the Westerplatte Fort, in Danzig. At the same time, German infantry divisions supported by squadrons of Luftwaffe airplanes began the invasion, and heavy bombings are currently rocking Warsaw.

The invasion follows Hitler's previous acts of aggression: the September 1938 forced transfer of the 'ethnically German' Sudetenland from Czechoslovakia to Germany and the March 1939 occupation of the rest of Czechoslovakia.

BRITAIN DECLARES WAR ON GERMANY

September 3, 1939

LONDON Following the expiration of the deadline for German troops to withdraw from Poland, British Prime Minister Neville Chamberlain has declared war on Germany. The French government has also declared war following the expiration of its own ultimatum to Germany. A new War Cabinet has been set up and Winston Churchill has been confirmed as First Lord of the Admiralty. King George IV, speaking on the radio, said: 'The task will be hard. There may be dark days ahead and war can no longer be confined to the battlefield. But we can only do the right as we see the right and reverently commit our cause to God.'

All men between 18 and 41 are liable for conscription.

THREE:
SNOW STORM

**LONDON—BERLIN—
WARSAW—LENINGRAD
1941—1945**

18. **LONDON** 1944

On rare shore-leave back home. Mother was still alive then; he was told Father had died a couple of years before. Didn't go to the funeral. Henry Fogg no longer existed. Even the register of his birth was gone from the church. The Bureau was nothing if not thorough.

He finds shelter in a dark cinema off Leicester Square. The uniforms keep away the roving bands of women handing out white feathers to civilians, a mark of shame, an echo of an earlier war. Why aren't you serving.

But he serves.

Huddling deep in his seat, the air freezing, the coat too large over his frame. The cinema is almost empty. Every time he comes back to London the city has changed further, become darker and more menacing. The Blitz had ended by forty-one, but it changed the city permanently, a madman taking a blade to someone's face. But savagery left Fogg numb, these days.

Huddling in his coat, smoking a Lucky Strike – American. The smoke rising before the projector, a blue, magical fog with light passing through it. Everyone smokes, in the war. A couple of kids courting in the back row. A veteran with a face like a quarry sitting in the front, eyes like boreholes. Fogg trying to forget the goddamned war, if only for a minute.

Instead, a newsreel.

D-Day.

American forces landing at Normandy. Grainy images in black and white. Warships crowding the sea. Landing craft beaching, soldiers pouring out like insects, aircraft flying overhead.

Gunfire. The reel is coy at first about showing us the dead.

Announcer: D-Day! Brave American soldiers are storming the beach at Normandy, coming under heavy enemy fire!

The veteran in the front is lit up by the projector, unshaven cheeks, lips moving without sound.

Announcer: The dastardly Hun fight desperately, but they are no match for American heroism!

Fogg smokes, fidgets. Knows what's coming next.

Announcer: Here comes Tigerman!

New landing craft has just beached. Painted garish colours, you can tell even in the black and white of the picture. Like something out of a storybook. The hatch opens. A man steps out onto the beach.

He looks like a circus performer. He is dressed in leotards. He has a long mane of blond hair. He is bare-chested, despite the cold. Tigerman roars without sound at the camera, showing teeth.

Wild eyes. Fucking *hero*, Fogg thinks. What makes a man. Tigerman roars again, *shifts*, half transforming – someone gasps in the back row of the cinema, the couple courting make their own sounds, oblivious. Fogg watches, Tigerman's face shifting, jaws opening, teeth like weapons, a tiger's canines. Roars. Hands extended to the camera, become claws. Stripes over his bare skin. What a fucking *animal*, Fogg thinks.

A smaller shape materialises out of the open hull of the landing craft.

Announcer: Here comes *Whirlwind*!

A female figure, slight, ears almost elf-like, dark hair, an impish smile – doesn't walk down but *jumps*, into the air, transforming into a localised storm, a cone of air, moving over the cold water of the English Channel. Bullets fired at it, the whirlwind takes them and fires them back, the camera jerks, a group of German soldiers die in a hail of bullets. Pans back, on Whirlwind: growing in ferocity, landing, at last, on the beach. Transforming, beside Tigerman, into a woman, barely more than a girl, Fogg thinks, that same half-smile on her face. She stands there.

Fogg leans back. Fascinated despite himself. In the back row the moans reach a crescendo and suddenly stop. An embarrassed giggle. In the front row the veteran moves his blind face this way and that, the light from the projector surrounding his head like a halo.

German soldiers dying on screen in a weird, speeded-up flickering. Announcer: The Electric Twins!

Two young identical men in overalls and helmets. Look like electricians, or miners. Serious faces. Neither smiling. Walk carefully off the ramp onto the beach. Stand next to the others. Reach for each other's hands.

Their bodies shake, convolute. Electricity like a living thing, coursing through them, surrounding them in a haze of blue, cold fire. They point in unison, forming an arrowhead, and aim. They discharge a lightning bolt, it leaves the tips of their fingers and cracks like a whip across the distance, hitting a German tank. There is a massive explosion as the tank blows up and the camera shakes wildly. When it settles it lingers, for a moment, on the remains of the burning tank, before returning to the Electric Twins. Their hands are back at their sides. They look into the camera. For just a moment. That self-satisfied look in their eyes. Then look away.

Americans, Fogg thinks.

It's one big fucking show, he thinks.

On screen, the announcer: The Greeeeeeeeeen Gunman!

Who's not even green. He's black. He steps off the ramp. Measured steps. A little older than the others. Wide-brimmed cowboy hat. Boots with spurs on them. Balls that clang as he walks, Fogg thinks. That swagger. The outfit must be green. Can't tell. Patterned with leaves. The boots, the belt buckle. Gun holsters each side of the belt. Unlit cigar in his mouth. Surveys the scene of battle. Takes his time. The camera pans out. German snipers taking aim. The Green Gunman smiles. Draws. Fires.

Not bullets.

Shoots. Vines. Green tendrils. Growing at an enormous speed. Sprouting from the Green Gunman himself. Looping around the German snipers. Taking root. They bloom flowers. They extend big, fleshy leaves.

Vegetation swallows the men. A hillside transformed. The Green Gunman holsters the guns. Not guns at all, Fogg realises. Props. The Green Gunman smiles. Fires up his cigar. Steps down the ramp. Stands with the others.

The League of Defenders.

Fogg shakes his head. Coughs. Drops the spent cigarette on the floor. Grounds it with his heel. Watches the screen. Announcer: Girl Surfer and the Frogman!

Last to the party. Girl Surfer first, board gliding on the water, over the waves, American soldiers watching from the beach, cheering.

Girl Surfer in a bathing suit, doesn't feel the cold. Holds twin machine guns, fires them, blonde hair cut short, a fringe, cold grey eyes like an alien sea. Out of the water bobs the Frogman, a toad-like human creature with scaly skin, in his deformed flipper hands a German diver. The Frogman crushes the diver in a hug. He dives back down, dragging the German diver with him. Surfer Girl lands on the shore. Pins the surfboard in the sand. The Frogman rises, dragging the German diver's bloodied corpse behind him. He deposits him on the sand. Steps over him. Joins Surfer Girl and the others. A line in the sand.

Announcer: Fritz can never stand in the path of the League of Defenders! The tide of war has turned, and *right* has *might!*

The camera turns, pans, the seven in their garish costumes stand, looking into it, a group photo, American power: Tigerman Whirlwind Electric Twins Green Gunman Surfer Girl Frogman. The image freezes, then disintegrates, the screen flashing, and Fogg sighs out, relief, a breath he didn't realise he was holding – the film's about to start, at last.

19. **THE OLD MAN'S OFFICE** the present

Remembers the film, now. *The Outlaw*, from the previous year. Holding his breath when Jane Russell walked onto the screen for the first time. Makes him smile, now. Watched it again with Oblivion, at some American camp halfway to Berlin, before the fall. Oblivion had made a comment, later. They were drinking the Americans' whiskey. Something about them being like the characters in the movie, Fogg and him. Doc Holliday and Billy the Kid. Fogg wasn't sure which was meant to be which.

Things he and Oblivion never talked about.

Too many things unsaid. One of the things they taught them on the Farm. Speak little. Say even less.

That had been Jane Russell's first screen appearance. Remembers watching her later. After the war. Hiding in that same darkened basement cinema off Leicester Square, until they tore it down in the Sixties. Calamity Jane, in *The Paleface*. Dorothy in *Gentlemen Prefer Blondes*. The Old Man says, What the hell are you grinning about? Fogg, jolted back into the present, says, Why did you bring me back?

But the Old Man just wouldn't start. Fogg knows the game, only it is not a game. His palms itch. Knows everything's been set up, ever so carefully. Says, at last, the words dragged out of him unwillingly, When we went past the cipher room, earlier . . . leaves it open, like a question.

The Old Man, eyes bright and predatory. Yes?

Fogg says, What happened in the North Sea?

– That is not your concern, the Old Man says. Waits. Fogg says, I heard them mention a name.

– Oh?

– Snow Storm, Fogg says.

The Old Man sits back. Like he's been waiting for this moment. Regards Fogg for a long while with those bright eyes. Eyes that saw you, wherever you went. Whatever you tried to hide. Says, at last, softly, But that wasn't what he called himself, was it, Fogg?

– No, Fogg says. Thinking, you bastard. Thinking, at least it's begun.

– What *did* he call himself, Fogg? the Old Man says.

Fogg looks to Oblivion. For help. But there's nothing there. Oblivion sits like a stone. His angular face pale and beautiful like a Greek statue. Fogg looks away.

– *Schneesturm*, he says. He called himself Schneesturm.

The words, like icicles, hang in the air. The Old Man smiles. Savours the moment. Fogg remembers him interviewing prisoners, after the war. The small, windowless room, breath fogging the air, a succession of German prisoners secured to the chair.

20. BERLIN—MARIENDORF DP CAMP 1945

A massive place, the throng of humanity is impossible to classify and tag correctly, but has to be, needs to be sorted, filed, questioned. Displaced Persons. DPs. There are similar camps all over Germany, and in neighbouring Austria, in places like Bad Reichenhall and Cornberg and Mittenwald and Pocking. Places no one's ever heard of, or ever wanted to. Fogg's never seen anything like it. The women like walking skeletons, skin over protruding ribs, bare feet covered in sores, heads shaved as the head lice crawled away on the cold ground. Men with that look in their eyes that said nothing could touch them any more. A school class where a dark-haired woman he knew slightly, her name was Anda Pinkerfeld, taught the children to sing Hebrew songs. Walking past the window with the singing coming from the inside, his feet leaving bootmarks in the dirty snow.

– Sorting and classifying, the Old Man says. Fogg nods politely. Sorting is done according to Supreme Headquarters Allied

Expeditionary Force guidelines. People from all over Europe are at the camp, sorted and tagged, by SHAEF guidelines, into: evacuees, war or political refugees, political prisoners, forced or voluntary workers, Todt workers, former forces under German command, deportees, intruded persons, extruded persons, civilian internees, ex-prisoners of war, and stateless persons.

With one category missing from the list altogether.

Fogg doesn't like the camp and doesn't like the work, which has nothing to do with either sorting *or* tagging where the Bureau is concerned. It's interrogation, pure and simple, with the solitary object of locating and holding on to any Übermenschen trying to disguise themselves in the civilian population.

Hence the line of bootmarks in the sludge, past the classroom and the children's reedy voices in song, past the lines of women and men waiting patiently and the soldiers watching them and smoking and around the back of the long one-storey building, and through an unmarked door (another Old Man favourite).

Inside, the cold seems worse. Air condenses out of our mouths when we breathe. We know. We've seen inside the place before. There is a metal desk and a metal chair nailed to the floor before it. Behind the desk another chair, more comfortable, without the leather restraints. A harsh glaring lamp on the table, but the Old Man seldom needs to use it. Makes a show of laying papers on the desk. Folders. Dossiers. The Old Man uses paper like other people use pliers and knives. Fogg's there as an observer. The silent figure sitting a little to the side. The one we don't know, can't read, can't understand its purpose there, the one we're afraid of because we can't figure it out.

– Bring them in, the Old Man says. Fogg does as he's told. Goes to the door. Signals to the soldiers. They let the first one in. A woman, in her thirties. Dirty-blonde hair. The nail on the small finger of her left hand missing. Sits down. Looks at the Old Man with . . . what? Defiance? Acceptance? The Old Man says, Well. Shuffles papers. Opens a folder. The woman's face, but younger, happier, looks out from a black-and-white photo.

Maria Becker, the Old Man says. The woman says, Yes? Her voice shakes. She keeps glancing at Fogg, who is leaning against the wall, arms crossed on his chest. Looking at him like she can't figure out why he's there. Do you have anything you wish to tell me? the Old Man says. Such as what, Maria says. The Old Man turns a page, another. Waits. Such as what? Maria says again. Keeps glancing at Fogg. Tell me about Schneesturm, the Old Man says. Suggests. Maria's face twists in old pain. She says, I don't know anything. The Old Man says, That's what everyone says. No one knows anything. Well, I don't! she says. The Old Man turns another page.

Cries outside. Some sort of a disturbance going on. Later, Fogg learns that some of the Jewish inmates have recognised amongst them a former kapo, a guard from one of the camps. By the time the soldiers get to them it is too late, the man is a bundle of meat and blood in the snow.

Schneesturm, Maria says, as though tasting the word. You don't owe him anything, the Old Man says. We just want to talk to him, the Old Man says. Silence in the room. A gunshot outside. Maria flinches. Fogg doesn't move. I met him in Warsaw, Maria says, at last, unwillingly. In forty-three. The words dragged out of her. Bursts – I don't owe him anything!

– You don't, the Old Man says. Agrees. Nods, encouragingly.

– But I didn't know what he was.

The Old Man leans back. Inviting her confidence. And Maria talks.

21. BERLIN—MARIENDORF DP CAMP 1945

Maria Becker cries without sound. So quiet in the interrogation room. Fogg notes dark stains on the floor. Some of it is dried blood, he thinks. Some of it is probably urine. Maria Becker cries and the Old Man sits on the other side of the desk, his hands with the palms down on the desk's cold surface. He's waiting.

– Tell me about Erich Bühler, the Old Man says.

– I met him in Warsaw. He was a handsome man . . . and I was lonely.

– What were you doing in Warsaw?

– I was a secretary working for Obergruppenführer Krüger at the Schutzstaffel.

The Old Man leans back. That glint in his eyes. Makes Fogg wonder what he was like before the change. What work he did. Questions they never ask. The Old Man says, That would be Obergruppenführer *Friedrich-Wilhelm* Krüger?

– Yes.

Schutzstaffel. The SS.

– SS and police leader for occupied Poland?

– Yes.

– Were you close?

– He was a good man, Maria says. He treated me decently.

– He committed suicide, the Old Man confides. In Austria. Did you know that?

– No, I did not know that.

Fogg knows the Allies have little enough interest in people like Maria. The hunt is on for the big fish – for people like Göring and Eichmann and Ribbentrop, Speer, Mengele. An SS secretary interests nobody, and Maria knows it. Her best bet is to talk, to give them everything they want. And what the Old Man wants, it seems, is Erich Bühler, codenamed Schneesturm, once upon a time an esteemed member of the elite Nazi Übermenschen Korps, and now a wanted war criminal, a fugitive from justice.

– I met Erich when he came to the offices. He was meeting with the Obergruppenführer. He stopped to chat to me on his way out. He had an easy smile. I did not recognise him at the time. Later, he showed me clippings. Schneesturm. Hero of Leningrad. Sometimes, when we made love, he made snow fall around us as he held me close, his naked body hot against mine . . . he could be very romantic. Do I shock you?

The Old Man smiles. I wish you could, he says, genuine regret in his voice. Maria glances at Fogg again, but his face is expressionless, it gives nothing away. Maria says, I thought he loved me.

The Old Man waits. Maria says, He used me. Like he used everyone else. He wanted information about SS operations. I brought him documents. Friedrich-Wilhelm – Obergruppenführer Krüger, that is – was very busy then. He had just been promoted. The Jews . . . she sighs, a long, suffering sigh. The Jews were rebelling in their ghetto. It was a mess. So much paperwork. The army had to get involved. They were like rats . . . She stops, catching herself. Starts to cry again, soundlessly, as though the tears offered some kind of protection from her interrogators. Fogg thinks, She must have been pretty, once.

The war made old people of everyone. We know.

– The Warsaw Ghetto uprising? the Old Man says, prompting.

– Yes. Erich wanted to know many things. Then, I didn't know why. But now I think I do.

– Why? the Old Man says.

– Power, Maria Becker says. That solitary word, like a fog, hovers in the still, cold air of the room. He needed power. He said to me, once, he had been drinking all night, we were sitting in my room, he was naked with his back to me, his buttocks pressed against the thin mattress. He was staring out of the window. It was snowing outside. He said, I no longer believe.

22. **WARSAW** 1943

We assemble this picture from conflicting reports, Maria Becker's testimony, what Fogg learned later. It is in no way accurate.

– I no longer believe.

Erich sits naked on the thin mattress. His skin is pale everywhere. Maria runs her nails down his back but he shrugs her off. On the small bedside table is a bottle of vodka. A taste he'd picked up in Russia, he says. Talks little about the Eastern Front. Even less of Leningrad, which is still under siege. Told her once of dead horses in the streets, frozen, and children hacking flesh from the horses' sides. There are no more horses in Leningrad. Erich stares out of the window. Raises the bottle to his lips. Drinks. Outside snow rages, snowdrops beat against the glass. Inside it is warm, the smell of their sex fills the air. Maria rises, presses against Erich's back, her heavy breasts cool against his feverish skin. You can't say that, she says. He doesn't reply, does not even appear to know she's there. She reaches around to touch him, her hand closes around his cock, but he shrugs her off.

– You're right, Erich says. Forget I said anything. Now she's frightened. Think of the future, she whispers. Jumbled images in primary colours. White and red swastika flags waving in the wind; gleaming rockets flying into the air; skyscrapers rise above the Danube, the Thames, the Volga and the Rhine, blond children play under a bright African sun, their uniforms ironed to perfection by their servant-slaves nearby, modern women work at factories assembling Volkswagens, in the mountains in a wood cabin Maria and Erich and their three children go on a skiing holiday, laughing, holding hands, one of the children comes across a strange object in the snow, a six-pointed star made of gold, on a chain. What is it, the boy asks. It is nothing, Maria says. Takes it from him, before throwing it away.

– I saw the ghetto, Erich says.

That damned uprising. The Jews won't leave the ghetto, the trains, ready to depart for Auschwitz, stand empty at the platforms. Maria stirs, uncomfortable. Tries not to look at the correspondence crossing her desk every day. Rumours of the camps. Letters from a Dr Mengele, seeking twins. It's almost a joke around the office. Later, the requests change. Classified letters, saying the unthinkable. *Are there Übermenschen in the ghetto? Can you confirm? Specimens urgently required.* Mad. Yet spoken about in hushed tones, almost as if speaking of Vomacht himself. Maria hates Warsaw. Hates the Poles, the way they look at her when she walks down the street, shabby men and women with the reek of the defeated, somehow not quite human, somehow other than her. What did you see? she says. Reaches around to fondle him again. This time he lets her. She feels him harden. I saw them die, he says. It's war, she says. War. It comes from the throat. *Krieg.* It is a throaty word. *Krrrriegggg.* War, he says. War. Stares out of the window. The snow storm outside rises in tempo, it swallows everything, it encloses them inside the room, like prisoners. War, he says. She strokes him until he comes.

23. **WARSAW GHETTO** 1943

Children with yellow Stars of David on their arms run down the street, seeking shelter. A nearby building is on fire. The ghetto is ramshackle, buildings crowded into each other, women in shawls peer behind windows, young men stand on the rooftops hurling Molotov cocktails at the tanks beyond the ghetto walls. We watch, we see, we tally. Schneesturm rises into the air above the ghetto, the running boys stop, point to the sky. His uniform is white, the twin lightning bolts of the SS entombed within a giant, umlauted U. A two-man team with a stolen machine gun on the rooftop open fire. The snow grows around Schneesturm, masking him, the boys, excitedly, Is it a bird, is it a plane? No, it's an honest-to-God German Übermensch.

Watching. Schneesturm does not engage. He is not here in an official capacity. But now a new figure emerges onto the rooftops. A man, bare-chested despite the cold. His skin is tanned, almost green. The boys, behind their shelter, whisper. Gunfire from the

German forces but they are being held in check, for the moment, by the Jews. The man on the rooftop begins to run. His feet are bare. He seems to grow as he runs, to expand. The snow dissipates, the white form of the German Übermensch reappears. Erich looks curious, hanging up there, suspended in the air. Watches the Jewish man running, growing larger, skin colour turning greener, feeding on the sun. Huge spikes suddenly shoot out of the man's skin, from his arms, his legs, his feet.

He leaps into the air.

Impossibly high. A roar of rage and defiance shakes the ghetto. A German sniper, unseen, fires at him, but the shot, if it hits, does no apparent damage and the sniper, his location exposed, is eliminated by a Jewish comrade hiding in one of the ghetto's apartments. But this man, this Übermensch flying across the skies, he seems half plant, he has inhuman power, the boys whisper, *Sabra, Sabra*.

Schneesturm looks shocked when the Sabra reaches him, holds out spiked, prickly-pear arms, wants to grab him in a deadly hug. Schneesturm sends a blast of frozen ice at the Sabra who roars, smashing the ice into snowdrops with his arms, the spikes make a sound like a needle against a gramophone when they crack the ice.

Schneesturm rises higher. Does not want to engage. The Sabra falls down onto the rooftops, the German forces fire at him, a wound opens in his side, green liquid oozes out but the wound closes, cactus-flesh sealing over, the Sabra lands on the roof, bent knee, one hand down on the roof, frozen like this, for just a moment, we see him in silhouette. Then he rises, shouts abuse at the German forces in their own tongue, and the ghetto cheers as one, the boys jump up and down, Schneesturm, watching from on high, wraps snow around himself and disappears, an apparition out of nightmare defeated, perhaps, by this Beyond-Man Jew.

Perhaps.

24. **THE OLD MAN'S OFFICE** the present

– Schneesturm, the Old Man says. Snow Storm. Turns his face from Fogg, for just a moment. We choose such fanciful names, don't we, Oblivion?

– Sir?

Oblivion stirs. Almost as if he had fallen asleep. Fogg isn't fooled. Not for a moment. The Old Man, too, shakes his head at such foolishness. Pulls out a folder, lays it on the table. Lets it rest a moment. Drums on it with his fingers. As though listening to invisible music. Opens it. A handsome young man stares out from an old photo. His hair so blond it's white. Clear, innocent blue eyes. Smiling at the camera. Snow behind him.

– His real name was Erich Bühler. You remember Erich, don't you, Fogg?

Fogg remembers. Doesn't say a word. The Old Man says, He was a handsome young man, wasn't he?

– He died, Fogg says, at last, unwillingly. He died in Berlin, in forty-six.

Remembers the first time he'd seen him.

25. **LENINGRAD** 1942

And again in the snow and the ice, the Old Man's two reluctant observers, Fogg and Oblivion, Oblivion and Fogg, walking slowly, dejectedly, across the ice. The sky is dark and clear. The sun sets ahead of them, the last of its rays falling on the snow-covered landscape.

– Observer mission to Eastern Front, on behalf of the Bureau for Superannuated Affairs, on His Majesty's Secret Service, bugger me it's cold, Fogg says.

– Report concluded? Oblivion says. It is cold but strangely beautiful, too, with Leningrad rising ahead of them in the distance, its rising spires of the Admiralty building and the Cathedral of the Saviour on Blood and Luftwaffe airplanes flying above like bats or eagles, colouring the sky a deep crimson, smoke rising into the sky, making Fogg want to reach out a hand and shape it, mould it into oblivion.

– Bugger the Old Man, Oblivion says, and bugger Russia, and bugger the buggering Nazis.

Fogg is so hungry he could kill a dog. Or something. There are no dogs. Oblivion keeps waving his hand in the air, obliviating snow and ice, as if he could do the same thing to the entire world. The air around him is clear and there are hisses of discharge and the tang of ozone every time he moves his hand. Bugger, Fogg says, agreeing. Goes back to composing the mental report in his mind. We are beyond the Nazi line of attack, he says. Leningrad lies ahead of us, at a distance of about – Oblivion?

– Damned if I know.

– Damned if we know, Fogg says, ceremoniously. But anyway it's there.

He looks ahead. Imagines what's inside the walls of this ancient city, this St Petersburg, this Leningrad. Starving children chasing a rat for their supper, skeletal men armed with guns patrolling the streets, women like emaciated storefront mannequins joining the fight, and thinking, can they hold on, thinking, this is something out of a bad novel, before the Revolution happened, before a man called Hitler rose to power and rewrote the world like a lurid paperback. Thank God we're not inside there, Fogg says.

– I'm hungry, Oblivion says.

– To conclude we believe the Nazis have made a mistake invading Russia, Fogg says—

– A big bleeding mistake, Oblivion says—

– And suggest leaving the Huns and the Ivans to slug it out amongst themselves while we go home to merry old England. Bugger me it's cold.

– Report concluded, Oblivion says. Fogg?

– Yes, Oblivion?

– Get down!

Fogg slips in the ice as Oblivion pulls him sharply by the arm, face down into the snow, he curses, but quietly.

– What!

– Look.

Lying on their stomachs they nevertheless raise their heads, looking at the sky:

And rising, from behind them, and heading towards the city, a fleet of rocket-men, spread out like a flock of black birds against the darkening sky, plumes of fire erupting from their backs, their metal helmets shining in the dying light of the setting sun.

Flying past, more and more of them, a horde of flying men, and the sound of their machines breaks the silence, there is a burst of gunfire, surface-to-air, and one of the men explodes, a bright flash of flame and a quick, dying scream, a Nazi Icarus dropping from the sky, his flame extinguished as he hits the snow and is still. And yet more of them come, until the sky is filled with these not-birds, not-planes soldiers of the Reich.

– My God, Fogg says.

– And his servant, Dr Vomacht.

Fogg breathes out. Look . . .

Rising from the city, into the air. The Union of Socialist Heroes, the dreaded *Sverhlyudi* of the USSR, taking to the air, defenders of the Motherland against the invading Hun:

Rising, growing larger in the sky, and Fogg can see their leader rising, the Red Sickle, and behind him all the rest, Rusalka and Koschei the Deathless and Baba Yaga in her green-grey colours, and the Molotov Cocktail, and the Great Soviet; and they unleash their powers on the hapless rocket-men, and the sky fills with the sound of tearing and explosions, and the dead rain down on the white snow; Luftwaffe planes arrive but the Red Sickle flies at an aircraft and grabs the pilot out of the cockpit, the man screaming and twisting, trying to escape, his face filled with horror. The Red Sickle lifts him easily, like a child, and flies away from the plane, which veers down and plunges, hitting two rocket-men too slow to get out of its way; and the Red Sickle, holding the captive pilot for a long, tender moment, drops him, in mid-air, and the man plunges down, screaming, down and down and down into the waiting ice and his cry is cut clean and there's a sick wet sound, like *splat*.

The sky is filled with planes and men and tracer bullets and eldrich lights and, down below, Fogg and Oblivion can see tanks moving, and foot soldiers, as if the apocalypse has come early; and Oblivion says, This damned war, and Fogg summons the mist to settle around them like a blanket, hiding them from view, This damned war, the fog wraps itself around them and the ice is their shared bed and for a moment they are together again, together and alone.

FOUR:

THE FARM

DEVON
1936

26. **THE FARM, DEVON** 1936

The wheels of the bus go round and round. Fogg sits pressed against the window of the bus, looking out. It's a beautiful day. Green fields lie under deep blue skies in which white clouds like swans drift past. The startling yellow of daisies breaks through the rolling green hills like a mirage. Music on the wireless. Cliff Edwards, 'I'll See you in My Dreams'. Fogg feels faintly ridiculous in his clothes. Khaki shorts, a blue shirt too tight, white socks, black shoes. Like a bleeding boy scout, what. Not alone on the bus. Others there. Collected early in the morning in London's Smithfield Market with the cries of butchers in the air, the smell of blood, the cold of refrigeration. Racks of pork ribs hanging behind displays. Cleavers rising and falling. Sausages like entrails. Standing there, still cold, that morning, breathing on his fingers to warm them, feeling faintly ludicrous. Eight or ten of them gathered. Waiting for the yellow bus – which comes, at last, the driver a hunchback, black thinning hair parted to one side, rough bristles covering his cheeks. Well, what are you lot waiting for? he says. They climb on board. No one talks to anyone else. No one looks at anyone else. Fogg stares out of the window, hypnotised by the motion of bus over road. Out of London, the sun rising, the fog he takes such comfort in stripped away. Not sure who the others are. Faceless boys and girls and one old lady, she seems out of place. Some strange ones on that bus, that's for certain.

Heading south. A folly of stone rising on a hill in the distance. Cattle in a field, chewing placidly. The giant in the seat behind Fogg sneezes. Almost takes Fogg's bloody head off. So sorry. A mumble from behind. A small voice for such a large guy. Where did they *find* these people?

– I'm here to take you to a special school. For special people. People like you. Where you will be happy, the Old Man says.

Fogg, wanting to believe. Hope in his eyes. How easily it's taken away. But wants it to be true, so badly it hurts. Says, Really?

– Of course not, boy, the Old Man says. Don't be bloody stupid.

Still. Hopes. They pass a sign for Exeter.

– Devon, the giant behind him says. They pass country lanes and mazes of hedges which open, suddenly and unexpectedly, and they come to a valley and descend the hill and there is a small brook and fields of grass and several long, single-storey white stone buildings dotted around, a fence surrounding the enclosure, some cows in a meadow and a guard hut at the gate and the bus comes to it and stops.

The guard looks bored, a thin man with skin the colour of nicotine stains. Comically wide ears. Talks to the driver, briefly. Nods. Opens the gate. The driver starts the engine, drives into the enclosure, follows the path to a large L-shaped building and stops before its wide stone stairs.

Other cars parked nearby; amongst them, a Rolls-Royce Phantom.

– Get off, you lot, the driver says.

Fogg hikes his bag on his shoulder and joins the others in the awkward shuffle off the bus. The giant is behind him, breathing heavily as he tries to fit his enormous frame through the narrow corridor between seats. They reach the door and Fogg hops down. Stands in the sun. Blinks against the sudden glare of sunlight. The others follow. The driver, climbing out from the other side, stands in the shade of the bus and rolls himself a cigarette. The air smells clean here. Fresher than the city. And it is very quiet. The hum of trains and people and carts is missing. Fogg can hear birds. A butterfly chases another butterfly towards a long building in the distance. Fogg sees other people standing there. Dressed in the same fashion, or lack thereof, as himself. The others are all off the bus. Mill around. Stretch. Fogg looks at them covertly. The giant, he stands well over seven feet tall, must be more like eight, Fogg thinks – wide, too, thick chest and arms, when they were standing in Smithfield he was drawing stares, more than anyone else, quite rightly, too. The man's eyes are green and watery. His face is soft, a strange contrast to his body, his enormous frame. He must be young, Fogg suddenly realises, he can't be any older than him.

Also in their group is the old lady. She wears the same clothes as the rest of them, the khaki shorts and a blue blouse and white socks over veined legs. She looks as out of place as Fogg feels. He's not sure what's supposed to happen next. Feels the attention of unseen eyes. Beside the bus the driver finishes his cigarette. Climbs back into the bus. Revs the engine to life. Drives away, down the path, out of the gate. Disappears in the distance, the sound of the motor slowly fading. Leaves them, stranded there.

The Farm.

A sound catches his attention. Fogg turns. Three men step out of the building. He recognises one of them. The Old Man.

The second: a young thin-faced man in a white smock, fresh-faced, clean-shaven. Early twenties. The third: a grizzled military man, in uniform, in his fifties, a thick moustache, eyes a startling green. Holds himself ramrod straight. The three of them standing there, on the steps, looking down. *Examining* them. Fogg and his companions turn, this way and that. Don't know what to do. The three above, as though having reached a decision, walk down to their level.

– Settle down, the Old Man says. I said, settle down! Form an orderly line.

Fogg joins the others. Line up. They each carry a single bag, and place them at their feet. Stand there, like on parade. The three men watch them and the man in uniform walks slowly up and down the line, glaring at each one in turn.

– I've never seen such a sorry bunch, he says.

The man in the white smock smiles. The Old Man says, Welcome to the Farm, boys and girls!

Looks at them. And lady, he says. Nods at the old woman, who nods back. The Old Man points at the man in uniform. This is Sergeant Browning, he says. He's in charge here.

Browning, if it is possible, stands even more erect than before. The Old Man turns to the other, younger man.

– This is Dr Alan Turing, he says. He is here in an advisory capacity.

– Hello, Turing says, shyly.

– I expect you to listen to these two men, the Old Man says. They are here to help you. They are here to make something out of you.

The Old Man surveys Fogg and the others. Says, Each of you has something unique. A quality. And you have a unique opportunity. To serve king and country. You should be proud.

The giant shuffles his feet. Fogg himself needs to go to the bathroom. Still, the words are real. They remain with you. To serve. To be something. Each of you unique. Every boy's secret dream.

27. KINGSTON UPON THAMES 1926

Henry, in hiding. Their house has an attic, the wind blows cold through the oak beams, the floorboards creak when the boy steps on them. A trunk in the attic, old books with the musty smell of age on them, foxed pages, water stains. Jim on Treasure Island, Huck Finn on the Mississippi River. Henry Fogg, a blanket around his bony shoulders, a paraffin lamp casting curious shadows over the slanting walls, reading. In the words he's free, on the page he can be anything.

A hero.

What makes a hero? the young boy asks. But answering is easy. A hero stands up to injustice. A hero triumphs over odds.

A hero fights pirates, sails a raft down a volatile waterway, a hero is a boy and a boy is a hero, good triumphing over bad.

Downstairs he can hear them fighting, screaming at each other. Father drunkenly threatens to stab the bitch through the heart with a knife. The sound of pots crashing to the floor. A scream. A hole in the floorboards, he can put his eye to it and look down, look at them, but he doesn't want to, he huddles closer to the wall, the book like a screen before his eyes. Closes his ears with his fingers, hums, rocks in place, in his mind he is free, flying, he has special powers, he is strong, super-strong, stronger than his father without lifting weights or barrels or crates of vegetables, he can push a wall down with a press of his fingers, he can leap tall obstacles, his mother cries with gratitude as he lifts his father up, effortlessly, tosses him aside, carries his mother in his arms and takes flight, into the clouds, into bright sunshine, and his mother says, Henry, you are the best boy in the world, I never knew you had this power and he says, I always knew but it's a secret, no one must ever know.

With the Three Musketeers in Paris, Henry Fogg with a blade in hand, fighting the Cardinal's men, his comrades beside him, he has friends, All for one and one for all! The villainous Comte de Rochefort strangely resembles his father, downstairs his mother screams, Put that away! I'll call the constables! Another crash, a table toppling over, his sister screaming, but Fogg with a whisper of blade disarms the Comte de Rochefort, On your knees, he tells him, and the villain obliges, Please, do not hurt me, I will never raise my hand against you and yours again, Fogg, magnanimous, You must depart hence, toad, downstairs the fighting stops, his father's voice, Oh, Gertrude, what have I done, doll, I'm so sorry, the sound of his mother crying, Get away from me you drunken lout, Gertrude, Gertrude, the sound of two bodies close together, Fogg hums louder, closes his eyes shut tight, despatches the Comte de Rochefort with a hiss of his blade, runs, alongside Parisian rooftops, leaps high into the air, sword in hand, flies, nothing can get him, flies to Neverland, fairy dust in the air, Wendy calls to him, Peter, she says, Peter! He lands on the deck of the ship, Hook turns with a grimace, his features strangely like Henry's father, but he has a hook for a hand, it flashes at Henry, he meets it with his sword.

– Henry, his mother calls from below, what are you doing up there, get down here now! He pretends no one can see him, he is like Griffin, he has the refractive index of air, he is invisible, he can walk through a crowd, pass like the wind, none can see him, but he can see them. He breaks into a bank, opens the safe, guards rush in but they can't see him, he disarms them and takes off with the loot, he can be anything, do anything, he has special powers, he is special, special, Henry Fogg come down here *this moment*!

28. **KINGSTON UPON THAMES** 1932

Standing by the train tracks in his special hiding place, the train from London journeys towards him and the air *ripples*, a wave of something he can't describe *hits* him and time slows, the world seems frozen, he can see each leaf on the trees, the movement of a worm under an upturned rock, small white blind thing burrowing into the earth, can smell each individual smell of fresh earth and rain and steam and oil and pupa, his hands raised as if he's dancing, fog clings like fur to his arms, when it comes it is not at all what he expects, it is what he dreamed of but never believed and, now that it's here, he is scared.

What makes a hero? the boy Fogg thinks. Time resumes, the train speeds past, deeper into Surrey, the people inside stare out of windows like eyes, did they feel it too, what has happened, what is happening? He raises his hand and the fog follows it like a dog, he lowers his hand and opens his palm and the fog spreads outwards, forms a shape in the air, seems to nod. Scared, Henry runs away. Runs for home. His feet leave muddy imprints on the bank. A trail for anyone to follow. The fog follows. He can't escape. It follows him to the house, to the attic, it crouches besides him and at last, exhausted, he wraps it around himself like a sheet.

29. **THE FARM, DEVON** 1936

– To serve, the Old Man says. Nods to himself. Says, I leave you in most capable hands. I trust in you. Don't let me down.

Walks towards the parked Rolls-Royce. His driver, Samuel, materialises by his side. Opens the door for him. The Old Man gets in the car. What has Samuel got? How can he appear like this, as though from nowhere? Never speaks. One of the changed, too, Fogg realises, with some surprise. Samuel gets into the driver's seat and starts the engine. The imposing black car pulls out, follows the path to the gate. Fogg looks after it. They all do. Their last link to the world beyond the fences of the Farm, it passes through the gate, which closes, climbs up the hill, goes around the bend and is gone.

– Atten . . . *tion*! Sergeant Browning says.

They all turn back. Look at him, the sergeant examines their faces, one by one. His face is darkly tanned, it is lined, Fogg instinctively thinks: He is not one of them.

Neither is Turing, standing beside him. A kid, looks like he belongs in a lab, a library, anywhere but here on this Devon farm, facing Fogg and the other changed.

– We will make something of you yet, Browning says. Paces slowly, hands behind his back. Walks past them again. Says, Show me what you can do.

30. **THE FARM, DEVON** 1936

The dormitory building is long, divided into boys' and girls' quarters, and different rooms for the different classes. It is cold inside. From the outside it is a low white stone house, with ivy growing over the cracks. Inside there are bunkbeds and shower cubicles, a row of clean white sinks, a row of sturdy wardrobes. Fogg shares a room with Tank and Mr Blur and a couple of the others. We know. We see. Mrs Tinkle sticks her head through the open door. Cooey! she calls.

– Hello, Mrs Tinkle, Mr Blur says.

Mr Blur is an achondroplastic dwarf. He has the head of a regular adult, a small body with short arms and legs. He is rather muscular and the blue shirt sits tight over his chest. He is busy shaving.

– So what do you do, big guy? he says, turning to Tank. It's easy to see what Tank does, though. He's a giant, and has the curious action of a very large person who tries to make himself seem smaller, without success. Tanks says, This, and plucks a steel bar from the windowsill, as if it were a twig of dried hay. Tank bends the steel bar, knotting it effortlessly, like the bow on a birthday gift.

– Name's Tank, he says, shyly.

None of them have been properly introduced yet. Browning dismissed them. Turing led them to a medical lab where they were each measured and tested. Then they were sent to the dormitories to settle down. Dinner's coming; they can smell cooking from the main building. Tank's stomach keeps rumbling, loud booming sounds as of the roiling sea. Mrs Tinkle, her head still through the door, making her look like a turtle, says, Big lad, aren't you!

Tank, shyly: I wasn't big before. The change made me big.

Tank looks at Mr Blur. Did the change make you small? he says.

– No, Mr Blur says. I was born small.

– So what do you do? Tank says.

– This, Mr Blur says.

Mr Blur . . . blurs. His features seem to distort, as if each molecule in his body is moving suddenly at exceptionally high speed. He seems to blink in and out of existence as the cloud of distortion shoots across the room, around Tank, returns before anyone's had the time to even move. The shape settles again, distortion easing, and Mr Blur stands there, grinning, holding a locket in his hand.

– Call me Mr Blur, he says.

– Hey, that's mine! Tank says.

Mr Blur smirks. What is it? he says. Girlfriend?

– Give it back! Tank says.

Mr Blur blurs. Disappears rapidly down the room. Tank chases with a roar, smashing things in his wake.

– Oh, dear, Mrs Tinkle says.

Her head disappears from the doorway. Fogg sighs, continues to fold his clothes over the neatly made bed. This wasn't quite what he had hoped for.

31. **THE FARM, DEVON** 1936

Food is served in a common hall. Students, if that's what they are, all these young men and women, serve the food from large metal trolleys that can be wheeled around. Everyone is in the common room. Fogg notices a very tall, pale man standing with a short, dark-haired girl. Both look in his direction for a moment, then look away. It's just like school, Fogg thinks. The same uncomfortable, childish, spiteful environment, the same quest for who to sit with, choosing a table, the hidden undercurrents of popularity and rejection. But he's not a child any more. None of them are. Fogg takes his tray and finds an empty table and sits down. Close to the window. A clear night outside. His fingers tense on the blunt knife, making a little bit of fog rise outside. Makes him feel better.

Has his schedule in front of him. Mimeographed, blue ink on thin rice paper. Digs into his food, without a huge appetite. Fish and chips and mushy peas. Heaps on a fork, puts in his mouth. Chews. According to the schedule he is to work in the kitchens as of tomorrow. The Farm is kept running by the students themselves. Others are on pots and pans, or dormitory cleaning, or working in the vegetable patch. Fogg didn't know there *was* a vegetable patch. Sits alone. Likes it that way. A shadow falls on his tray. Fogg looks up to see the shy face of Tank. Mind if I join you?

Fogg shakes his head. Tank sits down opposite. Out of nowhere Mr Blur appears. Takes a seat next to Fogg, without being asked. Suddenly Fogg isn't alone at the table any more.

A feeling he didn't expect. The fog clears outside. He says, So you two sorted your differences out?

Feels lighter. Mr Blur grins. Just having a laugh, he says. Tank fingers the locket around his neck. Us new kids got to stick together, he says.

Fogg smiles through a mouthful of food.

32. **THE FARM, DEVON** 1936

The adults, for lack of a better word, have a table of their own. Browning, Turing, a couple of other young men in smocks, the gatehouse guard, a few other faces: the staff at the Farm seem to be equal parts military and scientific, with a few Devon women working as cooks and den mothers. It is a strange mix of summer camp and military training camp, Fogg thinks, watching them.

A fresh-faced girl at a nearby table throws her water in a companion's face, following a remark Fogg didn't catch. The water flies in a curved line but does not hit the other girl. The water squishes together into a ball, in mid-air, it seems to shimmer like a cut diamond, then shoots up and explodes like fireworks, spraying water over the other diners, who shout out. The girl laughs. Browning glares disapprovingly from his own table but says nothing. The Farm, Fogg thinks. It is a place in which the laws of what is real seem suspended, for just a moment. It was beautiful in the daytime, the bright primary colours of blue sky and yellow sun and green grass and white stone. At night it is more of a chiaroscuro, the play of light and shade. The colours leach out of the day when night settles. The air feels colder, though inside it is warm from the cooking and the pressing together of human bodies.

Tank and Mr Blur are chatting. Fogg pushes the plate away. Look, I'll catch up with you two, he says. Need fresh air. Picks up his tray. Takes it to the bins, empties the leftovers, hands his tray and dirty dishes to a serious-faced boy in the uniform of the Farm. Walks out. Cool air. Fog rising from the ground. Comforting.

33. **MINSK, BELARUS** 1941

The two British observers are not meant to be here, not now, but the Old Man had decreed, and the Old Man always has his way. Fog masks them. German tanks dance across the ice like migrating geese. Artillery fire turns the old city into a demonic fairground, the air burns with sulphur, the city is awash with red light. Smoke and fire make a second sunset in the sky. Oblivion passes Fogg a bottle of vodka, liberated. Lines of civilians are being evacuated out of the city, Soviet artillery returns fire on the approaching Germans but each burst is like an apologetic cough, a tacit acknowledgement that the city is lost. What the hell are we doing here, Oblivion says, Fogg takes a sip of vodka. They'd been parachuted down, their only hope of getting away now lies in themselves and in what they can do. Does that make them heroes or fools, Fogg wonders. The truth is there is nothing they can do for the city or its people. They are here merely to observe. They had found shelter in this abandoned house, on a thick rug beside a massive fireplace. But the fire burns outside. Family portraits glare at them from the walls. What's this, Oblivion says. Fogg looks at the thing, says, It's some sort of Jewish candelabra, I think.

It's cold. Gunfire outside. They lie down on the rug. Cover themselves in liberated blankets. Huddle close, their bodies against each other's, for warmth.

– Miss the Farm? Oblivion says.

Outside, the city burns. The house is surrounded by fog. Invisible. Tomorrow they will make their way back through enemy lines, to the pick-up point. The Farm, Fogg says. Remembering.

They press closer against each other, trying to find warmth.

34. **THE FARM, DEVON** 1936

His steps make almost no sound on the thick grass. Night, from inside the dining room the lights shine behind windows but outside it is cool, dark, quiet. Fog surrounds him like a well-worn coat. Away from the buildings the field stretches out, a silver moon hanging like a pendant in the sky.

A voice startles him. Soft feet coming through the fog. A tall, slim figure, pale white skin, fine cheekbones. Even the ridiculous uniform doesn't change his inner silence, this sense of completeness in him.

– New boy, he says.

Fogg pauses, turns. What do you want, he says. The other one makes a motion with his hand. You're not in there with the others? he says. Fogg says, It's like a zoo. The other smiles. It *is* a zoo, he says. And we're the specimens.

Fogg reflects on that. How did they get you? he says. The other laughs. I volunteered, he says. Takes out a cigarette case. Opens it. Proffers it to Fogg. You want one? Fogg says, Sure.

The other lights the cigarette for him. Fogg takes a drag. Coughs as smoke enters his lungs. The other smiles. Like he knows things. Fogg's never really smoked before. He makes the smoke dance across his knuckles. A white snake of it, crawling. The other says, There's a girl in there, she can make fire. Clicks his fingers. Says, Like *that*.

– Must be handy, Fogg says.

The other shrugs. Takes a drag. Blows out smoke. Fogg, idly, makes it into tiny airships that burst apart.

– Girl in here, she can spit at stuff. Break it. Like she's firing bullets, the other says around the cigarette.

– That sounds disgusting, Fogg says.

The other looks at him. Those deep dark eyes examine Fogg. The other says, You're not very sociable, are you.

Fogg shrugs.

– It's Fog, isn't it? the other says.

– *Fogg*, Fogg says. With two Gs. Henry Fogg. Chews on it. You? he says.

– Oblivion, the other says.

Something passing between them. Fogg says, These names are stupid. Oblivion says, These names are necessary. Suddenly serious. Even angry. But his voice is even. Says, You want to use your real name? You want everyone to know who you are, what you do? You think they're going to like you? To thank you for it? I make things not exist. You know what would have happened if the Old Man hadn't found me in time?

He's in a rare talkative mood that night, as Fogg later learns.

Oblivion, usually, is a man of few words. Fogg just shrugs. Says, Why are we here?

– Training, Oblivion says. So we can be useful.

Fogg, a little petulantly, repeats himself. It's like a zoo in here!

Look, I don't know, Oblivion says. I don't like people all that much either. But you're an interesting case, Fogg. I don't know if I like you, but you seem all right. Keep yourself to yourself. Half these clowns, they'll be out in less than a week. And let me tell you, I don't know where unsuccessful candidates go, and I don't want to know. So this is just a word of advice. That Old Man, he didn't bring us here for fun and games. He's got a use for us. And he can keep us safe. From the others. Do you understand?

The others, Fogg thinks. The cigarette makes him cough again and he drops it. It falls on the grass and lies there. He crushes it with his foot.

35. **KINGSTON UPON THAMES** 1932

The others surround Henry. Caught up with him during the break. Five of them, two older boys and three from his class, their uniforms are dark and their faces are flushed with the excitement of the hunt. You, Fogg, the oldest boy, Roberts, says. Did I say you could run away?

Leave me alone! Henry says. The others laugh. Weird one, aren't you? Roberts says. He's the leader. That word. *Weird*. Already it has a new connotation. One Henry doesn't want to be applied to him. Just leave me alone, he says, I didn't do anything.

I didn't do anything, I didn't do anything. Roberts imitates him like an echo. The others laugh, their voices cruel. Shrill, they surround him. He feels the fog wanting to emerge, it is hiding in the roots of the trees, it is sending grey-white fingers out, questing. Henry says, Stay back. Doesn't know if it's the other boys or himself that he talks to.

– Give us your money, Roberts says. We know you have some.

– That's right! Thornton says. Roberts' second-in-command. Face twisted in excitement. That's right!

They come closer, pressing in on him. Fogg says, My father will beat you up.

– Your father's a drunk.

Haze rises. Fog clouds his mind. Small fists, landing on Roberts' face, his stomach, Thornton and the others trying to pull him away, drop him on the ground, a kick in his ribs sends sudden pain flaming across his body, the fog rises, it comes from everywhere at once, it reaches grasping fingers, the boys – What is *that*!

Land another kick, Henry closes himself into a ball, hands covering his head, but he can feel the fog, all around, it twists around the boys, someone cries, someone says, quietly, Please, please, no.

The boys run away. Their feet make little sound in the fog. Somebody cries, I can't see! But their voices lose their shrillness, become soft whispers, disappear in the fog that rises, covering the trees, the ground, blocking the sun, blocking escape. Henry lies there, hands covering his head. Scared of moving.

Waiting for the others to come back.

36. THE FARM 1936

– Do you understand, Oblivion says, again. And Fogg says: Yes.

Oblivion seems embarrassed at his earlier outburst. Fogg gets the sense, looking at him, of an intensely private world locked up inside him. Of a self-contained universe, letting very little in or out. Why do they call you Oblivion, he says.

Oblivion bends down, picks up a stone. It is a pebble, of the sort you'd find on a riverbank, made smooth and round by water and time. You might wonder what it's doing in the middle of a Devon field. It sits in Oblivion's palm. He has long, graceful fingers: a pianist's, as they used to say. Oblivion touches the stone, gently, with one tip of a long, tapering finger. The stone doesn't shimmer, doesn't melt, or turn to dust, or crumble gently in Oblivion's hand. It simply disappears, gone, as though it has never existed: one moment it's in his palm and the other, it has never been there at all.

It is surprisingly unimpressive. Like the magic tricks one sees as a child, an adult using the French Drop or palming a coin. There is nothing flash about it. Simply, Fogg thinks, it is a *negation.*

– Before I could control it, Oblivion says, and stops. Starts again. Before I realised, he says. Fogg nods. There are other things in the world, other than stones.

– How does it work? Fogg says. Oblivion only shrugs. It just happens, he says. Rubs his fingers together as though the absence of the stone had hurt them. Lets his hand drop to his side.

– Well, I guess I'll see you around, Oblivion says. Fogg says, Hey . . .

– Yes?

– Thanks.

Oblivion smiles. The expression is unexpected, it changes his face, lights it up from inside. Fogg awkwardly reaches out his hand. Something between them. Perhaps it is, simply, that they are both alone. Oblivion hesitates. Then he reaches across the space between them and takes Fogg's hand. They shake.

– Everybody needs a friend, sometimes, Oblivion says.

37. **THE FARM** 1936

And so on a lazy sunny afternoon, the Lost Boys and Girls of Never Never Land. Oblivion, Fogg, Spit, Tank, Mr Blur and Mrs Tinkle. Some we know well, some, less well. It is only the nature of things. There are others, too, though many will die in the coming war and other wars and others still are vanished, missing, location unknown: perhaps gone to their own implausible palaces of ice or bat-filled caves, hidden volcanic peaks on jungle-covered South Seas islands, forbidding chrome-and-metal skyscrapers or remote Gothic castles. Or perhaps more prosaically a cottage in Wales. The records are sealed and obscured.

Mr Blur sits under a tree, writing a letter. The notebook on his knees. He blinks in the sun, writes deliberately, a sweetheart back home, he fashions words like a man not used to grappling with diction, for whom punctuation lines up like soldiers in a trench. Tank lies on his back in the grass, nearby in the shade. He reads a book from the Farm's small library, *Tarzan and the Jewels of Opar*. His massive chest rises and falls, falls and rises steadily, his lips are pursed in concentration.

Some distance away, Spit teaches Mrs Tinkle to throw knives. Mrs Tinkle cackles in unholy glee, where is she from, this little old lady caught in the change, she is rare in that like the Old Man himself. For people like them, the extraordinary few who the change remade, ageing was slowing down, was halting. No doubt, Fogg thinks, Dr Turing has a theory to explain it. But sometimes one does not need reason, so much as a touch of magic, a sprinkle of fairy dust.

Mrs Tinkle's fingers wrap around the handle of a blade, manipulating it deftly, she hefts it in her hand, she throws and the blade thwacks clean into the centre of the target. Spit looks on, chewing a blade of black hair, for a moment the sunlight illuminates her face and she is lovely. Fogg glancing her way for a moment startled, she looks at him and he looks away, the fierceness is back in Spit's face. She hawks phlegm and spits at the target, which bursts open like a chest. The knife falls to the ground. Mrs Tinkle, with a tsk of disapproval, bends to retrieve it. Where are you from, dear? she asks. Spit shrugs, Up north and that, she says, vaguely. Oblivion sits cross-legged on the grass, contemplating a stone in his palm. Fogg paces, that restless energy, that discomfort of being in the open, exposed in the sun. Bees hum, birds sing, leaves rustle, gently. He glances at Oblivion and Oblivion looks up, and smiles, and the sun illuminates his pale, bleak face.

Perhaps it is always summer, in the place where we are young.

That day suspended in memory: a rare moment of peace.

FIVE:
SHADOWS IN THE SNOW

MINSK
1941

38. MINSK, BELARUS 1941

The city falls. It becomes obvious to them in the early morning, a sudden, eerie silence, which only lasts a moment. But long enough. They creep out of the mansion they had occupied. Fog covers them. German tanks are already evident on the streets. This is the start of Operation Barbarossa, we know: the German invasion of the USSR. But the speed at which the Wehrmacht enters Minsk is astonishing. The city falls sooner than Fogg and Oblivion had expected, and now they have to somehow make their way out.

Not that that's a problem. Not for Fogg and Oblivion, or is it Oblivion and Fogg? There's chaos in the street. Gunfire erupts nearby and a man stumbles into their fog, blood streaming out of his chest. He collapses at their feet, looks up at them, for a moment, before his eyes become glass and are still.

Oblivion steps over him, says, We need to get to a vantage point.

– You have any suggestions?

They pass a burning synagogue. Stained-glass windows showing a Star of David are still, somehow, whole. They should have sent fliers, Oblivion complains. Instead of us. I can't see anything in this fog.

– Neither can the Germans, Fogg points out. Or the Reds.

– Bolshevism has its moments, Oblivion says, without irony. And: Come on.

A German tank caterpillars by, too close. Oblivion reaches out, flexes his fingers. Does not quite touch it, just extends fingers like weaving a spider's web. The tank groans. The sound of metal twisting. Bending. Breaking. What the hell are you doing, Fogg says. We can't draw attention to ourselves.

–Who's drawing attention, Oblivion says, *twisting*, screams from inside the tank, the turret twists impossibly, Oblivion reaches and touches the metal, it falls away at his touch, opening a hole into the tank which grows, German soldiers inside like sardines in a tin, gaping at them, Well, do your thing, Oblivion says, irritably – quoting Emerson. Fogg forms a fist of grey fog. It reaches into the tank. Tactile fog, stroking, touching, feeling. The grey hand quests. Oblivion turns his hand, over and over, nothingness grows over the tank, one of the soldiers stares in bewilderment at a suddenly missing arm. Somehow, it's just not there any more.

– Why are we doing this again? Fogg says.

– To observe, Oblivion says. The Old Man said to observe.

Fogg follows his logic. They are not here to watch the Wehrmacht take over Minsk. No one in England gives a blast about Minsk. No one even knows where it is.

What they *do* care about, care about deeply, is Nazi and/or Soviet deployment of Bureau-equivalent personnel.

Übermenschen, to use another word.

–Your brief is simple, the Old Man had said. Observing them in his office, Fogg and Oblivion standing to attention. The Bureau had changed in the past couple of years. Expanded quarters. New personnel. Everyone in uniform. Or almost everyone. Not the Old Man. Who said, the Nazis are planning to invade Russia. Corrected himself. The USSR.

Nazis already control Poland. France. Treaty with Italy. Nazi expansion like ripples in a pond. Concentric circles expanding outwards. The Old Man: Your brief is simple. To observe.

– And if we can't?

– Then make them come to you.

Oblivion and Fogg make them come to them. Minsk at sunrise and the sun through the smoke like a prism. The tank groans. The soldiers cry out inside. Fogg makes the man appear, then. The Fog Man. Shapes him out of water droplets and ice crystals. Shapes him out of the smoke from burning cars and homes and people. Shapes him out of the nightmare that is Minsk.

Makes him tall. Makes him like Oblivion. Makes him tower over buildings, stand out like a beacon, makes him reach out grasping grey fingers over the smoke and the haze. Oblivion twists, the tank groans, a burst of radio communication, Fogg says, It's time to find that vantage point while we still can.

They shift. They move through haze and fog, running, and find shelter behind an intact Daimler. Watching. The Fog Man dissipates slowly in the breeze, returns to its constituent parts, smoke and water. The tank . . . Oblivion turns his hand, one last time, a frown of effort on that ivory face, glistening sweat, the more power you use the more it takes it out of you. Oblivion twists . . . *erases* the tank. Fogg can only stare. Does not understand Oblivion any better now than before. More tanks roll down the street. A sniper fires from a rooftop. Fogg sees a child, a boy, running down the street, towards the tanks. A woman runs after him, screaming. Fogg doesn't understand the words but understands their meaning. Come back!

Gunshots.

Smoke.

The boy rolls like a football. The woman flies after him, like a wounded bird, but she is not flying, she is falling, the tanks roll on and over them both, the sound they make is swallowed by the fog.

– Hold it together, damn it! Oblivion says. Fogg raises his head from the ground, wipes his lips.

– Watch.

A jeep arrives and a man climbs down from it. He is a short, wiry man, with close-cropped silver hair, a tanned face, as if he had spent time a long way from here, in one of the Mediterranean countries. He sniffs the air.

– What the . . . ? Fogg says.

– Shut up, Oblivion says. Tense, beside him. The man in the street stiffens. Turns his head, this way and that. Sniffs. Turns, slowly, in their direction. Fogg reaches his hand out. Finds Oblivion's. Cold. Presses it, hard, between thumb and forefinger.

Oblivion shakes his head. Minutely. They crouch, frozen. The man reminds Fogg of a wolf. The silver hair, the way he stands. Like he could be galvanised into motion without you even noticing. The way he smells the air. The way he seems to sense them. The man smiles. Slowly. Revealing teeth. His tongue snakes out. He licks his lips.

Fogg panics.

Later, he couldn't explain it. Irrational fear. Came from nowhere. Came on him like a physical blow, from outside. Seared him. Panicking, he runs. Behind him the wolf man grins, follows.

– Fogg! Fogg, you—

Oblivion grunting. Fogg turns, sees Oblivion and the wolf man facing each other, frozen, the wolf man's face in a fixed grin, Oblivion's hand raised before him, his face colder and harder than Fogg had ever seen it before.

– Kill him, Oblivion!

The fear is gone as quickly as it has come.

– I . . . can't. Oblivion's voice strained. Breathing harder now. The wolf man presses forward, one step. Oblivion takes a step back.

The scene seems frozen. Motes of ash suspended in mid-air. Flames on the horizon, not moving, smudges of red against grey. Then the horror comes back, worse than before, overwhelming Fogg, making him drop to his knees. His heartbeat escalates, it feels as though his heart is trying to escape his chest. His bare hands on the ice. He whimpers, like a wounded dog. The wolf man grins wider, presses forward again. Oblivion, sweat on that ivory skin, takes a second step back. Fogg thinks of Roberts, at school. The bullies. Fogg rises. Fury burns the fear. What makes a man. What makes a hero. Cries out as he runs, runs at the German, catching both him and Oblivion by surprise. Smashes into the wolf man, who grunts, in pain or surprise, and goes down on his behind. The fear is lifted as completely as it has come. The man on the ice growls, his face animalistic, strangely beautiful. Oblivion says, Run!

They run.

They run through the city of Minsk, the fog wrapped around them, gathering, as if Fogg by will alone could fill up the entire city with it, could hide this obscene invasion from view, the bodies in the street, the burning homes, the advancing tanks. They run and the fear reaches after them but it is weaker now, growing fainter in the distance. At last they reach the outskirts of town. Panting. Hot now. Sweating inside their winter clothes. I hate the goddamned cold, Fogg says. Still not used to swearing. Makes Oblivion smile. We need to get out of here, he says.

– Seen enough, then?

Oblivion drops the smile. Looks grim. I think we've seen enough, yes, he says. Quietly.

But they are not yet out of the city.

39. **THE BUREAU** 1941

– You did well, the Old Man says.

Fogg with a dirty grey beard, Oblivion somehow never needing a shave but his eyes look haggard, his face withdrawn. Their clothes stink. They stink.

Through Belarus to the Baltic Sea and a waiting fishing boat with signals flashing, through a nighttime journey to Uppsala county in Sweden and there a makeshift runway and a plane—

Hurried over to the Bureau from the military airfield, then made to wait as the Old Man was busy in the War Rooms. Were given tea. Fogg holds it now, his fingers wrapped around the mug. Shivering despite the warmth of this underground lair.

– Tell me about this wolf man, the Old Man says.

Makes notes in a folder. Pen with blue ink. Looks up. A spotter? he says.

Like himself.

– Yes, Oblivion says.

– But more than that?

– Yes, Oblivion says. Laconically.

– Do, please, elaborate, the Old Man says.

– A negator, Oblivion says. The Old Man raises eyebrows. Oh?

– Somehow he was able to stop my own . . . Oblivion hesitates.

– Your forces of disentanglement? the Old Man suggests. Oblivion shrugs. The Old Man licks a finger, turns a page.

– SS? he asks.

Fogg frowns. No, he says. The man did not wear uniform. Black leather, no insignia. A gun in a holster but he hadn't used it. Wore it casually, like decoration.

– Gestapo, the Old Man says, flatly.

Across the ice, they saw things they were not meant to see and survive.

The Old Man pushes the folder at them. A face looks out. Their wolf man. Fogg shudders again. The cold.

– Brigadeführer Hans von Wolkenstein, the Old Man says. A dreamy look in his eyes. The grey-haired man stares at them from the photograph. Honorary SS rank, the Old Man says. Attached to the Gestapo, the Nazi secret police. Department F.

– Department F? Fogg says.

The Gestapo has five departments. A for Enemies, B for Sects and Churches (primary amongst them department B4, dealing exclusively with the Jews), C for Administration and Party Affairs, D for the Occupied Territories (under which Brigadeführer Hans von Wolkenstein would otherwise be assumed to be working, per his appearance in Belarus), and finally E, the department of Counter Intelligence.

– Department F, the Old Man says.

– Übermenschen, Oblivion says.

– Aye, the Old Man says, some poor imitation of a regional

accent. Nazi equivalent of our own dear Bureau for Superannuated Affairs.

– I thought the Nazis show off their Übermenschen, Fogg says.

The Old Man smiles. They show off *some* of them, certainly, he agrees. The presentable ones, at least. The most suitably *Aryan*. For propaganda purposes they have a high value indeed.

– You really don't understand, do you, Oblivion says. Fogg says, What. The Old Man watches, that same tolerant smile on his face.

– The Gestapo is not the SS, Oblivion says. Fogg knows the SS have their own special Übermenschen unit. Their uniform is white, the twin lightning bolts of the SS on their chests within a giant umlauted U. The SS – Schutzstaffel, or Defence Corps – are a military entity. The Gestapo is police . . .

– They're the ones in charge of hunting Übermenschen, Fogg says, whispers, realisation sinking in. The Old Man's smile is grim. He nods.

– Brigadeführer Hans von Wolkenstein, he says. Austrian. Early supporter of the National-Socialist Party. A favourite of Adolf Hitler, advanced rapidly through the ranks of the Party before disappearing from view about a year ago. We can get very little information on Department F. We didn't even know von Wolkenstein was a spotter, until this moment, though we surmised as much . . .

– What was he doing in Minsk? Fogg says. Oblivion looks at him sideways.

– One of the Nazis' concerns is that little is known of the effects of the change in the Soviet Union, the Old Man says.

– He was hunting, Oblivion says. For people like us.

– And did he find them? the Old Man asks.

Fogg and Oblivion look at each other.

40. **BELARUS** 1941

Across the ice. The city sprawls in all directions, advancing
Germans on one side, the retreating Red Army on the other,
Fogg and Oblivion in the middle. Dogs howl at the sky. Fogg
raises ice particles like a screen to shield them. Word is out.
Sirens in the distance. The bark of guns. The sound of wheels.
They skulk from house to house, doorway to doorway. Nazi
soldiers everywhere. See Belarusians rounded up on the street,
sometimes led away, sometimes, more simply, shot. Burned
bodies everywhere. A man with his face peeled off. Fogg raises
the Fog Man again. It stalks ahead or behind. It scares people
away. The Fog Man is grey to black, it is as tall as houses, it
can reach into a tank, Fogg imbues it with enough force to be
physical, it can slap, it can stomp, it can hurt people. He had
never done this before. Had never extended the fog-sense this
far, this deep. Oblivion, beside him, doesn't speak. Sometimes
removes obstacles in their way. Obliviates them. People, buildings,
tanks. Oblivion is like a miniature Wehrmacht invasion all on his
own.

Running, they draw all sorts of attention to themselves. Eldrich
energies coursing through the air. Vomacht waves. The change.
The world is a white expanse of ice slashed with red. The red
of fire, the red of blood. Rising ahead of them, a monster forms
itself out of the ice. The ground itself pushing up, rising, forming
a grotesque ice golem, a malevolent thick-armed thing. Fogg and
Oblivion skirt around it, slipping on the ice, Fogg's Fog Man
losing substantiality behind them. The sound of engines and the
jeep reappears, a driver with the wolf man in the passenger seat.
A tank pierces through the smoke, a Panzer II, turret protruding
forward like an obscene appendage. It fires, once, a burst of
smoke and noise and a hole is punched through the ice golem's
chest, and the sky shows clear through the wound.

Oblivion swears, quietly. They lie on their stomachs on the ice, watching. The wolf man climbs out of the jeep. Smiles. The ice golem advances on him, towering over the Nazi, but each step becomes more hesitant, uncertain, and the golem begins to lose definition, to melt in tiny rivulets, as if it's sweating, until it stops, a mere step from the wolf man, and freezes there, an uncertain expression on its snowman face.

– What? Fogg whispers.

– Shut up, Oblivion whispers back.

– Get him, the wolf man says. Soldiers pour out of a truck behind them, hidden in the fog. Grey uniform, Gestapo getup, they stream across the ice, around the immobile golem. A man pops out of the ground, dressed in white camouflage, he raises his hands, snow erupts from the ground like fists, it punches the soldiers. The man moves his arms like a conductor, playing the snow. The wolf man bares his teeth, reaches out his hand, palm open, concentrating, the man in the white camouflage reels back, the snow falls, the soldiers recover themselves, make for him.

– We can't let them take him! Fogg says.

– We're only here to observe! Oblivion says.

– To observe something is to change it, Fogg says. He concentrates; like the Nazi. He makes the Fog Man come back. Like a giant doll. Clumsy, on the ice. Says, Come on, Oblivion. Through tight lips. The fog condenses. Ice in the air giving it weight, presence. Shouts behind. The wolf man turns but too slowly. The Fog Man, this fog golem if you think about it that way, swipes a long grey hand made of icy crystals. Aims it at the wolf man's head.

It connects with a crunch. Drops the wolf man to his knees. Suddenly the man in white is free again. His ice concerto rises, white arms shooting out of the frozen ground in a mockery of a Hitler salute. Grab the Gestapo men. Drag them down, into the ground. The sound of screams, of crunching bones. Fogg feels ill. Arcs of bright blood on the snow, arcs of red staining the purity of white.

41. **THE FARM** 1936

– How far can you extend your range?

Fogg concentrates. Dr Turing makes notes on a clipboard. They are in the large field beside the main house. It is a sunny day. Few clouds. Fogg concentrates hard. Raises a light fog in the air. It hovers. Thickens.

– Would it be fair to say it is dependent on local meteorological conditions? Dr Turing says.

– How the hell should I know? Fogg says. Dr Turing ignores him. Try extending it in a straight line, he suggests.

Fogg concentrates. The fog forms into an arrow, coalesces. Drifts from where they stand. Thirty feet is easy. At fifty there is a slight hesitation. At seventy feet the fog loses definition. Fogg feels sweat on his skin. The sun shines down. Dr Turing makes annotations on the paper. Good, good, he says.

Fogg lets his arms drop. How? he says. How does it happen?

– Quantum entanglement, Dr Turing says. Think of the mind as a . . . hesitates. As a machine, he says. A *computer*. Do you know what a computer is?

– A calculating machine?

– Of course. Quite right. A shy smile on Dr Turing's face. Think of the brain as a calculating device existing in several probabilities at once.

– I don't think I know what you mean, Fogg says, dubiously, but Turing keeps on, regardless – Fogg has the sense of a young, lonely man, used to carrying out conversations in his own head.

– The brain can be viewed as a biological quantum computer, Turing says. As such it interacts with the world on a subatomic level as well as the observable world. That means that your brain tells your hands and feet what to do – the body you feel yourself inhabiting – but it also works on a smaller scale, as well – a scale well beyond our ability to observe. Formerly beyond our ability to control. The world that is ruled by probabilities.

– I really don't—

– The Vomacht wave was a probability wave, Turing said.

– Well, whatever you say, Fogg says. Feels nervous. On edge. The fog thickens around him. Turing smiles, makes a note on the clipboard. Interesting, yes, he says.

42. **THE BUREAU** 1941

– The *Gibor* organisation, the Old Man says.

– The what?

They are still briefing the Old Man. He paces the room. Irritable, somehow. Says, A Jewish defence organisation. Gibor, meaning 'hero' in their Hebrew. Some, it appears, operate as partisans, supported by the NKVD – the People's Commissariat for Internal Affairs. What did you say his name was?

– Anton, Oblivion says. But he called himself Kerach.

43. **BELARUS** 1941

The man in white looks in their direction. Fogg can see his face for the first time. It is an extraordinarily ugly face. The man has no hair, not even eyebrows. His face is pockmarked and scarred, like a lunar landscape after millions of years of meteor impacts. His eyes are a pale blue, so pale they're almost white. He flashes them a sudden, unexpected grin. It transforms his face, lighting it up. Blood and guts on the ice, the wolf man rises to all fours, his face lean and hungry, red eyes look at them, moving from the man in white to Oblivion and Fogg.

Oblivion says: Run. There seems nothing else to say.

They run.

It is difficult running on ice. The fog follows them, hiding them from view. The sound of feet slapping the ground at their side. Fogg turns his head, sees the man in white keeping pace with them, that extraordinary grin still on his face. Happy to see them. Like they'd been friends forever. Just happened to run into each other here, in Belarus, during a Nazi invasion.

They find shelter away from the city, behind a fallen Soviet tank half buried in the ice. Lean their backs against it. Breathing hard. The man in white takes out a small packet, extracts a long strip of something grey or brown. Offers it to Fogg.

– What the hell is that?

– It's some sort of beef jerky, Oblivion says. I think. Accepts it from the man in white. Chews. It's not bad, he says.

They sit there with their backs to the metal, enclosed in fog, chewing.

– American? the man in white says. He has a deep, guttural voice.

– British, Oblivion says.

– Americans aren't even *in* this war! Fogg says. Somehow disliking this man, with his powers of snow and ice. Oblivion elbows him, hard. I'm Oblivion, he says. Speaks clearly, slowly. This is Fogg. You?

– Anton, the man says. Grins that crazy grin. Big guy, Fogg realises. Large square teeth with small gaps between them. My name Anton! Slaps Fogg on the shoulder. But you call me . . . hesitates, as if coming to a decision then, at last, says, Kerach.

That guttural sound, that *ch* stuck in the throat. Kerrrrrach, the man, Anton, says. Points at the ice. Makes it shake – makes Fogg jump. Jesus, he says.

– Kerach – ice? Oblivion says.

– Da! *Ice*, Anton says. Pulls up the sleeve of his coat. Shows them his naked arm. A tattoo there. A raised fist, embedded within a blue Star of David. Fogg says, Jesus, again. Anton nods enthusiastically. Jesus, he says.

– We need to get out of here, Oblivion says. Fogg wholeheartedly agrees. Anton, as if understanding their meaning, if not their words, nods. Points at the two of them. Then points to the distance. Points at himself. Points back where they came from. Kill Nazis, he says, complacently.

Oblivion nods. Stands up. Fogg and Anton follow. Oblivion reaches to shake the Jewish Übermensch's hand.

– You're crazy going back there, Fogg says. Anton grins again, and Fogg thinks it is almost like a grimace of pain. Kill Nazis, Anton says.

– Yes, well, Fogg says. Plenty of them about.

He and Oblivion make their way across the ice. Anton stands, watching them go, but he is soon swallowed up by the fog.

44. **THE BUREAU** 1941

– That tattoo is a special sort of encouragement dreamed up by the NKVD, I would think, the Old Man says.

– How so? Fogg says.

– Gives them an extra incentive not to get caught.

Fogg thinks of being a Jew and being caught by the Nazis. No, not Nazis. The wolf man. Wonders what happened to Anton. Thinks, he would have opened up a hole in the ice and jumped inside rather than be taken alive.

Didn't like the way Anton and Oblivion had looked at each other. And didn't like what the man could do to the ice.

The rest of their escape was red and white and grey.

They fled across the frozen terrain. Slowly. Tortuously. But no more Übermenschen. Fog surrounded them. Fogg's every moment a pained focus, a quantum entanglement with ice and water particles, with smoke, with dust. Oblivion cleared the way when they came on hostile forces. Anything alive was hostile.

Mostly they passed by undetected. They were just two shapeless figures in the mist. But once they hit a group of infantry, soldiers in a semi-circle, a group of Belarusian civilians digging a hole. The soldiers fired before the hole was dug deep. The bodies piled up soundlessly, it felt to Fogg at the time. Soundlessly. They should have walked away, just skirted the hole, the pile of corpses. Instead they didn't even use what they had, only their knives, all discipline forgotten, days on the Farm, the drills, the Old Man's orders: gone.

They had come at the soldiers with knives, like berserkers. War robbed you of heroics as much as of humanity. Serrated edges. Remembers burying it in the commanding officer's gut, and drawing it out, entrails spilling on the ice, steaming, the fog rising into the air like a dagger. Remembers running the edge across a man's neck and feeling the geyser of blood, warm on his hands and face. When the soldiers at last brought up their weapons, they had suddenly realised what they'd done. Breathing heavily, almost as in sexual congress, Fogg shaped the air around them into a weapon. Oblivion punched holes of unbeing through men whose flesh melted.

The rest of their escape was uneventful.

– We nullify each other, the Old Man says. Has already dismissed them. Speaking to himself. Oblivion says, Sir?

– Had there been Übermenschen on just one side, the Old Man says. If only the Nazis had them, for instance. Then the war could go a different way. But having them on every side nullifies the advantage. I'm afraid, gentlemen, that in this war, we are merely common soldiers.

Seems to lose interest. As if their mission, after all, had not concluded favourably. Dismisses them with a wave of his hand. Good work, he says, as they leave. But half-heartedly. Outside, Fogg lights up a cigarette. Oblivion too. It's war. Everyone smokes. Leave the Bureau, walk down Pall Mall, heading to the river. Cold on the embankment. Stare into the water. Green-grey and murky.

– What would you do . . . hesitates. What would you have done, in life I mean, if the Old Man hadn't found you?

Oblivion looks surprised at the question. Doesn't answer. So little that Fogg knows about him, so little we have been able to dig up. Where had he come from. You? Oblivion says. Fogg shrugs, the question bouncing on him, shapes in the fog from the lights of river traffic, trapped ghosts projected on a screen. Maybe a carpenter, he says. Doesn't know why he says it. It makes Oblivion smile. A carpenter, he says. Yes, Fogg says. Oblivion says, Really.

Fogg tries to imagine a world in which he is not standing by the railway tracks, the expanding wave rushing towards him, the frozen faces behind the windows of the approaching train, that crystalline shimmer in the air, the gathering fog, the onrush of probabilities hitting him, altering him on a micro-scale, a change he's not even aware of until it is a done thing, and the faces unfreeze behind the windows, and the train rushes on, and the fog gathers around him like a living thing . . . no, he can't imagine it, this alternate present is a blank in his mind. What would he have become? Follow his father into the market stall, off-loading vegetables, shouting, A pound for a pound! Fresh apples, darling, still with the dew of morning on them! Saying, There you go, mate, closed-cap mushrooms in a brown paper bag, the scales, the old cash register, drinks in the pub, slap the missus around on a Friday night, church on Sunday, God looking down on a world unchanged.

– Fogg? I lost you there, Oblivion says.

– Vomacht or not, Fogg tells him, there on the embankment, as an air-raid siren begins to sound, we'd still be soldiers, Oblivion. And there would still be a war.

SIX:
TRANSYLVANIAN MISSION

TRANSYLVANIA
1944

NAZI FORCES ENTER HUNGARY

March 19, 1944

In a surprise action, Nazi forces have taken over Hungary in a
bloodless operation, code named Margarethe. Hungarian
Prime Minister Miklós Kállay, a long-time ally of Adolf Hitler,
was invited by the Führer to the palace of Klessheim, outside
Salzburg, Austria, on March 15 for negotiations. It appears
Mr Kállay has been secretly negotiating with Allied forces in
order to reach an armistice.

As Mr Kállay was in Austria, Nazi forces moved quietly into
Hungary, occupying the country without a fight. Mr Kállay
returned to Budapest March 19, where he was welcomed by
German soldiers. Hungarian Regent Miklós Horthy was faced
with no choice but to surrender.

45. TRANSYLVANIA 1944

There is an ancient grandeur to the Carpathian mountains. Sleepy
villages sit under distant, snow-capped peaks. Smoke rises peacefully from chimneys. Trains chug-chug-chug along the mountain
pass, their sound like a lullaby.

. . . at least if you read your trusty old *Baedeker's*.

Which manages to forget the train wagons going to Poland, the
thundering industry of factory-produced boots hammering on
the harsh winter ground on their searches door to door, locating
and assembling the Jews of Transylvania, like so much extra luggage,

to be shipped to the camps. As for the gypsies of Transylvania, their fate is not unlike that of the Jews. Camps are broken up in pre-dawn raids, children torn from the arms of parents, wagons set on fire, horses confiscated for the war effort and men, women and children sent on the trains that leave laden and return empty. Up in the mountains the forests are dark and deep and hide the men Fogg had been sent to find. Up there in the mountains the snow sits on the dark leaves and the bears make their way through forest trails, huffing and puffing, and the wolves howl at the moon like a lament. This is where we come from. But this is not our story.

Fogg sits huddled by the fire. Cursing winter and this back-woods arse-end-of-nowhere dump of a godforsaken country. *Baedeker's* glowing words of ancient Transylvanian grandeur lost on him, if truth be told. Curses the Old Man for sending him here. Peers around, from side to side. Spooked by the shadows. The sounds in the trees. His first night a bear came ambling into the clearing where they slept. Drawn by their meagre supply of food. Wasn't detected until he was so close that Fogg, who was miserably asleep, woke up to the smell of wet fur and the rank breath of the bear, and the sight of teeth.

– He is hungry, the poor thing, Drakul explained. He had materialised in the clearing, a gaunt shadow. Frankly, he gave Fogg the screaming abdabs. Drakul had walked right up to the bear and laid a hand on the bear's neck and the bear came down on all fours and sniffed the air, and then followed Drakul meekly out of the clearing, into the forest.

– But so are we, Drakul said, later. They were eating steaks by the fire. First red meat in weeks, from the way the other partisans attacked their food. Fogg didn't have the heart to ask where it had come from. Didn't need to.

Poor bleeding bear indeed.

Drakul is an emaciated man, unnaturally elongated, stretched, no meat on him, his skin like leather, his eyes black holes. His English is surprisingly good. Learned it from the two previous recon officers.

Fogg doesn't need to ask where *they* had gone. War is a one-way ticket to a place where the train tracks end. The partisans had an Englishman recon officer before, Mallory, and before that an American, or an Armenian, Fogg isn't quite sure, but they both ended up in holes in the snow.

Drakul is a Jew without faith. He is a man without passion, and almost without anger. When he kills it is almost with regret, with an apologetic shrug. His men sit around the fire sharpening sticks. It isn't easy to impale a man. One needs stout wood, sharp and strong, and enough power to spit a man on it, an animal force as the man struggles in the hands of his captors, screaming or cursing or begging. But there is no mercy.

Fogg had been with the partisans earlier that day, on the road to Marosvásárhely. Though the Germans know the partisans operate in this area, they can't always spare the military escort necessary to fend against them. The partisans stopped a truck coming through and dragged the two drivers out. They had come across from the town of Cluj. Their cargo was useless. Building materials. Didn't matter to Drakul. Gave the order. The stakes were erected; the two men: impaled. Fogg watched the wood penetrating the men, into their anal cavity straight through their guts to their mouths. Spitted and left to rot on the side of the road, an old familiar message in an ancient script.

– Like Vlad, Drakul tells him. Materialises by the fire, sits down to chat. Like they're in some tea parlour in Budapest. Fogg listens to the night sounds, things moving in the foliage. Lookouts around their camp. High vantage point. The city of Marosvásárhely nestled far below. No SS should be able to sneak up on them. Though Fogg has private doubts.

– Vlad? Fogg says.

– Vlad the Third, Drakul says. Vlad Țepeș. They called him the Impaler. Rubs his hands mournfully together. The sound of dry leather, like pages turning in a book. It is an ancient message for my people, he says. Vlad was a Christian. It is said here in Transylvania that he was a hostage of the Turks as a boy. They raped him many times. When he grew up to be a man he fought them, impaling them as a warning and a message.

Drakul makes a curious noise, somewhere between a spit and a laugh. Through the anus! he announces. His men laugh.

– Your people? Fogg says. Yes, my people, Drakul says. Transylvania is a land of its own. Magyar, Romanian – here he makes as if to spit again – gypsy or German or Jew, we are first, all of us, of Transylvania. It is in the blood, my friend. It is in the soil.

Germans, too, Fogg thinks. A minority in this mountainous land, like the Jews – but their fate in this war is very different. He says, You style yourself after him?

– Of course! Vlad was defender of Transylvania.

Fogg isn't sure what to make of that. Had found a beat-up old volume of Stoker's *Drakula*, in English, that the partisans, for whatever reason, kept. Two names, handwritten inside it, suggested both previous recon officers had had it in their possession at some point. Fogg saw it as an ill-omen. Avoided the book.

– The land and the forests shaped me, Drakul declares. I am of this soil. I *am* the soil!

He tends to speak in this fashion, when he speaks at all. Declaiming insane proclamations. His men hanging on to his every word. An assemblage of misfits, crooks and the damaged. See this Übermensch as some demi-god, as Vlad Third Reincarnate. Fogg, shivering despite the heat from the fire, tries to draw the conversation, if you can call it that, back to more pressing matters.

– Brigadeführer Hans von Wolkenstein, he says.

A sudden silence around the fire. The men turn black gazes, black as night, on this Englishman, this *Fogg*. Drakul is still. A piece of night, of old leather, a bat man in this land full of ancient horror stories.

– *Der Wolfsmann*, he says. But quietly. His voice so soft it makes Fogg shiver. As soft as when he speaks the order to impale his prisoners.

– Yes, Fogg says. Into that silence. Wraps his coat around him tighter. Nervous. The fog hovers at the edge of the clearing. When Fogg is nervous the fog responds. Though it is strangely different here, in the high altitude of the mountains. The fog here responds more clearly, almost eagerly, its touch on the skin is like the touch of silk. Yes, der Wolfsmann, he says, whispering the words.

– What of him? Drakul says, at last. There is a nervous relaxation around the fire. The men turn back to their own affairs, the silence broken. But in this renewed conversation, Fogg nevertheless knows that they're listening.

– My masters in London are very interested in *Herr* Wolkenstein, Fogg says.

– So, Drakul says. Seems to lose interest. Examines his nails in the light of the fire. They are long and jagged like talons. Fogg once again wonders what he was like before the change. Before Vomacht. The name brings uncomfortable feelings back. Feelings he had hoped to forget. Had pushed deep inside, into the dark recesses of the mind.

– So, Fogg says.

– He is a bloody Nazi, what, Drakul says. A bad imitation of Fogg's accent. His companions laugh, dutifully. Come on, Drakul, Fogg says. Hates that name. Give me something I can use.

– Yes, he is here, Drakul says. Herr Count von Wolkenstein. Der Wolfsmann. *Ja?*

No more laughing. The fire casts a pale ring of light. At the edge of darkness, a young boy – Pèter? Something like that – whispers: *Wolfskommando.*

The boy's eyes as round and pale as moons. Drakul throws him a glance like a dagger. The boy flinches.

– *Ja*, so, Drakul says. Wolfskommando.

Sounds studiously bored.

Department F of the Gestapo. Übermenschen hunters. Made up of the worst of Nazi Übermenschen themselves and the dregs of European society, a band of Germans and Ukrainians and

Poles, a couple of Frenchmen, a plethora of Scandinavians. The wolf man found them, the wolf man trained them, the wolf man set them wild and free on this godforsaken corner of the world. Das Wolfskommando.

– He wants you, Fogg says. Understanding dawning. Drakul smiles, his teeth like filed stakes. His men laugh. As though at the punchline of a joke.

– Ach, it is so, Drakul says. Nodding.

Wolf versus fucking bat, Fogg thinks, but doesn't say. And I, Drakul says, and pauses, flashing again this smile, this almost boyish grin. And I want *him*, he says, so softly it is hard for Fogg to catch the words.

46. TRANSYLVANIA 1944

When Fogg thinks of the Carpathians, years later, it is with a mixture of horror and awe. Of the sun rising over a barren hillside, over men like scarecrows impaled on stakes driven into the frozen ground. No flies to mar their faces, frozen in screams of agony. The bodies preserved almost beautifully, in that cold, clean air.

But he tries, very hard, not to think of Transylvania at all.

– Here they come.

The first trucks of the military convoy come around the bend, down below on the mountain road. Drakul and his men high above, concealed from view. Fogg tagging along. The sun high in the sky. Sunlight breaking through ice crystals in the peaks high above. Trees bathed in sunlight. The river Maros snaking in the distance in the valley where the city lies. Fogg shifting weight on the hard ground. Binoculars hard against his skin, his eyes feel trapped within them.

– Are you sure?

Drakul laughs, softly. The smell of earth and dust. Has a

network of informants spread out across the towns and villages of Transylvania. The same devotion that his men show him. Admiration or fear, Fogg doesn't know. A mixture of both. You don't cross Drakul.

Fogg watches the convoy. It goes slowly, the mountain pass is dangerous, the curves sharp, no rails to stop them from plunging hundreds of feet down. Heavy armoured trucks. In the middle of the convoy a jeep, a ramrod figure in the passenger seat, Fogg focuses the binoculars, sees. A mixture of loathing and that fear he can't quite control. Bad blood, a history. History is made of cut-up pieces, like raw meat. Like open wounds. This one hurts. Paris. Things it's better not to think about. Too dangerous. Still. Paris. Like a gaping wound in Fogg's soul.

– I want him dead, he says, whispers, doesn't even realise he's speaking aloud. Beside him Drakul chuckles, something obscene in the sound. Oh, we would not want him to die too quickly, he says. Would we now.

– Can you take him? Fogg says. But they are too high, they are strictly observers here.

– Perhaps, Drakul says. They watch the convoy drive across the mountain pass, then slow. Stop. Men peek out of the roofs of the trucks. Guns at the ready. The jeep in the middle. The wolf man climbs out, Fogg watches, the man looks a little leaner, his close-cropped hair perhaps a little greyer at the temples. Looks this way and that. Smiles. Canines flash white in the sun. Scents the air.

– Son of a bitch, Fogg says.

– I can't take the shot. One of Drakul's men, leaning against a rock with a rifle perched. Drakul dismisses him with a wave of the hand. Watch, he says.

Too far for sound to carry. But the wolf man's lips move, he issues an order, evidently. Men come out of the trucks. Spread out. Fogg watches them. Not the white uniforms of the Übermenschen Korps. Not army either.

Gestapo.

It is hard to watch them. Their features shift, blur. There is every manner of the change here, on display. For this is what it is, surely. A display, for Fogg's benefit. Or a challenge, to Drakul. One man is an obese creature, fat seems to ooze from his arms, his legs. His belly contrasts and expands. No. All of it does. Like a toad, inflating.

Then the one beside him; Fogg recognises him from his dossier, with a start. *Blutsauger.*

Years later he will see him again . . .

Fogg can feel Drakul's reaction, can feel his own at the sight of this deformed creature, leathery skin like a bat's, short ugly wings between his arms and side, as if the skin of his armpits had been hideously stretched, and the long narrow bald head and those dark eyes, a face as crumpled as a newborn baby's, a name to go with the visage, another Carpathian horror come alive: *Blutsauger*, blood sucker, and he opens his mouth impossibly wide in a yawn or a grin and there are too many teeth inside, and he licks his lips with a long leathery tongue, Blutsauger, he flaps his wings and grins and sniffs the air as if scenting for blood.

– Bloody hell, Fogg says.

The partisans are quiet, watching:

Another man down below reaches hands into the air. As if searching for something. Drakul whispers, Lie low. Fogg does. There is a movement in the air. The leaves rustle on the trees. The man down below is a tall, pale Scandinavian. Thin blond hair. Eyes like pale blue marbles. Leaves fall down on their heads. As if invisible hands had reached this far up the mountain slope and shaken the trees, grasping, searching for them.

But withdraw, at last. A short, light-skinned man with Slavic features shapes circles in the air. The air shimmers, firms, becomes elliptical mirrors. Another man is shaggy, like a dog. Turns on all fours. Opens a mouth impossibly wide, teeth coated in shiny saliva.

– Wolfskommando, someone says, uneasily. The partisans

glance at each other. Beside Fogg, Drakul grins without humour. Down below, the wolf man gives a nod. His men go back in their trucks. The wolf man gets back in the jeep. The trucks start their engines, the sound reaches Drakul's party delayed and magnified. Fogg watches the convoy ride along the mountain pass until it disappears from view.

Fogg breathes out. Removes the binoculars. What was that about? he says. Drakul grins. Moves from lying to standing up with nothing in between. A piece of shadow. Der Wolfsmann, he is showing off, Drakul says. Fogg doesn't ask for whose benefit. Looks at Drakul. The Jewish partisan looks back. Understanding between them, like a spark.

47. **SIGHIȘOARA, TRANSYLVANIA** 1944

They enter Sighișoara at the dead of night. A sliver moon, a sickle moon, a blade lighting their way in the dark sky. Stars like holes punched into the dome of the sky with a knife. Sighișoara is a pleasant medieval town. Charming old churches, cobbled streets, the cool clean air of the mountains is beneficial for people suffering from consumption. At least if *Baedeker's* anything to go by. The Jews of Sighișoara had been herded over to the ghetto in Cluj, before they were put on the trains. The Gestapo make their headquarters in the Sighișoara citadel. One-time home of Vlad III, Son of the Dragon. Charming medieval citadel, built by Saxons. Castrum Sex, to give it its Latin name. Meaning the six-sided castle.

The partisans are ghosts in the night. Skulk from shadow to shadow. The streets are deserted, a curfew is in effect, patrols are scarce and the soldiers doing the patrolling bored. Fogg's value seems to have gone up in the eyes of the partisans. The fog rises from the cobblestones, thickens about them, like milk becoming cream. They pass closed shops, few street lights. The city is quiet with desperation. Drakul flickers from shadow to shadow. He moves like a bat in the night. Fogg does not know what drives him, what makes him go on. A sort of fatalism has taken over Drakul. We will try, he says, with a touch of humour. For you, Mr Fogg of London, we will try to take the citadel.

A suicide mission. Drakul's partisans are no match for the Wolfskommando. No sign of life from the citadel but Fogg knows it is far from deserted. Feels the unseen eyes watching from inside. Wonders if, somewhere deep inside himself, Drakul *wants* to be caught. Longs for an ending. But Fogg is swept along with the plan. Something to bring back to the Old Man. Anything to justify this sojourn to the outer realms of the war, where nothing much happens but for the mass transportation of the Jews.

Tendrils of fog creep towards the citadel. Gently, gently – do not spook the unseen enemy, make the fog a natural phenomenon. Dark shapes moving over the citadel. Bats, flying without sound. The fog creeps. Drakul and Fogg, watching from the doorway of a bakery. Drakul, pointing wordlessly, first at himself, then at Fogg. His meaning clear. You and I go. The others stay behind.

The partisans circle the citadel, hiding as best they can, in doorways and staircases, on rooftops, the boy, Pèter, with them. Fogg didn't get his full story. His dad and uncle shipped to the camps. Mother and two sisters smuggled over the border, hidden in the cart of a Romanian neighbour. Why Pèter was left behind, Fogg doesn't know. The partisans regard him as their mascot. The boy doesn't speak much. Seems in awe of Drakul. A distant cousin, somehow. Born after the change: for him, Übermenschen are as natural as gas chambers.

Fogg walks the short distance to the citadel. Masked by the fog. Drakul flickers into being beside him. Guards on the steps. Conversation in bad German. It's fucking cold. Stop complaining, Toad, you're so fat you probably can't even feel it. A laugh, a grunt in reply. Fogg looks at Drakul. They split up.

Snatches in the fog. Fogg cuts the throat of the tall Scandinavian, the one with the reaching arms. Soundlessly. Just walks up behind him and does it. An expert now, after all these years. Holds the man, gently, as he falls. Wipes the knife clean on the man's uniform.

The curtain of fog parts, momentarily. Fogg sees the corpulent man called Toad. Drakul appearing beside him. Toad opens his mouth to cry out. Reaction kicks in, he inflates, engorged. Drakul pokes him. No. Drakul's talon like a blade. Punctures the Toad's skin, ruptures the heart. The man sags, deflates. A second strike to the throat, he gurgles without sound and drops with a soft wet plop. Drakul raises two fingers in a silent salute. Two down. Many more to go.

The door opens for them. They slip inside.

48. SIGHIȘOARA, TRANSYLVANIA 1944

There is an echoey stillness to the vast hall of the citadel. Tendrils of fog drift through the large dark space. Moonlight penetrates through high windows, illuminating ancient tapestries, grotesque paintings. Fogg finds himself staring at a portrait of Vlad the Impaler. A narrow face, pronounced cheekbones, a hawk's nose, large, piercing eyes. The face dominated by a wide moustache, arched eyebrows. Vlad has long hair that falls over his shoulders. He wears a felt hat crowned with precious stones.

The painting hangs against the far wall. As he comes closer, Fogg sees holes in the painting, jagged wounds. A throwing knife protrudes from Vlad's forehead. Beside him, Drakul chuckles, softly, startling Fogg. He can't get used to the partisan's way of suddenly appearing.

A sense of unease overtakes Fogg. Something wrong. The citadel too quiet, the hushed darkness has a sense of unseen eyes watching. Drakul, beside him – Follow me. They walk softly across the stone floor, towards a staircase leading down. Nothing stirs. Drunken laughter suddenly wafts across the space, coming from upstairs, and Fogg freezes. Drakul brushes against him, pushing him, a restlessness overtaking the normally taciturn man.

Don't be a hero. That's what the Old Man told Fogg, when he sent him here. The Bureau has no place in it for heroes. Go, don't get caught, and bring me back the information I require.

Fogg shivers. The cold seeps into your bones, your soul. It is worse than the Eastern Front, almost. But no. Nothing was as bad as that. They reach bottom. A heavy metal door set into the wall. Brand new. At odds with its medieval surroundings and yet, strangely, a part of it, too. As if whatever is behind it belongs in a Grimm Brothers' tale. Fogg looks at Drakul, a question, How do we get in? in his eyes. Drakul pushes the door. It moves, soundlessly. Fogg shakes his head. Motions: Let's go back, he seems to say. The door should be locked. There should be guards down here. Too easy. Too easy to get in, at any rate. Might not be so easy to get out again.

Drakul seems to battle with himself. Pushes the door a little more. Darkness beyond. No way to tell what is in there. Fogg, suddenly, has no desire to find out. Mouth dry, rats gnawing his inside. We go back, he says. *Now.* Begins climbing back up the stairs. Drakul gives in, flickers behind him.

– Damn and blast and *fuck*, Fogg says.

Almost the last thing he says. The hall of the citadel is flooded with sudden light. It burns through Fogg's eyes, momentarily blinding him. When his eyes adjust, every mote of dust can be discerned in the air – as can the Gestapo men on the higher level, aiming machine guns at Fogg and Drakul. Fogg looks helplessly to the doors to the outside, but more men stand guarding them.

A trap. He should have known. Waits for a bullet, but none come. A strange silence. No one moves. Fogg looks at Drakul. The man's face twisted in something like a smile. Fogg pulls at the other's sleeve. Back down, he says, quietly. Facing the Gestapo men they climb backwards, cautiously. Back down the stairs. Back to the door. No one moves. Drakul, almost contemptuously, pushes the door open all the way. Darkness beyond. They pass the threshold and go inside.

Into the dark. Fogg's heart beating faster, his hands clammy, for once he doesn't even feel the cold. Takes him a moment to realise it isn't his reaction to their situation, it is the temperature in the room. The heat hits them fully a moment later. Warm, almost tropical air. A cloying smell. Like cloves. The door shuts behind them. Fogg turns a moment too late, just to see a sliver of light being extinguished. Anyway there is no escape that way, only death.

Takes a step forward. Another. Hits something hard. Runs his fingers over it. A rounded wall, smooth and glass-like. Drakul somewhere close by. Breathing in short, hard bursts. Angry. Fogg traces the object before him. It appears to be a column of some sort, but wide, and tapering upwards. Like a bell jar, almost. Fogg takes a step back. Takes out his cigarettes, and a lighter. Puts a cigarette between his lips, more bravado than need. Can barely feel it against his lips. Flicks open the lighter. Pushes it to life.

Light floods the chamber. Electric bars, arcs of light high above. Fogg takes a step back, the tiny flame of the lighter lost in the glare of light. Nevertheless he applies it to the tip of the cigarette, draws what he assumes might be his last breath of smoke. Blinks tears against the glare. Takes another step back.

Details come into being around him. The room is a long cavernous chamber. It has a high ceiling. The floor is white and clinical, and cables snake across it like dark reptiles. But what makes Fogg swear, what makes him draw a nervous breath on the cigarette, are the objects dotted around the otherwise empty room.

They are, indeed, bell jars. Giant bell jars, made of hardened glass, bolted to the floor with massive iron screws. Inside each one . . .

Fogg shakes his head, from side to side, like a wet dog. Drakul is so still beside him, it is as if he's become one of the things inside the jars.

Suspended under glass . . .

Fogg finds himself staring at the nearest bell jar, the one he hit in the dark. It is filled with water. The water is blue, rich with bubbles, as if it is oxygen-enriched. Inside the water is a man.

The man's skin looks hard, unnatural. It is an armour. A carapace. The man's skin is blue-green. His hands, pressed against the glass in mute appeal, are webbed. Around his neck fleshy vents open and close soundlessly. Gills, Fogg thinks, numb. The man is like an ancient story of mermaids, he is like some mountain river crustacean, a human prawn. His eyes stare at Fogg. Is he alive? Is he somehow suspended there, in animation, within his glass prison?

Fogg doesn't know. Looks around the room. At the other inmates, specimens, caught within the bell jars.

A girl with ivy growing out of her hair, her fingers. Leaves like a bracelet over her wrists and neck. Thick vines beating against the glass. Her eyes stare at Fogg. He turns away. The bell jars spread out across the room, there are so many he does not know where to look, it is a menagerie, a lab, a prison: a mixture of all three. In one jar a man constantly reconstitutes himself, his human shape shedding and re-forming, a blob that can't stay still. In another a man looking as young as a boy has a beak and green-feather wings that beat against the glass. Fogg can't look. Has to get back to London. To the Old Man. Tell him.

Tell him what?

– My people, Drakul says, beside him. Turns this way and that. Trapped like a bat. My people. What have they done to you.

– Keep it together! Fogg says. So hot in that room. The smell of cloves or something else. Orchids. The place is like a hothouse, a greenhouse, but there are no plants, no shadows either with the bright electric bars overhead.

Fear so sudden and cloying it makes Fogg shiver and draw in

on himself. Waiting for the punch. Something sordid, something unnatural about this place, these jars. Would rather die than find himself in one of them. Takes a sudden run at the nearest bell jar. Impacts with it. Pain flaring. Reinforced glass. No way to break it. No way out for those inside.

– Gentlemen, a voice says. Over on a balcony, at the far side of the room. Cautious, if nothing else. The wolf man.

– I will kill you, Drakul says.

The wolf man grins. It is an honour I have waited a long time for, he says. Vaults off the balcony. Cheap villain in a cheap book, Fogg thinks. Still numb. Wolf faces bat across the well-lit floor. This is ridiculous, Fogg thinks. Says, Drakul, don't—

The Jewish partisan flickers. One moment he is there, the other he is gone, his figure reappears halfway through the cavern. The wolf man howls, sprints at him. They meet mid-air, Drakul is repelled, falls on the ground, winded. The wolf man a negator, Fogg thinks. Remembers. You can't fight him that way.

Takes out his gun. You know where you are with a gun. Takes aim. Fires.

The gunshot is loud in the room. The wolf man is no longer in the place he was. Someone taps the gun away from Fogg's hands. Holds him, arms twisted painfully behind his back.

– Drakul!

But the Jewish partisan is on the ground, the wolf man stands above him, holding a long device, a metal arm with curving grasping fingers at the end, a cattle prod made for humans, Fogg thinks. Drakul lifts his face to the ceiling. Opens his mouth. A cry, a wordless cry, in the high register, ultrasonic, it makes Fogg's ears hurt, the man holding him loosens his hold for just a moment –

Fogg turns, it is a man he'd not seen before, a giant, reminds him of Tank. Memory of Tank brings hatred, anger – Fogg forms the remnants of fog around himself, a fist of hot air particles, punches the man in the gut, the giant stumbles, looks confused, his ears leak blood.

The wolf man kicks Drakul in the ribs. Hard. The tortured

scream ends. Enough, the wolf man says. Barks orders. Men appear, everywhere at once. Put them in the jars, he says. We'll ship them to Poland for the doctor to study. Loses interest. Oh and round up the rest of his boys outside.

Trapped. Men surround Fogg. He knows he can't take them all. Risks a look at Drakul. The partisan looks back at him. Fogg can't read his eyes. The men come for Fogg. Slowly. He turns and turns. Like in a game of tag.

Turns and turns and turns.

49. **THE OLD MAN'S OFFICE** 1944

When it was over, during his debrief . . .

– That was a bit of a cock-up, wasn't it, Henry? the Old Man says.

– Sir?

– Transylvania, Henry. *You*, Henry.

– Sir.

– What did I tell you? What do I *always* tell you?

Fogg feels like he's back on the Farm, suddenly. Like an errant pupil. That we are only observers, he says.

– Do you understand *why*?

Fogg sighs, a long suffering sigh. Because even to observe something is to change it, he says.

50. **THE FARM** 1936

A classroom. A blackboard. Alan Turing behind the teacher's desk. Looking at them with an expectant face. That shy smile.

To observe an event is to change it, he says. On the quantum level.

That level below atoms, those strange mysterious particles. In later years the physicist Murray Gell-Mann would call these quarks, after a word in the novel *Finnegans Wake*.

When Vomacht pressed the button, Turing says, everything changed. The Vomacht wave was a probability wave.

A girl raises her hand. Spit. Fogg knows her vaguely, like he knows the rest of them now. The Old Man's orphans. Turing says, Yes? Spit says, Mutation.

– Very good, Turing says. Yes. The wave made genetic changes on the subatomic level. Another word for that is indeed mutation, and mutation occurs naturally in – he coughs – nature.

– But not this one, Spit says.

– No, Turing says. He coughs again. His eyes find Oblivion's, for a mere moment, then look away, and Fogg feels a sudden, inexplicable surge of jealousy. When the wave hit, Turing says, everyone changed, *everything* changed, from butterflies to crops to humans. But for most the change was undetectable. Tiny. Minute. Of the billions of humans on the planet, perhaps a few hundred became . . . you. Suspended in a moment in time.

51. SIGHIȘOARA, TRANSYLVANIA 1944

Fogg stares at the specimens of Übermenschen, suspended in time under the glass bell jars. We observe, the Old Man told him. We watch. We are the shadow men of a shadow war. But what about the Americans, Fogg protested, their Übermenschen have the uniform, the *colour*, they are on all the newsreels, in the magazines! The Old Man waved his hand, dismissing them. Propaganda, he said. You're more use to me unseen.

– Drakul! Fogg says. The Jewish partisan is on the ground,

they are hunched over him, Fogg sees a syringe going into the other's arm. The wolf man stalks towards Fogg, smiling, and once again Fogg feels that overriding fear emanating from the man, crippling him.

– Paris, Fogg whispers.

The wolf man's smile grows wider in recollection.

Fogg retreats from him, cowering away, the fear eats at his insides. Don't be a goddamned hero, the Old Man said, before sending him out here. Now they're going to put him in one of the jars and send him to Poland, where Tank went. Please, Fogg says, let me go, I won't, I won't—

– Won't what? the wolf man says. Please, Fogg says, please—

And the ceiling explodes overhead.

It showers stone and electric wires down and a body drops between Fogg and the wolf man, one of the guards, a hole punched through his head. He's very dead. The wolf man loses the smile, the fear suddenly evaporates, like fog. The wolf man looks up, What is the meaning of this! Pulls out a gun—

A shadow overhead, standing over the hole in the ceiling. A familiar sound – familiar to Fogg. A wet, hawking phlegmy sound and something wet and hard shoots through the air and hits the bell jar where the man with the gills is trapped and the glass explodes.

Water floods the room. The man falls onto the hard concrete floor and flops there. The wolf man fires but there's that whistling spitting sound again and a second bell jar explodes and the ivy girl emerges in a shower of glass and she reaches out, ivy growing like a weed, choking a hapless German soldier, tightening over his neck and crushing his larynx. Then two figures drop down from the ceiling and Fogg can hear gunfire overhead and then he sees them, and he can't comprehend where they came from, or how they came to be here.

Oblivion, and Spit.

The wolf man howls with rage, he runs to his men, Oblivion says, Goddamn it, Henry! Fogg has never seen him so angry.

What were you *thinking!* Spit says, Come on, we need to get out of here!

– Drakul! Fogg says. Then the partisans come in through the doors, firing, and the Germans retreat, the bell jars explode and the Übermenschen trapped inside are released.

– They'll look after him, Oblivion says. Let's go.

– And the others?

Oblivion shrugs. Come on! Spit says. She grabs Fogg and they run up the stairs, Spit hands him a gun, a fire-fight is going on but no one notices them in the confusion and they run into the outside, into cold clear air, and starlight, and fog.

– You blooming idiot, Oblivion says, when they're away, beyond the city, and there's a car waiting for them, to take them across the border and into Romania, You blooming idiot, and he hugs Fogg, hard, almost crushing his bones, Fogg can feel Oblivion's hot breath on his shoulder, You blooming fool.

– I'm sorry, Fogg says, I'm sorry. Then they get into the car and drive away, lights off, Spit in the passenger seat, a taciturn Hungarian driving, Fogg and Oblivion in the back, close, Oblivion saying nothing the whole way just sitting there, turning sideways, looking at Fogg, looking away. He only speaks once and he only says, Paris. It is not a question and so Fogg doesn't need to answer.

SEVEN:
VOMACHT

PARIS-AUSCHWITZ
1943

52. **PARIS** 1943

He watches the girl. Huddled in the doorway of a building, the fog around him, smoking a cheap French cigarette, Fogg watches the coffee house, he watches the girl.

53. **PARIS** 1943

The smell of rain. Distant gunfire. An outline in a high window, a woman in profile, dressing. But Fogg has eyes only for the girl in the coffee house.

She leans over to her companion. Places her hand on his. A tall glass of hot chocolate between them. An ashtray, though neither of them smokes.

Love cannot be understood as a quantum construct. Or can it? Some say consciousness is a quantum process. In the sub-atomic world, events are merely a spectrum of infinite probabilities. It takes an observer to collapse them into one.

Rain. Fogg, watching the girl in the café. Is love merely a chemical construct? A spiritual connection of a religious sort? Fogg doesn't know. Can't stop watching the girl. Follows her, when she leaves the café, to the small hotel in the maze of streets, a hotel reserved for high-ranking German officers only.

Watches her, watches the old man with her. Sometimes it seems to him that the girl knows he's there. The way she turns her head, the way she looks into the fog.

Gives him a frisson of excitement, when she does. Something in her eyes, like the sun in a clear blue sky. Like a perfect summer's day.

54. **PARIS** 1943

Watches her across the street, sitting behind the glass window, drinking hot chocolate, the old man opposite her. Watches her turning her head and looking out of the window, looking at the fog.

Watches her companion, watches her.

Kill the one, kiss the other.

A moment of uncollapsed probabilities.

The girl looks out of the window, as if she can see him. She smiles, a hopeful, tentative smile.

And everything, for Fogg, changes.

55. **PARIS** 1943

There might be a war on, there might be Nazi tanks on the Champs Élysées and Jews rounded up in the Marais, but this is still Paris, damn it. There are still fresh baguettes baking across the arrondissements, and if the cinemas have to occasionally show a German film to please the troops – H. A. Lettow and Ernst Schäfer's documentary of the SS expedition to Tibet, *Lhasa-Lo – Die verbotene Stadt*, for instance – then so be it. Paris is still gay, there is still music in the cafés and wine in the brasseries, and aren't some of those German soldier-boys *handsome*?

Paris fell quickly, we know. 'With indescribable joy, deeply moved and filled with burning gratitude, we share with you, my Führer, your and Germany's greatest victory, the entry of German troops into Paris,' wrote Leni Riefenstahl in a nineteen forty telegram to Hitler. 'You exceed anything human imagination has the power to conceive, achieving deeds without parallel in the history of mankind.'

For Fogg the city is a living thing. The music and the smell of cheap cigars mingle with the ever-present fog, the sound of Luftwaffe planes flying overhead, fresh bread, the damp of the flat, the crinkle of the pages of the book he's listlessly leafing through as he waits.

Oblivion, at the window, watching with binoculars. Fogg lights up a cigarette.

– Spit's coming, Oblivion says.

– It's about bloody time.

Closes the book, gets up. Moseys over to the window and looks out.

The Latin Quarter. Somewhere beyond the narrow street and the tall brick buildings is the Seine, and from a distance you can still hear the bells of Notre Dame. Outside on the street: a second-hand bookseller's stall, a florist, a bakery, men in raincoats walking with their heads lowered, a group of German soldiers laughing as they pass in the opposite direction, a café with the prices chalked on a blackboard. Beyond the window, directly opposite the flat, is a restaurant: *L'Auberge*.

It is raining, the rain streaks the frosted glass windows of the restaurant, a small dark figure glides down the street and disappears into the building's entrance. Fogg blows out smoke, cold air blows it away. Oblivion like a statue by the window, all white marble and chiselled angles. Footsteps on the stairs. The door opens. Spit comes in.

Oblivion and Fogg both turn. Wet black hair tucked behind Spit's ears. A serious face, a slight figure, Oblivion is a giant beside her. Well? Fogg demands.

Spit grins. It's a go, she says.

Oblivion and Fogg seem to loosen up, all of a sudden. A tension they didn't even know was there, leaving only to be replaced with a different kind, a sort of anticipation. They grin at each other. Fogg says, When?

– Seven o'clock, Spit says. Grins at them too, suddenly, a ferocious expression on that studious face. Says, It's confirmed.

Fogg stares out of the window. Stares at L'Auberge. Dribbles smoke. And the party? he says. Doesn't turn around. Spit says, They're all going to be there.

Tense again. That little accent she put on *all*.

– It's a big shindig, apparently, Spit says. SS-Obersturmbannführer Lischka himself is hosting it.

Fogg nods, distractedly. Had studied the file. Had studied all their files. Lischka, Kurt. Son of a banker. A law and political science graduate, an unassuming man with a receding hairline and thin round glasses. Head of the Paris Gestapo. In charge of the mass deportation of Parisian Jews to the camps.

– Big cheese, Spit says, with that lopsided grin. Americanisms creep into everyday conversations. Americans in the war, now. Americans seem to have a different way of walking, of talking. Bigger and louder than anyone else. They walk, Fogg thinks, like people who own everything they see around them. Like people who have already won the bloody war.

– All of them, Oblivion says. The hint of a question mark.

– It's a regular medical conference, Spit says. Pretends to consult an imaginary guest list. Herr Doktor Carl Clauberg, she says. On a visit from some camp in Poland . . . Auschwitz?

No one gives a rat's ass about Herr Doktor Carl Clauberg, Fogg thinks, remembering the man's dossier. A *gynaecologist*, of all things. Served in the First World War. Became Professor of Gynaecology at the University of Königsberg. In forty-one approached Heinrich Himmler about a radical new scientific opportunity: how best to mass-sterilise women. Jews made useful subjects, there were enough of them in the camps by then. Part of the research involved injecting liquid acid into the women's uteruses. The budget did not extend to anaesthetics.

– All? Oblivion says, again.

Spit makes a show of consulting that list again. Herr Doktor Wernher von Braun, from rockets, she says—

– Who gives a damn about these guys, Fogg says. Turns from the window. The fog collects in the street. Presses against the window.

– Von Braun? Oblivion says. The name rings a bell.

– Some sort of rocket scientist, Spit says.

– Nasty things, rockets, Oblivion says. Fogg stares at him as if to say, *What?*

– Come on, Spit, Fogg says. Almost begging. She lets him stew, then expels a breath.

– And Herr Doktor Vomacht, she says.

The name hangs cold in the air.

56. THE FARM 1936

The classroom is long and narrow, the chairs are all chipped wood and peeling paint fold-outs, there is a blackboard and a teacher's desk and sunlight from outside. Fogg still feels uncomfortable in those ludicrous clothes. Like an oversized schoolboy. Sitting there with the others, as if time had peeled away, as if they are all children again.

Dr Turing is in the front of the class. No older than they are. Wearing that white smock. Writing on the blackboard with his back to the class, the chalk making rending sounds that set your teeth on edge. Turns, at last. Moves aside so they can see. A single word in Turing's handwriting. Hangs there like a *Closed* notice in a store.

Vomacht.

Silence in the class. The only sound is of Tank, at the back, shifting on the too-small chair. Fogg mouths the word without sound, exhales it softly. Vomacht . . .

– Have you heard that name before? Turing says.

No one answers. It is as if the name has cast a spell over them, a sort of awe.

– You are all here because you are different to other people, Turing says. But all people are different. The difference is that you're different in a different way.

Some of the other pupils laugh. Not Fogg. Remembers again the train tracks, the fog. The day it all changed.

– Why do you think you are different? Turing says, softly.

57. **PARIS** 1943

– Vomacht, Fogg says. Wonder in his voice. I never thought he was real.

Oblivion is pacing the room. We'll wait for them to arrive, he says. Spit and Tank will bookend the road.

Says, Fogg and I will hit them before they enter the restaurant.

Fogg nods. The plan seems simple enough. What could possibly go wrong?

Everything, he knows, but doesn't say. Goes back to his chair. Picks up his book.

What did he think about all that week in Paris, waiting for the call? In occupied Paris he passed like a shadow, the fog, ever present, masking his existence, hiding his being. An informant deep within the Nazi administration of Paris had contacted the Bureau, had told them of this summit about to occur. It sounds, if truth be known, almost too good to be true.

Vomacht! Reliable intel suggests Vomacht is indeed in Paris.

Fogg briefly wonders what he has to do with a rocket scientist and a man reputed to experiment on human beings: an unholy trinity of German science and technology, it almost seems to symbolise this new, third Reich.

A week of watching, of waiting, as the unnamed mole prevaricated, location changed, times, dates – at long last, here they are, on Rue Boutebrie, off Boulevard Saint Germain, watching the restaurant – a full Bureau contingent, minus Mrs Tinkle, who is otherwise engaged. It's a shame, Fogg thinks. Her peculiar talent would have come in useful.

Spit moves to the centre of the room. A low table sitting there. She places a folder down. Photos. Fogg gets up to study them, even though he already knows them off by heart.

Kurt Lischka, the Gestapo Paris commander, looks like a seminarian. His hair is shaved short at the sides. His cheeks are clean-shaven. His face is well proportioned, Aryan. His mouth is slightly turned upwards, suggesting he might smile easily.

In contrast the doctor, Carl Clauberg, is nothing an Aryan would be proud of. He is unshaved, wears large-framed dark glasses, he has an elongated skull, badly receding hair, a petulant double chin. His mouth looks like it is wrapped around a sweet.

But Von Braun, now . . . even Spit's impressed, and she's not usually expressed an interest in men that way.

Von Braun almost looks like an American. He has that easy poise, a handsome, chiselled face, a movie star's good looks. He has a full head of hair, combed back, and piercing eyes. Oblivion fingers the photo, then lays it down: almost reluctantly, it seems to Fogg.

Finally: Vomacht. A photo taken from a distance, blurry. No photos of the good doctor circulating. A private man. Here he is by a lake, holding a young girl's hand in his. He is in a suit. She is wearing a dress. There is a boat by the shore, on the water. Hard to make out his face. Hard to make out anything about him. Just a man.

Herr Doktor Vomacht.

58. **PARIS** 1943

When it is over, the operation blown, they scatter. *Abort and evacuate.* They flee from Paris singly, Oblivion and Spit.

Not Fogg.

Fogg stays behind.

Fogg lies on the hard single bed in the hotel watching the cockroach scuttling across the dirty bathroom floor. The window is raised a few inches and a chill wind comes through but Fogg isn't cold. He tosses and turns, the blanket pushed away from him. He's sweating. Grinding his teeth. When he closes his eyes he can still see it, in confused snatches.

Fogg and Oblivion, watching the restaurant.

The black Mercedes pulling to a stop.

The three men come out.

Lischka. Clauberg.

Von Braun.

Gestapo man. Nazi doctor. And rocket-man.

No Herr Doktor Vomacht.

In the hotel room Fogg twists and turns and the bedsheets crumple underneath him. The fog calls out to him from the Seine. He is hiding in an anonymous hotel under a brand-new identity, a Swiss merchant, in Paris on business. He should be safe, he thinks. He should be back in London but he can't. He has business of his own, first.

Fogg stares at the cockroach, which seems to be watching him back, standing there, a black armoured figure, like a Panzer tank, on the line between hotel room and bathroom. A hidden army behind him. What makes a hero, Fogg wonders, biting his lips, his hands balled into useless fists. Whatever makes one, he isn't it.

– Oblivion, stop! It's a trap!

Lying in bed, shivering, but not from cold. Earlier he'd run the water, stood under it naked, the water lukewarm, low pressure, he stood like that until it ran as cold as ice, as if it could somehow freeze his body clean.

– It's a trap—

Von Braun lifting his arms. A handsome man, not a hair out of place. Raises his hands not like a prisoner.

Like a conductor.

A flash of lightning. Smoke. Fogg raises his eyes to the sky.

Sees them coming.

Von Braun raises his hands like a conductor, and out of the sky come rocket-men. Fogg curses and pulls out his gun. He starts firing. The rocket-men's faces are obscured by the masks they wear, these Greco-Roman constructions; they are like some ancient legionnaires granted the power of flight by a modern-day Daedalus.

The rocket-men descend in a blaze of fire and rising smoke. For once Fogg is useless here. The smoke, acrid and heavy, masks everything but the flames and the gunshots, and Fogg is as blind as the rest. He fires high and hits a rocket-man's tank. For a moment nothing seems to happen, then the man explodes in a fireball that rips him apart. Dark rain falls on their heads and Fogg's face is splattered with gore. He wipes it off with his sleeve and keeps shooting.

Rocket-men pop like fat flies. Rocket-men pop like flies buzzing too close to an oil lamp. Later, Fogg will learn that more people died constructing Wernher von Braun's rockets than had ever died in the rocket attacks themselves. So it is with the rocket-men, he comes to realise. They hover in the air on lethal flames, young boys metal-covered, machine guns cradled in their arms, their short blond hair hidden behind their faux-historical helmets. Oblivion lets out a shout of rage or disgust and removes his glove and his hand aims at these sky-borne Lost Boys. He makes their rocket-packs vanish and they fall down, one by one, one drops over the black Mercedes and impacts on its roof, bending and tearing it, the sound of crushed bones, the corpse sprawls on the roof, one arm splayed over, blood pouring down the arm, the lifeless pointing finger, and onto the ground where it gathers in a small puddle.

Von Braun, in a half-crouch run, disappears inside the restaurant under cover of fire. The Gestapo man, Obersturmbannführer Kurt Lischka, doesn't, though. Instead, as if this is the Wild West in a Karl May novel, and as if he were Old Shatterhand facing some unruly Injuns, he pulls out twin guns and starts blasting. At Fogg.

Fogg ducks, rolls on the ground as the fog gathers desperately around him, trying to hide him from view. The fused bodies of dead rocket-men litter the ground, an unholy melange of men and machines.

Fogg rises, in his hands, too, are twin guns. For a moment he faces Lischka across the black Mercedes, both their faces lit up with the fires of the dying rocket-men. Lischka's mouth opens in a twisted grin, his teeth are predator's teeth. They fire together.

Fogg lies on the bed but he can't sleep. Flashes of light from outside periodically wake him. The sting of the bullet on his shoulder still hurts. A red raw weal where Lischka's bullet had grazed him.

Fogg tries to sleep. Tries to think of *her*, of seeing her again. Instead all he can see is Lischka falling down, a surprised look on his face, blood blooming like a thousand night flowers on his chest. Oblivion reaching out a gloveless hand and touching the SS doctor, Clauberg, almost gently, like a lover. Sees the Nazi unmade, obliterated. Nothing of him. Fogg, breathing hard. A sudden silence in the street. The bodies of nameless faceless Nazi flyboys on the ground. Fogg looks at Oblivion. Oblivion looks at Fogg. And cold. It's suddenly so cold.

That's when he sees him. Dressed in the white of the Übermenschen.

The twin lightning bolts within the red umlauted U.

Recognises him from his file in the Bureau.

Schneesturm.

Snow Storm.

Then the snow hits them like a shovel.

Wind smashing ice at them. The ice, like darts, cuts and penetrates. Fogg can hear Schneesturm laughing. He drops low. He tries to raise the fog to him, to do battle with this force of nature, this snow storm raging about them, a localised storm in the middle of this Parisian street. Everything is white, so white. He can no longer see Oblivion. He rises and a fist of snow smacks him on the side of the head and sends him reeling. Again he hears that laugh. Fogg fires his gun, but he has no idea who or what he could be hitting.

– Oblivion?

– Fogg!

Fogg shakes his head, touches his hand to his shoulder. It's bleeding. He tries to focus, tries to summon that thing deep within himself that responds to the invisible essences of that thing which is a fog. Half summons a half-shape: a loping, ungainly fog golem, insubstantial, tall and thin. Fogg watches and there is a mirror image to his own creation, a snowman. The snowman is bulky, a veritable giant. It grins a snowman grin. For a nose, someone with a twisted sense of humour has stuck a rotting carrot onto it – from the restaurant's bins, Fogg realises. The snowman swings a heavy south paw. It connects with the fog and passes through it, dispersing it. Fogg feels as though he himself has been punched. He reels back and his fog man fades.

– Oblivion? Oblivion!

Fear grips him. He can't see. He is snow-blind. He stumbles against something at once soft and hard and falls. Looks down at his friend, who has been fetched a heavy blow to the back of the head. Oblivion lies on the ground, useless, and Fogg realises they are both lost.

When he looks up the snow moves, just a little, and he can see the man in the white uniform. The Übermensch.

– Herr Fogg, the man says. He is blond and with a pleasing face, handsome and bland. One hears so much, he says. He smiles and aims his finger like a gun, at Fogg.

– Schneesturm, Fogg says. Defenceless.

– Meeting one's heroes is always such a disappointment, Schneesturm says.

He makes a firing motion and a dart of ice, long and sharp, condenses at the tip of his finger and shoots at Fogg, missing him by inches. It shatters against the ground. Schneesturm shrugs. He aims again. He is no longer smiling. His eyes, blue and cold, look into Fogg's, and Fogg knows he is going to die.

In the hotel he gives up sleeping, gets up, opens the window all the way and stares out at the street. The wood on the windowsill is rotten and chipped, the white paint faded and peeling. Fogg shivers and recalls the snow man looking at him, aiming that ridiculous make-believe gun. And Fogg knows he is about to kill him, kill Oblivion—

Then, a roar, a familiar voice, the sound of giant footsteps crushing ice and snow as if they were mere inconveniences and Schneesturm turns his head, no longer sure, and a massive, angry figure bursts through the falling snow and it's Tank, it's Tank to the rescue—

He swings a giant fist and it whistles through the air but Schneesturm is quick, he ducks and then the snow howls harder and Schneesturm is gone, vanished in the blizzard, and Tank gives a cry of rage and—

Fogg grabs Oblivion, shakes him. Oblivion opens his eyes, mumbles, Wha—

– We've got to get out of here. Can you stand?

Fogg half supports him, Oblivion's hand on his shoulder, and he looks at him and says, You've been shot?

– It's nothing, Fogg says.

– Henry . . .

– Let's go. We've got to get out of here—

In the snow, blindly. As if they were back in Minsk. But they don't get far—

The snow clears, creating a globe enclosing them. Within it they see the snowman, Schneesturm's golem, larger even than before, the details lost within its frame: its two small boxer's ears made of lumps of coal, its nose a rotted carrot, its eyes swastika buttons picked up from the dead rocket boys' sleeves. It faces Tank. They trade punches. Grunts of pain from Tank, nothing from the animated snowman. Oblivion stops. We've got to help him, he says. We can't, Fogg says, we've got to get away. The mission failed. I'm not leaving Tank, Oblivion says. We don't have a *choice*! Fogg carries him onwards. Looking back at Tank. For one moment Tank looks back at them, and smiles a goodbye.

59. **THE OLD MAN'S OFFICE**   the present

– Tank, the Old Man says, heavily.

– Yes, Fogg says.

– You got out all right, though, the Old Man says. You and Oblivion.

– Yes. We made it away. Tank bought us time. Still, it wasn't easy. The Gestapo had the street covered. We escaped in the fog. Oblivion was in no shape to . . . do anything. I killed one – no, two – Gestapo men. That was it. We somehow made it out to where Spit was waiting in the car. We drove to the safe house. We split up the next day.

Something else, though. Stepping out of the snow cone into a clear Parisian street. Bright lights suddenly shining into their eyes, half blinding them. Fogg, with the last of his power, raises the fog around them, letting them escape.

But just before the fog rises. Squinting against the glare, he sees him, standing with his armed men behind the spotlights, waiting.

Brigadeführer Hans von Wolkenstein.

Der Wolfsmann.

– Well, the Old Man says. Consults his folder. Turns the pages.

We failed to get Vomacht that time, he says. Shrugs, as if all this is of little consequence. But we got Lischka. He was supplying Clauberg with French test subjects. And Clauberg was working for Vomacht, wasn't he, Fogg?

– What was Vomacht doing? Fogg says.

– Research, the Old Man says. Sighs. Lischka and Clauberg. Of course, both were immediately replaced. And we had under-estimated von Braun's importance.

– Rocket-man.

That was their old code for him. The Old Man shrugs again. Rockets were never our priority, he says. Unlike the Americans.

– And the Americans got him all to themselves in the end, Fogg says, remembering.

60. **PEENEMÜNDE ARMY RESEARCH CENTRE, USEDOM ISLAND** 1945

We watch it from above, the way it was photographed by Allied spy planes: it looks like an ant colony in black and white, dug into the island. The island lies in the Baltic Sea, between Germany and Poland. Your mother, Emmy von Braun (*née* von Quistorp) suggested the location: It's just the place for you and your friends, she said. Slaves dug the secret tunnels and built the base. You hand-picked them yourself, from the Buchenwald concentration camp.

It can be a lot of fun having your own private island hideaway. Designing rockets, controlling their manufacture and launch. V2s, weapons of mass destruction. It can be a lot of fun playing at being a villain in a moving pictures serial: you feel invincible.

Not in the spring of nineteen forty-five, though. Not with the Russians advancing steadily, so close, your colleague says, mourn-fully, you can almost smell the vodka fumes. You have no loyalty to the Nazis. Hitler is a madman. And you have a dream, a dream more important than rockets for war or those ridiculous rocket-men – one of the Führer's less tenable ideas, you always, privately, thought. No. You won't miss them when they're finally gone. Not when what you dream of is outer space itself: space, and the stars.

And if the Nazi era is over, nevertheless there are others desirous of your services. There is no reason to become unduly panicked. The Nazis are uncivilised, you secretly feel. But you're a pragmatist. Working for Hitler got you an island, a secret base, the best minds Germany could produce (well, no, not the *best* minds, you concede, as your Jewish colleagues either fled to America or were murdered in the camps), but some of the very best, anyhow, not to mention a limitless supply of slaves for the work. Too bad, almost, that the time has come to change sides. The time has come to surrender.

It's spring and the air is filled with the smell of flowers and munitions. You gather your men. The decision is reached. You will not surrender to the Soviets. They are animals, the Russians. They might treat you like prisoners of war. Worse: they might treat you like *criminals*.

There is only one thing to do, at this stage.

You must find yourself an American.

The withdrawal takes time. Peenemünde must be abandoned. Already the Nazi high command is suspicious of you – they never trusted you to begin with, if you're honest with yourself. And Peenemünde is too exposed, the Soviets are too close. You and your men mobilise, you get shipped by train to the Alps, to Oberammergau, where the SS can watch you and make sure you remain loyal. Your brother, Magnus, is with you.

It is Magnus who facilitates the surrender. Magnus who ends up chasing a US private from the 44th Infantry Division on his rusty bicycle, calling out, in an English thick with his German accent: My name is Magnus von Braun. My brother invented the V2. We want to surrender!

We want to surrender.

By the end of the war, we know, *everyone* wanted to surrender.

61. **THE OLD MAN'S OFFICE**   the present

– Still, the Old Man says again. You got out, in the end. And Oblivion, of course.

– But not Tank, Fogg says, and the words fill the room like smoke. They won't go away.

– No, the Old Man says. Not Tank. That was . . . regrettable.

– They shipped him out, Fogg says. They shipped him to Poland.

Thinking of Tank, fighting Schneesturm, knowing the Gestapo were waiting just beyond the snow. Knowing that, even if he won, he had already lost.

Knowing only that he'd bought Fogg and Oblivion the time they needed to get away.

And smiling back at them, one last time, as they walked away.

– Yes, the Old Man says. They shipped him to Poland, Fogg.

Not letting him off. Forcing it back. The memories. The knowledge of what he'd done, or not done. The knowledge of walking away.

– To our old friend, Dr Mengele, the Old Man says.

And: As I said . . . regrettable.

Fogg closes his eyes. It is so quiet in the Old Man's office. It's deep underground. There's no one to hear him scream.

62. **AUSCHWITZ, POLAND**   1943

This is the thing about closing your eyes: that, not seeing – this act of *unseeing* – does not stop the things you don't want to see from happening. Tank does not close his eyes. Shackled like an Androcles taken into captivity, Tank sits hunched inside the armoured truck, alone in his cage, waiting. He has nothing to do now but wait. It is very cold inside the truck but that's one thing about Tank, he doesn't feel the cold easily. He's drowsy, both from the beating and from the drugs the Gestapo man, von Wolkenstein, ordered to be administered to him, back in Paris. Then, when they took effect, von Wolkenstein came and stared at him for a long moment and put his hand on Tank's shoulder, solemnly, and said, 'What a pity you were not born a German.'

Then comes the inside of the truck, and more drugs, and no food, and the long, slow drive across Europe, in the snow. The two drivers in the front take turns driving, stopping only to pee and refuel, and even that hurriedly. It makes Tank smile. They are afraid of him, afraid that he'd escape or that there'd be a rescue. But neither is forthcoming, and then Tank nods off again.

Then the truck stops. He can hear the drivers just sitting there, for a moment. As if they're taking a breath. Or waiting for something. Then the sound of doors opening and feet hitting the ground and coming around. He wants to tear off the shackles and hit the men with them when they come but he has no power left in him, he can barely keep his eyes from closing.

The doors open. Sunlight floods the dark interior, hurting Tank's eyes. Then they're pulling him and he staggers out, and stands on the cold ground and straightens himself up for the first time. He can feel them moving away, and he grins. He lifts up his hands and the shackles clang as they hit each other.

Tank blinks in the light. The drivers are backing away but now soldiers approach, guns pointing at him, almost a dozen of them. There's a short exchange. He doesn't get much of it.

– What's this?

– That one's for Dr Mengele.

The drivers get back in the truck and drive off. The soldiers stop at a safe distance and keep the guns pointing at Tank and wait. That's all.

The first thing Tank notices after the soldiers are the train tracks. They disappear over the horizon but they terminate right where he's standing. A last stop and destination.

The rails terminate at the gates to a camp. That's the next thing he notices. The camp. Barbed-wire fences, guard towers, low, grey brick buildings. It's a massive enclosure, like the biggest prison camp he's ever seen. Then there's the sign over the gate, in wrought-iron letters. *Arbeit Macht Frei.* Tank's lips form the words without sound. He doesn't speak German, much. They learned some on the Farm, but . . . The letters are not straight, either. They're arranged in an arc over the gates.

Arbeit . . . Work? He thinks.

And *Frei* he knows, it means freedom.

Arbeit macht frei. Macht – makes. *Work makes you free?*

Just working this out leaves him tired. The soldiers just stand there, watching him. He must have nodded off because, when he opens his eyes again, a train has pulled into the station and is being offloaded. Tank stares. The passengers all wear shabby clothes and all have a yellow Star of David stitched onto their sleeves or to their breasts, and so he reasons that they must be Jews. Most of them are very thin. They get off the train, old people, children, mothers and fathers and youngsters. Officers are barking orders at them, and there are many more soldiers, hurrying them along. They all head into the camp. The gates are open and they all go in, an exodus of Jews. None of them looks at Tank. That's one thing we notice, about the scene. None of them looks at Tank, not even once. Like he's not there.

Like they're trying very hard to not notice he's there.

He sees them walking through the gates. Carrying nothing. Parents holding their children's hands. Sees a man in the distance. Crisp uniform. A horsewhip in one hand, beating rhythmically against his thigh. Thump. Thump. And pointing. Sorting the incomers into two streams. Left. Right. Left. Right. Thump. Thump. Thump.

Black smoke rising in the distance. We notice that, too. The black smoke. Tank notices it as well. It's impossible not to. The smell. The air is choked with it. It makes a contrast with the smell of fresh hay and trees from the outlying areas. It's a charming sort of place in the Polish countryside, with a small village nearby, just out of sight, and forests, and that black smoke, that damnable black smoke rising.

After a while the Jews are all sorted left or right and the man with the horsewhip comes walking through the gates. Not hurrying. He's got all the time in the world. The horsewhip thumping rhythmically against his leg. Thump. Thump. Thump bloody thump, Tank thinks. The man comes over and looks at Tank and smiles a small and satisfied smile. Tank returns his gaze. Thinking the drugs are wearing off. Thinking maybe he can make a go at it. Tests the shackles, casually. The man's smile just grows a little wider.

– I'm Dr Mengele, he says. You must be Tank.

Tank looks at the man. Looks at the soldiers with their guns trained on him. Looks at the distance. Figures he can't do it. Does it anyway.

The shackles drag him down. He swings one at the doctor but he's too far away and it whistles before his face but doesn't connect. Mengele doesn't even move. Just stands there, smiling. 'What a beautiful specimen,' he says. Then he gestures with his head and someone fires, not a bullet, a dart. It hits Tank in the neck and he feels himself going numb.

– Take him to the menagerie, Dr Mengele says; the last words Tank hears for a while.

63. **AUSCHWITZ. DR MENGELE'S LABS** 1943

We can't now tell whether it is night or day. There are no windows. Tank opens his eyes, regains consciousness as they come inside. The room reeks of shit and piss and cleaning fluids and sweat. Mostly it reeks of an animal sort of fear. Tank isn't often afraid. But he knows the smell, and like an animal it makes him want to whimper.

He is not alone in the room.

It is a long corridor brightly lit by white electric lights. On each side of the corridor are cages. In each cage there are specimens.

Like with animals in an exotic menagerie, the floors of the specimens' cages are littered with their own excrement. The specimens are very thin, Tank notices. Or rather, he tries not to notice. Like the Jews going through the gates of Auschwitz, trying to unsee Tank. Tank blinks his eyes. Dr Mengele, ahead of him, turns and smiles reassuringly. 'Superb recovery,' he says. He nods at someone behind Tank. Something touches Tank, lightly, on his bare skin and intense pain flares up through Tank's body, spreading like a liquid, making his whole body ring out like a bell. Then the touch is removed and the pain goes away. Tank turns and sees men in white smocks holding long cattle prods. Electricity. They'd just shot him up full of electricity. He looks back at the doctor. The doctor is smiling. Do we understand each other? he says.

Tank understands electricity. He nods. What else is there to do? He looks at the cages as he passes them. They make a slow progression, Dr Mengele and Tank and Dr Mengele's assistants with their electric cattle prods. A slow exhibition, Tank thinks, staring into the cages. A woman with multicoloured skin looks back at him. Swan wings erupt out of her naked shoulder blades. Her hair is wild and matted, crusted with dirt. Her hair is black and so are her eyes. In another cage a man is on fire, like a human torch. In the next a woman is a statue of glass, her body is transparent, Tank can see the dirty wall behind her, through her.

Übermenschen.

Tank wouldn't describe himself as much of a thinker but when he looks at Mengele's specimens he can't help but think and none of his thoughts are pleasant. Übermenschen. He looks at these poor misshapen creatures in their cages and wonders what it means to be an Over-Man. What it's like to be a hero. He doesn't know how they all ended up there, in Auschwitz. Collected like curiosities. Scars on the man in the next cage. An average-looking man. Naked. Scarred everywhere. Scars on his face, his arms, his torso. Scars like a script. Some pus-ing. Some sealed and healed. Scars on his tummy, his abdomen. Scars on his thighs. Looks at Tank. Says nothing. Scar Man.

In the next cage a pale man in a world of ice. Ice frosts the walls and the floor and the bars. The man wears a tattered yellow Star of David on his sleeve. The man has pale blue eyes. He, too, looks at Tank. Smiles. The smile transforms his face. My name is Kerach, he says. What's yours?

The assistants step forward. Stick the cattle prods through the bars. Hit the ice man with them. He shudders, falls back. Keeps the grin. Keeps his eyes fixed on Tank. Blasted Nazis, what, he says. Mengele pauses. Looks at the man with a frown of displeasure. Schedule Mr Kerach the Jew for tomorrow's opera-tion, he says. Kerach ignores him. Where are you from? he says. English? I learn English in prison, he says. Camp with English officers, before Herr Doktor bring me here. English good!

Tank wants to reply but then the cattle prod is on him again and the electricity sings through him and he near passes out. Enough, Mengele says. Take him to the operating room.

They drag Tank the rest of the way. Past the cages and the specimens and into a brightly lit room with a metal table in the middle of it and a harsh light above it. They strap Tank to the table. The leather straps dig into his skin. They remove his clothes with a scalpel, leaving him naked. The light hurts Tank's eyes. It shines directly at his face. He can make out Mengele's face swimming above him. The man has gained back his good humour. Excellent, Mengele says. He strokes Tank's skin. Of the English specimens we get so few, Mengele says. He holds up something for Tank to see. A scalpel, Tank realises. It shines in the bright light. He tries to fight the restraints but he has no power left in him. Mengele feels him, strokes him. Such muscles! he says. Such a body!

He lowers the scalpel. The tip of the blade touches Tank's chest. It begins pressing into his skin. The light shines into Tank's eyes. The blade presses in and with it comes pain. Eventually Tank screams.

EIGHT:
SOMMERTAG

PARIS
1943

64. **THE OLD MAN'S OFFICE** the present

– These things happen, the Old Man says. As if he's trying to console Fogg. They happened to Tank, Fogg says. The Old Man sighs. In war there are casualties, Fogg, he says.

Silence reigns as they look at each other. The Old Man, as if trying to bring back this meeting – this interrogation – onto its right track, turns another page in the dossier before him. The Paris operation, he says.

– Yes?

– It failed, the Old Man says, because intelligence cannot always be relied on. I can assure you the informant was dealt with, later.

Fogg thinks of the corpse of a man, floating face down in a body of water. Is that what the Old Man meant? Or a quiet assassination in a curfewed street, in the dark, a bullet to the head, a body left behind.

Or a simple disappearance. A Nazi functionary who happened to go missing, one day. So much space in the catacombs under Paris, and dark quiet places to store such offerings in. Whichever way this nameless informant was dealt with, it doesn't matter to Fogg. It doesn't change things. And it makes facing the Old Man easier, somehow. As if, momentarily, Fogg has gained the upper hand. The point, the Old Man says, is that you came out of it, Fogg. Alive.

– Was that the point? Fogg says.

The Old Man regards him with his head tilted, like a bird's. Makes Fogg uncomfortable. The Old Man says, Vomacht was never there. It was a set-up, we both know that now. The others were decoys, sacrificial pawns, and Vomacht was kept clear away. Correct?

– Yes . . .

And now the Old Man smiles, a small, tight smile. As if this momentary shift in their relationship has ended, and he is once again holding the tiller on this ship, and it is heading into hidden reefs where Fogg has no desire to go.

– You had a hunch though, didn't you, Fogg?

The Old Man's voice is soft, almost a whisper. Fogg feels hypnotised, it is so hot in the room, the Old Man's eyes hold him in their stare. You stuck around, the Old Man says, matter-of-factly. Even when we recalled you and the others. You stuck around, in Paris. Watching in the fog. What were you watching for, Fogg? What did you *find*?

The Old Man's voice rises then, becomes a whip, demands an answer. Fogg moistens his lips. Nothing! he says. His voice is small and alone in the room. Nothing, he says. I found nothing. The Old Man looks at him and Fogg looks away.

The door, miraculously, opens. Ah, tea, the Old Man says.

It's his old driver, Samuel. As unchanged as they all are. Gives Fogg a tight-lipped smile. Nods at Oblivion. Carries a tea service on a tray. He places it on the desk and pours three cups, carefully. Cream? Sugar? he says.

Fogg just shakes his head. Cream and sugar, the Old Man says. For both of us, please, Samuel. Oblivion holds up two fingers, silently. Samuel serves the tea and departs. Fogg holds his cup of tea on his lap. The Old Man takes a sip from his, sighs with contentment. Then:

– Paris, the Old Man says. Nineteen forty-three.

– Old history, Oblivion says. Takes a sip of tea.

– Funny thing, history, the Old Man says. It has a curious tendency to come back to life when you least expect it.

65. **PARIS** 1943

Fogg, watching. Just like we're watching, now. The smoke from French cigarettes curls like fog. He makes shapes with the smoke. Releases tiny smoke men into the air. They float overhead and slowly dissipate. You're a good watcher, aren't you, Fogg. The Old Man, after three months on the Farm. You're a watcher, Fogg. A hider, not a seeker. Lays a fatherly hand on Fogg's shoulder. We could use men like you, he says.

And, later, in a bookstall on the Charing Cross Road in London, leafing through colourful American magazines. Like *Thrilling Tales of the Beyond-Men*. The text written by a Jacob Kurtzberg, in a tone of thrilled adoration. And yet the eye is drawn to the pictures, the bright uniforms in pixelated garish four-colour. There's Tigerman, framed dramatically on top of the Empire State Building, holding onto a cowering criminal mastermind. There's the Green Gunman chasing outlaws in the wilds of Texas. The Electric Twins in Detroit capturing Al Capone. Fogg is mesmerised by the images, their brashness, their colour. It is raining on the Charing Cross Road. A grey morning, people hurrying past with black umbrellas over their heads. You're a good watcher, Fogg, the Old Man says, his voice is in Fogg's ears. We need men like you. Do not be tempted by the Americans, the loudness, the colour. We are the grey men, we are the shadow men, we watch but are not seen.

What did you see in Paris, Fogg? What were you so diligently watching?

A girl, Old Man. I was watching a girl.

Fogg rolls smoke like quarters between his fingers. Watching the coffeehouse and the girl and the older man she's with. The way she leans over and touches the back of his hand with her fingers. The way she holds her hot chocolate. Watches the rain streaking down the glass, hiding her face. There are just the two of them, the girl and the older man. No Gestapo minders, no

SS shadows. No Übermenschen. Just the two of them. Just the two of them and Fogg.

66. **THE OLD MAN'S OFFICE** the present

– Unaccounted-for days, your stay in Paris, the Old Man says. Oblivion shifts beside Fogg. Fogg doesn't answer.

– It's understandable, the Old Man says. Fogg looks up. Oblivion crosses his legs. The Old Man's voice is soft, compassionate. You were looking for Vomacht, weren't you, Fogg, the Old Man says.

Vomacht, Vomacht. That name again. Hanging like smoke in the room. Fogg doesn't reply, neither confirms nor denies. A note of finality in the Old Man's voice. We are not here to tell stories to each other, he seems to say. We are here merely in pursuit of the truth.

– You figured even falsified intelligence must have a kernel of truth in it, the Old Man says. Turns another page in that damned dossier on his desk. Nods his head wisely. Hitler said something similar, once. For a lie to work it must have some truth in it to begin with. Or something of that nature, anyway.

Pauses. Oblivion looks sideways at Fogg. For a moment their eyes meet. Fogg looks away. The Old Man takes a sip of tea. Rests the china cup back on its saucer. Delicately. A chime as the two meet. The Old Man, softly: So what did you see, Fogg?

Like a hunter done with the laying of a trap. You were my best watcher, Fogg. The very best. A silence. Into it the Old Man's voice, a whisper, an insinuation.

What did you see, Fogg, that lost week in Paris?

67. **PARIS** 1943

He shadows the girl for two days, in fog and rain, trying not to think of Tank, of that botched operation, of rocket-men lying like broken mechanical toys on the ground. Late at night, lying on the narrow bed in a room too hot and too cold at once. Thinking of his mother back in England. Of the whistle of a train. Of the smell of wet leaves. Of a faraway place called Auschwitz, of which not much is known, somewhere in Poland where only the Jews, like lemmings, go.

But it isn't the thought of Tank that keeps him awake at night, tossing and turning, it isn't the thought of the operation; not even of Vomacht.

Fogg is thinking only of the girl.

Fogg had a hunch. Fogg stayed on in Paris, arguing with Oblivion, a bitter fight.

Standing there at the Gare du Nord. The whistle of a train. The smell of wet leaves. The smell of rich perfume and cheap cigarettes. Oblivion's long body clad in a raincoat. Fogg is just Fogg. Bored German soldiers patrolling. Spit had gone separately, was already out of the country. Oblivion says, We need to get on the train. Come on, Fogg. Reaches for him.

Fogg shrugs him away. I told you I'm not going, he says. Oblivion's white face seems chiselled of marble. He has that classical Roman statue look. Anger in his eyes, though. His voice is cold as the rain. You don't know what you're doing, he says. Fogg, listen to me—

– No. I have to—

– Damn it, Fogg!

– Leave me alone, Oblivion!

A soldier turns to look. Nudges his friend, who also turns. Two men shouting at each other on a platform attract attention. Fogg makes himself relax. Body language. Smiles. Oblivion smiles back. Pats him on the shoulder. You're not leaving me a choice, he says, quietly, through the smile. The soldiers turn back, bored. Men yelling at each other in France are a common occurrence. What do you expect. No, Fogg says, I'm not.

A conductor whistles. Oblivion's hand still on Fogg's shoulder. His fingers digging, hard, into flesh, into bones, hurting Fogg. Get on the train, Oblivion says, quietly, still smiling. Now, Fogg. We have to leave.

– Get your hands off me, Oblivion.

– Damn it, Henry! A different note in Oblivion's voice. Hurt, Fogg realises. It makes him feel peculiar. He's almost giving in. No, he says, but softly. He puts his hand on Oblivion's wrist. Feels the pulse of Oblivion's heart through his skin. I have to, Oblivion. I have to do this. Please.

– Please.

Oblivion looks at him. What's behind those pale blue eyes, Fogg wonders, Oblivion's eyes are as clear as windows, nothing but empty sky behind them. Blue sky and clouds. Fogg feels the pressure on his shoulder easing. Feels Oblivion's heartbeat, faster, then faster still. Hears the conductor whistling again. Smells wet leaves, oil, a woman's perfume. I just have to do this, he says. Oblivion nods. His face never changes. Only the beating of his heart against the tips of Fogg's fingers betrays what's inside. Goodbye, Henry, he says.

Fogg shifts in place, suddenly awkward. Things to say, no way to say them. Cover for me, he says. Oblivion nods, once. Then he turns and boards the train and is gone.

Fogg stays on the platform. Watching as the wheels start to turn. As steam rises into the air and the train starts its motion, accelerating along the platform. Watches as it disappears into the distance. Then he walks outside.

Into light and air and rain. Walking along the Seine with the rain falling around him. The sun peeks around a cloud, for just one moment, its light breaking through the drops, and Fogg can see a rainbow, an illusion of colour blossoming out of water and light. It stretches over the Seine, over Notre Dame, like a message he can't decipher, a sudden explosion of colour in a black-and-white world. For just a moment he stops and takes a deep breath, as if he could inhale not just air, but light and colour, with that physical act; as if he could make himself come alive, gain substance, gain shape and definition and scale.

But it's just air; and he stands there, by the river snaking below, and stares, transfixed, at the rainbow, rising over the river, a bridge in the sky, an impossible dream of colour; and then a cloud covers the sun again and the colours fade, and Fogg remains standing there, in the rain, in a world washed grey.

Again he picks up the pace, the Seine on his right, Notre Dame rising in the distance, the fog wraps around him, hiding him from German patrols and unfriendly Parisians, he is the shadow man and he stalks towards his target. He'd found her by instinct, by a whisper, by a sense that the informant *hadn't* been wrong.

This is what Fogg reasoned:

What, he thought, if the information was genuine? If Vomacht really *was* visiting Paris?

What if, instead of betraying them, the informant had been captured by the Gestapo and they, in turn, had then used it to their advantage? The operation could have been in its late stages by then. Fogg and Oblivion already in Paris, the backup team waiting, everything ready and then Spit comes back with the details – but by then the informant had been turned by the Nazis, and it's a trap, Vomacht kept clean away as the British Übermenschen walked right into the ambush. It was just dumb luck they got away.

And then: Tank didn't get away, did he, Fogg.

No.

Well screw Tank, he thinks, with sudden savagery. If it's flavoured with guilt or shame then so what. Screw Tank, he knew the risks when he signed on to do this job. Screw him. No one asked him to help. No one asked him to take the fall. Fogg doesn't want to think about Tank.

Instead:

If Fogg is right then Vomacht may still, in fact, be in Paris.
And so he goes looking.

He goes looking but, instead, he finds the girl.

68. **THE OLD MAN'S OFFICE** the present

Silence in the room, and warmth, and motes of dust. Fogg suddenly craves music. Something to break that oppressive, waiting silence. Reminds him of the interrogation room in the Berlin-Mariendorf DP Camp, in forty-five.

Echoes from the past, faint voices like dry leaves. Tell me about Erich Bühler, the Old Man suggests to Maria Becker. Tell me about Schneesturm. The sound of Jewish children singing outside. The sound of someone getting shot. The sound of a blackjack hitting a jaw, the sound of teeth spat on the floor. Only now it isn't poor Maria Becker, secretary for SS Obergruppenführer Krüger in Warsaw, who is in the chair. It's him, Fogg. And the Old Man still asking the questions.

Fogg wants to stand up. To shout. Get it over with! Remains sitting. Remains silent. The Old Man wets a finger and turns a page in the dossier before him. Vomacht, he says. Oblivion, stirring. Vomacht. The Old Man pulls out a photo. Pushes it towards Fogg. It's the same photo they were given in Paris, before the mission. Shot with a long lens, and blurry. No good photos of the good doctor. He is by a lake, beside him is a young girl. He is holding her hand. Fogg takes the photo. Glances at it, casually. Puts it back on the desk. The tea warm where it rests on his knees. Waits. So does the Old Man.

– Well, it's of little consequence, the Old Man says. Takes back the photo. Drums his fingers on the surface of the desk. Vomacht, despite our best efforts, kept eluding us, he says. Didn't he, Oblivion?

– Sure, Oblivion says. Noncommittally.

– He wasn't alone, either, was he, the Old Man says.

– Sir?

– Rumour had it that he had a daughter, the Old Man says. An only daughter.

– Rumours, Oblivion says. The Old Man laughs, shortly. Quite, he says. Still. Do you remember what else the rumours said, Oblivion?

Ignoring Fogg. Excluding him from the conversation. Fogg's fingers tightening on the china cup in his hands.

– Yes, Oblivion says. Unwillingly, it sounds like. But playing his part. They said he had a daughter, didn't they. And that she was there, with him, when he activated the device, in thirty-two. When it changed.

– Vomacht's girl, the Old Man says. Yes. Spreads his hands, fingers splayed, as though searching for meaning, an answer. What was her name? he says. Vomacht's girl. Do you remember, Oblivion?

Oblivion shakes his head. Perhaps a no, perhaps a criticism. Doesn't look at Fogg. But the Old Man is. Fogg? the Old Man says. Perhaps your recollection is better?

But Fogg has had enough. Fogg feels a sort of red fog descending. That anger that's been building up, the pressure, a kettle having to let out steam or it will explode, simple mechanics—

He shoots up, it feels so good to – just – *let* – *go* – to breathe out that anger, he lifts up the tea cup and the saucer, warm tea slushes on the floor, runs down Fogg's arms, he turns, like a discus thrower, lets fly the cup, the saucer – they fly through the air and hit the wall and smash satisfyingly into bits. He stands there, breathing hard, tea running down his arms.

– Klara! he says. Shouts. Her name was *Klara*!

Stands there, breathing heavily. Fingers curled into fists. A tea stain on the wall. Fragments of china on the floor. A silence. The Old Man takes a sip of tea. Puts his cup down. Nods. Klara Vomacht, he says. That's right.

Interlaces his fingers. Regards Fogg thoughtfully. But we used to call her something else, didn't we, Fogg? he says. She had another name. Do you remember it, Fogg?

Fogg looks at the Old Man, and the Old Man looks back at Fogg. Who sits back down. Wordlessly, Oblivion gets up and brings him a tea towel. Fogg wipes away the tea on his arms. Oblivion accepts back the towel and drops it on the tray and sits back down.

– Yes, Fogg says, tiredly.

The Old Man waits.

– Sommertag, Fogg says. Drained. But not yet defeated.

– We called her Sommertag, he says.

69. **PARIS** 1943

But what do we really know about Sommertag? About Fogg? The dossiers are left carefully empty, the pages blank. We can only see her through his eyes. Does he lie? His fantasy, his summer's day. Her innocence, that word we keep circling around. But there were no innocents in that war.

Can we trust him?

Can we trust anyone?

We sift through this account, but do we believe it, do we accept Fogg's recollection at face value? The fog of history rises to obscure. Details lost in the mist.

Fogg, a watcher.

Watching the girl through the mist and the fog.

That week in Paris. Can you truly fall so wholly in love? Fogg burned by war and treachery: perhaps he needed something to believe in. Something to cling to. A dream, a flame. Something to burn bright and pure and true.

Everyone needs something to believe in.

And yet. And so.

Paris. Fogg. The girl:

For once, she is alone. The third day of watching and the girl sits alone in the café, her companion nowhere in sight. Fog creeps along the gutters and crawls up the windows of the café, obscuring Fogg. Obscuring the girl. She is drinking hot chocolate. Yellow and red leaves litter the ground on the street outside. Somewhere a violin plays, an invisible street performer teasing out lonely, haunted tunes.

Fogg watches the girl, spellbound by some invisible force. Turing, at the Farm: talking of gravity and electricity, the motion of atoms, nuclei and orbiting electrons, mimicking the movement of planets around stars. The very small matching exactly the very large. Things we don't understand, Turing says, in his quiet voice. The way he sometimes looks at Oblivion. The way Oblivion sometimes looks back at him. And then going smaller, into the things electrons are made of, a Never Never Land of uncertainty. That's how Fogg feels right now, if he had to describe it. Watching the girl the way Turing sometimes watched Oblivion. And perhaps, in that quantum fluctuation that no one can see, some connection, like an electric charge, is made. And the girl gets up and leaves some money on the table and walks out, and she's alone. She pauses for a moment in the doorway of the cafe, smells the air. Looks ahead. Looks, in fact, directly at Fogg.

Who moves as if he has no control of his destiny. Perhaps, we wonder, somewhat uneasily, none of us ever does. He moves with a slow, wondering inevitability. Like swimming. Towards the girl. Like lodestones being pulled together by that mysterious energy, the motion of invisible particles that is electromagnetism. The girl is wearing a summer dress, with a coat over it. Her eyes are blue like the sky, her hair is the colour of the sun. Fogg is grey beside her. Then he stops and she does, too, and they stand there, in the middle of that Parisian street, having run out of room, and look at each other.

Fogg's throat is dry. His palms are sweaty. The girl is very calm. He can't read her face. Her eyes. She says, You are the shadow man.

Matter of factly. As if, by the very act of speaking, she has made him known.

– What? Fogg says.

– Wherever I turn my eyes, I can see you.

– You're the Vomacht girl, Fogg says, and then the words are out there; they have been said, and cannot, now, be unsaid, unthought.

The girl looks at him quizzically. Yes, she says. Yes, I suppose I am. My name is Klara.

– Klara.

She laughs. It lights up tiny fires in her eyes. Fogg moves in place. The fog rises around them, blankets them in their own special world. You are English? Klara says.

– Yes, Fogg says.

She nods. Her eyes examine him. His face. You have come to kill me? she says.

– What? Fogg says. Takes a half-step back. Like he's dancing. What do you mean? Why would I? Words taper into nothingness. She just stands there, looking at him. The intensity of her gaze acts on Fogg like gravity. He says, How could you see me? I was never visible.

– You are . . . changed, too, are you not? Klara says. I can see all the changed. We are brothers and sisters, my father's children. He made all of us.

– You will forgive me, Fogg says, and he can't say where the words are coming from, from what deep, hidden spring they well. The boldness of them. You will forgive me but . . . I do not look at you as one looks at one's sister.

Oh, she says. For a moment it seems to him she is hiding a smile. Oh, she says, looks away, looks back at him. She is very near to him. He can feel her warmth. I do not see you as a brother either, she says, softly.

What *does* she see? We know many things, but even we do not entirely understand love. Perhaps love is need, and love is selfish, it is self-preservation. Perhaps she can see the future and she does not like it. Everybody needs somebody, we think, uneasy again.

Fogg looks at her face. Her skin is pale. He strokes her cheek with the back of his forefinger. His trigger finger. Leans in closer. He can smell her hair. It smells like summer. You have not told me your name, she says, whispers, the words are soft and light against his cheek. It's Henry, he says. Henry, she says, as if tasting the word. Henry.

– Klara, he says. Yes, she says. She smiles, and it transforms Fogg, there is nothing wistful or reflective about her smile, it is so . . .

Innocent, he thinks. Like something from another time. She leans into him and her lips touch his, lightly at first, then harder, pressing against his, and he presses back as they kiss, surrounded by the fog.

70. **THE OLD MAN'S OFFICE**   the present

But was she ever an innocent?

None of us, we think, are.

The Old Man studies Fogg. Like an etymologist studying a fascinating word. Turning it around and around, looking for its flaws.

The older you get, the more conscious of time you become, the Old Man says.

Oblivion stirs.

– Sir?

The Old Man looks to Fogg, who doesn't reply. Who closes in on himself, like a card player facing another man's not-yet-winning hand.

– Time used, the Old Man says. Time wasted . . . time unaccounted for.

The tea cups are empty. No one seems inclined to refresh them. And Fogg's is on the floor, smashed. The Old Man is suddenly more expansive. Seems in a philosophical mood now. Leans back. Supports his head with his hands behind him. But his eyes are hard, Fogg thinks; Fogg, who had seen the Old Man do this hundreds of time, from the Berlin-Mariendorf DP Camp in forty-five, to barren rooms in nameless towns, tents in no-man's-lands, prisons, cells, detention centres, the Bureau's own interrogation rooms. Fogg, who knows every move and step of this dangerous dance. No. Fogg isn't fooled.

– Time unaccounted for, the Old Man repeats. Like a lost week in Paris, he says. Looks at Fogg, who shrugs. Well, the Old Man says. It is of little enough significance, I suppose. It *was* wartime, after all.

– Yes, Oblivion says, as if he'd just woken. Looks at Fogg, looks away. Not giving anything away either. The Old Man looks from one to the other. As if he is weighing all their actions, all their tiny giveaways.

– Still, the Old Man says, and his voice hardens, it matches his eyes. Still, he says. There must always be an account.

71. **PARIS** 1943

They draw apart, breathless from the kiss, this moment frozen in time. Klara takes Henry's hand, laughing. Come on! she says. She pulls him with her and he follows.

We too remember what it is like, we too remember Paris, in our own time, the quickening of our blood, the beating of our heart, our young bodies, the sense of promise, the feeling that anything and everything is possible. Perhaps we are a little jealous, even, now.

Through a Latin Quarter alive with revellers; Paris, City of

Love, City of Lights, transforms into a magical place with one kiss, a Sleeping Beauty awakening, awash with light and love. Night transforms it into carnival. Paris! Through open doors the smells of cooking waft out: butter, garlic, mussels, saffron; cream, eggs, sugar, vanilla; chocolate, white wine, pastries and glacés. By a bakery, men queue patiently in their suits and their hats for baguette and demi-baguette; nearby they sell jambons, olives, brie and camembert; an old woman sells flowers on the corner of the Boulevard Saint-Michel and Henry buys a red rose and hands it to Klara, who laughs and tosses it in the air.

She is so beautiful at that moment, Fogg thinks, captivated. He is encased in amber, like an ancient, vanished unicorn fly from the early Cretaceous. He is caught in her moment, her unchanged timelessness, she is a message from an earlier, happier, more innocent time and he responds to her with need and desire and greed.

A German soldier turns and smiles at the lovers. An old man selling newspapers grins at them affectionately without teeth. An accordion player follows them around with a cheerful tune and Henry throws him some coins, which the man snatches deftly from the air. Laughing, they run arm in arm, Henry and Klara, Vomacht's girl and Fogg, through the narrow, winding streets of the Quartier Latin, with no destination, it seems, in mind; floating on light and air in a city untouched by war, a city healed by love.

– Come on! Klara says. Through here! They cut through the garden of a small stone church and emerge on the other side, a quiet street, a stray cat skulking by the rubbish heap, a smiling moon in the sky. A closed and shuttered bookshop on the corner, opposite the church. She leads him to a plain wooden door set into the wall, next to the bookshop.

– Here? Henry says.

– Anywhere and nowhere, Klara says.

Henry holds his breath as she speaks. The moonlight catches her features, casts them in a bewitched light, and Henry thinks of magic, that maybe it is real. Klara reaches for the handle, her hand engulfs the metal and she presses it down, her white hand on the silver of the metal, and she pushes the door open and a bright, an impossibly bright light bursts forth from the opening door, bright impossible sunlight and the smell of fresh hay and grass and the humming of insects and flowing water: the smell of summer. Klara laughs delightedly. Come on! she says. Sunlight transforms their corner of the street. She pushes the door fully open and goes in, pulling Henry after her.

72. **DR VOMACHT'S FARMHOUSE** then

The sun warms Henry's face. He takes a deep breath of clear mountain air. The sun on his face. Insects humming. He opens his eyes on a perfect summer's day. Blue skies with white clouds like trails of smoke. Mountains in the distance, almost blue in outline. Green grass all around him and a white path of pebbled stones leads onwards, towards a white stone house just ahead. Faint music comes from the direction of the house, an old French chanson. Klara pulls Henry along the path then lets go of his hand and turns, laughing, swirling in the grass with her arms stretched out. Henry stands there. He looks back, sees nothing to show how they came to be there, at that no place, at that no time. Where are we? he says, his voice filled with wonder. Klara stops dancing. This is just . . . she says. Just the place I go away to.

Henry just looks at her. The music comes wafting from the house. A butterfly hovers near Klara's outstretched hand. Klara regains her smile, as innocent and beatific as the day is.

– This is what it was like before, she says, with new confidence. Like a child sharing her favourite toy. Before things changed.

Her smile turns wicked and she jumps on Henry, she is

surprisingly light but she pulls him down and he lets her and they fall to the grass together, Henry on his back, Klara straddling him. She leans down and kisses him on the mouth and he responds hungrily, engulfing her in his arms. She presses him down and looks into his eyes and her eyes are the colour of the sky, her smell is the scent of summer.

– It's better here, she says, softly. And – We can stay here, forever.

73. DR VOMACHT'S FARMHOUSE then

It never gets dark in this place. The sky is a perfect blue, the air is warm and scented. Insects hum outside, in the green grass. Henry stands at the window bare-chested.

– I have no power here, he says. There is no fog.

He turns to Klara, who smiles up at him from the bed. We can't stay here forever, Klara, he says. This is madness. I could be court-martialled for this.

Klara pats the bed invitingly. There are no court martials here, she says. Come back to bed, Henry. We have time. We have all the time in the world.

– Where *are* we? Henry says.

– This is where it all happened, Klara says. This is where it started. You, me. The war.

– Where is your father, Klara? Henry says.

– He's outside. He can't come in here. Klara smiles, happily. This is my secret place, she says.

She jumps out of bed. She wears her nakedness comfortably. She is young, Henry thinks. She will always be young. Do you want to see it? Klara says. Grinning. Like a kid sharing a wonderful secret. Henry collects his clothes, which are strewn across the room. See what? he says.

Klara jumps up and down in excitement and grabs Henry's hand. Come on! she says. She takes him by the hand and leads him out of the bedroom, down the stairs and into the kitchen. It is a spacious, airy room, flooded with sunlight. Strings of garlic hang on the wall alongside iron pots and pans. On the long wood table sits a small machine, about the size of a briefcase. It is impossible to say what it is, what it does. Klara stops and Henry stops with her. He stares at the room, at the silent machine. What? he says, at last.

– This is it, Klara says. This is the device.

– But . . .

– I remember it like it was today, Klara says.

She laughs. She spreads her arms wide and dances on the spot. It *is* today! she says. It is always today. Oh, Henry.

She throws her arms around him, nuzzles his neck. It is always today, she whispers, against his skin. One perfect summer's day. She pulls away from him, growing serious. Points at an empty chair placed at an angle by the table, beside the strange machine.

– He was sitting right there, she says.

– Your father?

– Yes. Tinkering. Always tinkering. With his quantum box. Muttering about Heisenberg. He was a doctor my father worked with for a while, before they fell out. Muttering about cats in boxes. I used to have a cat. Dinah.

– Dinah, Henry says. Klara's face crumbles. Oh, what does it matter! she says. What does any of it matter.

– Klara, I—

– What? she says, with sudden savagery. You don't want to be here? You don't want to be with me? Look at you, in your shadow man clothes! What's so important out *there*?

– Klara, Henry says, wait—

But she is angry, a sudden and scary transformation, as if a switch had been flipped on, or off, with nothing in between. Just *go!* she shouts.

Henry looks to all sides, like a trapped animal. Klara makes a pushing motion with her hands. Although she doesn't physically touch him something forces Henry back, like a gust of air, like he is being sucked back, somehow. Everything – the farmhouse, the warm day, the sun – seems to dim, a grey fog opens behind and around him, engulfing him, and Klara grows small in the distance, standing there with her hand extended and Henry falls, falls into the fog, until it swallows him and he can't see her any more.

74. **PARIS** 1943

Fogg lands awkwardly, as if the ground was not quite supposed to be there. It is cold and the rising fog sticks, not unpleasantly, to his skin. He is on the Left Bank of the Seine. There is a new moon in the sky, a sliver moon, hanging like a scythe over Notre Dame. A German patrol drives slowly down the road. Fogg just stands there, stares at it, stares at the new, fragile moon.

75. **THE OLD MAN'S OFFICE** the present

– And that is it? the Old Man says. That is all?

Fogg feels the tense muscles, tiredness starting to take effect. Looks straight at the Old Man. His secrets out in the open, laundry left to dry in the sun.

– I never saw her again, he says.

The Old Man doesn't say anything. Leafs through the dossier on his desk. Humming.

– She was innocent, Fogg says, but we are not sure who he is trying to convince, the Old Man or himself.

Still the Old Man says nothing. His old tactic. Drawing Fogg out.

– I went back to London, Fogg says, answering an unvoiced question. And, fiercely – Don't you think I would have done anything to get back Tank if I could?

– Would you? the Old Man says. Would you have?

– She was innocent.

– No one is innocent, the Old Man says. Turns another page. Raises his eyebrows. Well? he demands.

– I made my way back to London, Fogg says. I submitted my report—

– A false report, the Old Man says – almost reproachfully.

– Everyone lies a little, Fogg says.

The Old Man, silently, turns another page.

76. **PARIS** 1943

Curfew.

But what does Fogg care for curfew, for the Germans' patrols? The hushed air of deserted streets is his background music, the fog that rises and clings to the walls is his to do with as he will. Like a restless shadow he prowls the city, anger and need intermingling, and shame. The shame of seeing Tank captured. The shame of being pushed from that secret place, that summer's day. Anger at her. Her name, Klara, echoes through the city in the bells of churches still allowed to operate. Klara. Klara. Their lovemaking is echoed in the motion of the Seine. And Fogg's anger stalks along with him through the narrow cobbled streets of the Latin Quarter, a shadow to his shadow.

He comes across a group of German soldiers surrounding two girls. One light, one dark. Dressed in long army overcoats. What are they doing outside at this hour. An Oberschütze waving his hand angrily at the cowering girls, Your papers, where are your papers? *Vos papiers!*

One soldier grabs a girl's arm, laughing. She struggles against him as he pins her to the wall. The other screams, the sound pierces the night and Fogg is aware of all those faces behind windows and walls, hears everything. But who will come to her rescue, on this night, in this country, at this terrible time? The soldier presses close, his face leaning in for a kiss, the girl spits in his face. The soldier roars, slaps her, she falls to the cobblestones, the other girl seizes the moment and runs:

Towards Fogg, towards the sheltering fog, she comes towards him and the moonlight catches her pale, frightened face. She comes so close, Fogg could reach out and pull her to shelter, to safety. The girl's eyes open wide: she sees him. He reaches out to her. Two shots ring out. The girl drops to the cobblestones. A dark stain on the pavement. The Oberschütze holsters his gun, swears: *Verdammten Frauen,* he says. In sadness more than anger. Motions at the girl still living. Take her to the Gestapo, he says, this is not our business. His men pick the girl up and march her away. They pass by Fogg and the dead girl, so close. Fogg, wishing for a knife, a gun. For courage. But to observe something is to change it.

When they pass, the Oberschütze is left momentarily alone. He comes and stares down at the body of the dead girl. He shakes his head, says something too softly for Fogg to catch. The moon in the sky. Through a patch in the fog he can see the Sea of Serenity, forming one eye of the man on the moon. Something snaps in Fogg and he steps out of his hiding place. The soldier sees him stepping out like a ghost and his eyes open wide, like the girl's had. What— he begins to say, his hands begin to rise, too slow, as if to ward off Fogg. Fogg wraps his hands around the man's neck and squeezes, the soldier's skin soft and warm and the heartbeat inside it like a caged bird, struggling to break free, and Fogg helps it, squeezing, his thumbs digging into the soft pliable flesh, staring into the man's eyes; all the while he looks into the man's frightened eyes until the bird is free, is gone. He lets go and the body softly crumples to the ground, to lie beside the dead girl. The pleasant and the loved, in death as in life they were not parted, Fogg thinks, the half-remembered verse of a Bible song. Feels queer, something obscene in the two of them, the French girl and the German soldier, down there on the cobblestones. He feels bile rising in his throat, holds it down. He hears the soldiers calling out for their leader, coming back, but the fog rises, they become lost in it and Fogg walks away, walks past closed doors of shops and apartment blocks, walks and walks through the city like a ghost, his feet making no sound.

But then, as he comes to a cul-de-sac, and prepares to turn back, a door opens.

A door opens in the night, before him. The door to a shop or a house, he doesn't know. An ordinary door.

And light, so much light, comes pouring out of it. The bright light of a summer's day. And he stands there, entranced, and a lithe figure steps through the door and onto the cold pavements, into that occupied night.

– Klara, Fogg whispers, Klara, and she turns, and sees him, and her smile lights up her face. Look! she says. She points up at the moon, There's a man in the moon! and she laughs, delighted. You can't see it from the other place. She runs to him. Hugs him. That scent of her, something so pure. Fogg buries his face in the crook of her neck and inhales. I'm sorry, he says, I'm sorry.

For what? She is laughing. She pushes him back and looks into his eyes. He is a little taller and she must rise on her toes to match him. Let's not go back there, she says, not for now, not for a while. I want to be with you in your world. In the real world. But she says the word *real* dubiously, and perhaps she doesn't truly believe in it. It is too fantastical, this world, with its marching armies and its rockets and its death camps. It's just the world of a cheap novel, surely. She hugs him, then lets go and takes his hand, instead. She is dressed in her summer dress but she wears a thick army coat over it. Look, she says, reaching into an inside pocket. She brings out a document. My papers, she says, proudly.

And Fogg thinks, You are Dr Vomacht's daughter, and something cold reaches deep inside him and squeezes. But she puts it away and laughs again and her warmth suffuses him, this summer day taken human form, this Sommertag, and he lets her lead him by the hand, I want music! she says. I want to dance.

77. **PARIS** 1943

The night is a blur.

They walk down the quiet streets and run into a patrol. The soldiers cry *Stop!*, but Klara turns on them, barking orders, Do you know who I am, she says, Take me to Le Chabanais! One of the soldiers looks shocked, but the officer just looks resigned, Please escort Fräulein Vomacht and her companion to her destination, he says.

They are placed in a jeep and taken on a speeding ride, across the river and towards the Louvre. Fogg doesn't know where he is, what he is doing. He doesn't know who he is any more. All he knows is that the summer's light has worn away his fog.

They arrive at a brothel. There is no other word for it. Bare-chested women drape themselves over high-backed chairs and chaise longues. Bow-tied musicians playing Mozart in the high-ceilinged reception room. Toulouse-Lautrec murals on the walls. A waiter glides past with a silver tray bearing vintage champagne. Fräulein Vomacht! What a pleasant surprise. Fogg turns and finds himself face to face with Fat Hermann Göring: World War One ace fighter pilot, notorious art collector and Adolf Hitler's trusted Reichsmarschall and designated successor. *Herr* Göring, Klara says, with a curtsey. Fat Hermann downs a coupe of champagne and burps delicately. And who is your companion this evening? he enquires. Herr Schleier, Fogg says. The Reichsmarschall looks him up and down, then seems to lose interest. He disappears upstairs, accompanied by two of the young French women, both of whom have dyed black hair.

Fogg and Klara dance and drink champagne. From time to time senior officers stop by and speak to Klara. Fogg is a shadow man, he may as well not exist. I'm bored, Klara declares, later. They steal outside, into the night and the lights of the Louvre. They walk hand in hand through the Jardin des Tuileries. Oh, Henry, Klara says, I don't want tonight to end – she looks sad. Fogg strokes her face, her cheek is wet with tears. Everything ends, Klara says. Everything but us. She pulls away from his touch and runs away. Fogg chases. Down the gardens and they are all alone and it begins to snow, Fogg makes a grab for Klara but she evades him with a laugh, reaches for a gardener's shed door and pulls it open and the bright sunlight spills out onto the Parisian night and she disappears inside and leaves Fogg standing there, stupidly staring at an ordinary garden door.

78. **PARIS** 1943

But when he walks back to his hotel the door of the bakery right ahead opens and instead of the smell of fresh bread sunlight spills out and she is there again, standing in the snow. She is calm now, her face is beatific. She takes him by the hand. He leads the way, feeling a new urgency, a desire. They sneak into the silent hotel and tiptoe up the rickety old stairs into the dark room. How did you know who I was, he says, whispering into the skin of her neck, feeling her life beating inside. Light casts shadow, she says, whispering too. Perhaps it is as simple as that. It's wartime, there are no real answers. He strips her urgently, his hands seem to shake, she draws his shirt up over his head and runs her hand down his naked chest and Fogg shudders, Henry, she says, Henry, he whispers her name, pushes her back onto the bed, a boy, a girl, a night in Paris. He kisses her, all over. Her body is caught forever in that moment long ago. She tastes of blackberries and sun: though blackberries have the taste of autumn. The thought makes him sad, strangely. She pulls him up, kisses him on the lips. She draws him to her. I love you, she whispers, I love you too, he says, but what is love? Perhaps it is a way of unseeing.

Later, they lie in the bed, drowsy. The snow beats against the window, it makes Fogg think of Schneesturm, and of Tank, and that shame and hatred rise in him again. He realises he barely knows Klara. Barely knows who she is, what she likes and dislikes. She is different things all at once, she is both changed and unchanged. How do you explain what he feels? It isn't rational, not something you can quantify or study in a lab.

Or can it? Can love, too, be distilled, explained away, used as a weapon?

– Hold me, Henry, she says. He draws her close, she is so warm, so real. It is the war that is make-believe, it is the Luftwaffe and Hitler, the whole damned thing. He holds Klara until they both fall asleep, and in the morning she is gone, and the door to the room is left just slightly ajar, letting the sunlight through, and he fo—

79. DR VOMACHT'S FARMHOUSE then

—llows, into that other place.

But later, much later:

– I have to go back, Fogg says.

– You could stay with me, here. Forever.

– You know that's not true. You belong in the real world too.

– I could withdraw, seal the door, she says. I can! This moment is mine but I can make it yours, too.

– You are going back to Germany, he says. And I must go back to England.

– I don't want you to. England is cold and the Führer says we will soon win the war. And then what will happen to you, Henry? she says with a cold, childlike logic.

– You're not like them, Fogg says, you're not one of them, you could come with me, you could help—

– My father needs me. Her voice is small when she says it. Henry, she says. If we lose . . .

– Yes?

– Will you find me?

He holds her tight; he never wants to let go. I will find you, he says.

– I do not want it to be over, she says, and for a moment he doesn't know if she is talking about their being there, together, or about the war; and a shudder runs through him.

– Promise you will find me, she says.

Fogg strokes her hair, there in that place where it is always a summer's day.

– I will find you, he says.

NINE:

THE LOST DECADE

LONDON
1954

GERMANY SURRENDERS

May 7, 1945

REIMS Following the death of Adolf Hitler on April 30, by suicide, and the fall of Berlin to Soviet forces on May 2, on this day in Reims, France, General Alfred Jodl, Chief of Staff of the German armed forces, has signed the unconditional surrender document on behalf of all extant German forces, thus ending the War in Europe.

ATOMIC BOMB DROPPED ON JAPAN

August 6, 1945

WASHINGTON American President Harry S. Truman has announced today that an atomic bomb has been dropped over the city of Hiroshima, in Japan. The President was on board the cruiser USS Augusta in the mid-Atlantic. He said the device was 2,000 times more powerful than any conventional bomb ever before deployed. Hiroshima is one of the chief supply depots for the Japanese army.

The bomb was dropped at 08:15 local time from a B-29 airplane nicknamed the Enola Gay. A vast, mushroom-shaped cloud engulfed the city of Hiroshima and it is currently impossible to assess the damage caused by the blast. 'If they do not now accept our terms,' the President said, 'they may expect a rain of ruin from the air the like of which has never been seen on Earth.'

Speaking in London, British Prime Minister Clement Attlee, who has replaced Winston Churchill at Number 10, read out a statement prepared by his predecessor to MPs in the Commons. He said, 'By God's mercy, Britain and American science outpaced all German efforts. These were on a considerable scale, but far behind. The possession of these powers by the Germans at any time might have altered the result of the war.'

President Truman said the atomic bomb heralded the 'harnessing of the basic power of the universe.'

ELIZABETH II CROWNED QUEEN

June 2, 1953

LONDON Following the death of King George VI, ending his reign after sixteen years on the throne, the crown has passed to his 25-year-old daughter Elizabeth. The young Queen served as an ambulance driver and mechanic during the War. She was crowned by the Archbishop of Canterbury at a coronation ceremony in Westminster Abbey. Eight thousand dignitaries and heads of state attended the ceremony, while thousands of Her Majesty's subjects lined the streets to catch a glimpse of the new monarch. Millions more watched the ceremony around the world in a special broadcast by the BBC.

80. BATTERSEA POWER STATION, LONDON 1954

The machines hum inside Battersea Power Station, behind the dull brown bricks the coal never stops burning, the steam boilers humming with suppressed energy, the barges along the Thames docking at the jetties, this endless song of the loading and offloading. The lights always shine over Battersea Station, the steam turbines never cease. Out of the tall chimneys their smoke rises into the night.

Oblivion waits in the shadow of the station. A new moon. A new Queen. Prime Minister Churchill on his way out, again.

The Nineteen Fifties. The post-war years. Powdered eggs, how he hates the taste of them. The Bureau wrapped in shadows. Spit somewhere in Kenya, a Mau Mau uprising. Oblivion turns his head, sharply. The moonlight catches his pale cheekbones. Footsteps on gravel. The fog makes it hard to see who it is.

– Oblivion.

– Fogg. I didn't think you'd come.

– I almost didn't.

They hug, awkwardly.

– They told me you'd left. I'm sorry I couldn't be there for the service.

– I got a medal, Fogg says. From the King. Before . . . he makes a gesture. You know.

– You retired from the Retirement Service.

Fogg laughs, without much humour. Yes, he says. I suppose I did.

Oblivion looks at him but, of course, Fogg is unchanged. Why did you leave? he says.

– You know why.

Oblivion takes out a hip flask. Unscrews the top and takes a gulp. Passes it to Fogg. It's over, Fogg, he says. It's over. The Old Man doesn't know—

– Don't, Fogg says. They stare at each other.

– Come back, Oblivion says, at last.

– We don't grow old, Fogg says. We don't forget. The past never dies, not entirely. Not for us, Oblivion.

– You can't *bury* yourself in the past, Henry!

– Somewhere it is always summer, Fogg says, and drinks. He hands the flask back to Oblivion.

– Don't come back to see me again, he says, quietly.

But a vengeful spirit seems to take over Oblivion. One day I might have to! he says, and hates the sound of his own voice. Fogg, turning to leave, stops. He looks at Oblivion and his face is agonised.

– I know, he says.

He turns his head away. Goodbye, Oblivion, he says. He walks away and Oblivion does nothing but stand there, and watch him go.

– Damn it, Fogg, he says, but softly, to himself. Behind his back the steam turbines growl and hiss and burp.

An account, Oblivion thinks. Words they daren't say. But there must always be an account.

81. **LONDON** 1954

Oblivion walks away from the power station, walking along the south side of the Thames, crossing the river at last at London Bridge. It's late but there are people about and Oblivion misses the comfort of the fog. On the bridge he stops. He takes out a coin, newly minted, a penny with the young Queen on its face.

Turns it and turns it in his fingers. Berlin, in forty-six. The thing they can never talk about. So many things one cannot talk about, he thinks. He flicks the coin up and watches it arc over the railings. The moonlight catches the Queen's youthful face. Oblivion watches the coin tumble down to earth, down towards the dark surface of the river. It falls in with a tiny splash and is swallowed by the water. He makes a wish; we suppose he makes a wish.

He walks on. A cold night but he welcomes it. Past the Tower of London where the ravens stand guard over the Empire, crying fiercely into the night. A lone prostitute calls to him but he shakes his head and hurries on, into the night, the dark twisting streets of the East End.

The fog grows around him. Rubble in the streets. Houses still demolished by the bombings, not yet rebuilt. A dismal decade. Things moving in the abandoned houses. He doesn't quicken his pace. Let them come, he thinks, with savage anticipation. It isn't like him. But he feels angry, and lost. Fogg's damned *selfishness!*

Walks on. The river on his right, the city on his left. A pub ahead, lights inside and laughter, a figure lurches drunkenly out of the door and into the street, near colliding with him. He growls, Watch where you're going, old timer!

– Sorry, son, sorry. Hands pat him, the drunk steadies himself. His beery breath on Oblivion's face. Say, aren't you—

– Aren't I what – tries to push the old man but he won't budge. The old man's eyes open wide. Mrs Cable's boy, he says. From down that way – he jerks a thumb at the opening to a narrow lane. From up by Stepney, he says, Mrs Cable, the midwife.

– I'm afraid you are quite mistaken, Oblivion says, coldly, and the man takes a step back and looks him up and down, the Savile Row suit and the cane, and shakes his head, I'm sorry, sir, he says, You look the spitting image of her boy, but he would be much older now, and not . . .

– Yes?

– A gentleman, begging your pardon. She was an honest woman but her boys, none of them were gentlemen.

– Push off! Oblivion says with sudden vehemence, and his fist rises, pale and menacing, and the old man shrinks from him. He raises his hands up defensively, palms open, and Oblivion, as though ashamed, lowers his hand.

– What happened to her? he asks. The midwife.

The old man lowers his hands, which are shaking. The look that he gives Oblivion is queer. Died in the war, didn't she, he says.

– How?

– Bombing raid. Didn't make it to the shelter in time. The old man spits on the ground. Lost my wife the same way, he says.

– I'm sorry.

The old man shrugs. Well, there you are, he says.

Oblivion just stares. The old man looks back, uncomfortable. Here, Oblivion says. Reaches into his pocket. Comes back with a shilling. Take that, for your troubles, he says.

The old man takes it haltingly. Thank you, he says. But still looks at Oblivion's face with that puzzled expression.

– Go! Oblivion says and the man, startled into action, walks hurriedly if unsteadily away. Oblivion stares after his retreating back.

82. **LIMEHOUSE, LONDON** 1954

A restless spirit animates him. He walks with long strides. Along the river, the docks, the ships coming and going. The sight and smell and sound of empire. The call of sailors, porters, the lights. The lights attract him like a moth.

The pub is called Charlie Brown's, from outside you couldn't even say if it were open or not. A dockyard pub, a seamen's pub. Oblivion hesitates outside. There are fancier places, now. The Royal Vauxhall Tavern. The Spartan Club. But they are in the light. This place is all in shadow.

He goes inside.

Dim lights and cigarette smoke, the smell of wine and beer. Men only, in this pub. A gramophone playing, Doris Day singing, 'Secret Love'. Oblivion finds a chair at the bar and orders a pint. Drinks as if to wash away the night, the dusty streets. Half turns in his seat. A couple of dockers standing by the men's loos – one makes eye contact, Oblivion turns away. Drinks his beer. Turns again. One of the dockers has disappeared, the other stands there still, their eyes meet, an understanding. Oblivion drowns the last of his drink as though steeling his courage. Stands up.

83. LIMEHOUSE, LONDON 1954

Their lovemaking is a chiaroscuro of light and dark, hurried, furtive, the other man pressed against the wall, their naked skins, Oblivion licks the sheen of sweat off the other man's upper lip. When it is over they exchange no words, they go their separate ways, Oblivion adjusts his belt and his cufflinks, when he steps out onto the docks the sky is overcast. And a wild hunger takes flight in him, a form of nostalgia, for what has been, and gone, and is no more.

COMICS CODE ESTABLISHED

September 23, 1954

NEW YORK Following the public hearings before the United States Senate Subcommittee on Juvenile Delinquency in April and June this year, on the subject of graphic crime and horror 'comic books', the Comics Magazine Association of America (CMAA) has been established to self-regulate its members' publications. The new Code states, in part, that good 'must triumph over evil'; that the criminals must always be punished; and that 'scenes of horror, excessive bloodshed, gory or gruesome crimes, depravity, lust, sadism, and masochism' will not be tolerated.

In addition, 'profanity, obscenity, smut and vulgarity', as well as illicit sex relations, must be neither portrayed nor hinted at. All romance or love stories must 'emphasize the value of the home and the sanctity of marriage.' Quite rightly, too, the new Code states that 'passion or romantic interest shall never be treated in such a way as to stimulate the lower and baser emotions.'

Finally, stories which take as their focus the issue of evil must only be published 'where the intent is to illustrate a moral issue'. Evil must never be presented in a glamorous fashion or in any way 'as to injure the sensibilities of the reader.'

It is this newspaper's sincere wish that all other publications, be them the lowly form of the 'comic book' or the more lofty form of the novel, follow similar guidelines in future.

TEN:
THE TRIAL

JERUSALEM
1964

ADOLF EICHMANN EXECUTED

June 1, 1962

JERUSALEM Convicted Nazi war criminal Adolf Eichmann, widely considered one of the main architects of the Jewish genocide initiated by the Nazi regime, was hanged last night in Ramla, Israel, in the prison in which he was incarcerated. Eichmann, who carried the rank of SS-Obersturmbannführer, had been one of the prime movers of the 'Final Solution of the Jewish Question.' He had attended the Wannsee Conference, in which the Nazi policy of genocide was set down, and was appointed in charge of the transportation of the Jews to the death camps. He was convicted of crimes against humanity in the Jerusalem District Court on December 11, 1961. The three judges handed down a unanimous verdict.

Eichmann's body was cremated. His ashes were scattered in the Mediterranean Sea, beyond Israel's territorial waters, 'to ensure that there could be no future memorial and that no country would serve as his final resting place.'

Eichmann had lived for some years in Buenos Aires, Argentina. It has been suggested he is but one of many high-ranking Nazis to have escaped to South America under new identities, and that many more remain in hiding.

84. **JERUSALEM** 1964

The Old Man arrives in Tel Aviv on a British Airways flight, and a man from the Consulate picks him up.

– Hot, isn't it, the man from the Consulate says.

– Is it always like this? the Old Man says.

– Most of the year, the man from the Consulate says, apologetically.

They drive up to Jerusalem, through a landscape that changes rapidly, from the coastal plains to low-lying hills to sudden mountains, a sharp incline. The Old Man checks into the King David Hotel, on the edge of Jerusalem's Old City, on the very armistice line dividing the city between Israel and Jordan. The King David is packed full, international visitors arriving for the trial, and the hotel bar is thick with cigarette and cigar smoke, hard-drinking newsmen and, of course, the Übermenschen.

– This is the largest gathering of Übermenschen ever assembled, an excited anchorwoman for CBS says to the camera. All but unheard of, for that day and age: a woman reporting the news.

She is standing just outside the hotel, the camera pans over guests arriving or leaving. A man steps out, an impressive physique, muscles like a body builder's, all packed into tight multicoloured Lycra. He has a bare chest, wild blond hair, flashing eyes, a flashing grin—

– Tigerman! Over here! Tigerman!

The man turns, that lazy grin following the lens of the camera. Something animalistic, magnetic about him. It seems to draw us, the viewers, we notice the anchorwoman is a little flushed. We might, if truth be told, be feeling a little flushed ourselves.

– Hello, Theresa, Tigerman says.

– Tigerman, are you here for the trial? Are you representing the State Department? Would you like to comment on—

– Thank you, Theresa, Tigerman says. He sweeps back his blond mane. His nails, we notice, are long and sharp. I am here,

Tigerman announces to the camera, as a private citizen. I am here out of one simple desire: I want to see justice done.

– Tigerman, is it true the United States government has lodged a formal complaint with the Israeli authorities over the arrest and kidnapping of de la Cruz?

– I couldn't possibly comment, Theresa, Tigerman says, and the smile he flashes her is feral, it is of a wild animal showing its teeth, and the anchorwoman shies back from him. But I am sure we all, Tigerman says, simply want to see historic justice done here over the coming days.

– Thank you, Tigerman—

But the Übermensch is already turning away from her and, as the camera zooms in on his back, we see him joined by a woman in a blue, tight-fitting costume, with dark hair, a slender figure, and we hear Theresa of CBS drawing in her breath as she says, And that was the renowned Tigerman, a national hero, and there with him, it can be none other than the famous Whirlwind. They, and many more, are here in Jerusalem, Israel, for what some are already calling the Trial of the Century. This is Theresa Conway, in Jerusalem, reporting for CBS.

The Old Man smiles without humour and watches Tigerman disappear into the narrow streets. The Old Man goes and sits in the bar and orders a scotch and swirls it in the glass. He is not looking forward to the trial.

Now he sits at court wishing he still had that Scotch to keep him company. Waiting. Watching. They have no juries in Israel, and the three judges sit alone, on a plain dais, overlooking the prosecution and the defence benches, and the rows of journalists and spectators. In the middle of the courtroom sits a transparent box made of bulletproof glass, with a chair and a microphone inside it, and that is where the man sits. Woven into the glass are fine filaments of electric wire, and a faint eldritch glow suffuses the box, as though a force field of some form is engulfing it, sealing the man inside and whatever power he may possess. They are taking no chances, the Israelis. Not after Buenos Aires . . .

He is not a formidable man, this de la Cruz. He is a grey man in a grey suit, with grey short-cropped hair and old-fashioned spectacles and an impeccably knotted grey silk tie. He, too, looks hot in his glass aquarium box.

The Old Man sits down at the very back, so he may watch without being observed. Each chair has a pair of large earphones plugged into a socket by its side. The proceedings are conducted in Hebrew while witness interviews may be done in the witness's native tongue or in English. For the benefit of the journalists and audience, a simultaneous translation is broadcast in real time, directly into their earphones. The Old Man doesn't put them on yet. Instead he watches the journalists and the photographers and the television men. They are here from all corners of the Earth. Americans mix with Chinese, Russians with West Germans, everyone wants to cover this trial, everyone wants the scoop on the man in the glass box.

The courtroom is filled with Israeli officials in cheap, worn suits; of newspapermen with open collars and ink-stained fingers; and it is full of the costumed heroes, who sit still and silent, for the most part, lending the only colour to this otherwise rather drab courtroom. The man in the glass box, this anonymous de la Cruz, sits quietly, hands folded in his lap. The only thing in motion are his eyes; they scan the courtroom rapidly, back and forth, and the Old Man knows he is missing little. The eyes are alive with a fierce intelligence. The judges gather their papers. A hush slowly settles on the court.

The court clerk stands up. Clears his throat.

And the trial, *The State of Israel vs. Joachim Vomacht*, at last begins.

85. **JERUSALEM** 1964

There's a murmur of interruption, a moment during Anton Gerasimov's testimony. The Israeli soldiers scattered along the walls, even they stand to attention, and the judges perk up, and the foreign correspondents turn this way and that as if unsure exactly as to the nature of the interruption. The doors to the courtroom open and in comes a large, barrel-chested, as they say, man. He wears dusty khakis and what the Israelis call a Tembel hat, a cotton, bell-shaped hat that shades his dark face from the sun. The man's skin is indeed dark – no, not dark, not so much dark as a peculiar shade of deep green. He pauses and looks around the courtroom and the murmurs rise, and someone gasps, The Sabra!

The Sabra's eyes pan across the room until they find the man in the glass box, and there they linger. The Old Man watches from the back of the room. A tension in the courtroom, like an electric current (but not from the Electric Twins, only one of whom is present). The Sabra moves his head, his neck is thick, he raises one arm and thorns burst out of it, and in a ring around his neck, and out of his back. Then they deflate and disappear and the Sabra walks to the back of the room, quietly, where a nervous young man vacates his seat for the great man, this hero of the Warsaw Ghetto Uprising and the War of Independence and of Operation Kadesh and, of course, of the Vomacht kidnapping itself. The Old Man looks at the Sabra and, for just a moment, the Sabra looks back. Recognition floods his eyes. He nods, wordlessly. The Old Man nods back.

On the witness stand, Anton Gerasimov resumes his testimony. He is wearing white, a plain one-piece white suit. He has no hair. His face is deeply scarred. His eyes are blue and cold.

– You were a partisan? the counsellor for the prosecution, a tall, thin man in his sixties, wearing a yarmulke and a conservative suit, says.

– Yes.

Gerasimov has a deep, hoarse voice.

– Against the Germans.

– Yes.

– Where was this?

– I operated in Belarus. I was at the fall of Minsk. Later, I led a group of comrades against the Nazi animal and the Einsatzgruppen.

– Einsatzgruppen? the counsellor says.

– Death squads, Gerasimov says.

The counsellor nods, half turning to the audience, to make sure they got the point.

– You are changed, Mr Gerasimov?

– Kerach, Gerasimov says.

– That is your moniker, correct?

– That is what you will call me, the man on the witness stand says.

The counsellor colours, a little. Of course, he says. Kerach. A half-laugh from the audience, primarily, the Old Man notes, from the costumed Übermenschen.

– You are changed, Kerach? You are an *Übermensch*?

– Yes.

– Could you . . . could you show us?

– Here? Now?

– If the court has no objection? the counsellor says, turning to the judges.

– We'll allow it, the lead judge, a white-haired man with reading glasses on a string around his neck, says. On the witness stand, Kerach shrugs. Very well, then, he says.

He raises his hand, his palm upwards, open, as if to capture unseen snow. The temperature changes in the courtroom, it drops. The Old Man's breath fogs in front of his face. Ice crawls along the windowsills and the sunlight breaks through the glass into rainbows. An icy sheen covers the parquet floors. Kerach moves his hand, gently, the cupped fingers turning, outstretching towards the man in the box. A crack like gunfire echoes in the still courtroom and the bulletproof glass breaks. Shouts break out and soldiers rush towards the box. Stop! Someone shouts. Stop! Kerach's fingers move as though composing a silent symphony. Ice crawls over the glass witness box and the man inside it is trapped without sound, sealed within. IDF soldiers jump on Kerach and wrestle him to the ground. He does not fight them. They pin his hands behind his back and cuff them and still he does not resist. Do something!

– Perhaps I can help, someone says. Who the hell are you, the lead judge says. The man is wearing a flaming red outfit and has a Texan accent. I'm Flame Beast, he says. The judge nods, reluctantly. The Texan clicks his fingers and a flame comes alive in his hand. Gently he reaches towards the box and blows on the flame, which shoots out, expanding, engulfing the box.

– This is a bloody disaster, someone says, groaning. But a moment later Flame Beast extinguishes his fire and the glass box appears to be defrosting. Water puddles cover the floor and inside the cage the prisoner is breathing again, his hands grasping his neck; his colour is slowly returning.

– A bloody *disaster*, someone says again.

– Order! Order!

– Take him away to calm down, the judge on the left, a portly man with brown hair, says. *Honestly.* And fix the prisoner's stand. The court will adjourn until tomorrow.

The gavel comes down. The audience stands. Soldiers lead Kerach away. He is still unresisting. A cheer rises from the ranks of the Übermenschen as he passes amongst them, and many clap him on the back as he walks.

The Old Man shakes his head in disgust and gets up. A drink in the air-conditioned hotel bar would be just the thing to salvage what's left of the day.

86. JERUSALEM 1964

– The court will rise!

– Please sit down.

– Counsellor, I trust that the witness will not be in contempt of court again this afternoon?

– The witness has assured me there will not be a repeat of yesterday's unfortunate events, Your Honour.

– Very well . . . the judge rubs the bridge of his nose wearily. The witness is yours, he says.

The counsellor paces. The man in the repaired glass box sits stoically. Anton Gerasimov – Kerach – is back on the witness stand.

– We have established, the counsellor for the prosecution says, that you were a partisan, operating in Belarus during the war. You are – as I think we have all quite conclusively seen—

A small laugh from the otherwise-silent audience.

– An *Übermensch*. One of the changed. Is that correct?

– That is correct, Kerach says.

– I see, the counsellor says. And how long were you in operation, during the war? he asks.

– I was captured in the beginning of nineteen forty-three, if that's what you mean, Kerach says.

– Captured?

– By the Nazis, Counsellor. By the degenerate Nazi animal. He makes as if to spit. Wolfskommando, he says.

The counsellor makes a show of consulting some papers, fooling no one. You are referring to Gestapo Department F? he says.

– Yes.

– That would be the special department within the Nazi secret police established for the purpose of capturing Allied Übermenschen?

– Yes.

Whispers in the court. The counsellor ignores them.

– Can you tell me how you were captured? he says.

Kerach shrugs. We had gone to a village the Nazis had marked for extermination, he says. The village had a special school for the disabled. Our information suggested that a Nazi death squad had been sent to purify the school.

– Purify?

– Exterminate. The death squads used mobile gas trucks. They would lock the children inside and gas them to death. It was considered humane.

– I see.

The courtroom is deathly quiet. The counsellor says, What happened when you got there?

– We were too late. The school was empty. The Einsatzgruppen had already been, hours before. We found the children buried in a nearby field, in a mass grave. It was . . . not dug deep.

– I see.

Again the counsellor for the prosecution lets a moment of silence pass. What happened then? he says, gently.

But there is nothing gentle in Kerach's reply.

– We were set up, he says. It was an ambush. They had been waiting for us and once we were there they closed the trap. They killed my men. Shot them over the same common grave they had dumped the children in. But they didn't kill me. He smiles, without humour. They went to great lengths not to kill me.

– They?

– Brigadeführer Hans von Wolkenstein, Kerach says. Again that chilly smile. Der Wolfsmann.

A sigh, a gasp from the audience at the mention of that name. Tigerman growls in the front row and Whirlwind lays a hand on his shoulder until he settles back. The counsellor looks at the audience, at the judges, and turns his attention again to the man on the witness stand.

– That would be the head of Gestapo Department F? he says.

– Yes. He is a nullifier.

– Nullifier?

– His presence nullifies other Übermenschen's abilities.

– So you were not able to—

– No.

Kerach smiles that icy smile again. We met before, he says.

He and I. I do not need *powers* to take a man on. When he says
powers, he looks to the man in the glass box. All I need is a fair
fight. He shrugs. That was not something I was given.

– You were captured.

– Yes.

– Then what happened?

– At first they put me in a POW camp on the Polish border.
It was a general camp. They didn't keep me there long. I got
the sense it was a temporary arrangement. A few months after
I was captured they transferred me again. This time to Auschwitz.

A silence in the court. Auschwitz, the counsellor says quietly.

– Yes.

– And there? the counsellor says.

– I was given into the charge of a Dr Mengele, Kerach says.
Dr Josef Mengele.

A murmur in the audience. The name is well known.

– And what did that entail? the counsellor for the prosecution
says.

– I was kept in a special quarters separated from the other
inmates of the camp, Kerach says. It was referred to by both
inmates and camp staff as the Menagerie. It was a secure
facility, housing only Übermenschen. Dr Mengele had a special
dispensation from the Reich to experiment on the nature of
the condition. In another lab he kept twins, he had an obses-
sion with twins – twins and midgets. I don't know how many
people went through his labs during the war. But there were
many of us in the Menagerie.

– And you say he experimented on you?

– On all of us. He gassed us. He cut us open. He tested us
with electricity, acid, wanting to see how much damage we could
take. Some – many – of us didn't make it.

– Can you tell us of some of the things he did?

– I remember the twins, Kerach said. They weren't changed.
They were nothing. Roma. Gypsies. He . . . for the first time
here Kerach pauses. He blinks. Mengele sewed them together,

he says. He wanted to see if he could make conjoined twins. They survived the surgery but the infection killed them, later. He had child patients. He used to call himself Uncle Mengele when he came around to see them. He gave them sweets. Once, he took fourteen pairs of identical twins and injected chloroform into their hearts and once they were dead he cut them open on his operating table and measured up and compared their organs. What he did to us was easy by comparison. We were Übermenschen, we were harder to come by. Still, we didn't all make it. Those who didn't were carted off to the crematorium. I will always remember the smell. You can't wipe away the smell of three million dead. It never goes away. We? Kerach says. We who lived? We were the lucky ones.

A silence in the court, the counsellor for the prosecution turns his head this way and that like a stork. Comes to settle on the man in the glass box. I want you to think carefully now, he says. Speaking to Kerach but looking at the man in the glass box. Did you ever get visitors at the . . . Menagerie? Nazis?

– Often, Kerach says. Hitler himself came once, to stare. It was not considered safe for him to go inside. We were deemed too dangerous. Instead we were paraded out to him, one by one. Kerach shrugs. Hitler looked bored, he says.

– Anyone else?

– Martin Bormann, the same time as Hitler. Eichmann, twice. Alfred Rosenberg came – he was the main figure behind Nazi philosophy, the Party's spiritual leader. He argued with Mengele, I remember. Said the Menagerie was a disgrace, and that we should all be exterminated immediately. It was the only time I saw Mengele lose his temper. He was close to tears. It is my life's work, he kept saying. My life's work. I guess Rosenberg didn't get his way, though, because we were still there the next morning. I had rather thought that we wouldn't be.

– And this man? the counsellor for the prosecution says softly. And in the total hush of the courtroom we realise all of this, the questions, the back-and-forth, were all, simply, a lead-up to this one single question. This man, the counsellor says, in his soft cultured voice, and his hand rises, pointing at the man in the glass box. Did you ever see this man at the holding facility in Auschwitz?

Kerach looks at the man in the glass box. Looks at him for a long moment. The man in the glass box doesn't look back. He sits quietly, his hands in his lap.

– Yes, Kerach says.

– Silence!

Kerach is stoic, and so is the man in the glass box. But the court is anything but. The counsellor for the prosecution patiently, with a sense of theatrics, waits for order to return.

– Could you identify him for the court? he says at last.

– We were never . . . *formally* introduced, Kerach says – which draws a few laughs.

– However, I overheard Mengele referring to him as Dr Vomacht, Kerach says, and again there is noise.

– Vomacht, the counsellor says.

– Yes.

– Has he visited more than once?

Kerach shrugs. Two or three times, he says.

– Can you be more exact?

– Three, Kerach says. Three times.

– And you are sure this is the man you saw?

– Yes, Kerach says. Looks at the man in the glass box, who finally, calmly turns his head then, and looks back at him.

– Yes, Kerach says. I'm sure.

87. **JERUSALEM** 1964

– No, he says. Shakes his massive head. No, I won't do it. I can't.

The Old Man wipes his brow with his handkerchief. From the Friday evening and on through Saturday Jerusalem becomes a veritable desert: shops close, public transport ceases, and a hush descends on the Israeli side of the city. The Old Man and many of the foreign visitors flock to the handful of open bars catering mostly to tourists and visitors. Now he sits at one such place, Mike's, waiting for the air-conditioning to kick in, drinking a twelve-year-old scotch and rather wishing the whole interminable affair were over.

– So how have you been, Tank? he says.

– Living, Tank says. One day at a time.

The Old Man examines him. We don't age, he says, but quietly, almost to himself. He'd seen Tank after the war, after the liberation of the Auschwitz-Birkenau camp by the Red Army. The once-giant man had weighed less than eight stone – under fifty kilograms. He was a walking skeleton, his loose skin hung in folds from his bones, his teeth and his hair had fallen out. The Old Man had found him in a Red Army field hospital and pulled him out, shouting at the Russian officers in attendance, who glared at him mutely. A British Übermensch, they seemed to imply, was not high on their list of priorities.

The Old Man had seen Auschwitz, too. The people who died when they were freed, not from violence but from the food the liberating soldiers gave them. Too much, too soon, it killed them. At least they'd died free, the Old Man thinks. He'd seen the crematorium and the mounds of ash and human bones. Had seen the gas chambers. A pile of gold teeth extracted but not yet shipped, which had then been looted by the soldiers. It wasn't even war, he remembered thinking. He didn't know what it was. He took Tank from the Soviet hospital and nursed him all the way to base, and thought he'd lost him. But Tank clung on to life. Stubbornly. His hair never grew back and his teeth had been replaced with gold prosthetics. No one had asked where the gold teeth came from. He put on weight again, slowly. Grew back into himself. He never quite healed but he wasn't dead, either, which must have been something, the Old Man thinks.

– It isn't Vomacht they should put on the stand, Tank says. It's Mengele.

– They would if they could, the Old Man says. He . . . his whereabouts are unknown.

– Bullshit, Tank says. He's in Argentina, in South America, like the rest of them who left on the ratline.

The Old Man sighs. South America's a big place, he says.

– Vomacht, Tank says. He was there, in Auschwitz, yes. Two, three times? He was a Nazi. Everyone was a Nazi, Old Man. If you weren't a card-carrying member you might as well have given up then and there. Why is he really on trial? Is it simply for being a German at the worst time in German history? What choice did he have?

– He could have stood up to—

– And been summarily executed? Tank shakes his massive head. What is he really on trial for? he says, softly. For not being a *hero*?

The Old Man takes a sip of his Scotch. For what he did, he says. Looks at Tank's ravaged face. For us, he says, with sudden vehemence. He is being judged for what he did to *us*.

Tank shakes his head. I won't do it, he says. I can't. I won't testify.

The Old Man breathes out, seems to deflate. He lays a hand on Tank's shoulder, gently.

– You don't have to, he says.

He finishes his drink as Tank walks away.

88. JERUSALEM 1964

– Please state your name for the court.

– Stanley Martin Lieber, the man on the witness stand says. The Old Man has removed the heavy earphones with the translator's voice whispering in his ear. This interview is being conducted in good old-fashioned English, at least.

– Your occupation? says the counsellor for the prosecution.

– Historian and author.

The man is thin and wiry, in his early forties, with even white teeth and a tanned face and a New York accent.

– More specifically, says the counsellor for the prosecution, you are the author of the reference work *Le Dictionnaire Biographique des Surhommes*?

– Yes. The man grins; you get the sense he smiles easily.

– A work never published in English – in fact, banned in both the United States and England?

– That . . . yes. It's unfortunate—

– And which would otherwise be titled *A Biographical Dictionary of Super Men*?

– I expect so, Lieber says, which draws some muted laughter from the audience. *Übermenschen*, he says. What do we mean by that term? Beyond-Men? Heroes? The changed?

– You tell me, the counsellor says.

Lieber shrugs. It is a field shrouded by secrecy and superstition, he says. Filled with apocryphal misinformation and banned histories. I attempted to, if not clarify, then to at least *systemise* what we know. Or think we know. Even after the war – *especially* after the war – it is not a subject approved of by my government.

– Why is that? the counsellor says quietly.

The atmosphere in the court is tense. Muted. Lieber, for the first time, looks nervous. I'm not sure that I should – he begins.

– Remember, Mr Lieber. You are under oath.

– It's to do with Operation Paperclip, Lieber says. Lets the words out quickly, in a rush, as if to be rid of them. The noise level rises in the court but quickly subsides. The Old Man sees the journalists focused, intent. This, clearly, is a juicy moment for the newshounds.

– Operation Paperclip, Mr Lieber?

– It was an operation carried out by my country – by the US military – in the immediate post-war years, Lieber says.

– And its *purpose*, Mr Lieber?

– Its purpose, overtly, was to locate and . . . and *repatriate* to the United States the, ah, the cream of the crop of Nazi scientists, Lieber says.

Shouts in the court. Silence! the lead judge shouts.

– To be taken to America and given new identities? the counsellor says.

– Yes.

– Despite what crimes they might have perpetrated during the war?

– Well, yes. It was felt that their knowledge – their expertise – would be best utilised in service. Rocket scientists, in particular, Lieber says, and now his cool is gone, and he seems to be sweating a little. But not only them, he adds.

– You said *overtly*, the counsellor says in that same soft, patient voice. But it had a second purpose, too, didn't it?

– Yes.

– What would that have been, do you think? the counsellor says.

Lieber laughs, as if to make a joke of it. Wipes the sweat on his forehead with a monogrammed handkerchief. Well, I suppose it's never been exactly a *secret*, he says. And these *are* the Sixties, so . . .

– Mr Lieber? Could you answer the question?

– Übermenschen, Lieber says. Its second – but some would say primary – objective was to locate and repatriate German Übermenschen deemed to be of potential military use.

The court's in an uproar. The Old Man pinches the bridge of his nose. Feels a headache coming on.

– I see, the counsellor says, when the court quiets down. Tell me, Mr Lieber. Do you know – as a historian, as an expert in this field – can you tell us which name was at the top of both of those secret lists? Who was at the top of the Most Wanted list in this Operation Paperclip?

Lieber bites his lips. Looks at the man in the glass box. The man looks up and meets his eyes. Something between hatred and admiration twists Lieber's face. He raises his hand, points at the man in the glass box. They were looking for him, he says. They were looking for Dr Joachim Vomacht.

– Silence! Silence in the court!

– You identify this man as Dr Joachim Vomacht?

Lieber swallows; his Adam's apple bobs up and down. From all the evidence I have seen, he says, and such photographic material as could be found – yes. There is no doubt in my mind that this man is Joachim Vomacht.

– I see. Tell me, Mr Lieber. You are a Jew.

– Was that a question? Lieber says, and the audience laughs. The counsellor smiles patiently.

– During the war, you served in the Signal Corps?

– Yes.

– And there you worked on various propaganda campaigns?

– Yes.

– Specifically ones relating to the superiority of American Übermenschen?

Lieber shrugs. Our heroes were always made to be larger than life, he says. We merely helped them along.

– Is that when you became interested in the changed, Mr Lieber?

– I was always fascinated by the change, Lieber says. What happened in nineteen thirty-two changed the world. *This man* changed the world.

– Do you not, as a Jew, see the acts of Dr Vomacht – in view of later Nazi racial theory and the attempted wholesale extermination of your own race, Mr Lieber – as the supreme crime?

– Objection! the counsellor for the defence, who mostly, the Old Man notes, remains silent during these exchanges, says.

The judges silently confer. We'll allow it, the lead judge says at last. Mr Lieber?

A strange look enters Lieber's eyes. A fervent light, which

transforms his face, makes him seem, for just that moment, like an innocent; like a child.

    – With great power comes great responsibility, he says, softly.

    – Excuse me, Mr Lieber?

Lieber shakes his head, but his eyes are far away, as though seeing something only he can see. I think the change, he says . . . I think it was the greatest thing to ever happen to mankind.

    – Mr Lieber!

The counsellor for the defence smiles.

    – No more questions, the counsellor for the prosecution says, sourly.

89. JERUSALEM 1964

    – Let us talk of your . . . associates, the counsellor says. The Old Man sits up, listening intently.

    – What associates? the man in the box says.

    – Did you know Dr Mengele, in Auschwitz?

    – Objection!

    – Your honour? the counsellor for the prosecution says, shrugging a bit, as if to say, *Really?*

    – Overruled. The witness will answer the question.

The counsellor nods. Thank you. Turns back to Vomacht. Raises his eyebrows as if to say, *Well?*

    – The man was an animal. A pig. His methodology was fundamentally flawed.

A murmur in the audience.

    – You knew him? How many times did you meet?

    – I will not answer that question.

The counsellor shrugs. Very well, he says. Makes a show of consulting his papers – it makes the Old Man smile, appreciatively. We will assume that you have—

– *Objection!*

– Sustained. The lead judge frowns at the counsellor for the prosecution, who raises his hands in mock-surrender. The audience laughs. The judge's gavel hits the bench. There will be *silence* in my court!

The counsellor turns back to the witness in his enforced glass box. The shimmer of the electric force field surrounding the box seems almost to hum. Makes us think, for just a moment, of bees in the grass, of a warm summer's day.

– Now, please think carefully, the counsellor for the prosecution – not, it seems, in the very least deterred – says. Cast your mind back to the war. There was a man who supplied Dr Mengele with many of his . . . specimens. The head of Gestapo Department F.

A silence from the witness box.

– Do you know the person I mean? the counsellor says, softly.

A silence, still.

– Brigadeführer Hans von Wolkenstein, the counsellor says, still in that same soft, dangerous voice. But they called him the wolf man.

A silence.

– Yes? No? You see, we do rather wonder where he is, Doctor Vomacht. Many people are quite *anxious* to have a word with him. Over – how shall I put it? Over alleged war crimes?

A silence.

The counsellor shrugs. Very well, he says. Let the record show that the witness did not answer the question. Turns a page, looks down, looks up at the man in the box. There is one other, small matter, he says.

A stubborn silence.

– You had a daughter . . . the counsellor says.

The witness stands up in the box. For the first time showing emotion. His face contorts in fury and he shouts, You will leave my daughter out of this!

– What happened to her? the counsellor for the prosecution

says, softly. What happened to your daughter, Herr Doktor Vomacht?

– Objection!

– Sustained. Be careful, counsellor. The lead judge rubs the bridge of his nose, sighs. Court will adjourn until tomorrow, he says.

90. **JERUSALEM** 1964

A final memory from that trial, a few weeks later:

– I was not! You do not understand!

Vomacht had been quiet, almost placid, the Old Man thinks, throughout the trial. A parade of witnesses had come and gone, Übermenschen and scientists, but so few who had known Vomacht, had ever met him. He is a shadow, cast not by people's testimonies but from their own perceptions of him, of the change. Vomacht seemed a recluse, the Old Man remembers the war, it was impossible to even get a good photo of him. A shadow. One of them.

Cool, until that last round of questioning. And now he is no longer cool. As if sensing the trial coming to a close, that soon there would be no more speeches, no more opportunities, Vomacht now stands up in his bulletproof glass box, glaring at the audience of Übermenschen and reporters, shaking his fist as he speaks, a well-preserved, unchanged man, a shadow finally dragged out into the light.

He glares at the counsellor for the prosecution. You ask who I worked with? he says. You ask who my *associates* were? He draws a deep, angry breath. I worked with *Planck*, he says. With *Heisenberg*! With Dirac and Bohr! I was a scientist, and we were penetrating the very heart of the universe!

– Dr Vomacht, please, the counsellor says.

– No! You do not understand! What we did – what we sought to do – it was to know God himself! The device was not meant to – was not meant to—

– Dr Vomacht, please answer the question!

Vomacht shakes his finger, as at an unruly pupil.

– The uncertainty principle—

– Dr Vomacht!

– What happened later was not, could not, be my fault! Vomacht says. Herr Hitler—

An eruption of noise in the audience.

From the bench: Silence! Silence in the court!

But they won't be quieted, these spectators, these Übermenschen.

– Order! Order!

– Dr Vomacht will answer the question presented to him by the court!

The counsellor for the prosecution puts his hands on the dais, his fingers on the dark surface of the wood. Dr Vomacht, he says, in his soft, cultured voice. Were you, or were you not, a member of the Nazi Party?

An expectant hush descends. Vomacht glares. He reminds the Old Man of a butterfly, suddenly; a butterfly trapped in a glass jar.

– I was a scientist, Vomacht says. I did not—

– Did you not meet with the Führer on three separate—

– What I did, I did for science!

– Order! Or—

And it fades, colour leeched out of old memory, the courtroom and the men in their old-fashioned haircuts, and the garish costumes and the bad suits, and the parquet floor, disintegrating into the black-and-white snow storm of a dead analogue television signal.

And are gone.

FIGHTING INTENSIFIES IN VIETNAM

October 5, 1967

SAIGON American presence in Vietnam has risen to near 500,000 military personnel. Large-scale battles have taken place near Da Nang and Ia Drang in recent months. Heavy bombings by US airforce planes, including the use of napalm, continue. Protests have broken out across the United States. Four hundred thousand people marched from Central Park to the UN building in New York City to protest the war in April this year. In his State of the Union Address, President Lyndon B. Johnson said: 'I wish I could report to you that the conflict is almost over. This I cannot do. We face more cost, more loss, and more agony. For the end is not yet.'

ELEVEN:
JUNGLE FEVER

LAOS
1967

91. BANGKOK, THAILAND 1967

Oblivion flies London to Bangkok, first class, with a linen suit for the tropics custom-made on Savile Row. In Bangkok, a meeting with Jeffries from the Embassy, a tall nervous man with a pencil moustache. They have drinks at the Siam Intercontinental. Ceiling fans move lazily overhead, and the setting sun paints the sky in vivid reds and blues and yellows. They are surrounded by foliage. The gardens of the Siam are legendary. Mosquitoes buzz as lazily as the fans and the man from the Embassy lights up a Pall Mall with quick nervous fingers and waves it in the air – For the mosquitoes, don't you know, old boy.

Snaps his fingers at the waiter, Boy, bring us two G&Ts, chop chop, turns with an apologetic shrug, It's the tonic, you see—

– Quinine? Oblivion says.

– Got it in one, old boy. Got it in one, Jeffries says. Turns his head, this way and that, Well, he demands of the waiters, or the air, Well? A waiter hurries over, two tall glasses on a tray, lays them down on mats, already the glasses have a sheen of perspiration on their sides. Cheeky bugger, Jeffries says, affectionately, the waiter grins obediently as he walks off. Jeffries raises the drink, Cheers, old boy, Oblivion's fingers curl around the glass, the clink they make when they touch is like the chime of hours. When he drinks the bubbles tickle his tongue, and the taste of the tonic, bitter and cool, slides smoothly down. Cigarettes for the mosquitoes, gin and tonic for the malaria, Jeffries says, grinning again, and Oblivion wonders: What is the man so *afraid* of?

– Tell me about the war, Oblivion says. Takes out his cigarette box, taps one out on the table, lights up. Watches the man from the Embassy through the smoke. Jeffries fidgets, stubs his cigarette out in the ashtray provided, lights up a new one, says, It's the Americans' show, old boy. It's the Americans' show all the way.

– Yes, yes, Oblivion says, patiently. Jeffries sighs. We have no official involvement, he says. Our main interest is commercial.

– Commercial?

– Someone has to make guns, Jeffries says, as if it's the most obvious thing in the world. Which perhaps it is. Ammo. Airplanes. Helicopters. Waves his hand through the smoke vaguely. What have you. Bombs, he says. Lots and lots of bleeding bombs.

Oblivion waits. Vietnam, Jeffries says. What a mess. His glass is empty. He signals for a replacement. Oblivion covers his own glass with his hand. Jeffries shrugs. But you're not going to Vietnam, he says. You're going to Laos. It's a shit-hole, frankly. You know what the problem with this whole place is? he says. That we let the French take over. Should have taken Laos, Vietnam, Cambodia for ourselves. Goddamned frogs. No. Now look at this mess. Communism, Jeffries says, what do these yellow bastards know about Communism, what they need is a firm hand. Says, Malaya is ours, at least.

Oblivion waits him out, his face revealing nothing. Jeffries says, Laos. It's in the middle of an ugly civil war. The Royals are desperately trying to hold on to power, the Commies – they call themselves the Pathet Lao – are Soviet-backed. The Americans have no official presence in Laos. Unofficially, though . . . he smiles. His teeth are yellow, and crooked. You'll see, he says. Not pleasantly.

– Tell me about our involvement, Oblivion says, and this time the *our* has a different meaning, and he sees Jeffries flinch. That's for you to find out, Jeffries says. That's what you're here for, isn't it? Challenging him. You don't like us, Oblivion says, and Jeffries laughs, an almost hysterical sound, and the realisation hits Oblivion, like an old remembered pain, what is he scared of, he is scared of *you*.

92. **DONG MUANG AIRPORT, THAILAND** 1967

– You're the Brit?

The pilot is tall and tanned, with white even teeth and green agate eyes. Mike! he says. Oblivion says, Oblivion. They shake hands. Pleasure to meet you! Mike says. His hand sweeps the airfield. Welcome to Air America, he says.

They're at an airfield outside Bangkok. A dozen Bell helicopters sit alongside a similar number of cargo planes, twin-engine de Havilland Caribous and Fairchild C-123s. It is early morning, but already hot. The pilot, Mike, examines Oblivion in admiration, his linen suit, his wide-brimmed hat. I dig your style, man! he says.

– Thank you, Oblivion says, gravely. Mechanics swarm over one recently arrived plane, its side peppered, Oblivion notices somewhat uneasily, with bullet holes. Mike follows his glance and laughs. Don't worry about that! he says. I'll get you there safe and sound. Oblivion shrugs and follows him down the field to a makeshift square building with the door open. A handwritten note on cardboard, in crude letters: *Air America: Anything, Anywhere, Anytime.* They go inside, where the light is dim. A television flickers in one corner of the room without sound, it shows the American president, Lyndon B. Johnson, talking to reporters in the White House, the image replaced with that of planes flying in formation, replaced again, something about the Israel-Syria War. A group of men in civilian clothes sit inside the room on upturned crates of beer. The air is rife with marijuana smoke. A radio plays Jefferson Airplane's 'White Rabbit'. For a moment Oblivion feels ripped out of time, transported to this alien place, this alien time. A couple of the men nod greetings. Mike, Someone says, Who's the spook?

– Passenger, Mike says.

– One of ours?

– No, Oblivion says, with a slight apologetic air. I'm afraid not.

– A Brit? Then they seem to realise and suddenly the atmosphere changes, heads turn away, minutely. It's funny, Oblivion thinks. Or – no, not funny. Strange. That the Americans, as much as they celebrate their heroes in public, in private shy away from them, as though they are unclean.

– Spliff? someone says, passing it around. Oblivion waves away the offer, accepts a beer instead. It's warm. Don't worry, Mike says, we'll get you to Laos in no time.

– What's it like? Oblivion says.

– Laos?

– The war, Oblivion says.

– What war? Mike says, and the others laugh – it has the feel of an old, worn-out joke. Don't you know there's no war on in Laos.

– I'll tell you for free, one of the pilots says, I'm glad as fuck I'm not in the army. Fucking *jungles*, man. Viet fucking Cong.

– Yeah, Mike chimes in, it's OK as long as you're in the air, right?

A chorus of assent. Mike shakes his head. But down there? he says. You might as well be fighting fucking *ghosts*.

Ghosts? Oblivion says; a little sharply.

The others note his tone; look uncomfortable. Pilots, Oblivion realises. These guys are all pilots. An odd assortment, and he wonders how they'd all ended up here, working for the CIA.

– Ghosts, someone says, but softly.

– Yeah, someone else says. But they're not looking at Oblivion. Looking away. Bad luck, someone mutters, and Oblivion knows it is him they are talking about.

– Come on, Mike says, standing up. Don't mind these guys, they're fried. Too many flights, too many joints.

– Not enough, someone says, and they all laugh. Oblivion smiles. Nice to meet you all, he says.

– Yeah, you too, spook. That laughter again – relief, he thinks, that he is going. The music changes, the first notes of the Monkees' 'Daydream Believer' start up on the portable radio.

They emerge out into the sunlight. Mike talks briefly to a mechanic, nods. It's ready, he says. They go to the plane, You can sit in the cockpit, Mike says, Oblivion says, What's at the back?

Mike shrugs. Cargo, he says. Guns, bombs, dope, food, you . . . everything is cargo.

Oblivion stands there, takes a deep breath of the air, machine oil and fuel and that heavy, humid smell, and salt and tar from the sea. What is he doing here? This war is not their business, their war was a lifetime ago and in another place. And he is alone, he's been alone for what, sometimes, very late at night, awaking in the cold, fog misting the window, feels like forever.

93. ISAN, THAILAND 1967

Mike's playing 'Lucy in the Sky With Diamonds' at full volume and Oblivion stares out of the aircraft's grimy window, looking down at flatlands, the wind roaring outside. Flatlands and small villages of thatch and bamboo, herds of cows, banana trees, smoke rising from cooking fires – and again he feels that disconnect, that sense of being torn from time.

– Here it comes! Mike shouts over the engine noise and Lennon's singing, and suddenly the land is cut by a deep gushing wound and the plane swerves, following it, and Mike shouts, The Mekong!

Empty land ends and a city begins on the other side of the river, as if, simply by crossing, they had transitioned from one world to another. Oblivion sees streets, colonial French buildings, Buddhist temples with golden roofs, a black stupa squatting like an ancient toad, cars and carriages and pedestrians, palm trees, the swimming pool of a modern hotel. The plane swoops past the Mekong and over the city and Oblivion can see other planes in the sky, rising overhead, a flock of ravens.

– Our city, baby! Mike shouts. Our city, our planes, our fucking war. The plane swoops down towards a landing strip, the Beatles stop singing and the music changes, and it takes Oblivion a moment to recognise the song – it's Johnny Rivers' 'Secret Agent Man'.

94. **VIENTIANE, LAOS** 1967

Oblivion lands at Wattay Airport and the sky is full of wings. He can hear English spoken in a variety of American accents, as well as French and Lao. He'd not expected there to be so many people, so many planes, so much traffic. Hmong, Mike says, pointing at a group of men coming off a large helicopter, carrying heavy-looking boxes. Hill tribes. Oblivion says, What's in the boxes? Mike shrugs, looking shifty, Shit, he says. What do I know.

A man in civilian clothes hurries over to them, Thank you, Mike, he says, you're dismissed, Mike says, Jeez, we're not in the army here, Bob, Bob says, Yeah, yeah, turns to Oblivion with a tired smile, says, Pilots, right?

In moments they're in the city. The jeep stops sharply, jostling Oblivion. Come on! Bob says. Oblivion wonders if that's the man's real name. They're outside the Samlo Bar, on Setthathirat Road. Inside it is dark and dim and full of smoke. There's a long wooden bar and a pool table at one corner and a group of drunk pilots surrounded by girls, who all greet Bob effusively as he and Oblivion walk in.

– Come on, Bob says. He buys two pints of beer and carries them to an empty booth. There is no one else around. The juke box is playing the Beatles' 'Paperback Writer'. So, Bob says. Takes a long sip of beer and sighs when he's done. The Old Man sent you.

– Yes.

– That fucking asshole, Bob says, and laughs. He has an easy, comfortable laugh. He's been a pain in our ass for years, Bob says. No offence.

– None taken, Oblivion says.

– How's the beer?

– Good, Oblivion says. Almost, we suspect, beginning to lose his patience. The beer's good.

– Best in Southeast Asia, Bob says, with pride.

– I'm sure, Oblivion says, with his patience running increasingly thin. Now, tell me about your Übermenschen, *Bob*.

– It's hardly *our* Übermenschen you're interested in, though, is it, Oblivion? Bob says. Oblivion stares at him, the fine tanned wrinkles around the man's eyes. Used to the outdoors, and smiling. And not to be underestimated, Oblivion thinks, a Company man, Central Intelligence Agency, the guys who won the last big war and can't imagine losing one, ever. Although in that, he thinks, a little uneasily, it's just possible they may be wrong.

– I understand the Viet Cong utilise Übermenschen in combat operations? Oblivion says, bluntly.

– And the Pathet Lao, Bob says, though there seems to be a bit of an ideological issue, there.

– How so?

– Remember your Orwell? Bob says. Smiles. Lights up a cigarette. War, Oblivion thinks, remembering. Everyone smoked in the war. All animals are equal, Bob says. But some animals are more equal than others.

– What does that mean?

– It means they don't *trust* you, Bob says. Over-Men. Beyond-Men. Fucking *Übermenschen*. Whatever the fuck you guys are. All animals are equal but you're – what are you? Are you even an animal, in this fucked-up metaphor? He was a Brit, wasn't he, Orwell? I prefer Hemingway, myself. *The Sun Also Rises*? Fucking *great* book. Did you read it?

– No.

– Oh. Really? Bob looks a little surprised at that. You should, you know.

– I'll make a note of that, Oblivion says.

Bob shrugs. Cigarette? he says.

Oblivion reluctantly accepts one. Not smoked in years, now this new mission, this new war. Takes him back. He says, So they do not employ Übermenschen on a regular basis?

No. Only—

Then Bob stops, as if he were about to say something he was not supposed to. He smiles and waves the cigarette in the air and downs the rest of his pint as if it were water. Listen, buddy, he says, standing up. He lays a hand on Oblivion's shoulder, all friendly, but there's steel in his grip. Stay a couple of days, he says. A week. Hell, stay as long as you want! Take in the sights, shoot some pool, find yourself a girl. Smirks at Oblivion. Or a boy. Whatever. Gestures at the bar. Just take your pick. Then go home. There's nothing to see. Hell, boy – Laos is a neutral state. We don't even have a *presence* here! Bob laughs. Lifts his hand, pats Oblivion on the back. See you around, he says. Leaves Oblivion sitting there, blinking in the darkness of the Samlo Bar.

95. **VIENTIANE, LAOS** 1967

What does it feel like to be Oblivion? Not Oblivion and Fogg, Fogg and Oblivion? Just Oblivion: Nothing to mask him from the world, no one to share the burden of the long years?

– *Have there been any new ones, Oblivion? Fogg says.*

– *You know the answer to that.*

– *Then no.*

– *No, Oblivion says.*

Alone, and yet not alone, for in the night, he doesn't remember quite how it happens, the bar, too many drinks later, and a meeting of two strangers, about to become lovers, that knowledge between them, and then going back to the cheap hotel and making love on humid sheets and then.

The pipe. The ball of resin. That sweet and cloying smell, spreading over the room. He accepts the pipe, puts it to his lips, draws the sweet smoke of it into his lungs. Feels far away from anyone and anything.

He feels his world shrinking, the room compresses around him, becomes two-dimensional, a frame; it traps him inside it, and he tries helplessly to flee, the square like a window squeezing him inside.

He makes to *move* and is at once caught, suspended, in a new frame, and then again, each movement a frozen moment inside a panel. In the next his mouth opens in a helpless cry, the words emerge from his mouth: *EEEIIIGGHHH!*

What the— he thinks, and the thought bubbles above his head in the next frozen frame, like a cloud. Oblivion, scared, punches as a shadowy figure materialises beside him, KA-BOOM THWK! The shadow dodges, fires at him, BLAM! BLAM! Oblivion rolls, ahead of him is a light, an opening, he crawls through ever narrower frames, his body passing from one to the other, etched between cages of black ink, POW! A gunshot explodes, somebody screams, *AAAARRGGHH!* Oblivion crawls to the light and it opens, sucking him in, the frames, the shadows, all the black and the grey and the white—

He passes through blinding light into a world of rich primary colour. A red sun shines in the sky, tall skyscrapers rise into the air like silver rockets, men in hovercars jet jauntily through the sky, a man in blue walks past wearing red underpants and a cape, a woman like a cat with a mask on her face. Everywhere he turns, Oblivion sees masks.

A giant question mark forms over his head. He crosses the

street, he can see people's thoughts hovering over their heads, he sees a man with a giant smile etched into his too-pale face. He sees a man climb like a spider up a wall.

He falls.

Down into an opium darkness, he tries to open his eyes, a part of him is still in that hotel room, lying on the mattress on the floor, the naked body of another holding on to him, a pipe still burns, the night is humid, full of minute sounds, the lazy buzz of a mosquito but he falls, his eyes close and the inner world takes him and he:

Is bitten by a radioactive spider, falls into an acid vat, is trapped inside an Intrinsic Field Subtractor, is given a power ring by a dying alien, he is strapped to a table and experimented on by military scientists until he becomes the ultimate warrior, he is sent as a baby from his dying planet to Earth, he sees his parents murdered in front of his eyes leaving the opera, he is bombarded by cosmic rays, he dials a number in a telephone box, he is exposed to a gamma-ray bomb as it detonates, he eats spinach, he discovers a strange meteor, he finds an ancient mask that belonged to a god, he . . . he . . . he . . .

Oblivion whimpers on the naked bed, the bedsheets soak his sweat. A warm hand on his brow, Hush, hush, Oblivion whispers Hold me, another body presses into his, caresses, comforting, Oblivion thrashes, No, no, until at last the frames which hold him blow open, like windows, and set him free. Hush, now, the other man says, and Oblivion settles, like a child, on the bed and closes his eyes until, at last, he sleeps.

96. **VIENTIANE, LAOS** 1967

Rough hands shake him awake. We watch, we see: Oblivion on a mattress on the floor, the open window, the last remnants of a burning mosquito coil, that thick, nauseating smell, the humid bedsheets, rumpled, that nude sleeping form beside Oblivion, the pale flesh of a beautiful boy. Oblivion opens bleary eyes, they're gummed together, his head, what happened to his head, thieves came in the night and took it, memory won't come, where had the missing hours gone?

– Get up, you lazy son of a bitch, a voice says, the hands keep shaking him, they irritate Oblivion, he swipes a hand, it hits a table and obliviates the wood, a lamp comes crashing to the floor, the voice says, Whoa there, buddy, the sleeping form beside Oblivion stirs to life, alert, the voice says, Scram; the young man blinks sleepy eyes and smiles and touches Oblivion, briefly, on the shoulder; and scrams.

Oblivion sits up, leaning his back against the wall. The door slams shut. He stares.

– *Tigerman?* he says.

– Hi, buddy.

– It's been a while, Oblivion says.

– No shit it has.

– What the hell are you doing here? Oblivion pats the mattress with a vague air. Where's. . .? he says and trails off. What time is it?

– Time to get up, Tigerman says. Hi ho, hi ho. It's off to work . . . and so on. Here, drink this.

Oblivion accepts the bottle of water. Drinks. The cold water revives him. So what, he says, you're a spook, now?

– I'm me, Tigerman says. Oblivion examines him. Does not look any older than when he'd last seen him, when was it, forty-six? Forty-seven? Same arrogant grin, that mane of hair, that muscled physique. But something different about the eyes. The look in them is older, colder, hard. It feels, to Oblivion, for just a moment, like staring into a mirror. A sensation like falling. Whatever happened to that partner of yours, Tigerman says, Oblivion says, Who, Fogg?

– Slippery character, never trusted him, Tigerman says. Do you know, in forty-six . . . trails off. Never mind all that, he says.

You're here sniffing about for the Old Man, I know, Bob told me, sniffing for Übermenschen.

– Are there any? Oblivion says.

Tigerman shrugs. Sure, he says, Thai, Lao, Vietnamese . . . who the fuck cares?

The balance, Oblivion thinks. The Old Man's old maxim. Übermenschen on both sides cancel each other out. So? he says. Stands up, starts to gather his clothes. What *had* he done last night? he thinks. Tries to remember.

– So I've got one you *will* be interested in, Tigerman says, and when he speaks his mouth shifts, lengthens, his teeth become a tiger's teeth, wet with saliva. Who? Oblivion says, and the other grins and says, Der Wolfsmann.

97. LAOS 1967

The chopper rises beyond the city, the Mekong left in the distance. Mountains ahead, peaked in snow.

– The Soviets are supporting North Vietnam, Tigerman shouts over the sound of the rotors. Warm air rushes inside. Oblivion nods, more politeness than interest. Money, training, equipment, Tigerman says. The usual deal. Jerks a thumb at the pilot and grins a feral grin. These boys, our very own Air America, they're flying bombing missions over the Ho Chi Minh Trail, on the Lao border—

At Oblivion's questioning look, Tigerman explains – The trail links North and South Vietnam, passing through Laos. Jabs his finger in Oblivion's face. That's where *he* is.

– The Wolf man.

– Working for the fucking *Russians*, can you believe it? Tigerman roars with laughter. Of all people, he says. Oblivion shrugs. So what's the difference, he seems to be implying. What is he doing for them? he says. Tigerman says, Same as he always did. Hunting Übermenschen. Only difference, he's got a different paymaster now. He has a whole new gang working for him. A couple of old comrades from the war, the ones who didn't die or go on the ratline to Argentina or were—Tigerman stops, looks, if that's even possible, a little sheepish.

– Were not picked up in Operation Paperclip by your own government, you mean?

Tigerman shrugs it off. The rest are all locals, he says, Vietnamese, Lao, some Chinese.

– So what's the problem? Oblivion says. Why the interest?

– He's stopped taking orders from Moscow, Tigerman says. Shrugs. I don't know how he ended up with them. Somehow they'd pulled the wolf man out of the war. They saved him: but that meant he was theirs, for good.

– The *Russians* want him dead? Oblivion says.

– Once he stopped taking orders there was only one thing they could do, Tigerman says. And that's to try and get rid of him.

– So let the Russians do it, Oblivion says.

Tigerman grins at him and lights up a joint.

What, Tigerman says. And miss out on all the fun?

98. **LAOS** 1967

Chop, chop, chop, chop, the helicopter rises over crags and narrow dirt tracks, terraced rice fields, their yellow is startling to the eyes, *chop, chop,* the rotor blades swish through the air, down below Oblivion can see a boy leading goats, women with wide-brimmed hats sheltering their faces from the sun, *chop, chop* the helicopter rises, higher, higher, these mountains seem immense to Oblivion, what is he doing here?

– Kill that motherfucker, Tigerman says, Oblivion feels odd,

Tigerman's eyes are like two yellow moons in a dark sky, rising. What *did* he do the night before? Tigerman is smoking a joint, it's an enormous thing, a tapering cone, the smell fills the inside of the helicopter, Tigerman passes it to Oblivion who takes a drag – how many now, he thinks. And can't remember.

'The Age of Aquarius' plays full blast inside the helicopter. Oblivion starts to giggle, what do the people below them make of it, I'm a hero! he screams. I'm a fucking hero! Tigerman growls, his eyes are enormous, that smell of weed, seductive and sweet, fills the mind, You had some opium last night, didn't you, Tigerman says, and Oblivion, as though it's the funniest question in the world, laughs so hard as memory suddenly returns. Man I had the craziest dream! he says.

The helicopter drops suddenly, the landscape changes as they come around a bend in the mountain, the fog lies over the distant land, clouds below them, could Fogg shape clouds, Oblivion wonders, the laughter leaves his body like alcohol leaving a drunk's. The fog clears in snatches and a bright red shines below, as far as the eye can see the slopes are covered in deep-red flowers, and Tigerman sobers up, too, The poppies, man, he says. The fucking *poppies!*

The helicopter descends, out of the clouds there rises a village of low-lying huts built against the side of the mountain, men appear behind a rock outcrop, they're carrying guns, someone fires, into the air, Tigerman swears, the pilot, all this while, cool. Not much of a talker, maybe as stoned as they are, Bill, Oblivion thinks, was his name Bill, or Tom, something like that, anyway. Lands the helicopter right there on the slope, turns, There you go, sirs! he shouts. Oblivion and Tigerman climb out, the pilot gives them a thumbs-up, in moments they're surrounded by men with guns, all around them are poppies, red as blood, a river of blood flowing down the mountainside. Oblivion hears footsteps, the men, silently, part. A short figure, stocky, muscled, the material of his costume tight over his chest—

– *You?* Oblivion says.

– Me, the Red Sickle says.

99. **LAOS** 1967

Crates and crates and crates inside a bamboo hut, the men, Hmong, carrying them up to the helicopter. No one pays Oblivion any attention. He opens one of the boxes and things fall into place at last.

The opium bars are stacked up tight inside the box, the processed opium packed and sealed in bags. Its smell still tingles Oblivion's nose, that musk, that sweet or sour scent. The smell of dreams.

Glances at the chopper. So Air America is shipping opium, he realises. Tigerman materialises by his side, smoking a cigar. So you found out our little secret, he says, his teeth bite into the leaf in his mouth. You wouldn't tell on us now, would you? Oblivion.

– What do you do with it? Oblivion says, Tigerman shrugs: Funding the war effort, he says. From here to Wattay Airport or Long Chen, from there onwards – I don't know.

Oblivion thinks of men in white smocks in secret labs, beakers in hand. A special kind of science. Turning opium into what the Germans, when Bayer first marketed it in eighteen ninety-five, called *Heroin* – from the word for hero.

– So *this* is why the CIA want the wolf man dead? he says.

– He's burning down the poppy fields, Tigerman says, and shakes his head like he just can't believe it. He has a Vietnamese comrade working for him, Mr Van, a fire starter. They're costing the CIA millions in lost revenue.

– That's why he has to go?

– That's why he has to go.

– And you're teaming up with the Russians. With the Red Sickle.

Tigerman smiles, almost wistfully. Remember Cecilienhof? The Potsdam Conference. He used to sit with Stalin and the rest of the Russian team.

– I remember, Oblivion says. Remember Berlin in forty-six. Thinks of Fogg, who was always scared of the wolf man. Everybody has a bogeyman.

– So you're going to come along? Tigerman says.

Oblivion thinks of Fogg. He should be thinking of Tank in Auschwitz, of the botched Paris operation or bloody Transylvania, but all he can think about is Fogg.

– I'll do it, he says.

100. **LAOS—VIETNAM BORDER** 1967

They walk through dirt trails across the mountains, their guides with machetes, Oblivion can hear furtive sounds in the forests, bears and wolves still live here, clouds hide the world down below.

Besides Oblivion, Tigerman has transformed. He stalks ahead in animal form, and there is that smell, a wild musk coming off him. Almost as if for him, it is sexual, Oblivion thinks uneasily.

Three days on the trail . . . somewhere on the Lao border, a no-man's-land. At some point even the guides left. There are only the three of them, Oblivion, Tigerman, the Red Sickle. A mini-United Nations of Übermenschen. Poppy fields give way to rice paddies, give way to wild, primal forests. They are alone, the heat is unbearable, mosquitoes savage their skin, Oblivion waves his hand desperately, erasing them, but more and more of them come. We don't age, the Red Sickle says, and grins. But we can die.

Tigerman stalks ahead, the human form abandoned. The night before he left them to make camp and disappeared into the trees, at night they heard growls, the scream of an animal, in the morning there was fresh, bloodied meat waiting for them. He won't change back to human form, has gone feral. Crazy Yank, the Red Sickle says, the blood around his mouth as he eats is a darker shade of his uniform. He still wears the crossed-sickle-and-fist legend of the Russian Sverhlyudi. Oblivion thinks of a slender woman with haunted dark eyes and eternally wet, long black hair, a blue uniform with that same legend on. How is Rusalka? he says, the Red Sickle scowls, Siberia, he says, and says no more.

On the third day they reach the camp.

Oblivion is alone in the forest. Tigerman is prowling, the Red Sickle is in his own vantage point. They have triangulated the camp, gone into deep cover. Oblivion thinks longingly of hot showers, soap, food. The stench of his own body startles him.

The first one he kills is a boy. Oblivion is by a brook and the boy comes with bottles to be filled. He does not even feel Oblivion approaching behind him, Oblivion lays his hand on the boy's head like a benediction. He rips a trough of nothingness through the boy's skull and holds him, gently, as he falls. Later he buries the remains as best he can. It's easier than trying to erase the entire body.

In the night he hears a growl in the distance and a scream, cut short.

The next day no one comes out alone from the camp. They come out in groups, armed men and Übermenschen. Their talents are odd, startling. Oblivion hides. In the distance he hears shouts, and gunfire, the Red Sickle laughing, the sound of sharp metal tearing into human flesh, screams, then silence again.

The third night no one comes out of the camp.

We can't touch the wolf man, Oblivion says.

A negator, Tigerman says. Shrugs. We wait, he says, and the Red Sickle grunts assent beside him. We wait for the wolf man to come to us.

On the fourth night Oblivion is woken up to the stench of smoke and the crackle of fire. He makes his way through the trees cautiously to a rise, looking down. A short man, dressed in pressed khakis, stands before the wolf man's camp, a wall of fire rising before him, spreading rapidly away from the camp. Oblivion curses. That must be the famous Mr Van, the Red Sickle says, materialising beside him. The fire roars below. No, Oblivion realises. Not the fire. Engines. Jeeps burst out of the camp, men with machine guns, he seems to recognise one of them, a tall blond Scandinavian, another Nazi Übermensch escaped from that other war. But no sign of the wolf man.

The jeeps split up. They're hunting, the Red Sickle says. Laughs. Tiger hunting! he says. The fire rages below, spreading towards them. Oblivion looks to the Red Sickle. So what do we do now? he says.

– Now? the Red Sickle says. Now we go hunting back. And with that his giant sickle appears in his hand, and he grins, and the metal flashes. The Red Sickle takes to the air, the way Oblivion had seen him, all those years before, in the sky above Leningrad. He is left alone. He can hear the sigh of the fire, the crackling of trees, the hunting call of a tiger in the distance. Oblivion sighs. Cracks his knuckles. Then makes his way into the trees, into the oncoming fire, his hand outstretched before him, erasing fire, trees and earth as he goes.

101. **LAOS–VIETNAM BORDER** 1967

Dawn spreads over the place late, the sun having to rise over the peaks to at last be seen. When it appears it casts its light over a scorched land of desolation. The air smells of burnt organic matter, of bark and leaf and human flesh and small animals caught in the fire. It had rained in the night and the ground is wet, it has a smell like an unwashed dog. An upturned jeep lies half buried in the mud. Mr Van, the Vietnamese fire starter, lies awkwardly next to it, his skull cleaved cleanly in half.

Oblivion stumbles into the clearing before the camp. He is

covered in mud and blood, his heart beats fast in his chest, exhaustion rising inside him like damp.

– So you made it, he says, as a figure materialises by his side. The Red Sickle, left eye shut and bruised black, his costume ripped, a wound on his right arm clumsily tied with a hastily made tourniquet now soaked in blood.

The Red Sickle shrugs. Übermenschen are hard to kill, he says. To their left, lying in the mud, is the big Scandinavian, his body savagely torn, teeth marks on his chest and arms. Oblivion can't, for the life of him, remember the man's name. From Oblivion's other side comes the sound of soft pattering feet and a tiger hovers into view. It stops and sniffs the air and sneezes. The prodigal returns, the Red Sickle says, drily. The tiger turns its head and blinks. Then it slowly shifts, sheds its fur, rises, and then Tigerman is standing beside them, looking grim and somewhat bedraggled.

– Hard night? Oblivion says.

– Just couldn't sleep, Tigerman says.

The three of them stand, facing the silent camp. Oblivion, flanked by the Red Sickle and Tigerman.

They wait.

Silence creeps over the ruined forest. The sun rises over the mountains, slowly, already it is growing uncomfortably hot. They wait in silence, the weight of the sub-machine gun is comforting in Oblivion's hands, beside him Tigerman checks his own weapon, only the Red Sickle is still. Their strange talents will be of no use against the wolf man, but a gun's a gun.

Then he comes. Oblivion senses movement before he sees it. The man who approaches them is wearing plain khakis and his hair is grey like a wolf's. He is a man of medium height. Not at all the monstrous figure of one's imagination. Oblivion remembers Minsk, Paris, tries to think of Tank in the concentration camps. But the truth is he feels very little. To the Old Man he was the mind on the other side of a chessboard. Only to Fogg he was the bogeyman, a thing out of nightmare. Now, in the light of day, in the silent clearing, all Oblivion sees is another ageless, tired man.

The wolf man approaches the three of them in silence, then halts. They range before him in a semi-circle, guns at the ready. An execution squad. The wolf man smiles.

– Jury, judge and executioner, he says. But which of you is which?

– Hans von Wolkenstein, Tigerman says, solemnly, you are under arrest for the war crimes of—

The Red Sickle says, Nazi.

Oblivion says nothing.

Von Wolkenstein turns his gaze on the Red Sickle. Ah, the drunk, he says.

– I no longer drink.

– No? A shame.

There is a gun in a holster on the wolf man's hip. An old gun, Oblivion notes: a German Luger. The wolf man's hand is on the butt of the gun. Tigerman says, take the gun out slowly and throw it on the ground.

– Really, the wolf man says, this charade is unnecessary.

– Do it!

The wolf man's eyes are cold and grey as the sea. It's what Oblivion remembers later, that and his face without the smile, a tired face, and the silence in the trees. The wolf man slowly lifts the gun up. Then, before they can react, he calmly turns it on himself, puts the muzzle of the gun in his mouth like a pacifier and pulls the trigger.

TWELVE:
RED POPPIES

BERLIN-AFGHANISTAN-NEW YORK
1976-2001

MAN LANDS ON MOON

July 21, 1969

FLORIDA Mankind has made history today with the landing of the first manned mission on the moon. Mission Commander Neil Armstrong stepped onto the lunar surface and into the pages of the history books. His first words on an alien world were, 'That's one small step for a man, one giant leap for mankind.'

Armstrong was followed onto the lunar surface by astronaut Edwin 'Buzz' Aldrin.

The historic Apollo 11 mission, the pinnacle achievement of an American space programme, began with a military rocket programme that later became NASA – the civilian National Aeronautics and Space Administration. Apollo 11 was launched from the Kennedy Space Center in Florida on July 16, using a Saturn V rocket. Director of NASA's Marshall Space Flight Center, Dr Wernher von Braun, who headed the team developing the Saturn V, was on hand to watch the launch. Originally from Germany, Dr von Braun is now a naturalised American citizen.

In a historic telephone call to the moon from the White House, President Nixon said, 'Because of what you have done, the heavens have become a part of man's world. And as you talk to us from the Sea of Tranquillity, it inspires us to redouble our efforts to bring peace and tranquillity to Earth.'

CONSTRUCTION BEGINS ON BERLIN WALL

August 13, 1961

BERLIN At midnight last night, Soviet authorities closed down the border between East and West Berlin. Over eight thousand East Germans had travelled to West Berlin in the immediate lead up to the closure, and are now unable to travel back. East German troops have begun to dig up streets on the boundary to prevent the passing of vehicles, and installed barbed-wire fences. Armed guards patrol the border. Unauthorised travel between East and West Berlin is no longer possible. Construction is set to begin on a massive, 140 kilometres-long separation wall.

102. **VIENNA, AUSTRIA** 1976

The Brezhnev years.

We assemble this piecemeal, from broken transcripts, classified intel, old men's recollections. Vienna, in seventy-six. A year that is important to us, for our own selfish reasons. But this is not our story.

Nineteen seventy-six:

Earlier in the year the Israelis swooped on Entebbe, in Uganda, where a hijacked plane with one hundred hostages was kept under guard by Idi Amin. We remember – we watched this – the Sabra, brought back from retirement, leading the troops, his thorns protruding, his feet shaking the ground with each massive jump and subsequent landing, he was wounded in the shooting, his blood ran green and red on that parched African earth. They say when he died, his last words were, It is good to die for one's country. A legend, a myth, like the story about the wolf man not dying in Vietnam, there had been sightings of him later, elsewhere, in Argentina, in China and Tibet, in Mozambique.

How does it start? It begins, we think, in Vienna, a few months after Entebbe, nine years after Oblivion's sojourn to Vietnam, and it concerns the Red Sickle, again.

Imagine an old woman. Not one of the changed. She would have been in her twenties during the war. Perhaps she'd been at Leningrad. We are not sure. Old now, stooped, the years have not been kind. Could be worse, though. She is alive. Her name is Galina Feldman and she is a mathematician, attending an international conference in this beautiful city.

A conference that Spit, for whatever reason, is attending.

Not as a mathematician, of course. Let us say, an interested observer.

For this is what they are, what they do, at the Bureau for Superannuated Affairs. They *observe*. Like sharks circling in the water around a juicy prize. And what's juicier than Russian scientists let out to play outside? No matter the heavy escort, there to ensure they don't misbehave. The scent alone is tantalising. It's the scent of blood.

Go to Vienna, the Old Man had said. Looked Spit up and down. Didn't approve of the miniskirt. Old-fashioned, the Old Man. Think of it as a holiday. Take in the sights. Spit had nodded. Report back on anything of interest, the Old Man had said.

The usual, Spit had thought.

Instead she had found Galina. And Galina, as it turned out, was eager to find her, in turn.

Spit sits in the audience as Galina delivers her paper. 'A Statistical Analysis of Change Distribution, from 1932 to the Present Day'. At first Spit is bored, the mathematics are incomprehensible, Galina is uncomfortable speaking in front of an audience, she speaks in German, Spit has a problem following. And yet. At some point she sits up straighter, adjusts her miniskirt, the Sixties have not passed Spit by, she had loved the new era, though the Seventies, so far, are a bit of a drag.

On the podium Galina argues via mathematical symbols that the Vomacht wave had not been a single, observable occurrence. It emerges from a point of time and space, Galina explains, the audience of mostly older men and women avidly scribbling in their notebooks. But that point of space–time is a floating referent, Galina says, it is a sustained confluence, it did not happen and then pass. It is *still* happening, *has* happened, *will* happen – the audience burst out in shouts, a clamour, arguments and counter-arguments as Galina stands up there, alone, holding a piece of chalk like a weapon, tracing arcane symbols that seem to prove the wave is still happening, that minute mutations in the general populace prove it, but how? How, an ancient Hungarian mathematician says, banging his walking stick on the floor, and Galina says, apologetically, But I'm afraid *that* is something I simply don't know.

A floating referent? Spit thinks, What does *that* mean?

And we think of Paris, we think of Klara, of one perfect summer's day. Is this what this, all this, is about?

But wait. Now is not the time. And so—

Spit watches Professor Galina Feldman over the next two days. The professor has two escorts, a man and a woman who accompany her at all times. KGB, Spit thinks, following as the professor visits a variety of cafés, moving restlessly across the city as if searching for something, someone.

As if she is looking to make contact, Spit thinks.

Could be a trap.

Little lost Galina going all over Vienna, stopping, starting, the two Moscow goons trailing after her bored – it seems almost too obvious.

But Spit can't resist.

Who can tell. Maybe she's bored. In any case, Spit decides to make contact.

Spit trails Professor Feldman across the city, to a smoky bar off Rauhensteingasse. What the Professor may be seeking there is anyone's guess, but her two shadows, who seem, over the past

few days, to have grown quite attached to one another, are happy
with the choice. Spit walks in, old stone walls and a roomful of
smoke, dim lighting and nooks and crannies and she thinks, Good
choice. Galina sits on her own, a glass of brandy before her. She
sips from it slowly. Her two shadows sit in one corner, together,
paying more attention to each other than to their charge. Spit
scans the room. Mary had a little lamb, Spit murmurs, whose
fleece was white as snow. And everywhere that Mary went, the
lamb was sure to go. She hawks phlegm and spit-fires, tiny hard
pellets of gobby goo that hit the two shadows making out in the
corner. Not to kill. Just enough to make them appear to softly
doze, and to recover, later, with a hangover headache and
matching bruises on their necks. Spit walks over to Professor
Feldman's table and sits down.

   – Who are you, Galina says. Looks back, quickly, a motion
of her eyes, hard to make out the shadows in the gloom. Spit
says, They won't be bothering you for a while.

   – I . . . see. Galina smiles. Her eyes are bright and green. Let's
get out of here, she says. My thoughts exactly, Spit says. They
go the back way, through old cobbled streets, and find shelter
at last at the Café Drechsler, near the Naschmarkt, away from
shadows, stalkers and prying eyes.

   – You are Bureau? Galina says.

   – Yes, Spit says.

Galina seems to relax, slightly. A waiter brings over two hot
chocolates. Spit takes a sip. Galina says, Not CIA, not Mossad?

   – No. Disappointed?

Galina shrugs. I wondered, she says.

   – Jewish?

   – As a matter of fact.

Spit shrugs. Israelis not interested in you, then?

   – Look, Miss . . .

   – Spit. Just Spit.

   – *Spit*, then. I thought the subject of my lecture would arouse
some interest in the circles you move in. The changed. I am not

one myself and, I dare say, mathematicians are not in such huge demand on the secret service market.

Spit shrugs again. I won't argue with that, she says. Makes a moue of distaste at the hot chocolate. Too sweet, she says. So what *do* you want, Professor Feldman?

– I want to pass along a message, Galina says.

– A message.

– Yes.

– Who from? Spit says. And what about? Thinking, this has been a waste of time. Thinking, Is this what it has come to, playing nursemaid to batty old women in Viennese coffee bars?

– The Red Sickle, Galina says. And, into Spit's sudden stillness: He wants a meeting.

103. **WESTMINSTER** 1978

– Are you saying the Red Sickle wishes to . . . The Minister removes and polishes his glasses. When he coughs his whole body shakes, and the handkerchief he clasps to his mouth comes back bloodied. He replaces the glasses and stares over at the Old Man. Wishes to *defect?* he says.

– Well, the Old Man says – perhaps dubiously. If you recall the incident in Laos, minister?

– Yes, yes?

– Oblivion did have a little chat with him then, Minister. They discussed the possibility, as it were. At my request, naturally.

The Minister barks a half-cough, half-laugh. Naturally, he agrees. And the result?

The Old Man shrugs. He is very loyal, he says.

– I can't imagine why, the Minister says. It's not like the Union of Soviet Heroes is in the greatest of shapes. You remember Stalin's purges?

– Indeed, the Old Man says. The Minister barks another painful laugh. The Great Soviet himself ended up in a Siberian work camp, he says.

– Still, the Old Man says.

– Yes?

– Stalin is dead, the Old Man says, almost reproachfully.

– So they fared slightly better under Brezhnev, the Minister says, and waves a feeble hand. So what. The Minister sighs and looks across the desk at the Old Man. So what does the Red Sickle *want*? he says.

– To begin with, the Old Man says, he just wants a meeting.

104. **BERLIN** 1978

Had Fogg been there (and where *was* Fogg, in all this time, was he hiding at the Hole in the Wall, then, imprisoned in a fog of his own making?), he would have barely recognised this place, where once the Nazi ministries stood, this divided land, this Wall. Armed guards patrol on both sides and, right there where once a Russian checkpoint stood forlorn in the long night of post-war Berlin, now there are guard booths, banks of sandbags, vehicle barriers. The Old Man himself is here. The Old Man, having followed Professor Feldman's path, her papers, the way she had disappeared back to the Soviet Union and was never seen again. A meeting, yes, but it is harder to arrange, a delicate weaving of a web until this moment, the Old Man driving into East Berlin in the back of a Mercedes with blackened windows, the head of a delegation for an East–West meeting on UN resolution 1540, Weapons of Mass Destruction, Second Amendment, Übermenschen, and on the other side of the table, sole representative of the Union of Soviet Heroes, the Red Sickle.

Installed in an anonymous hotel with thick carpets swallowing sound, meeting in a once-grand ballroom, across a long table, the wood chipped but lovingly polished, two great crystal chandeliers dangling above their heads, coffee served in silver pots, and they are observed, of course they are, by functionaries on both sides. The Old Man gathers his papers together, tidies them, aligns the edges and with a decisive movement lays them down. Let us begin . . . he says.

How did they converse? Did they find a moment of privacy? The public bathroom, or over coffee and rich pastries, at recess time? Or was there no verbal communication, a note, perhaps, slipped into the Old Man's hands, which he opens in the car as they cross Checkpoint Charlie back into West Berlin?

We don't know. All we know for sure is that, at some point, the Red Sickle had communicated with the Old Man. A brief message, when it boiled down to it. Forget the logistics, the nightmare of trying to accede to the Red Sickle's request, forget even what's coming, another war, in another, more remote part of the world . . .

Help me get Rusalka out of Russia, is what the message says.

105. **WESTMINSTER** 1978

– We have to consider it is a trap, the Minister says. His cough rocks his skeletal body. He looks up at the Old Man and grimaces. How come you don't grow old and die? he says.

– I live to serve, the Old Man says, and the Minister laughs. A trap, he says.

– That's certainly the way I would have done it, Minister.

– What does he want?

– The Red Sickle won't defect, the Old Man says. But he is desperate to get Rusalka out of Russia. She is living in Moscow, at a State sanatorium. He wants to get her the medical help she needs, in the West.

– And in return?

– And in return, the Old Man says, he is willing to make us a deal. Sighs. To turn, he says, almost regretfully.

– A double agent? Him?

– It is strange, the Old Man murmurs, what men will do for love. Do I have your authorisation, Minister?

Pushes the forms across the desk. The Minister, with a sigh, reaches for a pen.

106. BERLIN 1979

And so, one year later: the River Spree. The Wall runs along its eastern shore. This is the point where it could all go wrong, the breaking point: the Wall, the guards, lights cutting through the darkness, the water lapping at the shore. From the Wall to the western bank this is still East Germany, to reach safety you must reach the western shore, emerge, alive and dripping, from the water. First you must scale the wall. First you must swim the Spree.

October 5, 1961. Udo Düllick. Drowned in the Spree.

October 14, 1961. Werner Probst. Shot in the Spree.

. . .

October 8, 1962. Anton Walzer. Shot in the Spree.

November 19, 1962. Horst Plischke. Drowned in the Spree. Body recovered four months later.

. . .

November 4, 1963. Klaus Schröter. Drowned in the Spree after being shot.

. . .

February 14, 1972. Manfred Weylandt. Drowned in the Spree after being shot.

. . .

And so on, through the years, history recounted as a series of failed escapes: they did not just use the Spree, everywhere you could scale the Wall they tried, and died: shot, shot, hit by a train, fell from the fourth floor of a building, shot, shot, suffocated, beaten with an iron bar, hit by a train, fell *off* a train, jumped off a roof, drowned, drowned, shot and, finally, in nineteen eighty-nine, Winfried Freudenberg, last of the escapees, crashed in, of all things, a hot-air balloon while trying to escape.

Sometimes, we think, you just couldn't make this shit *up*.

Like a lurid paperback the yellowed pages turn, the margins scribbled in, time passes for all, for you and us, for all but the changed.

For she is there. Somewhere, Klara V—

– Come on, the Old Man says, tense, his teeth around a Churchill cigar (though Churchill, too, is gone now, a stroke in sixty-five), come on, come on—

A cold night. A dark night. Fog creeping on the water and along the bank, the lights that cut through it are yellow and diffuse. Come on, come on!

And no Fogg, not even Oblivion, just the Old Man and an extraction team, but what can they do, they must wait on the western bank, on the far shore, wait breathlessly, nervously, the Old Man chomping on the cigar, those noxious fumes rising into the air, such a rich mixture, chemicals from East Berlin's factories, pork cooked in butter wafting in from the west, Come on, the Old Man says—

A flash of light from the other side of the river, once, twice, and is gone. The Old Man strains against the bad light, could that be a small, lithe figure crawling along the top of the Wall? For a moment it hesitates, suspended as it is up there, in the darkness. Then it falls, like a stone, it falls through the air and turns, gracefully, and hits the dark waters and disappears underneath. Silence, silence, and the Old Man's teeth break through the tobacco-leaf skin of the cigar, he drops it, never taking his eyes off the river, a shout in the distance, on the other shore, an alarm raised, shadowed figures appear on the wall, the sound of gunshots is deafening in the night, tracer bullets light up the sky and in their firefly light one can see the churning water of the Spree, punctured by bullets, Come on, the Old Man says, come on! until, right at their feet, a head emerges from the river, water streaming like tears down long, black hair, hands reach out, grab her, pull her to the bank, to the West, to safety, the gunshots cease, abruptly.

A silence, pure and precious, settles over the night.

Rusalka rises from the river, water droplets like precious stones caught in her hair . . .

Collapses into the Old Man's arms.

Her eyes are white, unseeing.

The Old Man carries her, as gentle as a lover, to the waiting car.

107. **LAKE GENEVA, SWITZERLAND** 1981

They walk along the lake shore, the Old Man and the diminutive Russian woman. Her black hair is permanently wet, her blue eyes turn, from time to time, in mute query to the man beside her. Rusalka, lithe and yet fragile, and something inside the Old Man will never be the same again.

– The water, Rusalka says. They stop and stand there, awkwardly. I listen but I can no longer hear the water, she says.

– Do you like it, here? the Old Man says, inanely. Rusalka tries to smile, fails, nods. Yes, she says. I thought you'd like the lake, the Old Man says, the water ripples under the stars. Rusalka strips off her clothes and enters the water, when she swims she is like a creature out of myth. I'm supposed to be debriefing you, the Old Man murmurs, but to himself, his breath is caught in his chest when she smiles at him from the water.

There was no publicity coup with her defection, nothing to serve them in the media. Did the Russians know? The Old Man suspects that they did, might have set the whole thing up. Got rid of Rusalka cleanly and got the Bureau to foot the bill for her care.

Just how the game has always been played, the Old Man thinks, sitting down on the shore of the lake, tossing stones into the water, Rusalka surfacing in the distance, her hair shiny under the light of the moon.

But it was worth it, he thinks. Not just for Rusalka, but now he has a private channel with the Russians, a conduit in the form of the Red Sickle. Rusalka waves at him and he feels a smile rising from some private place and he waves back. She swims towards him, rising out of the water slowly, her long hair clinging to her naked flesh. The Old Man removes his coat and wraps it around her and for a moment he holds her close. Then they walk back together to the sanatorium.

108. **LAKE GENEVA, SWITZERLAND** 1983

– I came as soon as I heard, the Old Man says. The director of the sanatorium touches him lightly on the sleeve. I'm sorry, she says. He shrugs her off. There is nothing to be sorry for, he says. His voice is gruff and the director nods and doesn't press him.

The funeral takes place in a nondenominational cemetery on the outskirts of Geneva. She should have been buried in water, the Old Man thinks, and the sudden anger makes him turn his back as the coffin is lowered into the hard ground, and he walks away.

He arrives back at the sanatorium alone. Remembers a body rising out of the Spree and into his arms.

The Old Man picks up a rock from the ground, turns it over

and over in his hands. His hands are old, they are covered in liver spots. He was old before the change, was caught, preserved, a living fly in slowly hardening amber. She killed herself. The words run round and round in his mind. He enters the building, walks to her room. The door is open, the bed is freshly made. No sign of the bedsheet she had pulled off the bed and ripped to tie into a rope. She hanged herself. No sign now, and he pictures her tearing up the sheets, her black hair streaming down her face, frowning in concentration. The way she bit her lips. Fashioning a rope and putting it around her neck. He should have found her a place by the ocean.

– I'm tired, she told him, the last time. She always said it but that time it sounded to him that she meant it. They had walked as they always did, by the lake. I can no longer hear the water.

Perhaps he knew all along. We all live on borrowed time. He looks vaguely around the room but she's not there, there is no sign of her, and he walks out and closes the door, softly, behind him as he passes.

RUSSIANS INVADE AFGHANISTAN

December 29, 1979

KABUL On Christmas Eve heavy Soviet forces entered Afghanistan. Commandos seized strategic installations in Kabul as armoured columns crossed the border. After a week of heavy fighting, tens of thousands of troops have entered the country by ground and air, with a new Soviet-backed leader installed in Kabul. A spokesman for the Kremlin confirmed Soviet occupation of the country is now complete. Fighting, however, is expected to continue for some time.

109. **WESTMINSTER** 1984

– Afghanistan? the Minister says. New minister, younger.

– The Red Sickle has requested another meeting, the Old Man says. The Minister examines him curiously. He is unchanged, externally. They never do change, do they, the Minister thinks, those bleeding Übermenschen. But who knows what they think, who knows what they are like inside. There had been rumours. He waves them aside. What's in bleeding *Afghanistan*? the Minister says, instead.

– Russians, the Old Man says. Does he sound more tired than he used to? the Minister wonders, uneasily. He shrugs. Send Oblivion, he says. Speak to our cousins in the CIA and see if they have an interest.

The Old Man's eyes are clear and dry. They bore into the Minister's eyes as if they can read the contents of his mind, the way one reads a cheap paperback book. The Minister, discomfited, turns his head away.

– Yes, sir, the Old Man says – ironically or not, we can't say.

110. **AFGHANISTAN** 1984

In Afghanistan the poppies blow, between the crosses, row on row, that mark our place; and in the sky, the larks, still bravely singing, fly, scarce heard amid the guns below.

Oblivion remembers the poem, modifies it as the chopper takes him over the fields, across the border from Pakistan, into the desert, flying low. John McCrae's 'In Flanders Fields', adapted for the new world, the new war, only it's Afghanistan, not France, and the poppies are opium poppies. And it's hot. Very hot, and dry, and he thinks, with sudden savagery, how much Fogg would have hated it here. He wonders fleetingly if there are larks in Afghanistan (there are).

Welcome to the Andropov Years.

In nineteen seventy-eight the communist party of Afghanistan assumed power in a coup d'état. In December of seventy-nine, the first Soviet troops were deployed into the country. In eighty-two Andropov – the main architect behind the Soviet invasion – had become leader of the Soviet Union following the death of Leonid Brezhnev.

And by nineteen eighty-four, the war had become full blown . . .

– Observer? Gus shouts. Gus is the CIA liaison officer to the Mujahedeen. What's to observe in this shithole?

Oblivion shrugs. I'll give you something to observe, Gus says, and his smile is unpleasant. He points down as the chopper takes a low sweep over sandy terrain, passing over a . . .

Over a . . .

Oblivion stares. The chopper drops low, blowing sand in all directions, lands with a soft *whoomp*.

They get out. Oblivion sees three human shapes in the sand. Unmoving. He comes closer, though something in him is reluctant to approach, there is a sickly smell in the air, he knows it well. Three human shapes, two men and a woman. He remembers Fogg's stories of Transylvania. Drakul. But this is not Drakul's work.

They are frozen in horrified death. One man, tall and skeletal, with his hand reaching out as if asking for alms, or a benediction. His face is frozen in a rictus of agony, his teeth had been broken and blood had pooled down on the sand. He had bled to death.

Impaled on a long, sharp stick.

The woman beside him had been garrotted before she was impaled, Oblivion sees. Her hands are scorched, her nails blackened with fire. He begins to understand. Übermenschen, Gus says, softly. The third man is half transformed on the spike, as if he had been killed while transitioning into some kind of impossible animal. Local Übermenschen, Gus says. Afghanis. I'm afraid our host does not approve of your kind.

– They were abominations, a voice says, calmly, reasonably. Good English. Cultured. A voice that has money behind it. He appears behind a bend in the narrow valley. Suddenly just there. Dressed in combat fatigues. A long thick beard. Piercing eyes. He exudes a powerful magnetism. As if he is more than a man himself. A Beyond-Man. But too young to have been remade by the change. They were abominations and had to be cleansed, he says. Who the hell are you? Oblivion says. Startled, to tell the truth. The smell of the dead beyond. Every year, he thinks, there are fewer of us left. And feels a sudden and painful sense of loss and doesn't know where it came from.

– Oblivion, Gus says, ceremoniously, meet our esteemed ally in this most holy war against the Soviet invaders in Afghanistan, supreme commander of the Mujahedeen, friend of the Company, Sheikh Osama bin Mohammed bin Awad bin Laden.

Oblivion stares.

Who is he? He had asked Gus, earlier. The CIA case officer just shrugged. The rich, spoiled son of a rich and powerful family, he'd said. Playing soldiers in the desert. Shrugged again and said, He's just another guy. And, philosophically: No one really gives a damn about Afghanistan.

– You bring one of them, *here*? bin Laden says. Oblivion stares into his eyes. Oblivion is taller than the sheikh, as slim. Not taking his eyes off the man he walks to the impaled figures. Lays his hand, gently, on the first figure's head. It begins to fade away, to disappear. He repeats the same action two more times. Stares at the other man all the while. Smiles, faintly. Bin Laden nods. Turns on his heels, quite abruptly, and begins to walk away. Gus looks at Oblivion, shrugs, and follows.

Around the contour of the mountain and they come onto a camp in the desert, pitched tents, goats grazing, a child runs up to bin Laden, who lifts him up, laughing – My son, he says. Come. He puts the child down and they follow him to a large tent. Armed men stand guard outside. Bin Laden goes in and Gus and Oblivion follow him inside.

– Our British colleagues, Gus says, believe they can help with intelligence regarding Soviet actions.

– We need more guns, bin Laden says. Talking to Gus. Ignoring Oblivion as if he's not there. We need more surface-to-air missiles. The Soviets are beginning to use armoured helicopters. We need more guns and we need more ammo and we need you, *Gus*, to deliver them.

– Now hold on just a goddamned minute! Gus says, reddening. For a moment he seems so interchangeable to Oblivion, just another young, brash American with a name that isn't his, in a war in which he doesn't really belong. He almost feels sorry for him.

– Come back, Gus, when you have what I need, bin Laden says. Our war is a righteous war. We will fight it with or without your help. As for him – he does not look at Oblivion when he speaks – no.

– No? Gus says.

– We do not want his information.

– But it could help—

– No. And never bring one of his kind here again.

Bin Laden says nothing more. Gus just stands there, breathing hard. Then he turns on his heels and stalks outside. Oblivion stays, staring at the man. Then he shrugs and follows the CIA man out of the tent.

111. **JERUSALEM** 1964

– But what's a hero? the counsellor for the defence says. On the witness stand, Joseph Shuster blinks through thick glasses.

– Indeed, Shuster says. What is a hero. His voice is sleepy, dreamy. It seems to me . . . he says, and stops. He removes his glasses and polishes them on the hem of his shirt. It seems to me . . .

– Let's backtrack, the counsellor suggests. Shuster seems grateful. You are, like Mr Lieber, a historian—

– *Not* like Mr Lieber, Shuster says. Not like Mr Lieber at *all*.

Some muted laughter from the audience. I am an artist, Shuster says, with more force. I have exhibited in Manhattan, Paris, London and elsewhere, and my work hangs in many modern art museums across the globe.

– And the subject of your work? the counsellor says.

– It is fair to say I specialise in . . . in a form of dynamic portraiture, Shuster says, shy again.

– Of Übermenschen, the counsellor says.

– Of the changed. Of Beyond-Men. And women. Of . . . for lack of a better word, Shuster says, I like to think my work focuses on *heroes*.

– But what's a hero? the counsellor says, again.

– It seems to me, Shuster says, it seems to me . . . you must understand, I think, yes, you need to first understand what it means to be a Jew.

– I think I have some experience in that, the counsellor for the defence says drily – which draws a few laughs from the audience. On the stand, Shuster coughs. His eyes, myopic behind the glasses, assume a dreamy look. Those of us who came out of that war, he says. And before that. From pogroms and persecution and to the New World. To a different kind of persecution, perhaps. But also *hope*. Our dreams of heroes come from that, I think. Our American heroes are the wish-fulfilment of immigrants, dazzled by the brashness and the colour of this new world, by its sheer size. We needed larger-than-life heroes, masked heroes to show us that they were the fantasy within each and every one of us. The Vomacht wave did not make them, it *released* them. Our shared hallucination, our faith. Our faith in heroes. This is why you see our American heroes but never their British counterpart. Ours is the rise of Empire, theirs is the decline. Ours seek the limelight, while theirs skulk in shadows.

He removes his glasses. Without them, his eyes are vulnerable. He turns them on the silent man in the glass box.

– Should we prosecute Dr Vomacht? Shuster says, softly. Turns his eyes on the silent audience in the courtroom. There is fervour in his eyes. Perhaps it is all the answer he will give. The only answer we need.

– We *need* heroes, Joe Shuster says.

112. **KANDAHAR, AFGHANISTAN** 1984

Years later, when they discussed it one afternoon, the Old Man had shaken his head. Of course, when he did give us good advice . . . I'm rather afraid we ignored it. Didn't we, Oblivion?

Oblivion had stirred, then. I'm sure I couldn't say, sir, he said.

The city is surrounded by Soviet troops. Planes with the symbol of the red star fly overhead when Oblivion arrives in the city. He arrives unremarkably, his papers identify him as an East German trade delegate, he checks into a rundown hotel, close to the Friday Mosque and the tomb of Ahmad Shah Durrani, in central Kandahar.

Oblivion is tired, tense. The sound of bombardment beyond the city reaches him in the room. There is a feeling of grim excitement in the air, young men with guns in the streets, beyond his window. Oblivion is lonely.

He wants to go home.

It was no surprise bin Laden mistrusted the information we offered, the Old Man had told him, later. We didn't trust it ourselves.

Oblivion examines the Red Sickle. He's changed, he thinks. Leaner, more tired. In Laos in sixty-seven he had told Oblivion he'd stopped drinking. If so, it didn't last. He is drunk now, but without enjoyment. He looks to Oblivion as if he is self-medicating: as if he is trying to drown Afghanistan in vodka.

– It's this war, the Red Sickle says. Waves the bottle with one hand. They are sitting in a bar full of Russian troops. This war. He leans close to Oblivion's face, his breath wafts like smoke from a factory. Heroin, he says. That's what my boys are on. All the heroin in the world is in this place. The poppies. This is how they grow, these Afghans. Like poppies. You can't kill them. You can't find them. They blow on the wind and rise somewhere else. We should have learned from your history. The British. Three wars and you lost every one. You can't win a war here. You couldn't, we can't, and whoever comes after us is going to lose, too. This land hates invaders.

– Did you ever give us truthful information? Oblivion says. Curiosity, nothing more. The Red Sickle laughs, slaps the table. The soldiers around them do not look their way, not once. I will give you one now, he says. This bin Laden. This Saudi. Kill him now. Kill him when you have the chance, or he will turn on you, and he will be stronger. Tell it to your Yankee friends, Oblivion.

– I saw him kill the changed, Oblivion says. The Red Sickle shrugs. We die like everyone else, he says. Only more slowly.

His eyes are red and haunted. There is a terrible, infinite weariness in his eyes. I'm *tired*, Oblivion, he says.

Oblivion can't get the Red Sickle's voice out of his head, that night. That awful tiredness that comes with too many unchanged years.

Too many wars, the Red Sickle says. Do you remember the war? he says, and Oblivion doesn't need to ask which one. There was only ever one war to matter, to Oblivion, to the Red Sickle, to all of them.

Everything else is a shadow of that war.

113. **NEW YORK** 2001

Were we standing underneath, on the streets of New York City, looking up—

It's a bird! It's a plane! No, it's—

It's a plane. Hitting, as though in slow motion, the top of the north tower of the World Trade Center.

That slow-moving destruction. That horror, that incomprehension we feel as we watch it, over and over, broadcast around the world, we watch and rewatch in slow motion, in high-definition, the moment the dream dies.

All that time we had expected a saviour. A man. A hero. But what's a hero? Someone leaping from the colour pages or from the silver screen, gun in hand, to rescue us. To make it stop. To disarm the hijackers, to land the plane safely. To avert this monstrosity.

It's a bird. It's a plane. No, it's—

Nothing. No one.

That day we look up to the sky and see the death of heroes.

THIRTEEN:
SECRETS AND LIES

BERLIN
1946

114. **DER ZIRKUS NIGHTCLUB, BERLIN** 1946

Big band music plays on stage. The air is thick with cigarette smoke and drunken conversation. The lights are dim. Ghoulish waiters in black tuxedoes move around like undertakers, pinched faces and undernourished arms, vampires amongst the living. There are soldiers at every table. Fogg is in a sergeant's uniform, sitting at a table with Oblivion and Spit, a couple of the others. An insignia on Fogg's shoulder: BSA. Beer steins dot the table. Saucer-sized ashtrays. Oblivion reaching the end of a story . . . and I said, with a face like that, darling, you've got nothing to laugh about!

Drunken laughter. Fogg sips his beer. Spit turns, looks at the door, says, Hey, look what the cat dragged in.

Fogg turns to look. The doors of the club open. Swaggering in: Tigerman, the Green Gunman, and Whirlwind. Stand in the doorway for a moment, for maximum effect. Tigerman throws back his mane of blond hair. Like he's posing for the cameras.

– Yanks, Fogg says. The Brits are all in army uniforms. The Americans are in their costumes, bright primary colours gaudy in the dark interior of the club. The head waiter rushes to greet them. Leads them away, to a table by the stage. A bottle of champagne in a silver bucket full of ice is brought over to the table, along with three glasses. The head waiter hovers, waiting. Tigerman acknowledges him with a nod. The head waiter opens the champagne with a practised pop. Pours. Waits. The Americans drink. Tigerman nods. Dismissal, this time. The head waiter bows his head. Departs, noiselessly. Spit says, They don't offer *us* any of the good stuff. Oblivion says, I prefer beer anyway.

Fogg never got to the bottom of where Oblivion came from.

His aristocratic air belying humbler origins. Sometimes his past slipped through. Or perhaps it's a calculated act, just further obfuscation. Fogg never knows.

He lights up a cigarette. American GIs get them as part of their rations. Along with nylon stockings and chocolate, they serve as the post-war currency in Berlin. Fogg pays informers with cigarettes, bribes officials with chocolate, courts elusive contacts with nylons. The Bureau in post-war Berlin, hunting Übermenschen.

The Americans look over to their table. Tigerman frowns. The Green Gunman nods, neutrally. Oblivion raises his drink at Whirlwind, who looks at him with distaste and looks away.

– What's with you and miss hurly-whirly over there? Spit says. Oblivion says, We had a thing.

Fogg looks at him sharply.

– You did not! Spit says.

– In Rome, in forty-four, Oblivion says. Smiles, a little ruefully. It didn't last, he says. Spit, leaning over, interested: What happened? Oblivion shrugs. You know those Italian girls, he says, how grateful they were for liberation.

Spit laughs. So what happened, she says, Whirlwind caught you with one?

– Well, Oblivion says. Yes . . . only there were two of them.

– You're disgusting, Spit says.

– That's what she said, too, Oblivion says.

Fogg drinks his beer. Only half-listening. Not saying much. Smokes his cigarette. Checks his watch. A commotion at the door. Turns to see a small slight figure trying to get in, the waiters closing in on it like crows. The man slips through them, heads directly to the British table.

It's Fogg's informant.

It's good old Franz.

A waiter follows, agitated. Fogg raises his hand. The waiter backs off. Franz stands there, looking at the table, the drinks, the well-fed GIs around the room. Something naked and hungry in his face. Fogg says, Outside. Now. Stands up. Drains the rest of his beer. Franz already walking away. He's not allowed inside. The big band finishes on stage. It darkens. Everyone quietens down as a lone woman comes on stage. Dressed in a masculine suit. Wears a black top hat. A strong face, sharp cheekbones. A solitary spot of light engulfs her. The rest of the stage is in darkness. At the doors Franz stops, face turned to the stage, captivated. The woman on stage approaches the microphone. She starts to sing. At the sound of her voice, Franz gives a little shudder. The room, the whole of Der Zirkus, is silent. The woman sings. An American song. 'My Dreams are Getting Better All the Time'. Fogg pushes Franz through the doors, outside.

115. **OUTSIDE DER ZIRKUS, BERLIN** 1946

Into the hell that is Berlin. The exposed skeletons of buildings jut at odd angles. Rubble like temple offerings piled up everywhere. A beggar slinks in the shadows. Outside Der Zirkus there are always beggars, a woman in a shawl holds a baby under one arm, or it could be a bundle of cloth, you can't tell. A blind man in dark glasses holds a tin cup and rattles it. Women wait outside, legs bare despite the cold, wear smiles like uniforms now, when they see Fogg. Try to get his attention. Can be had for a packet of cigarettes. Berlin. Fog in the air, he pulls it around him like a comforting cloak. As though hoping it will obscure the city, make it disappear, if only it could be unseen.

Berlin.

Franz's glasses crooked, held by tape. Fogg walks away, and Franz follows. Down that dead street, the road uneven, an American jeep goes past, the GIs cheering at the sight of the waiting women. Around the corner, at last. The fog thickening. Hiding them both. They stop.

– What do you have for me, Franz? Fogg says.

– The man you were asking for, Herr Schleier! he says. His name for Fogg.

Says: I have received word of him.

Fogg's heart, like a caged bird sensing freedom, beats faster in his chest. Bühler? he says; thinking of a man with blond-white hair; thinking of a snow storm.

Franz smiles. A sly smile. A calculating look. How much can he get off Herr Schleier, this time? Says, He no longer goes by that name.

Fogg doesn't reply. Franz stamps his feet, rubs his hands. Blows cold breaths that condense like fog. Says, Please, Herr Schleier, you have a cigarette?

– What makes a man, Franz? Their old refrain. What makes a hero? Fogg says.

– Please, Herr Schleier. A cigarette?

Fogg takes out his cigarette case. Silver. Belonged to a Nazi colonel, sold to him by an American GI. Opens it. Takes out a cigarette. Franz watching. Closes the case, taps the cigarette against it, thoughtfully. Franz watches, his eyes are like grey seas.

– Danke schön, Herr Schleier.

Franz accepts the cigarette like an offering. Fogg pulls out a Zippo, flicks it into life. Lights up for Franz. Says, Bitte, bitte.

Franz takes a drag. Coughs. Takes another. Fogg says, Where is Herr Bühler?

– He is hiding in the Soviet zone, Herr Schleier.

– Shit, Fogg says.

– He has been very careful, has Herr Bühler.

Sudden hatred illuminates Franz's face. Takes Fogg by surprise. Franz spits on the ground.

– I would give you him for free, he says. Herr Schneesturm. How you say? Snow Storm. I was on the *front*, Herr Schleier. I was on the Eastern Front and I saw the Übermensch and what he did.

Fogg regards him silently. Franz, frantically, smoking cigarette dangling in his mouth, reaches down, takes off his shoe. You see? he says. Fogg sees. Two of Franz's toes are missing.

– This is the Schneesturm's work, Franz says. To him we were like Jews.

Fogg lets him speak. Into the silence. His informer, bolstered by tobacco and hatred, has a need to fill it.

– I was a soldier, Herr Schleier. How you say Schleier? Fog? Waiting for a response. Getting none.

– Mr Fog, Franz says, and laughs. Stops. Fogg looks at Franz's foot. His missing toes.

– I was a soldier, Franz says. His voice is small. I served my country.

Fogg says, This God-damned war.

Franz nods his head, rapidly. Shrugs. Puts his shoe back on, takes a deep satisfied drag on his cigarette. Him I would give you for free, Herr Schleier, he says again. Looks at his nails, the hand holding the cigarette. Examines them thoughtfully. Says, But a man cannot live when a man has no food in his stomach.

Fogg sighs. Fogg reaches into his coat pocket. Fogg brings out a box of cigarettes and something else, something small and soft that flutters in the wind. Franz looks at it, transfixed. It is like a little green butterfly with dark spots.

– Ohhh . . .

It's a twenty-dollar bill.

– So, Fogg says.

But Franz seems captivated by the sight. Lips form into an O of wonder. Fogg hands him the cigarettes and the money both. Reanimating him like some mad scientist in a cheap horror film.

– Thank you, Herr Schleier! Thank you—

– There will be double that if I find him—

Fogg stops to look at his informant. The Yanks better not get there first, he says.

– I talk to no one! Only you, Herr Schleier. I swear on my honour—

He's made the money disappear.

– Now give it to me.

Fogg waits as Franz rummages through his own, dirty coat. Brings out a small piece of paper, folded over several times. Hands it to Fogg, who puts it away.

– Herr Schleier . . .

– Go away, Franz, Fogg says.

Franz looks at him, conflicting expressions crossing his face, as if he can't settle on one. With what seems like wounded dignity he says, I was a soldier, Herr Schleier. Fogg only looks at him, and so Franz repeats himself. Perhaps, we think, he is caught in a loop from which there is no escape.

– I was a soldier.

– We were all soldiers, Franz, Fogg says. Now get the fuck out of here.

116. **THE OLD MAN'S OFFICE**   the present

– He was just an informant, Fogg says.

– But he found Erich Bühler for you, didn't he, Fogg? The Old Man says. He found Schneesturm?

– He said Schneesturm was hiding in the Soviet sector, Fogg says.

– So you do remember, Henry.

Fogg makes himself relax. Even offers a little half-smile. Says, As I recall, I submitted a full report at the time.

– Quite, quite, the Old Man says. His face softens. I want you to know I really do appreciate you coming in on such short notice, Henry, he says.

– Sir?

– You've been out in the cold for too long, Henry. Too many years, the Old Man says.

– It was such a long time ago, Fogg says. Does it really matter any more?

The Old Man seems to let that one go. Perhaps not, he agrees.

Waves his hand as if to say, none of this is of importance any more. Pulls towards him a different folder. Opens it. Looks at it thoughtfully.

– Let's get back to Franz, the Old Man suggests. Franz Schröder. Your informant in Berlin in forty-six.

Fogg shifts in his chair. I really don't see . . . he says.

– Humour me, Fogg.

Fogg stares at him. What do you want to know? he says. Resigned again. Knowing that the questioning is not at all over. That it has, in fact, just reached its crucial point. What the Old Man has been after all along.

– Tell me about Berlin, Fogg, the Old Man says. Tell me about Snow Storm.

And Fogg, resigned, does.

117. **BERLIN** 1946

– *Berlin. You have to understand what it was like, Fogg says. Berlin in forty-six was an insane asylum. It was a circus of the grotesque. There were all manner of freaks. And ghosts . . .*

The snow falls over the grey broken-down streets, the shadows of the street-dwellers slink like rats along the walls, but there, in neon lights, a sign: *Der Zirkus* and, in only slightly smaller letters below: *Nachtklub*.

The cold permeates everywhere. Fogg's fingers feel frozen, unresponsive. The fog rises around him like a shield: from the watching eyes of the Berliner lost, of the shadow men and shadow women, the post-war living ghosts.

– *Every intelligence and acquisitions agency in the world was in Berlin that year, after the war, Old Man. We were looking for Übermenschen. We were looking for Vomacht. For the people who had worked with him in his labs. For the Nazi big shots who had so far managed to evade the Allies and stay free. We were looking for Nazi scientists. We were looking for rocket people.*

How long has he been outside in the cold? He'd met with Franz and Franz had given him a piece of paper, with an address written on it. He was so cold.

– Christ, Fogg says. Most of the time, we couldn't even find ourselves.

He walks to the club doors and pushes them open and goes back inside.

118. DER ZIRKUS NIGHTCLUB, BERLIN 1946

He steps into an air of luxury. Of cigarette smoke and beer, laughter and music. It's so warm inside after being in the cold. He stands still and savours the atmosphere. This little cocoon of life in the midst of all the death.

On stage the same lone woman as before stands, singing mournfully. He recognises her.

Machenstraum, Fogg thinks.

She is tall, she wears a man's black suit and a circus ring-master's black top hat. She is not conventionally pretty, though she could, if she wanted to, assume any shape she wants, Fogg knows. Machenstraum. Dream Maker. The spotlight engulfs her. The rest of the stage is dark, dark like an ocean. Fogg stands and listens to the music, 'I Had the Craziest Dream'. She had been singing something else before.

Fogg nods his head in time to the music. Lights a cigarette. The smoke curls around his arm like a snake. He looks at the occupied tables. The silent waiters gliding along the floor. The moth-eaten velvet drapes. Looks at the Americans still sitting there, at their usual table.

*And it is as if he is in two places at once, the past and the present,
a time-traveller split in half, and in the Old Man's office Fogg talks
rapidly, like a younger man, the words just come and come and come.
Suddenly he can't stop talking. Like something's been at last let loose.*

– *The Americans were crazy for rocket scientists, Fogg says. They
grabbed von Braun as soon as they could. He ended up running their
space programme for them. They were all over Berlin, spooks and
super-men – like Tigerman and the Green Gunman and Whirlwind.*

In the *then*, in Berlin after the war, Fogg looks at them, squinting
his eyes against the smoke, listening to Machenstraum's singing.

– *The Americans were always so* showy, *Fogg says. They showed
off their super powers like an English hostess shows off her best china.
The entire nation was a super power and they wanted everyone to
know it.*

– *As if everyone didn't already know, the Old Man says. Fogg*
snorts.

– *And they wanted what we wanted, he says. Vomacht, rogue
Übermenschen. There was a market in the changed. They double-
crossed us and we stabbed them in the back in return.*

Fogg stares at the stage. The song is ending. *In Berlin, in forty-
six? he says to the Old Man,* everybody *played the game.*

119. DER ZIRKUS, BERLIN 1946

Fogg rejoins the British table as the last notes of the song fade
away. The lights return, and with them the ambient noise.

– Champagne? Oblivion says. He is glowing, Fogg sees, with
some inner light, a happy drunkard stage which is rare for
Oblivion. Fogg nods and Oblivion pours him the drink. The
bottle, Fogg sees, sits in a bucket of ice on the table. He raises
his eyebrows.

– Compliments of the competition, Oblivion says. He gestures at the American table. Fogg raises his glass in salute and the Americans, Tigerman and Whirlwind and the Green Gunman, respond in kind.

– How very civilised, Fogg says.

On stage, the singer bows to muted applause then walks off stage.

– When are we going to arrest her? Spit says.

– Machenstraum? Oblivion says, in evident surprise. She is too precious to waste.

Spit snorts. Dream Maker! What a stupid name. She's a Nazi and she's got the Vomacht touch. We should have collected her a long time ago.

Oblivion frowns. If the war had gone the other way, he says, we'd be the ones being *collected*.

Spit stares at him. What, are you going soft, Oblivion? Are you getting all *sympathetic* because some Nazi super-*bitch* turns you on?

Fogg has his doubts about that last one, but he keeps them to himself. Oh come on, Spit, Oblivion says. Everyone knows who she is. She's hardly Adolf bloody *Eichmann*, is she.

– Isn't she? Spit says, darkly.

– No. She isn't, Oblivion says. If you must know, the Americans have already tagged her. She's theirs. Got a free pass out of the country.

– Really? Fogg says, surprised.

Oblivion nods. Spit's in that raging drunk stage. Like every other bloody Übermensch, she says, and Oblivion shrugs. Well, what did you think was going to happen to her? he says.

– I don't know, Spit says. And, more quietly – This war . . .

Fogg just sits there, drinking his champagne. Enjoying the warmth. Spit and Oblivion's bickering, as familiar as old leather. The band's background music. Thinking all the while of the note in his pocket, the address Franz had given him. Thinking of Paris, in forty-three, of a man called Erich Bühler, called Snow Storm. Of Tank in a hospital bed in a military field hospital, somewhere in Scotland. Finishes his drink in one gulp and stands up.

Spit looks up at him. Where the hell are you going *now*? she says, slurring the words.

– I'm going to see a man about a storm, Fogg says.

120. **THE OLD MAN'S OFFICE** the present

– You went to the Soviet quarter that same night?

The Old Man turns the pages of Bühler's dossier. Finger. Page corner. The whoosh of paper softly sliding against paper. No clocks in the room, Fogg notices, not for the first time. No way to tell the hour.

– I was restless, Fogg says. I didn't tell them. Not even Oblivion.

– No, the Old Man says, but dubiously, it seems to Fogg. Dubiously. Not even Oblivion, you say.

– Schneesturm, Fogg says. I remembered him, Old Man. I couldn't forget Paris. He was the reason we lost Tank. I couldn't stop thinking about Tank. What had happened to him. Auschwitz. We'd all seen the images by then. I was there, after.

– I remember, the Old Man says, softly.

– I needed to be the one to find him, Fogg says, pleads. The Old Man doesn't reply. Studies him with his head tilted. Blinks, once.

– Erich bleeding Bühler, Fogg says. Leans across to the Old Man's desk. Stares at him. Snow Storm, he says.

The Old Man nods.

– Yes, Fogg says. Yes I went to the Soviet quarter that night.

121. **BERLIN** 1946

Driving past the Tiergarten, Fogg and the driver he'd requisitioned outside Der Zirkus, the army jeep, cold night air on their faces, the fog trailing them like a pack of dogs.

– Been here long? says the driver. Something about him Fogg doesn't like. Not an Übermensch, regular army, a corporal, but something about him. Black hair slicked back, a cigarette dangling from his lips – American, not a rollie and not cheap. Looks by far too well-fed. Cheeky, is what it is. That grin, those even white teeth.

– Long enough, Corporal, Fogg says shortly.

– You know, sir, the corporal says, if you ever need anything, you can tell me. It gets lonely on the cold nights here, in Berlin.

They head east. The corporal easily avoids the potholes and the bomb craters. Their headlights are the only source of illumination in the Berlin night. People draw deeper into the shadows when they pass.

– And some of the *Fraus* are incredibly obliging, sir.

– Excuse me?

Fogg stares at him. The corporal's long fingers are steady on the wheel. The grin he turns to Fogg is white and cheery, positively American.

– Women, sir, the corporal says patiently. Girls. *Ladies*. Some of the Russians used them a bit rough, sir. When they took Berlin, you know. Some of them are a little used. Not my ones, sir. Each one's a bleeding masterpiece.

Fogg looks away. Closes his eyes, for a moment. Feels the night around him. The wind on his face like a benediction. Opens his eyes, takes out his cigarette case, lights up.

– I'll bear that in mind, Corporal, he says. Blows smoke. For just a moment it shapes itself into the shape of a stick man, waving its hands before evaporating into the air. If the corporal notices that, or the fog that follows the jeep, almost engulfing it, he doesn't say. And perhaps, Fogg thinks, the young man is used to the strange ways of the army's attached specialists from the BSA, from the so-called Bureau for Superannuated Affairs. Either way he flashes a grin again at Fogg.

– Or jewellery, sir? he says cheerfully. Maybe you have a girl back home, sir, who'd like some new jewellery? I can get you a very special price on gold, sir.

Fogg smiles. Blows smoke into the shape of a dove that flies away. A girl back home . . . he says. Yes, yes, I guess you could say that.

– Sir?

– Somewhere there's a place where it's always summer, Fogg says. Closes his eyes. Exhales smoke. A white stone house, surrounded by a meadow, he says. The grass is green, and bees hum lazily in the air. The light is soft, like music . . .

– Sir?

Fogg opens his eyes. The corporal has lost his grin. They're on Wilhelmstrasse, passing the huge Reichsministerium, Hermann Göring's Reich Air Ministry building. It is the only building left intact on that once-magnificent street. Everything else – the Reich Chancellery, built by Albert Speer for the Führer; and the grandiose former President's Palace occupied by Ribbentrop during the war; and the Propaganda Ministry, and all the rest of them – all these symbols, this *centre* of Nazi power, now reduced to rubble, by Allied bombs dropped from Allied planes. All but Göring's building: a lone survivor. It is eerily quiet, and the only light comes from farther ahead, where Fogg knows the Russians have their checkpoint.

– Stop here, Corporal, Fogg says.

The corporal seems glad to oblige. The sound of the engine dies, leaving them in silence. Fogg tries to remember the last time he'd heard a bird, and can't. Whatever non-human life there has been in Berlin it is all gone, died off or eaten by the human survivors. The city reeks of death but it reeks even worse of life.

– What's your name, Corporal? Fogg says.

The corporal swallows. King, sir, he says. Corporal King.

Fogg nods. Wait here until I get back, King, he says.

– Here, sir?

– Problem with your hearing, Corporal?

– No, sir.

– Good.

Fogg turns from him. As he walks away the fog gathers around him, rising from the ground until it covers him. In moments he disappears. Corporal King stares after him. Looks at the bombed-out buildings, the lights of the Soviets in the distance. Listens to that hush of post-war Berlin. Wraps himself tighter in his coat, pulls out a cigarette and lights it. He blows smoke into the darkness, stares at the rising fog.

– Rum old bird, he says, meditatively.

122. **THE OLD MAN'S OFFICE** the present

– Corporal King, eh? the Old Man says.

– Yes.

– What we used to call a useful chap.

– Quite, Fogg says.

Every military company has a man like Corporal King. A man who can get things done. A man who can get things, for the right price.

In Berlin it was chocolate and American cigarettes and nylons. It was women. It was drugs, or guns, or even identity papers. It was anything. Anything but peace. That was one luxury Berlin no longer had.

– Well, the Old Man says. Setting the matter of this King aside. He is not unknown to him. To us. So you went into the Soviet zone, the Old Man says. Not through . . . official channels.

– No.

– I take it that wasn't difficult for you, Fogg.

– No, Fogg says. It wasn't.

123. **BERLIN. THE SOVIET ZONE** 1946

– I didn't like going into the Soviet zone, Old Man, Fogg says. That split infinity: the present imposed on the past . . . Walking through the night, this lunar landscape of Nazi architecture reduced to rubble, all but for Fat Boy Göring's Ministry of the Air. Makes Fogg think, for just one moment, of the Eastern Front.

– No one did, he says. Too many scalp-hunters disappeared there. The Soviets were playing the endgame just as we were. They were hoarding up Übermenschen like a kid hoards candy and they didn't like to share.

Hears, as if through underwater, the Old Man's reply. He walks through that dark, dead land and the fog crescendos around him, and he slips past the Soviet checkpoint, unseen and unheard, a shadow man in a shadow world.

The Soviet quarter. The Soviet zone.

Not much different to the rest of ruined Berlin. Snow on the ground, treacherous puddles underneath frozen surfaces. Dark, dirty water. Fogg curses when his foot lands in one, breaking the thin ice, the cold water would soak into him if it could. He hurries his steps. Aware of tiny sounds, of eyes in the dark.

– Everyone knew the end of the war was just the beginning, Fogg says. The Soviets and the Yanks had carved up Berlin as a prelude to carving up the rest of the world. We were no longer important to them. We just tried to hold on and carry away as many crumbs as we could.

– Rule Britannia . . . the Old Man says.

Fogg shakes his head, trying to clear it. Makes his way along the ruined streets, past dark figures huddled around a fire, past a patrol of Russian soldiers talking in lowered voices, past a rat scurrying along the wall: rats, he thinks. The only other animals to survive in Berlin that winter.

What could possess Snow Storm to hide in the Soviet zone? Fogg wonders. He could have gone to the Americans, been given a new life, papers, a ticket out. He knew he couldn't come to the Brits. Not when they still had a personal score to settle.

And he wouldn't go to the Soviets, Fogg knows. Not voluntarily. No one ever did.

He takes out the note Franz had given him. Checks the address again. It takes him some time, but by trial and error he finally finds it.

This street is relatively undamaged. The smell of boiled cabbage wafts weakly out of an open window. There is a working street lamp outside. A row of double-storey buildings. The sound of mute conversation from inside. A handwritten sign on grey cardboard: Pension.

Fogg approaches the Pension's door. Waits for a moment, as if thinking. Then he raises his hand and knocks, with his fist, on the door.

124. **THE OLD MAN'S OFFICE** the present

– So far, the Old Man says, this tallies with your report.

He picks up another dossier. Opens it. Leafs through silently until he reaches a page where he stops, stabbing it with his finger.

– Let's see, the Old Man says. Yes . . .

He reads aloud from the page.

– I was approached by an informant of mine named Franz Schröder, the Old Man reads out. I had been cultivating him for some time. He was a native Berliner and had fought on the

Eastern Front. He had no love of the Nazis after that. He knew Berlin very well. He was a rat but he always brought me good information.

The Old Man raises his head. Looks at Fogg. Shakes his head.

– He was a rat but he always brought me good information?

Fogg shrugs, a little uncomfortably. What did you expect, he says, Shakespeare?

– I'd have settled for Marlowe, the Old Man says.

The Old Man picks up the report again and reads.

– Franz approached me at the Der Zirkus nightclub, a popular hangout – *the* Der Zirkus, Fogg?

The Old Man shakes his head again. He claimed to know the whereabouts of Erich Bühler, codenamed Schneesturm. Most concise, Fogg.

– Thank you?

The Old Man ignores him. Continues reading: The address was in the Soviet zone. I went there that same night. I found the address.

– Yes, Fogg says. Remembering. It was a boarding house.

125. **BERLIN. THE SOVIET ZONE** 1946

Fogg knocks loudly on the door. The sound echoes in the quiet street.

There is no answer. He can feel them behind the door. Waiting for him to go away. Whoever he is. Whatever he wants. Knowing that he won't. Knowing that a knock in the night will never lead to anything good. Fogg knocks again, louder. He bangs on the door. Saying, in effect, as clearly as he can – I am not going to go away.

Sounds behind the door. He stops banging. There's the sound of a key turning, latches removed, then the door opens. An old woman stands in the door, two frightened children peering from behind her. The woman wears a faded yellow dress and a worn military coat over her shoulders. Her hair is white and thin. Her eyes are the eyes of a bird. She doesn't speak. Looks at Fogg. Studies him.

– May I come in? Fogg says, in German. He doesn't wait for an answer though. Walks in. The woman retreats from him, her and the two children. Fogg closes the door behind him and turns to face them. Looks at the room. Not much in it. A small Primus stove. A pot on it. He walks to it, lifts the lid. The smell of cooking cabbage hits him fully in the face. He replaces the lid on the top. Turns back. Gestures at the children. Your own? he asks.

The old woman looks at him as if weighing her options. Finally, reluctantly: My sister's, she says. She is dead.

– I am sorry to hear it, Fogg says.

– The Russians killed her.

Fogg doesn't – quite – shrug. This is war, he says. And this is Berlin.

The woman looks at him. Not afraid. You blame *us?* she says. You think we knew? Before the war I had Jewish neighbours. We never had problems with the Jews.

– No, Fogg says.

– They left, the old woman says. Did I make them leave? Did I force them? She seems to be appealing to him. Her hands rise, palms open, old fingers with broken nails. I am a woman, she says. What power do I have?

Fogg looks at her. Wonders where she'd been, what she'd done. The smell of the cabbage makes him want to gag or light a cigarette. Stares at the woman, remorselessly.

– You are a German, he says.

All the answer she'll ever receive.

Reaches an officious hand towards her. Give me your papers, he says.

She stares at him. He stares back. Fog rising outside, closing on the windows. Quickly now, he says. The woman reaches into her dress and comes back with a worn ID book. Fogg opens it, looks at it perfunctorily. The woman's photo. The handwritten details of her life, in Russian and German. Fogg keeps it in his hand. Without the ID book, the woman is nothing. It is her life he is holding, her essence. The way witches and wizards were said to decant their soul into a material object, to keep it safe. He is holding the woman's soul.

There is something dangerous, illicit about it. That sense of power over another human being. Perhaps, he thinks, this is how the Nazis felt all the time. Perhaps that's why they did what they did, the death camps, and the Einsatzgruppen, the war. Something intoxicating about that power, whether over one person, or millions.

Fogg clears his throat. How many tenants do you have here? he says.

– Seven, the woman says.

– Seven people?

– Seven families.

Fogg holds the ID book. Moves it, idly. The woman's eyes are fixed on his hands, follow the ID book's movement.

– *All* families?

– Yes.

Fogg shrugs. Maybe I have the wrong place, then, he says.

He makes to hand the woman her ID book back. As she reaches for it, however, Fogg seems to change his mind. He withdraws it, with that same air of officialdom, of official boredom, and watches as the woman's hands drop to her side.

– I'm looking for a man, Fogg says.

It's the old woman's turn to shrug. There are many men in this city, her shrug seems to say. Many living. Many more dead. Too many men. Just take your pick. But there are none here to interest you.

– A young man, Fogg says. The woman's eyes slide to her ID book. Her broken nails are yellow around the edges. She looks up at Fogg, defiance in her eyes. Of young men we have no more, she is, perhaps, saying. We have used up our young men and now even their bones are ground to dust.

– Blond, Fogg says. So blond his hair looks white.

Watches her closely. Like snow, Fogg says, softly.

The woman shakes her head violently. There is no such man here, she says.

Fogg reaches into his pocket, comes back with money. United States dollars. The woman's eyes widen when she sees the notes. Are you sure? Fogg says.

– I am telling you, the woman says. There is no such man here.

Fogg holds the money. The woman watches it, as if hypnotised. The money in one hand. The ID book in the other. Fogg weighs them before her.

– An Übermensch, Fogg says. Watches her. The woman shakes her head, No, no.

Fogg's voice is low, confident. We can protect you, he says. The woman flares. Her hand shoots up. Like you protected my sister when your soldiers raped and killed her? the woman says. She was out on the street looking to get bread for the children.

– You said the Russians killed her, Fogg says, taken aback by her reaction.

– British, Russian, American . . . the woman says. You're all the same.

Fogg stares at the old woman. The old woman stares at Fogg. It's a stand-off. Neither of them seems willing to give in first.

Fogg, at last, smiles. Makes the money disappear. Like a magician. The woman stares at his other hand. Fogg courteously hands her back her ID book. She takes it quickly, pushes it into a hidden pocket in her dress.

– Well, thank you for your time, Fogg says. Sorry to have bothered you.

Nods. Walks to the door. Then stops. Turns back. Smiles again. Reaches into his pocket and comes back with a handful of American sweets.

– For the children, he says.

They peer out behind the woman's legs. A boy and a girl. Fogg stretches out his hand and they come to it, shy but determined. They take the sweets from him. Their little fingers are hot and sticky. Fogg straightens, nods. The children retreat to safety behind the old woman's legs.

– Gute Nacht, Fogg says.

He walks outside. Closes the door. Hears the old woman locking it behind him. He takes a deep breath of air. It feels so much fresher after that oppressive smell inside, that cabbage boiled to its death. He stares into the night, feels the cold on his skin. He raises his face. A whiteness, falling. Tiny kisses.

Fogg looks up, into the falling snow.

126. **THE OLD MAN'S OFFICE** the present

– I visited the boarding house but encountered no one but for the proprietress, who denied all knowledge of a man answering Snow Storm's description residing at that address—

The Old Man reads out loud from the page; his voice fills the room, its drone a soothing spell woven across dust motes and light beams, bouncing soundlessly at the speed of thought. Could you make your sentences any more convoluted? he says, accusingly.

Fogg doesn't answer. Perhaps he is half asleep, seduced at last by the night and the lateness of the hour and the heat of the room. Tea is a distant memory. The Old Man returns to the report. Wets his finger, turns the page. The sound of the page like the fluttering of wings. The Old Man reads. I made a search of the premises and was satisfied with the woman's account, following which I left.

Raises his head. Stares at Fogg. Shakes his head, slightly. And that's all she wrote, he says.

Fogg shrugs.

– That's all she wrote, the Old Man says, softly. Remember that? Something else to come out of that war.

Fogg raises his head at that. Nods.

Remembering.

– I knew a few guys like that, he says.

127. **NORMANDY, FRANCE** 1944

The bombs are falling, and overhead Allied planes streak low across the sky, De Havilland Mosquitoes and Supermarine Spitfires, Liberators and Hurricanes and Invaders. Fogg and Mr Blur sit in a trench, leaning against sandbags, and the sky is a maelstrom of coloured lights, a fireworks show. General army soldiers man the machine guns. The Germans are up ahead, only a short distance away, the invasion is a reality now but the Hun is giving back a bloodied fight, Fogg has seen more dead bodies litter the beaches of Normandy than he could ever forget, they will rise from the waves and from the sand in his dreams for years to come, bloated corpses shambling in their worn uniforms as giant poppies grow out of the ground until they envelop them in red.

Fogg smokes a cigarette. Mr Blur sits with his little legs crossed beside him, holding an envelope in one hand. The envelope is torn and crumpled and covered in mud and spots of what looks like rust but might, in fact, be blood. Mr Blur hesitates as he holds it in his hand. Fogg turns to him, raises his eyebrows in a mute query, Mr Blur shakes his head. Want me to read it for you? Fogg says. Volunteers. Mr Blur mulls it over. Shakes his head. No, he says. I'll do it.

Slits open the envelope. Carefully. His nails are long and clean despite the war. Withdraws a single sheet of thin paper, aerogramme-style. The ink is blue. Hesitates again. Someone shouts – Incoming! They duck instinctively for a moment, heads between thighs, as the bomb explodes. Well get on with it then, Fogg says. The sound of machine-gun fire fills the air, the smell of cordite, bitter like nutmeg. Well? Fogg says.

– Don't rush me!

The bombardment goes on all around them. Fogg ashes the cigarette. Mr Blur reads out loud.

– Dear Ron.

– There is no easy way to say this.

He stops. Looks to Fogg, who looks away. Giving Mr Blur the illusion of privacy. Another bomb, somewhere nearby, and a scream cut short.

– There is no easy way to say this. I met another man.

Fogg looks away. Smokes as Mr Blur reads the rest of the letter silently, to himself. It is not, Fogg notices, a very long letter. At last he is done. He holds the thin sheet of paper in both hands. Stares at it for one long moment. Then he folds it neatly and slides it back inside the envelope.

– And that's all she wrote, he says, with a sad smile. It is the smile Fogg remembers, for years afterwards. That sad little smile on Mr Blur's face, a moment before someone shouts – Incoming! And then they're both up and this time it's close, too close, the soldier ahead, Fogg never even learned his name and now he never will, the soldier is thrown backwards through the air as the machine gun explodes, the gunman is dead before he even hits Fogg and shards of molten metal spray across the dugout and it's the only thing that saves Fogg, that dead nameless soldier and that's all she wrote.

128. **THE OLD MAN'S OFFICE** the present

– So then what happened? the Old Man says. Looks at the page. Drums his fingers on the desk. Raises his eyes and looks at Fogg.

Who says, I don't remember.

The Old Man waits him out. It's all in the report, Fogg says. Reluctant.

– Which report? the Old Man says.

– The other report. The one I made directly to you. After the . . . after what happened then.

– When you left the old woman's boarding house.

– Yes, Fogg says. When I went outside.

129. **BERLIN. THE SOVIET ZONE** 1946

Snow falls like a benediction. It touches Fogg's upturned face. It turns the world white. It muffles sound, it blankets the world in silence. It makes Fogg smile, a hunter's smile, a smile of anticipation. Then there's a roar of wind, which he is only partly prepared for. He half turns, raising his hand to protect himself, and a figure comes flying out of the whiteness at him, like a ghost, like a white ghost; it knocks Fogg back, slamming into him and it is solid, a white thing of snow and flesh, and Fogg rolls, landing on the ground painfully.

He hasn't got the time to react. Wind and snow reach for him like hands, lift him up bodily, slam him against the wall of the boarding house. Fogg curses, angry now, punches upwards in an uppercut that connects with something soft and he hears the other grunt. The pressure eases, for just a moment. The white shape flitters back, disappears behind the falling snow. Fogg spits blood and grins and calls the fog to him and it comes, like an obedient dog. The very air is singing. It is a two-tone cry that rises, that vibrates like strings through the air and the moisture in the air, through condensation, water molecules, hydrogen and oxygen atoms, nuclei, quarks. An elemental music.

One tone, rising, thrums through Fogg's body, through his very soul: it is the sound of subatomic particles responding in a collapsing wave of probabilities, of molecules forming and re-forming around him, of a great and comforting gathering fog:

While the other, a discordant tone, is one he had heard once before, that night in Paris. It is a song of molecules not *dispersing*, becoming diffuse, but rather pressing together, forming into something hard and yet soft, a whiteness not a greyness, snow where there should be fog, ice where there should be smoke. Fogg launches himself from the wall, comes flying at the other, fog shards like blades sweeping before him, slicing through ice. For a moment both fog and ice clear and he sees the other cleanly, the blond hair and the blue eyes and the laughing mouth and he says, *Schneesturm*.

– Herr Fogg, the other says, mockingly, and his smile grows wider. Then he is gone and a blast of snow hits Fogg in the face, cold and smarting, and reminding him, strangely, so strangely of a winter before the change, when his father worked in the market and brought him along, and let him loose, and he played, with the other children, along the bank of the frozen Thames, making snowballs and throwing them at each other.

But that was a long time ago, he thinks, and the anger rises in him like the notes of a song and he laughs, and the fog rises around him, obscuring the world in a spectrum of grey. He launches himself forward but he can't see the other, the white one, and the snow dances around him, trapping him. Then a punch, out of nowhere, catches him in the ribs, a fist sinks into his belly and he gasps, doubling over, and for a moment the fog fades and the world is dominated by pain and snow. He is aware then of eyes at the windows, of the silent watchers, those defeated old Germans, those tired survivors behind their flimsy walls;

watching this silent re-enactment of the war, but they had already lost; and that knowledge gives him power, and he rises, twirling, indifferent to the pain, and raises up a being of fog, a simulacrum; and he can sense the hidden Schneesturm doing the same.

Their avatars meet in the middle of that bombed-out street of East Berlin. Snowman versus fog creature, Fogg's golem the more amorphous of the two. The snowman swings a great arm for a punch but it passes through the fog creature harmlessly and its own elbow, solidified by particles in the air, jabs into the snowman's abdomen, and it raises a mighty blade of fog and dirt and swings it. It cleaves the snowman's head clean off.

– You think you're a hero? Fogg screams, into the night. You think you're a fucking *hero*?

Somewhere, a cry of rage. The snowman's head flops wetly to the ground. Fogg hears tiny sounds and turns, a moment before Schneesturm appears behind him. Fogg blocks the German's arm, the blow glances off, then Fogg's own angry attack pushes Schneesturm back, step by step, he loses his mocking smile and Fogg swings at him and catches him on the side of the head and Schneesturm falls to the ground and then Fogg is over him, leaning over the man's fallen body, and somehow Fogg's gun is in his hand and it is pointing directly at Schneesturm's face, it is steady, Fogg's hand is steady on the gun.

– Don't, the man on the ground says. He is very still. Fogg is breathing hard. Give me one good reason why, Erich, he says. Looks at him. Remembers Tank. Remembers Paris. A moment of silence, stretching. Then . . .

– Sommertag, Erich Bühler says, quietly.

Fogg blinks. The gun wavers.

– Please, Erich Bühler says.

Fogg's hand shakes. The gun is light in his hand. He stares into the other man's eyes, as if searching for something there, something he had lost long ago and can no longer find.

– Sommertag, Erich Bühler says again. His face is pale, white, drained of blood. He is very still on the ground. Sommertag.

Like a prayer. Like a magic word. Like a promise. Fogg stares into his eyes when he pulls the trigger.

130. **THE OLD MAN'S OFFICE** the present

– I had to do it, Fogg says. As if trying to explain. As if weighing, all those years later, the balance of events, and finding it curiously uneven, with something missing, a false weight where there should have been a balanced scale. He left me no choice.

And again, into the Old Man's waiting silence, feebly: It was payback. For Tank.

But the Old Man seems mollified. Seems to dismiss it. Waves his hand, grandly. Quite, quite, he says. Closes the folder, in fact. Nods. Well, we couldn't have had *that* in the written report, now could we, he says.

Fogg squirms in the seat. The lateness of the hour and the relentless questioning getting to him. Just as the Old Man wants them to, no doubt.

– What is this about? Fogg asks, again, and knows it is futile. For the Old Man has no intention of answering. Not yet. Not until the narrative of these long-ago affairs reaches its conclusion, to his satisfaction. Looks at Fogg through hooded eyes. Do you know, he says. There's one thing that bothers me, Fogg.

– Sir?

– How do you think your informant – what was his name again?

– Franz? Fogg says.

– Right, the Old Man says. Franz. How do you think *Franz* found our Herr Schneesturm, Fogg?

Fogg shrugs. Why bring this up now, he seems to say. What difference does it make? You know informants, they're like rats, who knows where they go and what they hear. It is of no significance. That is what his shrug seems to silently suggest.

– I don't know, sir, he says.

But the Old Man isn't really listening. He opens another folder, reads through it.

– Franz Schröder, wasn't it, the Old Man says.

– Sir.

– That did trouble me at the time, the Old Man says, meditatively.

– Sir?

The Old Man sighs. Perhaps it is to express displeasure with Fogg's inability to give him the answer he seeks. Perhaps he is tired. Or perhaps it is calculated, like every other thing he ever bloody does.

– A few things bothered me at the time, the Old Man says. And, all those decades later, they still do, Henry.

The use of his name doesn't escape Fogg. Sir? he says again.

– You have gone very monosyllabic, Henry, the Old Man says.

– Sir?

The Old Man glares at him.

– I mean, what is this all about, sir? Fogg says.

– I was rather hoping you'd tell me, Henry, the Old Man says – rather disapproving of Fogg's innocent tone, if truth be known. For instance, this Franz Schröder of yours. He turned up the next day, as it happens. Near Potsdam, of all places.

– I wasn't there, sir, Fogg says.

– No, the Old Man says thoughtfully: it makes Fogg uncomfortable. No, you weren't, Henry.

131. CECILIENHOF 1946

Schloss Cecilienhof is a strange sort of palace, a Tudor English country house in the heart of the German countryside, outside Berlin, on the banks of the Jungfernsee lake. Its grasslands are maintained even now, and coming along the sweeping driveway one encounters numerous vehicles parked on the grounds, and armed soldiers guarding the place, for this is where the Potsdam Conference is taking place.

Although that cannot be, we suddenly realise, that couldn't have happened, not this way, for Potsdam was in summer, not winter, and the previous year, and Fogg distinctly remembers snow; but he wasn't there, was he, that was the whole point of it, and it was only by accident that—

Perhaps this is the Old Man's memory, then, or Oblivion's . . . but memory plays tricks on us all.

Potsdam, then: and the conference is in full swing, the greatest meeting of world leaders ever seen: and we zoom along the sweeping path and into the conference room where crystal chandeliers hang from the ceiling and the armchairs are leather and the table is round, like in some mythical time of chivalry; and the smell of expensive cigars hangs in the air, and the sound of clinking glasses, and the taste of velvety smooth whisky from across the Channel:

And there's Churchill, rotund and flushed, a cigar in his mouth, the bald dome of his head shining softly in the light; there on the British side of the round table, this island empire now, we all know, can all *feel* it in that room, declining; and next to Churchill, of course, is the Old Man; and beside him, in his army uniform, is Oblivion; and also, beside him, with a cup of tea by her side, is Mrs Tinkle in a flowery dress.

And then there's the American side, and Harry S. Truman with that combed-over hair and the round glasses and the lips that always seem to curl upwards in a smile, clean shaven and with a neat tie, this President of a rising global superpower, the U S of A; and on either side of the President, and sitting comfortably, seeming, in fact, to lay claim to this room, this meeting, are Tigerman, and Whirlwind and the Green Gunman – a lone black face in that room of white men and Over-Men – and behind each team their secretaries and spymasters and advisors and viziers—

And facing the two teams in this Mexican stand-off, at last, the man with the beautiful, thick hair, luxurious, luscious, combed back like a cockerel's crown, and that moustache, thick and vibrant, tapering only at the ends, and those eyes that miss nothing, Comrade Joseph Vissarionovich Stalin himself:

And beside him, almost as impressive, the Red Sickle, genuine Hero of the Soviet Union, in that distinguished red uniform that stretches over his well-toned muscles, those soulful eyes and there, on his chest, the unmistakable crossed-sickle-and-fist legend of the Russian Sverhlyudi, these guardians and protectors of Mother Russia and her colonies (soon to embrace many lands liberated from the Nazi fiend); and beside him Rusalka, in her uniform of blue foam-white and her own legend of the fist and sickle and her long wet black hair and her large startling eyes, this water creature, this deadly nymph, this *Sverhzhenschina*, this great heroine of the Battle of the Baltic.

Here the map of Europe is studied across the round table and drawn on, measured, new borders marked, it is argued over, but it is all a formality. Runners come and go, minutes are typed, and there is a sense that, in fact, this is not an end but a beginning; Churchill, puffing on his endless cigar, seems apprehensive, Stalin ebullient, Truman quietly confident.

Into that hushed atmosphere of business being conducted, a business nothing and no one must interrupt, there comes an MP, a captain, making for the British side of the table. He kneels down and speaks quietly in the ear of the Old Man, who nods and dismisses him. Churchill is speaking now, drawling in that famous voice of his, and the Old Man turns quietly to Oblivion and speaks equally quietly and it is Oblivion's turn to nod. He gets up and walks to the doors and goes out of the hall. He makes his way outside, where the MP is waiting for him.

132. **CECILIENHOF** 1946

Beyond the manicured lawns lies the Havel River, and it is to its banks that the military policeman now takes Oblivion.

– This is a bit of a potential embarrassment, to tell you the truth, old boy, the captain says. Lights up a cigarette. No rush, he seems to say. Offers one to Oblivion, who declines. Yes, bit of an embarrassment, I suppose, the captain says, thoughtfully. Lucky I was around when the Russians found him.

Oblivion seems equally oblivious. Russians? he says, with a sort of languorous, disinterested affectation.

– Yes, routine patrol along the riverbank, the captain says. Well, we can't have anything disturbing the conference, now can we.

– Why don't you just show me? Oblivion says.

The captain nods. Leads, and Oblivion follows. Down to the river, the ground sloping, Russian soldiers standing guard over a package lying on the wet grass.

No, not a package, Oblivion notices, coming closer. A corpse. He comes closer still and kneels beside the dead body. It lies in a pool of cold water on the ground. The man's thinning hair is wet. His eyes are pale and watery. His skin is white and clammy-cold.

– A Franz Schröder, sir, the captain says. Waves a small paper booklet in Oblivion's face. His ID book was in his pocket, sir, he says.

– So? Oblivion says.

The ID book is sodden.

– It's only, it's this, sir. You see—

Almost apologetically, the captain kneels down, lifts up the man's right hand. It is closed into a fist which somebody had partially forced open. A piece of cloth clutched still in the hand. A piece of cloth, in fact, of a British insignia, with the letters B and S just visible.

Missing the A.

The only designation the British otherwise give to their special operatives in order to distinguish them from regular army personnel.

BSA.

Bureau for Superannuated Affairs.

Übermenschen.

Oblivion seems to consider the implications. Then shakes his head. I'm afraid I don't see . . . he says.

– Sir?

Oblivion removes a glove. Gestures for the ID book. His fingers are long and slender. The captain hands him the book but, when it touches the tips of Oblivion's fingers, it simply disintegrates into nothing. The captain looks a bit shocked. Oblivion next reaches for Franz's hand, that strip of implicating cloth. When he touches it there is a hiss of water becoming steam. Then the cloth, too, is gone. Oblivion puts his glove back on. Straightens up.

– An unfortunate drowning. Please make sure to remove him before they break for tea, will you, Captain?

– Yes, sir.

Oblivion nods. Good, he says. He turns and walks away, back to the palace, leaving the captain, the bored Russians, and the nameless dead man behind him.

133. **THE OLD MAN'S OFFICE** the present

– Potsdam, the Old Man says. We were carving up the world like a cake at tea time and serving it up. At least, the Russians and Yanks were. We were just grateful for the crumbs.

Fogg inches his head. It was a shame about Franz, he says. Still, what can you do.

The Old Man seems to give his statement some consideration. You know what bothered me, Fogg? he says at last.

– Sir?

– What bothered me, Fogg, is that it was all so bloody *neat*.

– Neat, sir? Fogg says. His face is a perfect blank, a study in innocence.

– Neat, the Old Man says, then shrugs. Letting it go, it seems. I had more important things to deal with at the time, of course, he says. After all, what did I care for one dead informant?

– I would think not very much, sir.

– No, the Old Man says. And equally, how much attention could I pay to one missing Übermensch.

Fogg stirs. Sir? he says, as if not quite understanding the Old Man's change of subject.

The Old Man leans back in his chair. Because no one reported they had found a *body*, you see, Fogg.

– A body, sir?

– After you shot Bühler.

– I'm afraid I don't understand, sir, Fogg says. The Old Man shrugs again. At the time we put it down to simple Russian obstinacy, he says. They never did like to share information.

– Quite, sir, Fogg says, as if that should put an end to the matter. The Old Man smiles. Do you know, Fogg, he says, in music, one listens for the silences between the notes.

Fogg, with a sudden hint of anger: I don't even know what that means. Adds: *Sir*.

The Old Man lets it go. The notes were all there, he says. But the silences troubled me.

Fogg sighs. Silences?

– Unanswered questions, the Old Man says. And again, like a man unable to stop picking at an old, scabbed-over wound: Such as, for instance – who killed Franz Schröder?

Fogg opens his mouth. Perhaps to refute. Perhaps to argue. Oblivion's chair scrapes against the floor and both Fogg and the Old Man turn their eyes to the source of the sound.

– What? Oblivion says.

But both men, perhaps each for his own reasons, shake their

heads. Oblivion settles back, Fogg rubs his eyes with tiredness, the Old Man looks restless, almost annoyed.

– Well, never mind all that, the Old Man says, and for a moment both he and Fogg look to Oblivion again, and then back. Let us return to the matter at hand, Fogg. You say you shot Schneesturm. What happened then?

Fogg once flew in a DC-9 – what they called a 'vomit comet'. It was a name given to those planes that rise, in a parabolic arc, high into the atmosphere, before plunging downwards at speed, creating, for a precious twenty-five seconds or so, the sensation of free falling: of zero gravity.

The sensation he feels now, sitting there in that too-quiet, too-warm room.

Of course the Old Man knows, he thinks. He wouldn't ask unless he already knew.

And – could he have known all along?

134. **BERLIN. THE SOVIET ZONE** 1946

The snow evaporates like mist, leaving the quiet street clear, but already fog is rising, instead. Fogg looks at the man at his feet, then reaches down. Schneesturm clasps his hand and Fogg pulls him to his feet. They stand there, staring at each other. There's still a hole in the snow where Fogg had fired, and the smell of gunpowder is still dispersing in the air.

– It was Sommertag, the German says. She wants to make a deal. He laughs, quickly. His face is bruised and there is blood on his cheek. How do you think you found me? he says. I made sure you'd know where to look.

– Franz.

Schneesturm shrugs. Fogg says, Where is she? but the other shakes his head. Not yet, he says. He nods towards the boarding house's door. Let's go inside, he says. Fogg nods. They walk up to the door. We can talk in my room, Schneesturm says.

The old woman lets them in. The same smell of cabbage, maybe a few pieces of meat in there, not too fresh. The same two children hiding behind the old woman's dresses. Her face is impassive. She does not acknowledge their presence. They go up the rickety stairs to the upstairs landing and the smell of defeat, the smell of cabbage and bad meat, follows them up there. At the end of a dark corridor, a door. Schneesturm pushes it open and they go in.

No electric light. Schneesturm, with an embarrassed air, reaches for a box of matches on the bedside table. Takes three attempts to light a match and, when he does, he sets it to two candles, one on the table, the other on the windowsill. In their wan light Fogg sees the room: the single cramped bed, the mattress as thin as any survivor; the dresser, a pre-war marvel of Teutonic engineering, and the side table, and some clothes on the floor, the clothes of a refugee, a far cry from Schneesturm's white Übermensch uniform that he still wears, even now, but it is no longer white, Fogg notices, it is a faded grey, holes have formed in the material, it is held together by nothing much more than desperation. Tiny black droppings on the floor, rats, or mice, they look like question marks. Schneesturm shrugs. Sit down, he says, awkwardly. Fogg sits down on the bed, next to Schneesturm. There is nowhere else to sit. Schneesturm reaches for the bedside table and pulls open a drawer. He brings out a bottle, half full, and two grimy glasses. Puts the glasses on the table, opens the bottle. Vodka. He pours. Stoppers the bottle. Places it back on the table. Picks up the glasses, hands one to Fogg.

– This war, he says. This fucking war.

They clink their glasses and drink. Erich, Fogg says.

– Do you think I asked for this? the other says. To be this . . . this *Schneesturm*? *Germany for the Übermenschen. Ja.* The Master Race. Look where it got us.

He gestures around the room. Laughs. Stops. I want out, Herr Fogg, he says.

– Why didn't you go to the Americans?

– Ah, yes, Erich says. The *Americans*. Laughs a short, bitter laugh. Refills the glasses. For their famous Zoo, no? So they could put a collar on my neck and give me treats when I'm good? No, Herr Fogg. I want *out*. I want out for good.

Raises his glass. Fogg raises his in return. The war, he says. They both drink. There is sweat on Erich Bühler's forehead. The blue in his eyes is flecked with white. I want a small house in the Alps, he says suddenly. Where the snow blankets everything, and it is so quiet. Do you know what I mean? he says.

Fogg lets him talk. The other is drawn into the silence, the words come pouring out, they fall like snow. Here in this boarding house there is sound all the time, Erich says, I can hear them all around me, groaning, farting, crying, shouting . . . never laughing, Herr Fogg. Laughter has left Germany, now. I wake up to gunshots and sirens and wonder if they've come for me. I do not want to be Schneesturm anymore. I want to go back to being Erich. I want out. Of the war, of Berlin.

Fogg listens: to the sound of Erich's voice, to the footsteps down below, to a siren calling far away; to the snores in the next room, and someone else crying in their sleep, and the gurgle of pipes, and above their heads the scrabble of tiny rats' feet as they scuttle unseen.

– Wish in one hand, shit in the other, Fogg says. An expression he picked up from the Americans. Schneesturm – Erich – smiles. You can do it, Herr Fogg, he says. He leans towards him. Puts his hand on Fogg's shoulder. Leans in close, his breath in Fogg's face. Vodka fumes. Desperation. You will tell them I am dead, Erich says. Searches Fogg's face for a clue, an answer. Fogg says, And in return?

– I will give you Sommertag.

He pulls back. Tension seems to ebb out of the set of his

shoulders. He reaches for the bottle again but this time Fogg stops him with a gesture.

– Where is she?

– She's safe.

Fogg stands up. Let's go, he says. Erich looks up at him, shrugs, fills up his glass again and knocks it back. I will take you to her, he says, but then we are finished. Schneesturm dies tonight.

– If she's not there, *Erich*, that's something you can be sure of, Fogg says.

Schneesturm smiles, and touches his fingers to his forehead in a mock salute. He gets up and follows Fogg out of that small, dismal room, closing the door behind them softly.

135. **NEVADA** 1976

The Zoo, Fogg thinks. Wondering once again why Schneesturm didn't choose the Zoo. A memory plucked out from all the others. We watch. We examine it in our hands like a stone, Fogg in that cheap motel, why is he there, we no longer recall, a mission or a private arrangement, anyway waiting for someone or something, there on the edge of the desert, watching the television when the adverts come on.

Or perhaps – no. He was looking for her.

There was the thing about Operation Paperclip: those Nazi rocket scientists just . . . disappeared. And new men with kosher new identities appeared instead, in America, men who had nothing to do with the war. Kosher identities, Fogg thinks, a little drunk on cheap American bourbon, nothing else to do there in that cheap motel, drink and watch the telly, but still it makes him laugh. Then the adverts come on, shiny wholesome women with shiny impossibly white teeth promoting shiny kitchen appliances, a man smoking a pipe extols the virtues of Ford cars, and then it comes, an inevitable cereal advert, America's Breakfast of Champions, and it reminds Fogg, in his drunken maudlin state, of a joke from the war:

A Russian general and an American general argue about their troops' food. I give my soldiers *one thousand* calories a day! the Russian general boasts. The American says, Yeah? I give my soldiers *two* thousand calories a day. That, the Russian general says, is impossible! No one can eat *two* sacks of potatoes in twenty-four hours!

Not, admittedly, a very *funny* joke, Fogg thinks, and then another commercial comes on and there is something, almost like déjà vu, or a sense of wrongness, somehow, but he can't, at first, identify its source:

Light rises over gentle hills cut out of cardboard; a scenery in bright primary colours, a yellow sun over green hills, blue skies, white clouds, children – real ones amidst the fake shrubbery, and a lake in the distance – what does it remind him of? For a moment a twinge of pain curls like smoke around Fogg's heart, that place where it is always summer, that place he cannot, can never go back to, his paradise lost, replicated here, so garishly on the television screen – the children sit around a picnic cloth spread on the ground, singing happily, warbling in some alien childish tongue, but their happy voices turn sad, their enormous eyes look upwards and their hands rub their tummies, signalling to all of us watching at home: they're hungry.

But trumpets blare, big band martial music out of the air and there! The children look up, they raise their little hands to point at something approaching from the sky, from the air, it's a bird, it's a plane, no, it's—

Captain Cherry-Crush!

And this oh-so-American hero swoops down from the skies, from the clouds, materialising over the children, who welcome him with squeals of intelligible delight. Captain Cherry-Crush opens his mouth and grins at the children, so many teeth, so white and clean, an American's teeth, his ugliness is charming, the leathery skin and the bald elongated skull and it begins to rain, it begins to rain Cherry-Crush soda cans and the children all grab them from the sky and so does Captain Cherry-Crush and he bites a can with his impossibly sharp teeth and the dark blood-coloured liquid stains his lips and runs down his chin as he grins, then he links hands with the children and they dance, singing the Cherry-Crush Song.

And Fogg, slumped there on the bed with the faded covers and the cigarette burn in the pillow case, stares at the small screen and the monstrous figure dancing there with the children and he remembers, suddenly and with aching clarity, of the sort we only ever get for those moments we wish most dearly to forget: Transylvania, hiding in the bend on the mountain, and watching the Gestapo convoy down below, which stops, and they get out: the *Wolfskommando*.

Blutsauger. The name crystallises in Fogg's mind. The Blood Sucker. Details from the man's dossier: a Ukrainian, like the infamous Demjanjuk who was a guard at the Sobibor extermination camp and nicknamed Ivan the Terrible. But Blutsauger was one of the changed, one of Hans von Wolkenstein's hand-picked men, his Übermenschen. Never captured after the war, missing presumed – what, exactly? Gone on the ratline to Argentina like his one-time comrades? Blutsauger, who wasn't there when they had stormed the Sighișoara citadel . . . ancient history that gives Fogg heartburn.

On the screen this new, improved, white-toothed version of Blutsauger dances hand in hand with the laughing, shrieking kids, Cherry-Crush cereal loops now leaping into the air like purple popcorn, and Fogg, clutching his bottle of cheap bourbon, stares in morbid fascination until the advert's finished and *Happy Days* comes back on the television screen.

136. **THE OLD MAN'S OFFICE** the present

But the Old Man is not interested in television ads, for cereal or soda or anything else, or in any Nazis legitimately and lawfully repatriated to the United States by the United States government; the Old Man frowns and looks at Fogg the way a teacher looks at an errant pupil, perhaps; or as a disappointed father; drawing this back to Berlin, in forty-six, drawing it back to Bühler, Erich, codename Schneesturm, and he says, So you lied to us, Henry.

– Yes.

A silence. An expectation. Fogg shrugs. Yes, he says again, I did.

– You were conspiring, the Old Man says, with an enemy agent. With a Nazi, Henry.

Silence.

– A Nazi, the Old Man repeats. To protect another Nazi.

– *She wasn't a Nazi!*

Fogg, without realising it, has stood up. And is shouting. Oblivion looks over to him, concern written on his face. A silence settles again. The Old Man makes a 'sit down' gesture. Fogg sits down. She wasn't a Nazi, he says again, but quietly. And: She was one of us.

– One of us, the Old Man says, softly. You were forgetting which side you were on, weren't you, Henry?

Tilts his head and regards Fogg like a bird examining a worm. You would have been court-martialled, the Old Man says. And executed as a traitor.

– I knew the risk I was taking.

– Did you? the Old Man says. And you still went ahead with it. Why, Henry?

– Why? Fogg says. As if the question makes no sense. As if the answer is so clear, so obvious, it fills the room with its light.

And it is as if the Old Man senses it, too. Why did you do it? the Old Man says. Did you do it for *love*, Henry?

Fogg stares at him, as if he's mad. Love? he says. As if it is a new and unfamiliar word; or perhaps, he seems to be implying, instead, it is one the Old Man has never heard and never known. The word, like a dirty secret, hangs in the room. Oblivion moves uncomfortably in his chair. Come on, Old Man, he says.

– Stay out of this, Oblivion, the Old Man says, sharply. But Oblivion isn't willing to let go. Not just yet. And perhaps there is anger there, not sudden, but long-suppressed, because, for the first time, he rises, he raises his voice, even.

– Do you want to know why he did it? Oblivion says, it is impossible to mistake the anger, the hurt, in his voice. She was the mystery he needed, the enigma that kept him going. Something to believe in. Something precious and non-corrupt and good. Holier-than-thou *bloody* Sommertag. As perfect and unchanging as a summer's day.

Fogg looks at Oblivion. Misery in his eyes.

– I never believed she was an innocent, Oblivion says. That she didn't know what was going on around her. The war. The camps. She *knew*. She wasn't a little girl: she just played at being one. For herself. For Henry. He lifts his arms up and lets them drop. Deflated, after this unaccustomed speech. But I suppose that sometimes, everybody needs to believe in love, he says.

– Goddamned stay *out* of this, Oblivion! Fogg says. Angry now, too. Oblivion settles back in the chair, his expression unreadable. What do you know about love, Fogg says. Oblivion looks away. Fogg takes a deep shuddering breath.

– You want to know why I did it? Fogg says. They're both watching him, the Old Man, Oblivion turning. But Fogg is looking at neither of them, he is looking far away, somewhere he has not visited in years. You use the word 'love' like you've never known it, Old Man, he says. But that's not why I did it.

At that, for just a moment, Oblivion's face turns, an unreadable expression – surprise? hope? – etched on it for just a moment before it disappears. The Old Man is silent, waiting.

I did it because she *was* innocent, Fogg says. Stares at Oblivion.

Dares him to argue back. Oblivion minutely moves his head. Because Klara, alone in that damned war, was an innocent, Fogg says. He spreads his arms as though appealing to the Old Man. When Vomacht activated the device, the quantum wave hit her the hardest, Fogg says. It fused into her, somehow. It kept her *pure*. She was *never* like the rest of us.

Don't you *understand?* he seems to say. Like he could reach across and somehow explain, somehow justify, what happened all those years before.

– We don't grow old, outwardly, do we, Fogg says. But we age inside. We corrupt. She never did. Somehow, she is still there, in one perfect summer's day. You want to know why I did it? he says. This is why. And I would do it again, Old Man. I'd do it again if I had to.

– I'm sure that won't be necessary, the Old Man says. Seems almost embarrassed. Fogg leans back. Lets out a breath of trapped air. The Old Man shuffles papers on his desk. Straightens them. Tell me, Henry, he says. Do you remember when we first met? When I took you out of Cambridge and brought you here?

137. **LONDON** 1936

The Old Man's Rolls-Royce moves across London Bridge like a dream. Dusk, and the lights are coming alive everywhere; on the north side of the river the sun glints off the dome of St Paul's and, on the Thames, a lonely barge moves majestically, laden with trash.

– Stop the car, please, Samuel, the Old Man says. The car stops on the bridge and the Old Man opens the door and steps out. After a moment of hesitation, Fogg follows. The air is cool outside, and he can smell the city, the mixture of automobile fumes and the stench of the Thames and the smell of restaurants opening for dinner on the South Bank and blossom from the trees lining the river and women's perfumes and men's cigars and horses' sweat and manure. To the east he can see the docks, crowded with ships, with cargo, sailors, warehouses, porters, the wealth and breadth of Empire; and when he joins the Old Man against the railings of the bridge he can see Parliament House to the west. Hovering above the building is a mighty airship, the famous German-made LZ-class Graf Zeppelin, hydrogen keeping it afloat, its crew of thirty-six and its countless passengers, and its name in bold letters stretched across its rigid frame: the *Hindenburg.*

– Beautiful, isn't she, the Old Man says, following the trajectory of Fogg's eyes. He lays a fatherly hand on Fogg's shoulder. What you are – what we are – cannot be undone, Henry, he says.

Fogg turns, raising his face in the setting sun to look at him. What does the Old Man see in his eyes, what hope, what trust, what can he make of this young changed man, what use can he be put to?

– The world is on the brink of war, the Old Man says.

The boy's face registers confusion. Fogg looks at the city, the setting sun, the floating airship. The city is at peace. Tendrils of fog, but no more, rise timidly at his feet. War? he seems to silently say. How can it be?

– I wish I could tell you it is because of us, or the change, or man's fear of the unknown, the Old Man says. Henry. Look at me.

This boy – this young man – does.

– We cannot stop this war but we can fight it, in the shadows, the Old Man says. You have a choice. We all have a choice. We can give in to the darkness, or we can fight it, and elect to try and make the world a slightly less terrible place than it is. Perhaps we'll fail. If we succeed in what we do, no one would thank us. If we die, no one will remember us.

Fogg's lips part. The sun almost disappears on the horizon,

only its tip, its crown, visible still. From up here he can see the whole world, or what seems like the whole world. London. The seat of empire. The greatest and most powerful empire the world has ever known. And it is strange to him, it is exceedingly strange, to be standing here, with someone who knows his secret, who accepts him for what he is, a changed, a freak, this lone grocer's boy from Kingston upon Thames. And suddenly Fogg grins, as though the Old Man has just told a joke, and he says, War? and he gestures at the city all around them, he says, I mean – like it's the most ludicrous idea in the world, like something out of an illustrated storybook, he says – war?

The sun sets entirely. The sky, enormous over the city, is a battlefield of fiery reds and dying yellows, a blackness encroaching like a spider bite beyond, spreading out against the sky. The Old Man's hands hold on to the rails, and he looks out, away from Fogg, his eyes look far away, seeing something only he can see.

– A world war, the Old Man quietly says.

138. NORMANDY, FRANCE 1944

– Incoming!

Fogg and Mr Blur huddle in the trench, it is night and the temperature has dropped, it is freezing, but Fogg sweats inside his coat, the smell of unwashed bodies and fear and gunmetal, oil and blood stinging the nostrils, his fingernails are blunt but still somehow dirty underneath, there is a sense he would never be clean again, heaven becomes the memory of a hot shower—

The explosion rocks the ground and makes sand slide down the trench and the soldier manning the machine gun, a different one now, the other had been carted off by stretcher, to be bagged and tagged and, later, buried, and this new nameless gunner opens up a sudden frantic burst of bullets, screaming hysterically, They're coming! They're coming!

Mr Blur starts to laugh, there is something awful about the sound, Fogg's hands are moist and his throat is constricted, there is a Dionysian madness that rises in him like wine fumes, it rises in all of them and perhaps it is the effect of some madness-inducing hidden Nazi Übermensch nearby, it would be comforting to think so, in any case; though it's probably just war. They're coming! the machine gunner screams again, gibbering as the bandoliers of bullets feed into the machine and are spat out, bullet separated from cartridge in a mechanical inevitability, like chicken and eggs, the machine gunner is foaming at the mouth, Fogg gets up, shouts, Stop, Stop – trying to think of the man's name, what in Hell's name was his *name*, while beside Fogg, Mr Blur is hugging himself, going into high speed, his special power, his features blurring as he rocks back and forth, back and forth faster than anyone should be able to go—

The machine gunner's body rocks backwards, left and right his arms are moving, left and right as if he's dancing, falling backwards like a swimmer through water, a neat hole through his helmet, his brain leaking out, down his face like tears; and his hands, as though in some final, mystified shrug, leave the handles of the machine gun, which falls silent—

Fogg runs forward but the machine gunner hits the ground faster than Fogg can get to him, and anyway he's dead on impact. Fogg kneels by him but there's no time, he looks up and indeed they *are* coming, there is a mad dash across a no-man's-land between the German positions and their own, and Fogg stares in horror at these shambling living-dead, these uniformed skeletons marching across the battle field:

Bombs and shells explode around them, tossing them like dolls into the air. Machine-gun fire mows them down. Grenades pick them apart like pieces in a butcher's diagram. And still they come, their eyes drugged by tiredness and war, by sheer exhaustion, and Fogg knows it is an end they seek, those who are coming, crossing the line: an end to the war, by one way or another.

And a chill grabs his heart, for they are coming directly towards *him*: towards the dugout shelter, where he and Mr Blur are now alone but for the corpse of that nameless gunner, may he rest in peace, forever and amen. In horror Fogg stares for one long moment at the approaching horde of Nazi living-dead, for so they seem to him, these soldiers, shambling and stumbling over the corpses of their brothers, a slow yet mad rush towards the Allied positions, so many of them, he cannot keep track of how many.

And as dread comes he realises they must move, they must act, and he cries out, Mr Blur!

And Mr Blur stops rocking, slows down to normal human speed, and looks up at Fogg with crazed eyes, with only the whites showing, and Fogg says, We have to get out of here, we can't stop them! and, with desperation and fear, he echoes the nameless, dead gunner: They're coming!

– I'll stop them, Mr Blur says. He stretches to his full height, this small man, this Übermensch, this *friend*, and he pulls out a pistol, a huge polished-metal thing, and waves it, like an Old West gunslinger with a silver star over his breast, a sheriff come to cleanse the town, and he says, Leave them to me, Fogg. You get out. Advance backwards!

– Mr Blur, what are you doing—

– I said go, goddamn it! Mr Blur says, and turns his milky crazy eyes on Fogg and then he smiles, just like that, a normal smile in the midst of that horror, the living-dead advancing, these flightless lost boys, bombs falling and the dead gunner lying at their feet with his brain leaking out like spoiled Worcestershire sauce.

Then, before Fogg can cry out, there is that *blurring* in the air, that sudden bending of light, as Mr Blur accelerates into his unnatural – no, his changed, his super-human – speed, and he shoots off, up the dugout and into the no-man's-land, almost invisible, he is travelling so fast, only his laughter can be heard and the sound of gunshots, twining together into a sort of song, a music . . .

– Mr Blur! Fogg cries, but even as he speaks he is advancing, as they say, backwards, and raising fog, raising fog like a storm to follow Mr Blur, to mask him, to blind the advancing Germans, but they do not see, they move without regard to maps or vision, but on blind instinct that says only *forward, forward*, and as Fogg climbs up from the dugout, as he turns to flee, just once he turns, like Lot's wife or, perhaps, like Orpheus at Hades, or just like any person who would feel compelled to stop, and look back, and he sees Mr Blur, pausing in the midst of the advancing horde, slowing to normal, turning back, and his eyes find Fogg, and he smiles, and this is how Fogg always remembers him afterwards, how he stopped there and smiled, just before a random bullet found him and blew off his head.

139. THE FARM, DEVON 1936

And sometimes in his dreams it doesn't end that way. Sometimes in his dreams Fogg stands there, watching Mr Blur's head blown off and the very earth and air rebel against the wrongness of it, against the bloodshed and the death, and he summons the fog, it rises all around him, Fogg a lonely figure on a mound of earth, shaping out of grey fog an enormous five-fingered hand that reaches past him, past the trench and to the no-man's land, through the shambling hordes of desperado soldiers, the hand reaching out and grabbing, trying to take hold of Mr Blur, to drag him to safety, the vast hand reaching, futilely, until Fogg wakes up, sweating . . .

But this is nineteen thirty-six, the Farm, Devon, the sun shines down on the grassy field, bees hum amongst the flowers, the air feels thick and heavy with promise, with spring. The pupils are lined up in their khaki shorts, blue shirts, their white socks stretched up. Bending, fingertips to toes, stretching, one, two, one, two, Tank puffing, Oblivion cool, Mrs Tinkle surprisingly agile, Spit with her serious, intent face, Mr Blur moving too fast for the eye to see, Fogg just going through the motions, hard to summon fog in this sunny weather, a part of him craves city streets, dirty pools of water, the yellow light of street lamps, the sound of hooves on cobblestones, a flash of lightning. Sergeant Browning stands opposite them, his thick moustache quivering, a whistle around his neck, his face is red and he is screaming, You *will* be ready, you *will* be soldiers, if I have to kill you myself!

Fogg trying to touch his toes with his fingers and failing, feels the blood rushing to his head, it suffuses his cheeks and lips, he grunts and someone, no one knows who, exactly, farts loudly.

And they all, everyone loses discipline. Tank collapses on the grass with mammoth snorts of laughter and Mr Blur joins him, even Oblivion is smiling, Mrs Tinkle looks horrified but even Browning can't hide, for just a moment, his smile; and Fogg, with relief, drops to the ground, and he's giggling, he gasps, Tank, stop it, but he can't stop, it builds up, this deep, this belly-deep laugh, and he rolls helplessly on the grass, laughing until his stomach muscles ache.

140. **THE OLD MAN'S OFFICE**   the present

– And so we come to the final act, the Old Man says. Let's see . . . He arranges the papers on his desk with an air of finality. You met Erich Bühler, codenamed Schneesturm, in the Soviet quarter. You failed to kill him. Instead, you struck a bargain. He was to take you to Klara Vomacht, codenamed Sommertag. Am I correct so far?

Fogg looks at the Old Man. Steals a glance at Oblivion. No way out, he thinks, resigned. And what does it matter, after all those years? And so: Yes, he says. You are correct.

– What happened then? the Old Man says. Gentler, now. A hunter soft-footing the last short distance to his target.

What happened then . . . Fogg looks down at his hands. Looks up, meets the Old Man's old eyes. Everything started to go wrong as soon as we set out, Fogg says.

141. **BERLIN. THE SOVIET ZONE** 1946

Walking away from Erich's boarding house, Henry and Erich, Schleier *und* Schneesturm. *The night was full of shadows, Fogg says, it felt as though eyes were watching us as we walked. Everything was hazy, unreal.*

– *Do confine yourself to reporting on just what happened, Henry.*
Fogg shrugs—

Down the ruined alleyways of this part of Berlin, where once, not long ago, the opulent homes of high-ranking Nazi officers, their families and servants sat in splendour. The two of them pass the burnt shell of a Mercedes Benz 770K, the once-beautiful chassis a rusted skeleton, and Schneesturm pauses, places a hand over the ruined car, sadly: What a waste, he says. Fogg shrugs. Does not care much for cars, perhaps. Continues walking and Erich follows. Passing a street lamp that is still functioning. The butt of a cigarette, crushed by a heel some time back, lies on the ground. They continue onwards, two travellers through the fog, two white ghosts in the grey and the black, traversing a land of the dead.

We watch. The two men move ahead, the fog parting, there

is a strange sort of sound, a scratching as of a vinyl disc being pulled against a needle, skipping grooves, and then a shimmer, and a sudden loss of perspective—

– Did you feel that? Fogg says. Uneasy.

– Like a scratched gramophone record, Schneesturm says. Shrugs. They continue walking in silence.

142. **THE OLD MAN'S OFFICE** the present

– A sound like a scratched gramophone record? the Old Man says sharply.

– At first I didn't think anything of it, Fogg says.

143. **BERLIN. THE SOVIET ZONE** 1946

Walking away from the boarding house, Schneesturm and Fogg, two shadows in a shadow Berlin, walking past a Mercedes Benz 770K, a once-beautiful car, now reduced to a burnt shell, Schneesturm shakes his head, sadly, Fogg frowns, how many of them are there, he thinks. Continue walking, through the narrow streets, past a street lamp miraculously working, Fogg looks down, sees the crushed butt of a cigarette, Fogg's frown deepens, he opens his mouth to say something but doesn't, they continue walking and Schneesturm begins to whistle, there is a strange scratching sound and they're walking away from the boarding house, Schneesturm and Fogg, Erich *und* Henry, past a burnt skeletal car (but aren't all cars, once burnt down, the same as each other?) and into thick fog, and a street lamp, still burning, and the butt of a cigarette on the ground and Fogg says, Stop!

They stop. Schneesturm's whistle fades away into nothing. What was that? Fogg says.

– What?

– Be quiet.

Fogg stands still. Listens. Waiting.

144. **THE OLD MAN'S OFFICE** the present

– And then I remembered the Farm, Fogg says.

145. **THE FARM, DEVON** 1936

Fogg remembers that moment, for he was anxious, shy: they were all lined up before Browning and Turing, for the first time made to – asked to – show themselves.

To really be yourself. There was something terrifying about it, the way it was when the Old Man came to Cambridge, when Fogg tried to escape. To really be yourself, naked, helpless, to be judged by others. He was afraid.

– Oblivion?

Oblivion shrugs, and Fogg envies him his cool, his calmness. Oblivion picks up a stone from the field. Examines it in his hands. Shows it to Browning and Turing. Like a magician, Fogg thinks. Performing. The same way he performed for Fogg. Oblivion gives a half-smile, shrugs, passes one hand over the other and the stone, caught in between, disintegrates. Becomes a nothingness. Browning's face incredulous. Turing smiles, a delighted child's smile at a magic trick. Wonderful, he breathes. Do it again!

Oblivion crouches, runs his hand over the grass, the grass, like the stone, dematerialising, obliviated. And Fogg is suddenly jealous of his friend: not of his ability, for that is not something one can control, it is just part of the change, part of the indelible re-shift of quantum probabilities in the human genome: but of his *courage*, his ability to stand there, cool and composed, in control. Like a real hero, Fogg thinks.

– Mr Blur?

Mr Blur grins, in his khaki shorts and his blue shirt he looks like a boy scout. He gives a mock-salute and then streaks across the field, faster than a speeding bullet, crossing it to the gate and around and back, his blurred form moving like a smudge of colour until he reappears in position in the line, still grinning, but breathing heavily.

– Impressive, Browning says.

– Are you hungry? Turing says. Mr Blur says, I could eat. Turing makes a note on his clipboard. High metabolism, most likely, he says, but to himself.

– Mr Fogg? Browning says.

And then it is his turn and he is suddenly terrified, it is like being back at school, back with Roberts and Thornton and the others, the bigger boys surrounding him, and all he wants is to flee, to *hide*, and without even realising he is doing it the environment responds to him, those minuscule undercurrents of observation and collapsed waves of probability, water molecules and air and there's a wisp of fog, forming, only a wisp at first and then another, and another, beginning low, hovering on the ground, on the grass, but rising, forming, Fogg drawing it over himself, a memory of Roberts, or was it Thornton, saying, Your father's a drunk! Someone laughing, a cruel childish laugh, before the change, before he could hide, and the fog is rising, it surrounds him, expanding, blocking out the sun, and inside it he feels safe.

– That's enough, Mr Fogg!

Startled, the fog grows thicker, but the voices penetrate – I said, that's *enough*, thank you, Fogg!

Old Browning's voice, and Fogg takes a deep breath, forcing out the fear, letting the fog diffuse, slowly, shafts of sunlight cut through it, he begins to see again, Turing's kind face, nodding as he scribbles away on his clipboard, briefly looking up – Thank you, Mr Fogg.

Fogg nods. The others look his way. He looks down. Already missing the comforting protection of the fog.

– Ah, yes, Browning says. Frowning. Mrs . . . Dinkle, is it?

– Tinkle, young man. It's Mrs *Tinkle*.

– And what is your talent, dear? Turing says.

– I can do this, Mrs Tinkle says.

She raises her hand and makes a motion like scratching a record on a turntable. There is an odd, discomfiting sound, like a scratch or a tear. Fogg feels a strong sense of discontinuity, of things not fitting in.

– Ah, yes, Browning says. Frowning. Mrs Dinkle, is it?

– Tinkle, young man. It's Mrs *Tinkle*.

– And what is your talent, dear? Turing says.

Mrs Tinkle smiles. A shiver runs through Fogg.

– I . . . see, Turing says.

146. **BERLIN. THE SOVIET ZONE** 1946

Fogg and Schneesturm, under the street light. The butt of a cigarette under Fogg's foot. A clear, girlish laugh from the shadows. Fogg feels trapped under the pool of light. Schneesturm, alarmed, tries to move, but Fogg stops him with a gesture. There is the sound of approaching light footsteps. And then she's there, under the light, looking at them like a teacher staring down two errant pupils.

– Henry Fogg, she says. You've been a naughty boy.

– Mrs Tinkle, Fogg says.

She smiles. Fogg, with confusion and anger intermingled: What the hell are you *doing* here, Mrs Tinkle?

– Language, Mr Fogg. Language!

– Sorry, Mrs Tinkle . . .

– Who is this woman? Schneesturm says. A look of bemusement on his face. What is she doing here?

– What are you doing here, Mrs Tinkle? Fogg says, again.

– Watching you, Henry Fogg, she says, still smiling. Who is your friend?

– He's nobody, Mrs Tinkle, Fogg says. You really shouldn't be here.

– Nobody? She turns slowly and looks Schneesturm up and down. He doesn't look like a nobody to me.

– Who is this woman? Is she a changed? An *Überfrau*? The term seems to amuse Schneesturm. We must go, he says.

– You must be Erich Bühler, Mrs Tinkle says. The famous Schneesturm.

Schneesturm loses the grin. Looks at her again as if seeing her properly for the first time. Inclines his head. I was, he says. I am in the process of retiring.

– Retiring? Mrs Tinkle inclines her head as if puzzled, or merely, subconsciously, echoing Schneesturm's body language. We do not *retire*, she says. We serve, or we die.

Schneesturm shrugs. Smiles. Doesn't know how to take her. Well, he says, I do not wish to die.

– Too bad, Mrs Tinkle says.

Schneesturm frowns. Mrs Tinkle ignores him, turns to Fogg. He is the one who got Tank, is he not, Henry? she says.

Fogg, put on the spot: Yes, he is. But things have changed!

– Not for Tank, they haven't, Mrs Tinkle says.

– Tank is alive! Fogg says.

– Not thanks to this man, Mrs Tinkle says. Really, Henry. I am disappointed in you. Consorting with enemy agents? I will have to report this to the Old Man. After I deal with this one.

– How did you find us? Fogg says, stalling for time. Trying to think what to do.

– I was out hunting, Mrs Tinkle says, and smiles: she reminds Fogg of a predatory bird. There are many of us out tonight, she says. Now . . . she raises her hand, as if to scratch again, somehow she is able to affect temporality, causality, Fogg knows if she uses her power they would be helpless, trapped in her loop, he says, desperately, Mrs Tinkle, please, we can talk about this—

–You crazy old woman, you will not take me alive! Schneesturm says, and he too raises his hand, and the wind howls, a gust of cold Arctic wind and snow comes out of nowhere and hits Mrs Tinkle, she gives a surprised gasp and falls back on her arse, knocked back in the street under the street lamp, and Fogg, horrified, shouts, Stop it!

– Nazi scum, Mrs Tinkle says, her voice muffled by the wind and snow and then there's a gun in her hand, she aims it with an unsteady hand and a shot goes off with a bang, Fogg cringes, but the shot has gone wide; and then Schneesturm, too, has a gun. Mrs Tinkle squints at him from her kneeling position, and she takes aim, carefully, but Schneesturm raises his hand again and ice forms over Mrs Tinkle, a sheen of it over her skin and over the gun, her finger tightens on the trigger but slowly, so slowly, and Fogg can do nothing but watch and then there is the sound of a gunshot.

– No! Fogg cries, sees Schneesturm drop his gun and curse, clutching his shoulder, blood soaking his coat, his sleeve, but he's all right, he's alive, and Fogg turns back to Mrs Tinkle with a sigh of relief that turns to horror when he sees her; and he realises it was not one gunshot but two.

She lies in the street, in the pool of light, on the edge of the darkness. A sheen of ice covers her face, but it is hissing as it melts, for the blood, her blood, is warm, and it is gushing out of her chest where she's been hit. Mrs Tinkle! Fogg cries, running to her, crouching by her side. She looks up at him, for just a moment. Her lips move, trying to form a word. Then her eyes lose their humanity; her life is gone; and Fogg is left stroking the hair of a dead old woman in the melting ice of a cold Berlin street.

147. **THE OLD MAN'S OFFICE** the present

– You killed *Mrs Tinkle*?

For the first time since the interview started the Old Man sounds shocked. This, Fogg realises, is a part the Old Man did not already know. He says, Schneesturm did. And – We didn't have a choice.

– She was a little old lady!

– She was an assassin, Old Man, Fogg says, remorselessly. She was *your* assassin.

The Old Man sits back in his chair, sinking into it. Looks this way and that, almost blindly; Fogg almost feels sorry for him. At last the Old Man lets out a breath. I knew she disappeared, of course . . . he says, softly. I always had her down as a defector to the Russians. She had communist sympathies, you know.

Oblivion stirs. I didn't know that, he says.

– Yes . . . she came from a mining community. Welsh. There were rumours she was seen in Moscow, after the war . . . I never trusted the Welsh.

Fogg and Oblivion exchange an uneasy glance. The Old Man smiles wryly, shrugs, and seems to pull himself together again. He drums his fingers on the desk top. Well, well, well, he says.

– Sir?

– Well, you really are confessing everything *now*, aren't you, Fogg? the Old Man says.

– Do I have a choice?

The Old Man doesn't reply; leaves the answer hanging,

unspoken, in the air. Then: Please, proceed, he says. Schneesturm had killed Mrs Tinkle . . .

– Then it got worse, Fogg says.

148. **BERLIN. THE SOVIET ZONE** 1946

– I can't believe she *shot* me, Schneesturm says.

– I can't believe you *killed* her! Fogg says.

– What did you want me to do! Schneesturm says. She was going to spoil everything, Fogg!

Fogg sighs. He helps Schneesturm tie a torniquet around his arm. It's only a scratch, he says, dismissively.

– Yes, well, it hurts! Schneesturm says.

– You'll get over it. Let's go.

Down these dark streets Fogg must go, the snow man by his side, the fog rising to mask them both, but the night has eyes, the night is watching, and behind them a corpse is left, just one amongst many, there have been so many—

A scream cuts through the night like a blade, rises, and abruptly stops.

– *The city was full of screams that night, Fogg says. They were the screams of the dead, and the dying. The old world died and the new one was waiting to be reborn.*

– *Come, come, Fogg, the Old Man says. Stick to the details, please.*

– What was that? Schneesturm says.

– The scream?

– No. What—

The night is full of shadows and their shadow men. Moving, stalking. A shadow coming through the fog, human but immense, as if projected by a titanic being. They can hear it moving through the fog, coming closer, and they draw back:

Then the shadow collapses and out of the fog comes a man

in red, short and squat, with powerful muscles stretching the material of his red uniform, showing to good advantage his muscled torso, and the prominent symbol of crossed sickle and fist of the Russian Sverhlyudi on his chest.

The Red Sickle.

Who is swaying on his feet, Fogg realises, and is holding a half-empty bottle of vodka in his right hand, and his eyes are wild and bleary and he raises the hand holding the bottle and points at Schneesturm and he bellows, You!

Fogg looks at Schneesturm in bemusement. The Red Sickle knows you? he says.

– Leningrad, in forty-two, Schneesturm says, softly.

– Many times we met, in the air, snow storm against sickle, rising high above the ancient city, battling for domination! the Red Sickle says; still pointing the bottle like a weapon.

– Yes, well, Schneesturm says.

– While all the while my people were starving under the siege! the Red Sickle roars. Eating the corpses of horses, eating the dirt off the city streets!

– Now just calm down, will you, Schneesturm says; and his hand steals to the butt of his gun.

– German! the Red Sickle says. Pointing the bottle. Tonight we finish what was started!

Fogg decides it is time to intervene. The war is over, he says. Imbues his voice with an authority he doesn't have. I'm a British officer. This man's with me.

– British! the Red Sickle says. I spit on the British!

He seems to suddenly discover the bottle in his hand and lifts it up to his mouth, taking a deep slug. His eyes narrow as he looks at Schneesturm. Tonight we finish, he says. He shuffles towards them, his fist raised, a demonic, red-clad middle-aged man who – as Schneesturm shies away – stumbles. He totters and nearly falls on Schneesturm, who instinctively grabs him.

– My friend! the Red Sickle says. He grabs the surprised Schneesturm in a bear hug, nestling his head on Schneesturm's shoulder, and begins to cry, big, thick tears staining Schneesturm's shirt. Schneesturm winces in pain as the Russian's arms squeeze his wounded shoulder. Be careful, you oaf! he says, in English.

– My friend! the Red Sickle says, in the same foreign tongue, paying him no heed. We are the same, what do we care for the ones who live and die, like flies? Hitler or Stalin, we are but soldiers, we are brothers—

– Yes, yes . . . Schneesturm pats him on the back, awkwardly. Fogg looks on, bemused: these two battered Übermenschen in the fog, holding each other tight; they look like they are clumsily dancing.

– *Every spook and Übermensch was out on the prowl that night, it seemed, Fogg says. There was a new kind of war in the making, a cold war, and we were all out, for all that we could get.*

– *Fogg . . . the Old Man says, warningly.*

– *Next thing I knew, Fogg says, there was the sound of clapping . . .*

There is a sound of hands clapping. Fogg tenses as he hears footsteps approaching. Three figures resolve out of the fog, and he recognises them with a sinking heart.

Tigerman.

The Green Gunman.

And Whirlwind.

– What a beautiful friendship, Tigerman says.

The Red Sickle and Schneesturm pull slowly apart and look at the newcomers.

Whirlwind points. You are Erich Bühler, alias Schneesturm, she says.

The Green Gunman pulls out his guns. You are under arrest, he says.

The three Americans, lined up, stand facing the others. Tigerman tosses his mane back over his shoulders and grins.

– Who are these people? the Red Sickle says in apparent bewilderment. Yankies?

Fogg steps between Schneesturm and the Americans. Every

nerve in his body insists that he run, hide. This man's with me, he says, with a boldness he does not feel.

– Ah, Fogg, Whirlwind says. And just what is a British agent doing in the company of a known war criminal?

– You are overstepping your authority, Whirlwind, Fogg says; but it only makes her smile.

– Walk away, Fogg, Tigerman says. He is ours now.

– For your Zoo? Fogg says.

– For whatever we fucking say, Tigerman says. Almost pleasantly. Come on, Fogg. Walk away.

– No.

They lock eyes, Tigerman and Fogg. For a moment they seem to Fogg like a frozen tableau; he knows something must break, must happen, and he does not know why: all he knows is that he must continue following Schneesturm, he must protect him, until the German takes him where Fogg most desperately wants to go.

Until he finds Klara again.

– No, he says, again.

– Be very careful, Fogg . . . Tigerman says.

Fogg weighs his options. But the Red Sickle makes the decision for him. He detaches himself from Schneesturm, suddenly, and glares at the three Übermenschen facing them. Americans? he says again, and then, Yankies!

– Red Sickle . . . Fogg says, a warning in his voice. Tigerman grins.

– No! The Red Sickle says. He raises the bottle still clutched in his hand and aims it like a missile. This is the Russian quarter! You have no authority here, *Americans*. Leave!

Tigerman loses his grin.

– Make us, you drunk fuck, he says.

The Red Sickle growls with outrage. He smashes the bottle on the ground and the sharp smell of vodka permeates the air. The Red Sickle rises, the broken bottle, shard-sharp, in his hand, and in his other hand something flashes, and a sickle materialises there. He faces the Americans and grins. Tigerman, in response, brings out a handgun.

– Tigerman, no! Fogg says.

But he is ignored. And with a howl of pure rage, the Red Sickle attacks the Americans.

They scatter. But Tigerman is too slow, the gunshot goes wide and the bottle catches him on the shoulder, draws blood, sends him spinning. The gun drops. Tigerman growls, beginning to transform. Claws emerge from his hand and he swipes at the Red Sickle, who laughs and knocks him aside, easily. Tigerman rolls, remains on all fours, grows fur, his long blond hair spreads and expands to cover his body and he opens his mouth wide, showing his teeth. Whirlwind spins. She turns like a dancer and doesn't stop, moving faster and faster, becomes a hurricane in miniature, the wind howls and sucks into itself leaves, dust, fog and cigarette butts. The wind attacks the Russian, who lashes with his sickle, cleaving the wind in two.

But the wind howls laughter and re-forms, engulfing the Red Sickle, who roars, *Blyadischa!* – whore! – and the sickle flashes again, and then the Red Sickle is airborne, fighting the wind until his fist finds purchase, there is a heavy thud, and the whirlwind transforms, mid-air, into a young woman and drops down.

The Red Sickle remains hovering, underneath him Whirlwind lands hard and groans, holding an injured leg as she lies there. The Green Gunman, coolly holding on to his twin guns, begins firing; and green shoots emerge from his pistols and whip through the air and clasp the Red Sickle in their grasp, tightening, growing flowers and shoots as they imprison him. The sickle flashes again, and again, and the vines drop to the ground but more are fired at him and they are dragging him down, down to the ground where Tigerman waits, fully transformed, and growling.

Yob tvoyu mat! the Red Sickle swears, and Fogg, breaking at last from a trance, grabs an equally dazed Schneesturm and says, Run!

Behind them, the Red Sickle slashes his way from the vines

and pulls, bringing the Green Gunman violently to his knees. The Red Sickle kicks him in the face and laughs. Then he turns to face Tigerman, sickle in hand, and the tiger roars as it attacks him.

Fogg and Schneesturm run.

149. **THE OLD MAN'S OFFICE** the present

– The Americans did not share this information with me, the Old Man says, somewhat huffily, Fogg thinks. He shrugs. I suspect they never even made a report, he says. After all, they failed to get what they wanted.

Oblivion stirs; stretches his long legs in front of him mutely. Oblivion, you remember what it was like, don't you? Fogg says. Elaborates for the Old Man: It wasn't the only time we ran into each other like this. The city was swarming with head-hunters. If I recall correctly, Tigerman even bought me a drink the next night, at Der Zirkus. To show there were no hard feelings.

– What happened to him? Fogg asks. After Vietnam?

– Went into oil, the Old Man says. Shrugs. That's where the money is. He was never a fool, was Tigerman.

Oblivion smiles. And the Green Gunman became a hippie, he says. Protesting against the war while Tigerman was hunting in the jungle.

– The Green *Gunman*? Fogg says.

– Yes, I remember seeing him at Woodstock in sixty-nine. He was something of a symbol for the anti-war movement. And then the whole Green thing took off.

– You went to *Woodstock*? Fogg says.

Oblivion looks embarrassed. No, no, he says. I saw a documentary about it a while ago, on the BBC. They had footage of the Green Gunman on stage. He was quite a good speaker, you know.

Fogg shakes his head.

– I don't know what happened to Whirlwind, Oblivion says; trying to change the subject, perhaps.

– Last I heard she was running guns somewhere in Africa, the Old Man says, stirring. Went private, same as most of them did after the Cold War.

Something cosy about the three of them. Gossiping about old colleagues, adversaries, what everyone is doing now. No one mentions what Fogg's been doing the past God knows how many years. Burying himself in the Hole in the Wall, or elsewhere, a ghost, a shadow man. While everyone else's still busy being heroes.

The Old Man turns to Fogg. Places his hands on the tabletop, leans forward, says, So?

Fogg takes a deep breath. So, he says. We left the Americans behind, and . . .

150. **BERLIN. THE SOVIET ZONE** 1946

– *The night was suddenly quiet, and very cold, Fogg says.* We watch him: sitting facing the Old Man, deep underground in the Bureau's hidden offices; and we watch him walking through the streets of this post-war Berlin, Schneesturm leading the way.

– *I found myself missing the smell of pine cones, Fogg says. The touch of sunlight on my skin. The smell of the sea. Berlin after the war was Hell made incarnate. It was the heart of winter, and I wanted – needed – summer.*

– Stop, Schneesturm says. They pause outside a dilapidated building, no different from any other building in this part of town, remarkable only for the fact that it is still standing. A worn wooden door, with all the paint flaked off it, no lights in the windows, a sinister quietude in the street, a hungry, anticipatory silence.

– Here? Fogg says; whispers. The fog thickens around them, responding to him; trying to mask their presence, the anticipation of what might be lying behind that door.

– Shhh, Schneesturm says. Looks nervously left and right, right and left, but there is nothing to see, the fog is all but impenetrable. Schneesturm nods, then reaches for the door. He knocks, softly, once, twice, again, drumming a code onto the old splintered wood. Waits.

Fogg, tense, beside him. Nothing changes. Then: In there, Schneesturm says.

Fogg looks at him. Questions behind his eyes. Is it a trap? Some sort of trick?

– Well, go on, Schneesturm says, a little impatient. Fogg stares at the door. Reaches, slowly, for the handle, a rusted metal thing jutting out of the old wood. The touch of it is a shocking cold against his skin. He presses it down.

Presses further. Slowly the handle turns. Fogg hesitates. Lets out a breath of cold air. It hangs like mist in front of his face. Come on! Schneesturm says. Stamps his feet on the ground as if, for the first time, he too feels the cold. Fogg shoots him a glance and, as if Schneesturm can read the contents of his mind, he shakes his head and says, No. Only you. I have never . . . and holds himself close, shivering. Snow rises around Schneesturm, as if it could hide him from Fogg, from that door, from what's inside. Go, he says, and Fogg, with a burst of fear and courage, pushes the door open and it gives under his hand and, as he opens it, bright summer sunlight pours out of the door and the smell of cut grass and the humming of bees, spilling out onto the cold dark Berlin street.

151. **THE OLD MAN'S OFFICE** the present

– I . . . see, the Old Man says.

But Fogg knows he will never truly see. Not what Fogg saw, what Fogg knew. The Old Man, like Schneesturm, can only *imagine*. Which is a wholly different thing.

– I went back to our side the same night, Fogg says. Back to Der Zirkus. The Americans weren't there. I needed to find a way to get her out of Germany. Sommertag. Klara. She wasn't safe but then, none of us were.

152. **BERLIN** 1946

To Fogg's surprise Corporal King is still waiting for him by the jeep when he gets back from the Soviet zone. Fogg gets into the passenger seat without speaking. The corporal is smoking a cigarette when Fogg approaches. He seems neither surprised nor startled when Fogg appears. Nor does he comment on Fogg's somewhat ramshackle appearance. They drive in silence through the streets, away from the Soviet zone, until at last Fogg sees the lights ahead, of the bars and clubs and Der Zirkus, where he motions for the corporal to stop.

Fogg gets off and acknowledges the corporal with a curt nod before he goes into the club. It is late, and even in Der Zirkus things are winding down; the Americans, Fogg notices without surprise, are missing, their table vacant, and Spit, too, is gone. On stage Machentraum is singing, a slow, sad song: 'When I Grow Too Old To Dream', a Vera Lynn number. As Fogg enters, a shadow detaches itself from the walls and approaches him. Fogg turns, startled. It's Franz.

– Herr Schleier, he says, I must speak with you.

– Not here, Franz.

– I must speak with you! He seems agitated, his hands move nervously, tracing wide arcs through the air. Fogg puts his hand on Franz's shoulder, Be quiet! he says.

They confer in low voices. At last Franz nods. They disengage. Franz goes to the doors, disappears to the outside. Fogg goes to where Oblivion is sitting. Oblivion turns his head. Fogg leans his head close to Oblivion's. Whispers in his ear. For a moment they are as close as lovers. Oblivion nods, their shadows part.

They get up together; walk away – Oblivion outside, Fogg into the shadows, behind the stage.

153. **THE OLD MAN'S OFFICE** the present

– Out of curiosity, the Old Man says, which one of you was it who killed the informer, Franz?

Oblivion, startled, half rises from his chair. Sir, I must protest, he says.

– Settle down, Oblivion, the Old Man says.

– Sir, I—

Oblivion and the Old Man lock eyes. The Old Man wears a mocking grin. After a moment Oblivion sighs, and sits back down.

– I assume Fogg asked you to do it when he returned, the Old Man says.

154. **DER ZIRKUS NIGHTCLUB, BERLIN** 1946

– Fräulein Machentraum.

– You startled me!

She comes off stage after the last song; comes into the shadows where Fogg waits. There is no one else around. It is late and Machentraum is the club's only performer. Even the musicians are long gone.

– I apologise, Fogg says. She looks at him, recognises him and sighs, as though knowing nothing good will come of this meeting. Without the stage light she just looks tired; the makeup sits heavily on her face. Herr Fogg, she says, in acknowledgement. What do you want?

– I want your help, Fogg says.

– Oh?

– They call you Dream Maker, Fogg says. Speaking quickly. Machentraum.

– Yes . . .

– I need you to weave an illusion for me.

But Machentraum is already shaking her head. Herr Fogg, please! she says. I will get into trouble. I cannot do it.

Fogg opens his mouth to speak but she silences him with a gesture. They only let me stay here for my singing, Machentraum says. The Americans promised me a visa if I cooperate. I am wanted for war crimes! I have never harmed anyone, Herr Fogg, she says, pleading. The change was not my fault.

– None of us were responsible for the change, Fogg says. She pushes past him, goes to the mirror. Begins to wipe makeup from her face. Fogg says, Please. Will you help me?

Her face softens, for just a moment. She steals a glance at him. To do . . . to do what? she says.

– To give someone a new face, Fogg says.

155. **OUTSIDE DER ZIRKUS, BERLIN** 1946

Franz stands outside, pacing. Smoking a cigarette with nervous, hungry pulls. The doors of the club open and a long shadow falls on Franz. He turns as the doors close. There is no one around, it is late, so late; the deep darkness that comes before dawn. He turns, smiling; but the smile drops when he sees it is Oblivion standing there; Oblivion, not Fogg.

– You, Franz says. Gathers himself together, smiles a cocky smile. What do you want, he says.

– Me? Oblivion says.

– Yes, you. Did Herr Schleier send you? You can go back to him, lapdog. Tell him Franz does not deal with lapdogs. Franz wants what he deserves.

– And what does Franz deserve? Oblivion says.

– Life, Franz says, suddenly angry. A way out. You think you're all heroes, don't you, so mighty and superior. *Übermenschen.* Franz spits on the frozen ground. You're not different to the rest of us, he says. Grubby, dirty little men. No, you're worse than we are. You're nothing but shadows. You're the shadows of men.

Oblivion doesn't answer. His face is as pale and immobile as stone. Well? Franz says. Stabs the cigarette in the air. Did you bring me my money? What are you doing? What are you—

But Oblivion's long hands are reaching for Franz; and his long, thin, graceful fingers close on Franz's throat with an ease born, perhaps, we think uneasily, of experience. And he is choking Franz, choking the life out of him, giving him the only way out Franz will ever find. Franz tries to struggle, his hands flail in the air, to ward off Oblivion, to fight him, clutching, for one brief moment, at his military uniform, but Oblivion is unrelenting, his thumbs dig into Franz's soft skin, into his neck, blocking the passage of air, and the burning cigarette drops from Franz's fingers to the ground. In moments it is over. And

Oblivion lets the body collapse to the ground and stands there, looking down at it. A fleeting expression – of shame, of triumph, it is impossible for us to say – passes over his face and is gone. He picks up Franz's limp body by the arms and begins to drag it away.

156. **DER ZIRKUS NIGHTCLUB, BERLIN** 1946

– Why should I help you? Machentraum says.
And Fogg says, I don't know.

157. **THE OLD MAN'S OFFICE** the present

– I never knew why she did help us, in the end, Fogg says. Love. Perhaps she was a romantic. I think we all were, at the end. Failed cynics. We wanted to believe in love.

– You could have threatened her, the Old Man says.

– She already belonged to the Americans, Fogg says. She had her ticket out. I saw her once, after the war. Not in person. In a movie, it was on late-night cable television, when I was in the States, for . . . He blinks, sleepily. The long night catching up with him as it is coming to an end.

– Machentraum?

– She had a new name, a new face. She went to Hollywood, but somehow she never made it. Fogg shrugs. She had no reason to help me. Looks at Oblivion and looks away quickly. No one had.

– You had friends, Oblivion says, quietly. People who cared for you.

– Maybe. I shouldn't have . . . shouldn't have got them involved.

– Maybe it wasn't your choice to make, Oblivion says.

The Old Man looks at both of them. Scribbles a few lines in the folder open before him.

– What did you do then? he says.

Fogg rubs his eyes. Feels drained. Not much else left to confess. The night is almost over. Deep inside him he can feel the encroaching of dawn.

– We went at daybreak, he says. Took Klara from the safe house and drove her to the airport. Schneesturm was already waiting. He'd made his own way out of the Soviet zone. None of us ever had much problem with borders. It was a package deal. Schneesturm and Klara. Who else could I trust?

– No one, the Old Man says. Least of all him.

– Sometimes, Fogg says, you have no choice. Sometimes you have to trust *someone*.

The Old Man nods, conceding the point.

– I put her on the plane myself, Fogg says. Somewhere safe, Old Man. Somewhere far from the world powers who would reach out to grab her, if only they could. I said my goodbye. Or perhaps I said nothing at all. I no longer remember.

158. TEMPELHOF CENTRAL AIRPORT, WEST BERLIN 1946

The Douglas C-47 Dakota stands on the runway, starkly illuminated against the dark skies. They had driven in, it had been easy with Machentraum along; as far as the Americans now knew the flight was a part of Operation Paperclip and classified *Verboten*. Only the pilot knew the destination and the pilot, though he looked all-American in his military uniform and his Bob-or-Bill-or-Tom good looks, was Schneesturm.

Schneesturm in the cockpit, waiting, his features recast by the magic of dreams, by Machentraum. Who stands with Oblivion a short distance away. Machentraum's face pinched, her illusion weaving over the scene, reshaping Klara's face, and Fogg's. Oblivion alert, but relaxed, his hands gloveless, waiting in case anything goes wrong. Sometimes he steals looks at Fogg and Klara. Fogg can feel them, warm against his skin.

He stands there like a fool, holding Klara's hands, only it isn't Klara, it is some stranger conjured out of Machentraum's mind. She has the face of a stranger but her voice is still Klara's. Do they speak? We cannot tell. The plane's propellers start, the engine thrumming alive, all that coiled power. Do they kiss? All we see are shadows.

Then the shadows part, one goes to the plane, the other stands there, watching as she climbs the folding steps, as the door closes, as the plane executes a half-turn, ungainly on the ground, then accelerates along the runway, faster and faster, until, at last, in some miraculous act that seems to contravene the laws of nature, it rises into the skies; no longer ungainly, the metal bird flies; and it takes Klara with it, taking her away, and Fogg, down below, watches, his head raised, watches as the plane grows distant in the sky until it finally disappears.

FOURTEEN:
SHADOWS AND LIGHT

LONDON
the present

159. **THE BUREAU** the present

– And this is it? the Old Man says.
  – This is it.
  – This is everything?
  – Yes.
Fogg rubs his face. Feels drained, depleted. All those secrets, spilling out . . . but he always knew the day would come. So many years of keeping secrets, polishing them like precious stones until they shone, and now they were out, and they were tawdry, vulgar almost in the light. Had it been worth it?

But – Yes, he answers himself, it was, it had to be. Because it meant keeping Klara safe, all those years. Klara who was like a flame in the dark, the only thing ever to illuminate the shadows. Klara who was Fogg's faith, his belief, something good and unsullied in everything that happened – whatever the others said, he knew. The loneliness, the shadows, the Hole in the Wall – it had all been worth it, to keep her safe.

Until now.

– Come with me, the Old Man says, and Fogg rises, with a sense of doom, of an inevitability he has felt ever since Oblivion came for him at the Hole in the Wall.

Oblivion, too, stands up. Looks to Fogg, expressionless. The Old Man gets up slowly, supports himself on the desk as he rises.

The Old Man walks to the door. Opens it. Fogg feels aches in his joints. Sitting for too long. Follows Oblivion after the Old Man. Closes the door behind them.

The long corridor of the Bureau. It's very quiet. Bars of neon lights on the ceiling. The Old Man moves slowly, tiredly. He says, We caught Erich Bühler two nights ago.

Fogg says, Oh.

Tries to take it in. But a part of him already knew, he realises. Has known all along.

– He never did go away, you know, Fogg, the Old Man says. Not entirely. He surfaced during the Cold War. Running guns in Chechnya. Running drugs in Afghanistan. Bad Boy Snow Storm. We kept an eye on him. Tried to catch him in the early Eighties, as a matter of fact, but he got away . . .

The Old Man stops, abruptly. Fogg almost runs into him. The Old Man puts a hand on Fogg's shoulder to steady himself. Until now, he says, his eyes searching Fogg's face.

– Yes? Fogg manages to say.

– He tried to raid one of our North Sea installations, the Old Man says. The ones that don't, officially, exist. Only, this time, we caught him.

– Yes, Fogg says. Can't think of anything else to say. Can't even – won't – work out the ramifications in his head.

– Since then he's been singing like a bleeding canary, the Old Man says.

He releases Fogg. Singing for his supper, he says, with sudden savagery. Come.

They walk down the corridor, take a turn, and then another, heading even deeper underground. There is no escape, Fogg thinks, dazed. At last they reach the lowest level of the Bureau. A secure door, reinforced steel. A small utilitarian plaque that says, *Interrogation Room.*

– We never did make another Vomacht box, the Old Man says; and pushes open the door.

160. **THE BUREAU** the present

She sits slumped behind the glass wall. She is in a chair, behind a table, held in restraints, facing the glass; facing Fogg and the

Old Man and Oblivion. Her head lolls on her chest. Her eyes are half open, puffy. She looks drugged. Fogg goes to the glass wall. Presses against it. Klara! he says. She hasn't changed, he thinks. She is still . . .

– Why? he says. Turns back, turns on the Old Man. What has she ever done to you?

With sudden anger: No one even remembers the war any more. Why couldn't you let her *be*?

Fogg turns back to her. Can't pull away. His palms against the cool glass. Klara shifts in the chair. Tries to open her eyes fully. As if she can sense him there.

The Old Man ignores Fogg's outburst. Says: Tell me about Klara, Fogg. Tell me about Dr Vomacht's farmhouse, on a perfect summer's day.

Fogg leans against the glass. Closes his eyes. The memory so vivid still, it burns like a flame in his mind. A perfect moment, where it is always summer . . .

Do you want to see it? Klara says. Grinning. Like a kid sharing a wonderful secret. See what? Henry says. Klara jumps up and down in excitement and grabs Henry's hand. Come on! she says. She takes him by the hand and leads him away, into the kitchen. It is a spacious, airy room, flooded with sunlight. On the long wood table sits a small machine, about the size of a briefcase. It is impossible to say what it is, what it does. Klara stops and Henry stops with her. He stares at the room, at the silent machine. What? he says, at last.

– This is it, Klara says. This is the device.

– But . . .

– I remember it like it was today, Klara says.

She laughs. She spreads her arms wide and dances on the spot. It is today! she says. It is always today. Oh, Henry. She throws her arms around him, nuzzles his neck. It is always today, she whispers, against his skin. One perfect summer's day.

Fogg opens his eyes. The device? he says, wonder in his voice. Is that what all this is about?

It's still there, the Old Man says. That quantum bomb. That

whatever it is. It, or a copy of it. The only working model in the world.

Fogg shakes his head, realisation dawning. No, he says. Old Man, no . . .

– Vomacht himself said that he didn't know. That he would never have done it if he knew. There is naked anger in the Old Man's voice. Terrifying after the hours of patient interrogation. The technology is non-replicable, the Old Man says. We can't create a new change. Or undo the old one. The change is still happening, Fogg. A floating referrent. There's no way to *make it stop*. Not unless . . .

– No, Fogg says. No.

– I have to, the Old Man says.

– You mustn't!

– We don't *age!* the Old Man says. Fogg turns to him. The Old Man rounds on Fogg. His face is no longer patient, understanding; no longer a confessor's face, it is now that of an old, bitter warrior. And Fogg thinks: How could I not see it before?

– We don't *die*, the Old Man says.

His voice softer now; it breaks Fogg's heart.

– We stand still as the world moves on, the Old Man says. I don't know this world any more. I don't know the language people speak. I walk the streets of London and it's as if I am walking through a city on an alien world.

– What are you planning to do? Fogg says; but the Old Man ignores him.

– We won the war, Henry, he says. We won the war, but we lost ourselves.

– I can't let you do this, Fogg says.

– You don't, the Old Man says, get to decide.

Motion catches Fogg's eye. He turns back to the glass. A nurse enters the interrogation chamber. She is holding a syringe in one hand. No, Fogg says. Please. The nurse approaches Klara. Rolls up her sleeve. Cleans the skin with a pad of cotton wool. Primes the syringe. You're attuned to her, the Old Man says. He stands close behind Fogg. Says, softly, This will only last a moment.

The nurse pushes the syringe into Klara's arm, emptying it. Klara's body thrashes against the restraints. Fogg cries out as

161. DR VOMACHT'S FARMHOUSE

he finds himself standing in the kitchen. Bulbs of garlic hanging from the wall. Heavy blackened pots. Sunlight streams in through the open window, disorientating Fogg. He blinks and sees Klara.

– Henry!

The sight of her fills him with fear. Klara, he says. They go to each other. He holds her tight, burying his head in the crook of her neck, inhaling her scent. She is trembling in his arms. She pulls away. Her hand rises, strokes his cheek. I'm scared, Henry, she says. What is happening to me?

His hands on her arms, the warmth of her, he says, I'll get you out of this, I pro—

162. THE BUREAU the present

—mise.

In the chair Klara sits slumped, the nurse stands over her, she is reloading the syringe from a bottle on the table. Fogg can feel the Old Man at his back, a heavy, oppressive presence.

– Press the button, the Old Man says.

– No!

The Old Man is breathing heavily. It's time to end this, he says.

Fogg turns on him. You don't know what you're doing, he says. You don't know what it would do.

– I don't *care!* the Old Man says. I don't care any more. Henry, I'm *tired*.

Something snaps in Fogg. Disappointment. Anger. He makes to attack the Old Man. Oblivion steps between them, restraining Fogg. His fingers solid and hard on Fogg's arms.

– Oblivion, help me! Fogg says.

The Old Man says, Hold him, Oblivion.

Oblivion's face is unreadable. The Old Man pushes Fogg, turns him around. Fogg stares at the glass. In the interrogation room the nurse prepares the needle again, Fogg can only watch as the nurse plunges it into Klara's arm and this

163. DR VOMACHT'S FARMHOUSE

time he appears not in the kitchen, but in the field outside the house. The feel of the sun on his skin is shocking, strange. Klara is dancing, her arms spread out from her body, her dress rippling in a motion of air. A butterfly hovers in the air beside her. But it is wrong. Klara is frozen in the dance. The butterfly hovers motionless, dead. The sun disappears and the sky turns gangrene-black. The green leeches away from the grass, turning it sepia grey. A rumble shakes the ground. The air ripples. Klara stumbles, Fogg rushes to her, stops her fall. She looks up at him, terrified.

– Henry, what is happening to me? she says.

The ground shakes again, there is a sound like a rip in the sky. Fogg loses his footing and he and Klara both fall. Klara screams.

– Henry!

He holds on to her, desperately. Make them stop! she says. Please make them st—

164. **THE BUREAU** the present

—op! Fogg says. Let her *go*! Struggling against Oblivion's hold. The nurse pulls out the empty syringe. Begins preparing a third dose. The Old Man is breathing heavily, his face is crazed. It's happening, he says. At last, it's happening.

– Oblivion, please, Fogg says. He sags into his friend's arms. Please, Oblivion . . .

Oblivion is warm, hard. He releases Fogg. His hands are on Fogg's arms, he looks into his face as if searching there for something, something precious, something lost. Why, Fogg? he says.

– Because I love her, Fogg says. Oblivion's face like a stone statue. You dare to talk to me about *love*? he says.

Fogg feels the air knocked out of him.

– I'm so sorry, he whispers.

– Oblivion, what the hell are you *doing*! the Old Man says.

Oblivion doesn't even turn his head. All his attention is on Fogg. Stay out of this, Old Man, he says.

Fogg sees Oblivion, as if for the first time. He has the sudden urge to reach out a hand, to stroke his friend's pale face. Wishes he could unsee the terrible look in Oblivion's eyes.

– I helped you get her out, Oblivion says. I killed that *man* for you.

– I know. I . . .

– We were *together*! Oblivion says. Ever since the Farm, in the war, in the trenches, in Berlin. And you never even *asked*.

Fogg looks into his old friend's eyes. I didn't need to, he says, softly.

– That night in Minsk, Oblivion says. His voice is choked with pain. Fogg says, Don't, Oblivion. I never meant to . . .

But Oblivion is not yet done. You *left*, he says. You retreated from the world. For decades. Because you hurt. Henry, he says. Henry, you left even me.

Fogg finds nothing to say. Feels how useless and empty words will be. How useless and empty all words are.

They look at each other. What is there left to say? Fogg feels resigned to his fate. Just do it, he whispers. And again – I'm sorry.

But Oblivion shakes his head. And then his hands fall to his sides. He releases Fogg.

– Oblivion? What are you doing? the Old Man screams.

But Oblivion is still looking only at Fogg.

– Go, he says, and his voice is both brittle and hard. Go. You'll only get the one chance.

He turns to the glass. Touches it, gently, and it disintegrates, it disappears. Cold conditioned air from the inside rushes at their faces. He pushes Fogg through. Go! he yells. Fogg stumbles in. Surprises the nurse. Everything is moving sluggishly, as if he's swimming. Get away from me! the nurse says. Give me that! Fogg says, making a grab for the syringe, but the nurse waves it in front of her like a weapon and Fogg pulls back, wary. The nurse waves the needle wildly, panic on her face. Then, without a word, she drops it on the floor and turns and runs off, disappearing through the side door, which slams behind her.

Fogg picks up the syringe. He stares at it in his hand.

– What are you doing? The Old Man is wild, his voice rising. What is he doing? Stop him, Oblivion!

But Oblivion reaches the Old Man instead. Holds him, but gently. Fogg goes to Klara. Kneels by her side. Strokes her cheek. Her eyes flutter open. Henry . . . she says.

– We have to get away, Fogg says. Whispers. Klara's lips form the beginning of a smile. Can you do it? Fogg says.

Klara sighs. It is a struggle to keep her eyes open. There will be no coming back . . . she says. Fogg smiles back at her, tenderly. I know, he says.

Klara's eyes close. A haze of light, faint at first but growing stronger, seems to emanate from her, the bright sunlight of a summer's day.

– Stop them! the Old Man says. He pushes Oblivion, catching

him by surprise, and pulls free. Fogg turns back, still crouching. The Old Man runs at him, Fogg raises his arms, stands to intercept the Old Man: until they collide violently.

– Fogg? What did you *do*? Oblivion says.

The Old Man sags in Fogg's arms. Fogg lowers him gently to the ground. The Old Man is breathing heavily. Fogg turns, kneeling beside him. And Oblivion can see it, now.

Can see the syringe sticking out of the Old Man's chest like a knife.

– Fogg!

But Fogg doesn't hear him. He kneels by the Old Man, his face twisted in pain. The Old Man's breathing is ragged, laboured. He looks into Fogg's eyes.

– Old Man, I . . . Fogg says, and his voice breaks.

– Henry, the Old Man says. He raises his hand, touches Fogg, briefly, on the cheek. He tries to smile.

– I just wanted to be free, he says.

His hand drops to his side. He closes his eyes. A moment later, his breathing ceases. Fogg looks down, blinks. Looks up at Oblivion, his face full of grief. Oblivion nods wordlessly. Walks to him, offers Fogg his hand.

– I didn't know, Fogg says.

– He ran out of things to believe in a long time ago, Oblivion says. Everyone needs to believe in something, Henry. As implausible as that something is. Oblivion's eyes are blue and clear. You have Klara, he says. And I . . . He tries to smile. I suppose I have you.

He pulls Fogg up. Their hands part. Fogg nods, wordlessly.

Then: Klara! Fogg says. He turns.

The light suffuses her now. It brings with it a hint of the scent of fresh grass, of flowers in bloom. The sunlight grows until it forces them to shield their eyes and look away.

The sunlight emanates out from Klara, a blinding glare. Then it fades and, when Fogg looks back at the chair, it is empty: Klara is gone.

– Henry, Oblivion says.

Fogg looks at him.

– Don't go.

The words catch in his throat. Fogg walks up to him. He puts his arms around Oblivion. He hugs him. He is shorter than Oblivion, his cheek is pressed to Oblivion's chest. He can feel the beating of Oblivion's heart, the way he did all those years before, at the Gare du Nord, when they were leaving Paris. He releases Oblivion. Can't bear the look in Oblivion's face. He turns away. It always ends by us turning away. We know. We, too, have been hurt before.

Fogg whispers, I have to.

Oblivion says, I know. So quietly, we're never sure, later, if we heard it.

Fogg says, Goodbye, Oblivion. He doesn't look back. He walks to the interrogation room's door and pulls it open, and a flood of summer sunlight pours into the underground room. The room is grey and white, glass and concrete. But within the frame of the open door we see the suggestion of colour, of blue skies and green grass and white clouds and yellow sun.

Somewhere beyond music plays, faintly, and a girl laughs in childish delight.

The sunlight pours into the underground room.

Fogg walks towards the light.

A NOTE ON HISTORICAL PEOPLE AND EVENTS

While this is a work of fiction, care has been taken to present the historical events and personages within these pages as accurately as possible. Operation Paperclip was an American operation to locate and bring German rocket scientists back to the United States. Dr Wernher von Braun, the developer of the V2 rockets, in particular, became a senior member of the American space programme and eventually developed the Saturn rockets used to launch the Apollo missions into space.

Josef Mengele's horrific medical experiments in Auschwitz have been well documented elsewhere – one of the most wanted Nazis in the post-war period, he was never captured, and is believed to have died, peacefully, in Argentina, of old age.

Kurt Lischka was the head of the Paris Gestapo in 1944. He was responsible for the largest single mass deportation of Jews in Occupied France. After the war he was sentenced to ten years in prison. He died, a free man, in 1989. Like Mengele, Carl Clauberg worked in the Auschwitz death camp, where he horrifically experimented on human subjects – over a thousand Jewish women, many of whom died or suffered permanent physical damage. After the war he was put on trial in the Soviet Union, sentenced to twenty-five years, but released after seven and returned to West Germany. Boasting of his 'scientific achievements', he was soon rearrested, but died of a heart attack in his cell before the trial could begin.

Leni Riefenstahl, Hitler's devout friend and filmmaker, was never charged with any crimes. She died at the ripe old age of 101.

Arnold Deutsch, who spots Fogg in Cambridge for the Bureau, was in real life a Soviet spy of some renown. A Jew, he was an early recruit of the NKVD, the Russian secret service that preceded the KGB. While at Trinity College, Deutsch acted as a recruiter for the NKVD, identifying and 'turning' several promising candidates. These were Kim Philby, Donald Maclean, Guy Burgess and Anthony Blunt. A fifth member has never been officially identified. They were known as the Cambridge Five. Burgess and Maclean escaped to Moscow in 1951, followed by Philby (by then a senior member of MI6) in 1961. Blunt remained in the UK; he was later secretly pardoned.

Deutsch was recalled to Moscow in 1937, where he survived Stalin's purges, then in full effect. He disappeared in the 1940s: some say he died when parachuting into Austria, others that the ship he was on was sunk by a U-boat. His true fate remains unknown.

The Warsaw Ghetto Uprising took place in 1943, defying the Nazi forces for almost five months. Thirteen thousand Jews died in the uprising. The remaining 50,000 were sent to the death camps, the majority to Treblinka.

Paris fell to the Nazis in June 1940. Minsk fell in 1941, during the early stages of Operation Barbarossa, the German invasion of the Soviet Union. German forces had reached Leningrad (now St Petersburg) by September 1941, beginning a harrowing siege of the city. It lasted almost two and a half years, one of the longest and most devastating sieges in history. Hungary – and with it Translyvania – fell in 1944, leading to the mass transportation of the Jews of Hungary to the death camps in the year just before the end of the war. Some 600,000 Hungarian Jews died in the camps.

The Vomacht abduction and trial are loosely modelled on the abduction by Mossad agents, and subsequent trial, of Adolf Eichmann, a senior Nazi and one of the architects of the Final Solution. He was executed by hanging and his ashes scattered beyond Israel's territorial waters, in the Mediterranean Sea, so that there would be 'no future memorial and that no country would serve as his final resting place.'

Stanley Martin Lieber is better known by his pen name Stan Lee. The son of Jewish emigrants from Romania to the United States, he became one of the most influential creators of comic book heroes.

Joseph 'Joe' Shuster was the son of Jewish emigrants from the Netherlands to Canada. Jerry Siegel was the son of Jewish emigrants from Lithuania to the United States. Together they created the comic book character 'Superman' in 1932.

The Potsdam Conference took place in 1945 (not 1946), with Stalin, Churchill and Truman all in attendance.

The Berlin Wall was erected in 1961 and came down, famously, in 1990, almost three decades later. Over two hundred people died trying to cross the wall, the last of whom, in 1989, did indeed attempt to use a home-made balloon to cross.

By 1967 the American war in Vietnam was in full swing. Less well known is the so-called Secret War that American forces carried out in Laos. The CIA and its civilian airline, Air America, had established a major military base in Laos, carrying out mass-scale bombings over Laos and Cambodia. Some 260 million cluster bombs were dropped over Laos alone, of which 75 million remain unexploded, leading to some 300 deaths and injuries a year to this day. Rumours of the CIA using opium shipments to fund their operations have never been fully confirmed nor comprehensively negated.

Soviet forces invaded Afghanistan in 1979. The war against the Soviets drew a large number of Mujahedeen, many from the Arab world. One of their leaders was the young scion of a wealthy Saudi family. By 1984, Osama bin Laden had established an entire network of fighters, arms supplies and financial support, some of which was provided by the CIA.

ACKNOWLEDGEMENTS

No novel exists in a vacuum. My thanks first and foremost to Kate Myres, who first set me on the road to Oblivion: this book would not exist without you.

To Nicola Sinclair, friend and muse, for always pushing me when I need a push.

To my parents, for always being there, and for providing the space where I wrote the first version of what would at last become *The Violent Century*.

To Richard Kunzmann for friendship and help when it was most needed.

To Marcus Rauchfuss for graciously correcting my German, and to Ekaterina Sedia for help with the Sverhlyudi. Any mistakes are entirely my own.

Both Bella Pagan and Shimon Adaf read an earlier draft of the manuscript and offered much useful criticism. To them my thanks.

To Shimon, too, for inspiration, and to Nir Yaniv, for much patient listening.

To my agent and friend, John Berlyne, for sticking by me.

And to Elizabeth, always.